INTERSTATE

INTERSTATE

A NOVEL

Stephen Dixon

An Owl Book

Henry Holt and Company
New York

Henry Holt and Company, Inc.
Publishers since 1866
115 West 18th Street
New York, New York 10011

Henry Holt® is a registered
trademark of Henry Holt and Company, Inc.

Published in Canada by Fitzhenry & Whiteside Ltd.,
195 Allstate Parkway, Markham, Ontario L3R 4T8.

Library of Congress Cataloging-in-Publication Data
Dixon, Stephen.
Interstate: a novel / by Stephen Dixon.—1st ed.
p.   cm.
I. Title
PS3554.I92I57   1995   94-40174
813'.54—dc20   CIP
ISBN 0-8050-2654-1
ISBN 0-8050-5028-0 (An Owl Book: pbk.)

Henry Holt books are available for special promotions
and premiums. For details contact: Director, Special Markets.

First published in hardcover in 1995 by
Henry Holt and Company, Inc.

First Owl Book Edition—1996

Designed by Betty Lew

Printed in the United States of America
All first editions are printed on acid-free paper.∞

1   3   5   7   9   10   8   6   4   2
1   3   5   7   9   10   8   6   4   2
(pbk)

To Gusta and Gregory Frydman

Portions of *Interstate* have appeared in the following publications: *American Short Fiction, Antietam Review, Antioch Review, Arts & Sciences, Asylum Annual 94 & 95, Bakunin, Boston Review, Boulevard, Cream City Review, Florida Review, Georgetown Review, Glimmer Train, Kenyon Review, Paris Transcontinental, Pequod, Triquarterly,* and *Western Humanities Review.*

INTERSTATE

He's in the car with the two kids, driving on the Interstate when
a car pulls up on his side and stays even with his for a while
and he looks at it and the guy next to the driver of what's a
minivan signals him to roll down his window. He raises his forehead in an expression "What's up?" but the guy, through an open
window, makes motions again to roll down his window and then
sticks his hand out his window and points down at the back of
Nat's car, and he says "My wheel, something wrong with it?"
and the guy shakes his head and cups his hands over his mouth
as if he wants to say something to him. He lowers his window,
slows down a little while he does it, van staying alongside him,
kids are playing some kid card game in back though strapped in,
and when the window's rolled almost all the way down and the
hand he used is back on the steering wheel, the guy in the car

sticks a gun out the window and points it at his head. "What? What the hell you doing," he says, "you crazy?" and the guy's laughing but still pointing, so's the driver laughing, and he says "What is this? What I do, what do you want?" and the guy puts his free hand behind his ear and says "What, what, what? Can't hear ya," with the driver laughing even harder now, and he says "I said what do you want from me?" and the guy says "Just to scare you, that's all, you know, and you're scared, right?—look at the sucker, scared shitless," and he says "Yeah, okay, very, so put it away," and the kids start screaming, probably just took their eyes off the card game and saw what was happening, or one did and the other followed, or they just heard him and looked or had been screaming all the time and he didn't hear them, but he doesn't look at them through the rearview, no time, just concentrates on the gun and guy holding it and thinking what to do and thinks "Lose them," and floors the gas pedal and gets ahead of the van but it pulls even with him and when he keeps flooring it stays even with him and even gets a little ahead and comes back with the guy still pointing the gun out the window and now grinning at him, driver's in hysterics and slapping the dashboard, things seem to be so funny, and he thinks "Should I roll the window up or keep it down, for rolling it up the guy might take it the wrong way and shoot, if he's got bullets in there," and he looks around, no other cars on their side of the Interstate except way in the distance front and behind, no police cars coming the other way or parked as far as he can see on the median strip, and he yells "Kids, get down, duck, stop screaming, do what Daddy says," and sees them in the rearview staring at the van and screaming and he shouts "I said get down, now, now, unbuckle yourselves, and shut up, your screaming's making me not think," and slows down and rolls the window up and van slows down till it's alongside him, the guy holding the gun out and one time slapping the driver's free hand with his, and then the guy points the gun at the backseat with the kids ducked down in it and crying, maybe on the floor, maybe on the seat, for he can't see them, and he swerves to the slow lane and the van gets beside him in the middle lane, and then he pulls onto the shoulder, stops, shifts quickly and drives in reverse on it bumping over some clumps, and the van goes on but much slower and from about a hundred and then two and three and four hundred feet away the guy steadies his gun arm with his other hand and aims at his car and he yells "Kids, stay down," for both are now looking out the back, maybe because of the bumping and sudden going in reverse, and bullets go through the windshield. He screams in pain, glass in his head and a bullet through his hand, yells "Girls, you all right?" for there's screaming from in back but only one of them, and his oldest daughter says "Daddy, Julie's not moving, Daddy, she's bleeding, Daddy, I don't see her breathing, I think she's dead."

There's a funeral next day, and day after it, while his wife and their families are mourning at his house, he goes out on the same Interstate searching for those guys, wishing he'd done it in the few hours of daylight he had the day before. He drives on it every day after that looking for them in one of the road's rest stops or in the car they drove, a white fairly new minivan, Chevy or Ford, or in any vehicle they might have now, he wouldn't think it'd be that van, though they could be that stupid or devil-may-care—swashbuckling, he was about to call it, when he meant swaggering, the fucking hyenas. He knows their faces, what they look like and, he thinks, what they like to wear. Knows it's a long shot finding them, that they'll probably stay off this road if they have any reason to be on it again, drug-trafficking maybe if that's the right term for delivering drugs from one place to another, something he'd think they'd be in, or running guns, for another thing. But then they might think this route's the best of any because it's big and fast, for one reason, and it's the last the cops might think they'd be on after what they did, if they even know about it from the papers and radio and such. Because for all they know or care about later they might think they only got the windshield, big laugh, but didn't hit anyone or hurt anyone much except with maybe a little glass. Or maybe the driver had his eyes peeled to the road, and by the time the guy finished shooting the van was too far away for him to see if he hit anything, or the gun recoiled or whatever it does, banged him in the eye, even, no matter how hard he was holding it, so he didn't even look to see or just couldn't if he hit anything. They also might have been so far away from the shooting the next day that it wouldn't have been news in the papers of the place they were in or on the radio and TV stations there, not that he believes they read the newsier part of the papers or listen to radio or TV news even when it might relate to them. Or they might have been too drugged or drunk to read, watch or listen, if they do do those things with news, or just too busy getting rid of the drugs or guns they were delivering or picking up or whatever criminal activity they were going to, for certainly some kind of crime like that's what they're in. So, a long shot but the only shot he thinks he has at finding these men, especially the guy who seemed to start it or was most involved in it and could have easily stopped it, the one with the gun, and finding them and getting even and making them die if he can, at his hands or the state's, and if the state doesn't do it then he'll come with a gun to the courthouse last trial day to do it himself, or with a hammer, or better, a pick, and especially to that guy, is the only thing right now he wants to do.

He stays on the Interstate days for about ten hours each day for weeks, south at the big bridge through his state for eighty-four miles, direction he was heading that day, turning around at the state line and back north to the bridge, and so forth, north-south, south-north, every two hours or so stopping for coffee or a snack at one of the road's rest areas where he looks around for those men at the restaurants and fast-food places inside and then outside in the lots which he drives around looking for the van, and occasionally there for gas where he asks the attendants if they've seen a white minivan lately, Chevy or Ford—even though when he saw newspaper ads of the different vans he couldn't tell the two makes apart—he doesn't know what state's license plate but with one or two men in it looking like the ones he describes.

Hand gets better, for a while had to steer and shift with the right, which took some getting used to, at the start of the search his wife telling him it's understandable but a little crazy what he's doing, risking his health by damaging his hand further, raising the chances of an accident by driving so much and so many hours a day and with a bad hand and staying awake through most of it on coffee, deserting his family when they really need him, maybe losing his job and draining their savings and just doing something useless and futile, for he'll never find them, not one in a million will he ever even see them even driving the opposite way from him, and if he does hit that once and catches up with them they'll probably kill him first second they recognize him, for they're pros at it with no remorse at what they do while he's just an inexperienced hysteric, and continues saying what he's doing is crazy but not "a little" anymore or "understandable," but he still does it, and longer he does greater the chance he'll find them, he thinks— if they weren't on the Interstate before they'll be on it now, unless they got jailed or killed since because of the stuff they're into, for they'll feel it's all blown over or almost and they can ride the Interstate again because nobody's really out looking for them— takes a week-to-week work leave always saying he's still in a state of shock over his daughter, eventually they ask him to see the company psychologist, and when he refuses—one reason, he doesn't tell them, that it'll take time away from his search and another that he doesn't think the psychologist will believe him— then a private therapist he chooses who should send the report on him to them, and when he says rest's all he needs, no doctor, they let him go.

Few months after he started the search he sees a white minivan like the one that day going the other way on the Interstate and not unlike many he's seen on it and a few he's gone after because he thought he saw one or two of those men in it and pulled up alongside and saw he was wrong, and this one also seemed to have two men resembling the ones that day, around the same age as them and both with mustaches and fedora-type hats and the driver with dark sunglasses, more so than any guys he's seen so far in this kind of white minivan, and he crosses the grass median, tries keeping his eyes on the van while he waits for a slew of cars to pass, drives eighty miles an hour to catch up with it and is pulled over by an unmarked police car and though he says why he was driving so fast and asks the cop to go after the van, is told "You have to stay within the law, whatever you're after, and the car's long gone from here, if in fact your excuse is on the level," and gives him a steep ticket.

He continues his search another month, by this time his daughter and wife have gone to live with her folks in New York and he's down to the end of the little savings he asked her to leave him when she left, when he sees on the other side of the Interstate what he thinks is the same van from the last time, only one guy in it but with a mustache and he thinks a fedora-type hat but no sunglasses. A mesh fence separates the two directions so he has to drive about a mile before he can cross in the first don't-enter space between the fence, goes exactly sixty-five an hour in the speed lane till he sees a white minivan in the distance and hopes it's the same one he saw more than five minutes ago, catches up, maybe the guy driving at the maximum legal speed so as not to risk being stopped by the cops if he's the one, gets behind it in one of the three center lanes and jots down the license plate with the pen and pad he'd stuck to the dash just in case of this, from the back the driver looks like the one that day when the van drove on while the other guy shot at them, gets alongside on the left in the next center lane and looks inside. Same driver, he can't believe it, he's almost sure it's him and looks hard again, he's sure and shouts "Holy Christ, oh my God," and slams the passenger seat with his fist and stays alongside and thinks what's he going to do? what did he plan to?—follow him and then get the cops to grab him after he sees what house or store or whatever he goes in, no, scare the hell out of him first and then do what he can to give the guy an accident but not a bad one as he doesn't want to kill him for it's the other guy he wants much worse than him, and honks and the driver stays staring straight ahead, windows up, listening to some heavy beat it seems because his head's bopping back and forth and his mouth's moving as if he's singing or doing something to the music with it, and he honks again and again and the driver looks in the rearview and then when he honks again, to his right and he nods and says "Yeah, yeah, me," and lowers his window and indicates with his hand the driver should roll down his and the driver raises his eyebrows with an expression like "Hey, what's up, man?" and he says out loud to himself "Jesus, just what I did that day, the bastard," and honks repeatedly and the driver seems to say with his expression "What's with you, man, what're you going nuts for with your horn?" and he aims his hand out the window in the shape of a gun at the driver and the driver smiles and aims his hand back at him across his seat in the shape of a gun and then with his mouth seems to go bang-bang and he says "Bang-bang to you too, you rotten bastard, you scroungy rat, do you hear me?" and the driver laughs but a fake one and looks back at the road and he honks and honks till the driver looks at him and he jabs his thumb into his chest and says "Me, I'm the fucking father of the kid you killed, do you remember me?" and the driver smiles and points to his ear while shaking his head and then looks at the road again and he honks repeatedly and the driver keeps looking ahead though every thirty seconds or so sneaks a glance over to see if the car's still beside him and gradually picks up speed and while they're doing about seventy he crosses into the driver's lane and slowly gets close enough to the van to bump its side once with his and then veers right and straightens out just as he's about to lose control and drives parallel to the van about a foot apart and the driver looks alarmed and through his closed window seems to scream at him while shaking his fist "What're you, fucking nuts, you moron?—I'll kill ya," and speeds up and he follows but can't stay even as the van gets up to about a hundred and his car at the most can do eighty-five, so he just watches it till he loses it and then slows to sixty-five and keeps driving for miles, hoping a patrol car pulled the van over for going at such a high speed but either the van's off the Interstate by now or the police were only able to catch up to it once it was off or none had.

He rides the Interstate another two weeks and then gives up; they're probably not driving on it anymore, he thinks, or they got a different car, but now that they know he's out looking for them and no doubt told the police he actually saw them on it, or just the driver knows—the other guy could be anywhere else, even shot dead by now, being involved in what he had to be and having exhibited the kind of craziness he did—they're not going to chance that van or this road no matter how dumb or reckless they might be. He did ask the police that day to check on a white Ford minivan with the Florida license plate number he gave and which either has some damage to its right side or will be having body work done there, but they can't locate any van like that in any state they've communication with and the Florida plates were reported stolen in Georgia a few days ago.

He phones his wife and asks her to come back, "I'm done looking for those guys and am going to get a job first thing and get my life back in order," but she says she can't, it's all finished, it's best they get divorced, for he's shown something of himself in all this, no matter how terrible the circumstances might have been to provoke it, that she never wants to risk experiencing again. He's talked on the phone to his daughter almost every day since she and her mother left, mostly just "How are you?" "Fine," "What've you been up to lately?" "Things," "Anything in particular?" "Nothing much," "Maybe something new you want to tell me about?" "Not today," "How's your school doing?" "It's all right," "And your mommy?" "She's okay, I guess," "Why, something happen to her?" "No, everything's the same," "I love you, sweetheart," "I love you too, Daddy," and asks to speak to her now and tells her he loves her, "that's nothing new to you, I know, but like I love no other person on earth, not even your mommy, and I loved your sister as much as I love you and will always be a broken man because of what happened to her that

day with you both on the highway, do you know what a broken
man is in the way I said it?" and she says she thinks she does,
"it doesn't mean split in two like a stick but is about sadness,"
and he says "Though of course I also know how horrible it was
and must still be for you in what happened, as horrible as anything it is for me, and I wish you were with me so I could help
you and you, with just being with me and maybe in some of the
things you'd say, could help me, do you understand what I mean,
sweetie, or am I just being dumbly complicated again?" and she
says "I understand but can't do what you want as I have to be
with Mommy," and he says "I know, and I want you to, but I
wish we could all be together again, not just with Julie, of course,
but if that's impossible, then the three of us left," and she says
"Mommy says we can't, and I don't know how long for, but
wishes the same thing about Julie," and he says "Probably right
now you also don't want to just be with me alone—it's all right,
you don't have to answer that, I don't want to put you on the
spot, and do you know what that means—I mean, by that spot?"
and she says "I can figure it," and he says "Because you see it's
obvious I'm still all out of sorts over it, meaning unhappy, meaning miserable, that highway thing, which is why I say I understand
why you wouldn't want to be alone with me now, it might be
frightening, though please don't ever be of me, but I'll be back to
pretty near normal soon and then maybe almost completely normal, and almost completely normal and normal are just about the
same thing, though with always a little left out for your sister, of
course, which is okay and normal, and some also left out for what
it did to Mommy and you, but not altogether enough with those
to put me back to being even pretty near normal again," and she
says "Daddy, I don't understand anything you're saying now,"
and he says "Anyway, what I'm saying is that when I'm back to
being almost what I was, which should be soon, you can come
stay with me, half with your mommy and half with me," and she
says "We'll see," and he says "Then just weekends, or weekends
here and there and summers or a month of one every year," and

she says "I don't know about that either, you'll have to discuss it with Mommy," and he says " 'Discuss,' oh I love that, you're getting so big and smart that that's also why I want you to be with me now or very soon before you've really grown and won't need to be with your parents anymore that I'll just lose you natu-rally in a way I would have even if Mommy and you were living with me," and she says "Perhaps, I'm not sure of that." "You know," he says, "though maybe you don't unless your mommy's told you, but I almost caught the driver of that car—that van, a minivan, a Ford it turned out to be," and she says "No I didn't, Mommy probably didn't want me to," and he says "Well, she's likely right, but the van was much faster than our old buggy and I'm sure souped up, which is when they do something to increase the power of the car, so it got away. I was on the same highway also, though maybe I shouldn't go further into it or even remind you of anything connected to it, but I was going to, I swear to you, smash into the van to force it off the road—I'd already bumped into it with our car—and then strangle him till he almost died or club him with this kid's baseball bat I had right beside me in the car just for that, I didn't care, and then hold him for the police but not kill him, as I'd really want to, for I wanted much more to get the guy who killed your sister and I thought I might force who that guy was out of him or the police might or the courts when they got this driver on trial, but what do you think?" and she says "You mean the other man wasn't with him?" and he says no and she says "Still, you ought to stop worrying over it, Daddy—let those men alone, they might kill you first next time, they're so bad," and he says "Your mommy told me that so long ago I forget when, so she probably also told you, for those were almost her exact words," and she says "Even if she did, and this is only what I now think, what you want to do to those men won't do anything for Julie. She's dead and you should start knowing it," and he says "What do you think?—of course I do, but getting those men would do wonders for me, I'll tell you, because I can't live right knowing those guys are still around, enjoying themselves maybe, maybe even bragging about what they did and got away with and maybe even just that they forgot what they did till I bumped the van of that driver, or that they're still doing it to other cars, though I haven't read anything in the papers on it, though they could have switched those crazy killings to the street—that goes on all the time—or to highways in other states, which how would we have gotten news of unless it was to like ten cars in one day? but for your sake I'll do what you say and stop worrying over it. You're right, you're right on just about everything, sweetheart, boy do I have such a smart right kid, but I'll tell you a little secret—I gave up on ever finding those guys once that rat driver got away, so as I told your mommy, I'm no longer driving on the highway looking for them," and she says good.

He gets a job and about three months later is on his way to work when he sees two men getting out of a light blue minivan with no windows except in front, both looking from almost a block away like those guys in the white van: same ages it seems, sunglasses though he can't see from here if they're dark, and as he gets closer to them just their faces and smiles and the driver's big bulky forehead seem the same. He drives past slowly, they're talking on the sidewalk, smile a big conniving-together smile and slap their right hands in the air like he's seen athletes do after a real good play and then go opposite ways on the sidewalk he sees in his right side mirror and then in the rearview when he turns it to show more of the right and though they don't have mustaches and have on baseball-type caps instead of fedora-style hats, they're the ones all right, no mistake of it. He doesn't know what to do, slowing down to almost a crawl: get one somehow and best yet the guy who killed his kid and through him the police can get the other one soon, but he doesn't know if he's revved up enough to do what he thinks he could have easily done or at least made an attempt to on the Interstate when he was cruising for them and which with his bumping their van he almost did. "Fuck it, the bastards," he says, "they killed my kid—you fucking guys did and you're both going to get it in the head," and makes a sharp U, no cars are coming either way, which he didn't think to look for when he made that U, cuts across the street and the driver, one nearest and heading in his direction, stops and looks at his car, and he climbs the sidewalk and starts for him with his foot now all the way down on the gas and the driver yells "Hey, what the shit—Luke!" and quickly looks around where to run it seems but he hits him, driver going over the front of the car and landing in the street and he starts for who he supposes is Luke who's running across the street darting back looks at him, through the rearview and right side mirror sees the driver on both knees shaking himself off, front and Luke's on the other sidewalk running away from him with no looks back now and he drives off the sidewalk, doesn't know if he should get on Luke's sidewalk or stay in the street alongside him till he has a clear shot at him with the car, gets on, nobody else is there and gets to about twenty feet of him with the gas pedal all the way down when Luke jumps over the front of a parked car, foot clips the hood and he tumbles to the street, he cuts into the street second he's past the car in front of the jumped car, stops hard, looks back and sees the driver hobbling back to their van, and looking through his back window, Luke getting up slowly and holding his elbow, doesn't know whether to turn around and head straight for Luke or back up on him hard, knocking him down, and then turn around and drive over him, "Luke, over here," driver shouts by the van and Luke starts to run to it, almost falls and then limps to it and he shoots forward, stops, angles the car so it's diagonally across from Luke and backs up fast as he can and Luke lunges but he jerks the steering wheel that way and hits him. Luke goes down, driver's fumbling inside his pants pockets probably for car keys, Luke's pushing himself up with his arms and he shoots forward, backs up and goes over some part of him he feels from the bump, goes forward so over probably the same part though just wanted to get where he could see him, thinks "Yes? no? screw him, he killed my kid and if he gets up he'll probably try to kill me," and backs over him with both the back and front wheels now till, and doesn't know why he didn't think of this before, he's in front of Luke who's flat out and face down and maybe dead and he screams "Killer, killer," and floors the gas pedal and goes over him making sure not to hit his head, then makes a U, driver's on the sidewalk looking as if he's unlocking the passenger door, doesn't know whether to drive up on it and hit him or just ram the van from the street, stopping it from going and maybe hurting the man, or just pull up and jump out and grab him and pound him to the ground. People have come out of some of the ranch houses, workers are standing right outside the one-story computer-graphics place, the lawn sign says, between two ranch houses and which the van's parked near, cars have stopped at both ends of the street, driver's got the door open and is getting into the van and he rams into it from the street, is thrown forward but head doesn't hit anything and windshield doesn't crack and he flops back into his seat, driver's thrown down on the seat or floor somewhere or is looking for something there, "Gun, get him before he gets it," he thinks and jumps out of the car and runs around the van, driver's on his back on the seat with his eyes closed and opens them on him and he thinks "The kid's bat, left it where?" and pulls the driver out by his legs, driver shoots his hand back to protect his head but it bumps on the sidewalk and the driver yells "Oh shit" and looks in great pain, he gets down and grabs the driver's head, hands flinch from the blood in back of it but he says "No, fuck it," and grabs it again and hard and driver screams and he says "You remember me, right?" and the driver says "Hey, wha?" his eyes rolling and he says "Hey, hey, you remember me, don't you?" and the driver says "Hey, I'm hurt, don't, no more," and he says "But you remember me, you and your pal do, or he did, right?—open my window, roll it down, stick a gun in my face, aim it in back, shoot who the hell you want to, me and one of my dead little kiddies, right, right?" and the driver says "What? I swear. What pal? I haven't got one. I didn't do anything. What do you mean?" and he says "On the

Interstate here—white minivan—don't you remember me bumping
it?—where's your mustache and fedora?" and the driver says
"What fedora? Fedora, what's that?" and he says "This fedora,
this fedora, my daughter," and bangs the driver's head against the
car several times and people yell "Stop. . . . Don't. . . . Enough. . . .
Someone!" and he lifts the head high and bangs it against the
ground and again and hands grab him from behind and he tries
shaking them off while banging the head and someone gets him
in a neck lock and yanks him back while he drags the driver's
head with him till someone pries his fingers off one by one and
he lets go with the last fingers and someone catches the driver's
head just before it hits the ground and they still pull him back
and he says "All right, okay, I've stopped, you've stopped me, I'll
be good now and stick around for the police," and they let him
go and he sits a few feet away on the curb and wipes the blood
off him on his pants and shirt and just looks down at his feet.

"Jesus, did you do them," a man says, crouching beside him,
"what was it, like you said?" and he nods and the man says "One
in the street's dead, I don't know if you know, fucking face
crushed, and other's—" and he says "Didn't mean to run over his
face, in fact I intended—" and the man says "Well, your aim was
bad, but the other looks almost finished too—cops and medics
are on the way," and he says "They deserved it, hope the alive
one dies," and the man says "Listen, for some advice, don't go
blabbing that, say it was self-defense, defense," and he says "It
wasn't and at this point I'm not going to start bullshitting," and
the man says "Then say nothing, put your hands over your face
like you're sad, look disturbed, even, and wait for your lawyer or
one given you but don't sell yourself away and ten more years
for it," and he says "I'll answer what they ask and if they don't
buy it, fine, I'll swing," and the man says "That's what you think
now, but I've been inside, babe, and later when you're there you'll
hate every extra day for not doing what I say, but okay, I'm only
trying to help, and lots of luck," and the man stands and he
stands and hugs him.

Police and medics come, driver's treated on the street and taken away in an ambulance, guy's put in a bag and left there in a special medical van with the back doors open while the police ask him what happened though say he doesn't have to answer or can wait till he has a lawyer and he says "I was getting back at them, if I didn't nothing ever would have happened to them, like finding them, except by accident, it's all written down somewhere what they did to my kid that day on the Interstate, you'll see they'll fit the descriptions I gave minus the mustaches and there'll be nothing about their height for I never saw them out of their van till today."

The two have records, now wanted for this and that in other states, police photos showing them with mustaches, he refuses to hire a lawyer so is assigned one, his daughter can't be a witness for him since she can't even say what age around or color the men were that first time on the Interstate and thought there were three or four of them in the van, he's convicted and given ten to twelve years for killing an unarmed man and permanently damaging the brain of another, judge says at sentencing "If you had shown one iota of remorse or expressed some understanding of the wrong you've done I would have sentenced you to a few years or less, given what you've gone through over your daughter's death and that you've never been charged with a serious crime before and the men you attacked had a history of felonious activity and were wanted for robbery and murder though not of your child and who now ironically can't be tried for these other crimes since one is dead and the other will be a vegetable for life, but what you've done, sir, and how you've acted since sends the wrong message to others similarly victimized and bereft who might want to take barbarous revenge the way you did and then the streets would even be more menacing than they are today, so I must conclude that you're nearly as dangerous and perhaps even as ruthless as the men you call without proof your daughter's brutalizers," and he says "You could think that, I'm not going to take issue with you, though nobody's going to convince me I

didn't get the right guys, but personally I feel a hell of a lot better
for what I did, and to me, though it'll be a long time before I can
enjoy them, the streets have to be a little safer now, and for sure
the Interstate is, not with me off them but those guys, even if
that's not at all why I did it."

Some prisoners say they admire him for what he did for his
kid and proof's in the eye and those guys deserved it, but most
others say he shouldn't have gone so far as to try and kill them,
for look what he lost: wife, other kid and his freedom, and also
he couldn't have been sure it was them after almost a year and
maybe he still didn't get the right men who might even be in this
prison wanting to kill him before he finds out his mistake and
tries to get them and besides, you want someone killed you get a
pro to do it but you don't try it yourself in what always for an
amateur turns out to be a sloppy job or total bungle, like with
his braining for life that poor slob, and where you usually end up
dead yourself or in prison for years if not gassed by the state for
having killed some innocent bystander or the wrong guy or even
the right one. He usually says he had no time or money to hire
a hit man, not that he ever would have for he didn't want anyone
doing it except himself because only he had a reason to and money
for killing no matter how much someone would pay can never be
a reason, and some say "For ten thou? . . . for twenty? . . . for
fifty then? . . . you telling me you wouldn't knock off someone
you don't know for a half million if you knew it was fairly easy?"
and then if that's the case he should have let the matter go and
got on with his life and if he saw them by accident like on the
road then he just should have told the cops where it was and
leave it at that and at most hope for the best and if it was in
some place where the guys were still there, then where, but to
keep his body completely out of it.

His wife visits him a few months after he's in, though he
wrote and spoke to her answering machine plenty of times to
come, without hearing anything back, and she says she'd like a
divorce and hopes he won't try to stop it and he says he doesn't

want one, of course, but he put her through such misery like leaving her stranded and almost broke and with their oldest child, besides the even worse misery by far she had over losing Julie while at the same time seeing him go nuts in his own misery and over finding those guys, that anything she wants he'll give, every single dime in the bank and whatever assets and possessions they still might have and things like that and any arrangements she wants to make with him over Margo he'll sign, though he hopes she'll bring the kid to him here or have someone do it a few times a year, and she remarries a short while later and has a daughter who in a few years is the age Julie was when that guy killed her.

His ex–sister-in-law brings Margo to see him in prison about once a year once the girl turns twelve and then when she's eighteen she visits him on her own because she wants to or knows how much he wants her to and feels sorry for him and is just responding to his begging letters for her to come for she's all he has he says in them, all he ever will and just a few hours with her makes the next few months till her next visit so much better for him, and it's usually uncomfortable between them for the two hours she's there—they could have more time but he can tell by her fidgeting and face that those two hours are a little more than she can tolerate—and they don't talk to each other much and he mostly stares at her not looking or looking at everything but him and says when he says anything, and then it often becomes a sort of running-mouth thing, how nice she looks and bigger and even prettier she's getting, all things he knows daddies, or "fathers" now because she's of that age, are almost supposed to be saying but with her it's altogether true, and mature she's sounding and also mature in lots of other good ways and how nice her clothes are or how they're the perfect choice for her looks and physique and the weather today and how it's not so bad in here, she didn't ask but he'll give her his semiannual report anyway if she doesn't mind, the other prisoners still leave him alone for the most part for they know it's what he wants after all he went through, and how much it means to him that she's here sitting opposite him, he can hardly believe it after wishing for it so much the last three months and he apologizes if coming here was a lot of trouble and cost her more than she could afford or stopped her from doing something or being with someone she wanted to be with or do much more, it's okay though, he was a kid once, or a young man he should say if he's going to get their age comparisons right, so he understands and he won't ever forget that she comes here pretty regularly, that she comes here at all, even, and he knows it's not the greatest place to see one's dad and he appreciates the effort she made in coming here but he said that, and at least once every time she's there he suddenly starts bawling, first sniveling, then trying to hold it back, then flat-out crying or bawling but over nothing he later tells her, just happy to see her and he hopes his crying doesn't stop her from coming to see him more and she swears it doesn't but inside he thinks he's also bawling because he's thinking all he's missed not living with her the last eight years, nine years, ten and when he sees her he sees Julie for they looked almost like twins when they were kids except for the three-year age difference and he figures this is probably close to what Julie would have looked like if she hadn't died, or seeing her he thinks of Julie and what happened to her that day and what she looked like dead in the shot-up car, bullet hole in her chest just below her neck, expression, once he picked her arms off her face, no, that's not it, the hole was some other place, in her neck and it was car glass in her cheek and chest, why was she up? why wasn't she down? he'd told them both to be so why couldn't she have listened to him as Margo did? didn't he yell loud enough? wasn't there enough anger and power and force and alarm in his voice to scare them to stay down? and a minute or two before when he was driving side by side with the van and looked quickly in the rearview to see if they were okay and before that when they started out on the car trip, on their way back from a weekend in New York, wife staying with her folks two more days and then returning by train, talking during the start of the ride which rest stop they'd stop at if they didn't have to stop before that for one of them to pee, and then when they decided, which eating place there, Bob's Big Boy or Roy Rogers or Sabarro he thinks the Italian place was called or maybe a combo of all three? and one of the last times Margo saw him in prison and when they were silent a long while with her looking at anything but him she says, something she's always wanted to say but never had the heart or courage to or whatever it takes she says, she wishes he hadn't gone after those men so drivenly, and that's no joke, like her mother and she told him not to years and years ago, although okay she was just a kid then so he'd hardly listen to her but to his own wife? for what good did it do even if he'd killed both of them and they were the real men and almost more important and she's surprised he wasn't thinking this then, what good was he as a father after that when she really needed one, not just for the year or two after the shock of her losing Julie and all that blood and stuff but through her entire growing up, and even now he's not there the few times she could still use him for advice and bouncing off her views or just being there for her, with or without her mother, or driving her where she needs to be before she gets her own car, or whatever real biological fathers are supposed to be good for and do for their children besides the money she could really use for college and which her mother's husband doesn't have or if he does he's not going to part with so easily since he has his own biological kids with her mother and his first wife to support and he says "Money, what can I tell you?—I don't get paid a whole lot here and they don't have any college tuition plan for the children of their workers, but as for the rest—moral support and all—I'm here for you, I'm here, where else am I?—I'm not any ghost, and I write you almost every day, you're the only one I do, so in that respect you have more communication with me, and even more if you'd answer a letter every now and then, than maybe most girls your age do with their dads who are all out to work half the day and then bring it home with them and things like that—just not interested, lots of them, or only interested in the things they're not—but maybe you don't even read half my letters, which'd be all right, being I send so many," and she says "I do too, but not always so carefully, for I've a lot to do for school to earn future college money you won't be able to give, and let's face it, Daddy, you sometimes say the same thing in them or fairly close or repeat yourself in different ways where it becomes too repeatinglike and sort of boring if I can say—after a while there's not a lot to write about in prison, which I long ago figured out but I guess is what this place is supposed to be for—to make you wish you didn't do what you did to get yourself in here and to make you also want to jump back into the non-crimelike world once you get out where you can have something new to do and talk about and for gosh sake never to go back in again because of all the sameness and bad food and sleeping and no privacy and your horrible toilets and all the TVs on around you and dumb conversations and no summer vacations as you've joked a hundred times and that music the other prisoners play that you hate and I'm sure no women and even some fear of the other men," and he says "True, although it could be I haven't told you everything, though none of what I didn't say would make me want to stay, but I also call you whenever I can and am able to afford it and you can call me at the prescribed hours when you like too but unfortunately not collect, they don't have that advantage here either, or even from your mom's phone, why not?—I handed all we had and owned over to her without a gripe when we split up, not that there was much, I admit, or that I regret a single nickel of it, though a little house with a big mortgage is still something if a few years' interest on it have been paid off and the market hasn't dropped, so maybe the least she could do for both of us—and then if it makes you feel better it should make her too, right?—is let you call me from her phone now and then, or just tell her to tally all the calls you make to me and their cost— why didn't I think of this a thousand years ago?—and when I get out and really working, or even with the little dough I make a day here, I'll pay her back with regular bank interest whatever

that now is, but anyway, none of those I realize are the same as
my being there for you on the outside when you need me and it
never can be turned around to be made good, but what else did
you want to tell me?—you said there was something," and she
says "You're not going to like this," and he says "Just say, nothing
about yourself can make me angry," and she says "Sad, though,
that's what I'm afraid," and he says "If you're sick, but I mean
on your last leg or just very bad, then that of course," and she
says "Soon as I graduate in June I'm going to Seattle or some
West Coast place where young people go, to look for work and
room with girls I'll get from the ads and hopefully get residency
status there so I can go to college cheap, so to be honest I'll be
coming here even less than I have and today can easily be the last
time for a while, I'm sorry, Daddy," and he says "Well, that
wasn't too bad, I'm already recovering because I know it's what
you want and should be good for you if it's safe, and also, since
I'm out of here in less than two years, it won't be too long a
stretch between seeing you if you don't come again but tell me
where you are. Now as for what you both said not to do with
those guys who killed Julie, long as we're talking straight, going
after them so one-mindedly and blindly you can say, I shouldn't
have if only because it broke up what could have been considered
a fairly good marriage till then, though just losing Julie could have
done that, everything because of it thrown out of whack, but it
also separated me from you and then permanently when she left,
though if she had stayed who knows by then when I saw those
guys if I wouldn't have been over it, so to speak, so wouldn't
have run over them and banged the alive guy's head on the street,
but truth is, and thanks for calling me Daddy—you never say
that, not in ten years, so maybe it's like, well, your final visit, sort
of a planned keepsake for me—but I doubt I would've been *that*
over it when I saw them, even in a killer-animal way, so would've
done, even if your mom hadn't left me, what I did and been given
even more years because with you both not gone the judge could
have said 'Hey, he still had his family there, so his wife didn't

leave him because she thought he was crazy and he wasn't crazy in addition because she left him and took their only other child, so he even shouldn't more have done what he did,' or something— I can't put words into a judge's mouth, they're of another breed and their legalese is way past me. The other truth is I'm still glad what I did to those guys, the worst of the two for all time erased, for nobody in the world deserved it more but maybe Nazi butchers of a thousand kids in one day or the Japanese in World War Two with Chinese babies on their bayonets if that story wasn't just made up to get us to hate and kill the Japanese even more, and I lots of times wish, even sometimes for that driver-of-the-van's sake, though that feeling of good for him doesn't last long, because he could have told the gun guy to stop, you know—he could have shouted in the van 'Stop, there're kids in there, stop!'— that I'd finished him off too even if it would've no doubt given me a longer term, or maybe I don't wish that for I've probably done all the time here, plus the two years to go, I can just about take."

Has to serve his maximum sentence, minus a few months, and is let out, returns to his old city and rents a single room, gets a job in a cheap hamburger-steak place, work he learned in prison, not the hamburgers so much or steaks at all though they're easy enough, steaks a bit trickier, but just weighing and frying and grilling and boiling and recooking lots of food quickly and on a much larger scale and dishing it out all at once and where he was one of many cooks rather than the only one behind the counter now who has to do some of the dishwashing too. Daughter marries but doesn't tell him where or when—she stopped writing him a few months after that last visit and her mother, when he called for Margo's phone number and address when he got out, told him about the marriage and said "I'll tell her you called, next time I hear from her—it could be this week or next—and if she wants to get in touch with you I'll give her your phone number and address—what are they, and by the way how are you?" and he said "Exhausted, demoralized, done in, badly off, but couldn't you call her today and tell her I'm out and want very much to see her, at least hear from her?" and she said "I'll try"—has a baby very quickly he hears soon after that from his ex-wife when he calls again for Margo's phone number or address or even her city and husband's last name and who won't give it, "Once again, that's her business," she says, "she has her ways, which I don't necessarily approve of regarding you, but nothing I can say—I'll keep forwarding your letters and packages to her if you keep sending them here care of me or Dave, though with the packages, since we also aren't in great financial shape, maybe you can mail them first class instead of fourth or parcel post so we don't have to put out for the extra forwarding cost—and Margo says, well she still hasn't said anything about not wanting your mail, so maybe one day, I'm sure this'll be the case—she's still a kid, even with one of her own, and congratulations, Grandpa, I'm sure nobody's said that to you before, and kids change—she'll switch over," and he says "From what—seeing or hearing from me or something deeper I don't know about? Or just the obvious—she say she's ashamed of my having done time or frightened because I once pummeled and killed some guy, now that she has her own child?" and she says "Wish I knew, Nat, she's closemouthed on the subject, but you remember her as a girl—supersensitive and always a reader, never one for talk or introspection except about her dreams and books—she in fact reprimands me when I ask what gives over you," and he says "Plead with her, Lee, please plead with her for me—tell her prison neutered and weakened me and I've become the most harmless of men, slapping patties, going home and reading newspapers, on my days off taking walks and going to movies and museums and in the park looking at the kids playing in the playground till it gets to look suspicious and in the zoo throwing old restaurant rolls to those birds that stand on one leg, flamingos, and all kinds of no-flying ducks—sounds hokey, I know, but I'm not saying it to make me seem even more harmless to you so you can report back to her how much but because it's what I am, or have become—which is it? for I truly forget a lot of what I was like before I bopped those guys—for there are no friends or nothing else from before, the jobs I had where I knew people I got so far behind at in twelve years, and no doubt my prison and what I did to get in didn't help, that they wouldn't hire me anymore, all of which I've said endlessly in my letters to her, and about my harmlessness, but maybe she'll tune into it better coming from you," and she says "I'll try but not to the point where she then won't want to speak to me," and he says "So she lives nearby you?" and she says "No, why'd you say that?" and he says "I don't know—thought if she did I could trick you into saying so and maybe where and if she didn't and you said so, I'd know that too, which I now do and isn't any help to me and just shows how desperate I am to know even the slightest inkling of her and just to see her, I'm sorry," and she says "You ever think that perhaps desperation like that is what might be pushing her away?" and he says "Why should it be?—I'm just a familyless father showing normal loss and love after so many years with probably some holdover woe going all the way back to our poor Julie, for do you ever forget?" and she says "I don't want to talk about it," and he says "Okay, you got other people to do it to, which I'm glad for you, plus also you've another kid, but did Margo tell you that about pushing her away?" and she says "In all honesty, no," and some years later Margo calls him at work—he'd given her the number in his letters, always at the top left under his address along with his home phone number and what times and days he's usually at either place—and says "Hello, it's Margo, your daughter, how are you?" and he says "Margo, my goodness, oh-h-h, gosh, where you calling from, how are you?" and she says "I tried getting you at home the last few hours but nobody answered and you have no answering machine," and he says "My hours aren't others', and me, a machine? but I thought I gave my work and home hours in my letters in case you did call, and they haven't changed in years," and she says "I don't remember seeing them, and it's all right to talk to you here?" and he says "For the moment, sure, I practically run this joint, but don't hang up without letting me know where you are," and she says "You're the manager?" and he says "Just a cook and counterman but of long standing and so honest they know they could never get another like me," and she says "And that was a fib about the hours—I remember now—actually, I remembered when I mentioned them before, but I didn't jot them down, only your phone numbers and home address," and he says "It's okay, it's okay, and you're okay, everything at home okay? nothing wrong I hope with your family or your mother or other sister, the one between Lee and her new husband—new, old, her second husband," and she says "No, I'm just calling, and listen, I'm sorry I haven't contacted you sooner, haven't been in contact, period, I'm not certain why I haven't though I know it's inexcusable and more inexcusable why I didn't answer even a fraction of your wonderful letters," and he says "They weren't wonderful, they were mostly sappy and dumb and maybe too beggarlike, right?" and she says "They were very nice, no excessive demands or re-proaches on me, which I could have used to get me to write back, and also for the books and things for me you sent and birthday presents for what you thought were the birth dates of my boys," and he says "I didn't know the exact dates, and am only finding out now the exact genders, but just the approximate ones by a month or two which is all your mother would tell me—she said you'd have to tell me yourself and when I said 'What's the harm if I know the exact dates?'—though I'm not blaming her—'in fact it'll be clearer to her kids,' I said, 'why they're getting these gifts and if I know what sex they are I can get them even more fitting gifts, dolls for the boys, catcher mitts for the girls, et cetera,' only kidding, she said that's all she'd tell me, that she possibly shouldn't have even said you had kids, so I just guessed the sex and exact dates, hoping, sly devil I am, that you'd send a note back not thanking me so much as correcting me, but anyway, let's forget it, just hearing your voice is all and I'm talking too much to hear much of it, and you sound so different, nowhere near like you did, your speaking manner, use of words and proper diction—

you make me feel like a dolt in comparison—you sure this is my old Margo and not some practical-joker one? only kidding again—just put up with me, honey, I'm so excited I can't stop mouthing, but where are you, in your city, the country?" and she says "No, yours, with my husband and oldest son," and he says "That's right, three, and now boys, I know, and all of them you had while working plus going to school and then getting not one but two after-college degrees, your mother said, and in very difficult fields," and she says "Rigorous disciplines, perhaps, but not difficult—I must have had the knack, just as I probably couldn't have done the schoolwork for what you did before, what was that?" and he says "Before what?" and she says "The present job," and he says "Dental technician, something my father wanted me to do because he thought it a field where I'd always have a job, but by the time I got out, but wait a minute, the city? here? this one?" and she says "Glen, my husband, is attending a sales rally and the parent company of his firm wanted to have it here because of all the waterfront attractions and I guess the place caters to it, so I thought I'd turn it into a minivacation for me and sightseeing trip for our son and also a chance to see the few of my friends left here," and he says "Oh, and who are they?" and she says "People, but getting back to before, I suppose part of why, if you don't mind my saying, though I'd like to get it out right away—that's the way I've become, open like that, though I'm not saying it's the best quality or I'm boasting or occasionally couldn't be more diplomatic at it," and he says "Anyway, what were you saying?" and she says "That part of why I stopped having contact with you was that I wanted to cut myself off from my old life, childhood friends included, though perhaps not Mom—that would have been too radical a surgery—to develop on my own, if you can accept that," and he says "Okay, that's interesting, something to think about, but speaking of cutting off, honey, and this is in no way a reaction to what you said, for there's nothing more in life I want to do than speak to you and soon after that to meet Glen and your boy, whatever his name is," and she says "Saul," and he says "Biblical—any reason, or Glen's family?" and she says no and he says "And the other two?" and she says "Dyon and Carlos," and he says "Nice names too—after anyone I know?" and she says "No, we liked them as names," and he says "But I thought everyone's named after someone—I'm named after my mother's father Nathaniel, who I never knew—he died, that's why, before I was born, which is how you usually did it, and 'Margo' comes from my mother's brother Marvin who was killed in the war, and which your mother was kind enough to go along with, but you know this," and she says "Not the particulars, so go on," and he says "And who because I was so young when he died you could say I almost never saw, or actually as a result of injuries from it a year later—they say he blanked out at the wheel of his car because of being shell-shocked in battle, or something like that—it's funny how you forget—I do, when at the time it's the biggest thing existing—but anyway, being I was the only child I knew it's what my mother would have wanted—it pleased her till she died that you were named Margo after him," and she says "Well what can I say?—with each of ours we took the ten best names we found in the most complete namebook, considered Glen's surname in relation to it, and narrowed it down to two or three—" and he says "Excuse me but by surname do you mean last name?" and she says yes and he says "What is it?" and she says "I still go by my maiden name, even if it's yours, meaning a man's, but at least I didn't continue the custom I wasn't so keen on, adopting my husband's patronym," and he says "It's not a bad one, our last name—one syllable, confusing to spell if you think it's the spat or shred Fray rather than an *e*. But anyway, my sweetheart, I am suddenly in the thick of work with two customers, and hungry ones, judging by their faces—in fact, not wanting to be a fibber either, they came in more than five minutes ago and have been good about it but they got to get back to work too and business hasn't been that hot, so we need them, so give me your number where you are and I'll call back soon," and she says "I can call you at home later—when would be the best time?"

and he says "No, please, I don't want to miss you, long as you're here—to be straight open, you might change your mind or have a memory lapse for your entire time here, only kidding, or even lose my phone numbers—that could happen, people lose things— and not remember how to get them—place I work at is called the Corner Cafe, but no 'the' before it, just Corner Cafe, so listed in the directory under C, for Corner, then 'Cafe' after it, and on Abbott Street, like Bud Abbott and Lou Costello—Abbott and Costello they were called, but you wouldn't remember them, an old-time comedian team," and she says "Sure, I once saw a movie with them on TV, or maybe it was a video with my kids—some- thing with a ghost, the humor grossly dated and somewhat trite, but they didn't like it much either—you have to understand I'm not that young and you're not that old, you might have had me when you were past thirty but now I'm getting to be thirty," and he says "Not possible," and she says "I'm telling you, I'll even show you my driver's license," and he says "You mean you're old enough to drive?—only kidding, and I want to see it, you show it when you see me, and listen, Margo, if you don't call I'll only go from hotel to hotel looking for you and there has to be a couple of dozen of them by the harbor now, so wouldn't that be a waste of time? and I'd also be putting my job on the line or my bosses in a tough spot because I wouldn't go in when I'm sup- posed to and they need me, as I'd be out searching for you," and she says "I swear I'll call, or just meet us for lunch tomorrow," and he says "Lunch is so short—I know, fellas," he says to the customers at the counter, "I'll be right there—my daughter," pointing to the mouthpiece, then the ear part, "after I can't tell you how many years," and the men nod, say with their hands "Take your time," and he says into the phone "Excuse me, I had to pause for work stuff, anyway, lunch is too short and I don't think I could get off, so what about dinner tonight, out, my treat, all of you?" and she says "Dinner? tonight?—just a moment, Dad," and she starts talking away from the phone—"He wants to take us all out for dinner tonight"—and another voice talks,

but all garbled, and then he hears nothing, her hand must be
muzzling the receiver, and one of the men says "Long as you're
just standing there, Nat, start my regular," and he says "Hold it,
she might suddenly come back on, and when it's over I'll be extra
fast, making up for what time you lost," and another man says
"At least our coffee, or mine, heck with him," and he puts his
hand up for them to wait and she says "All right . . . Dad?" and
he says yeah and she says "Tonight, but our treat, Glen didn't
think he could get away from a cocktail party–dinner his company's throwing, but this comes first," and he says "Great, but
my treat, I insist on it," and she says "We'll meet only if you
abide by this one condition—it's on us," and he says "I'll abide,
I'll abide, I can't wait to abide," and she gives him the name of
a restaurant near their hotel that she heard was good—"You still
like seafood, or rather, did you ever?" and he says "Anything,
pizza, even, Crackerjacks—just seeing you all is all I want, food's
no consequence but I'll eat if that's your second condition," and
what time to meet and they meet at the front of the restaurant,
he's there fifteen minutes before, thinking maybe they'll get there
early, can't believe it's her when she comes in, knows though
immediately it is, very slim but not skinny, taller, even, and she
was tall then, filled out on top or maybe it's what she's wearing,
no, she was still developing when he last saw her, old as she was,
hips, longer legs, the fashionable clothes it seems, anyway, well
dressed, pretty as ever, prettier, beautiful and not just because
she's his daughter, any man would fall for her, a decent honest
intelligent man but he bets the horns also can't take their eyes off
her when she walks down the street, a kid before, woman now,
nice-looking son, tall, like him and her but not his father who's
a couple inches shorter than her and she's not wearing heels, kid
a little scared of him or just shy, almost no smile, fish handshake
but he's still very young, he likes the way they dress him for the
restaurant or the occasion he could say, jacket and tie, husband
seems nice, dignified, polite, bright, comes from money or made
it on his own ethically, somewhat square or so it seems at first

meeting, clothes, haircut, company man looks like, she hurries over to him second she sees him and kisses his cheek, "I know you, you must be my dad and practically unchanged," smiling, stepping back, "Absolutely none, you're amazing," introduces her husband and son, he's dressed up too, his one tie with his one suit he got married in almost thirty years ago and wore day after day in court and it still looks good, wore it into prison just to have it when he got out, they only allowed one outfit to bring in and for them to store, dry-cleaned it soon after his release but hasn't worn it once till now, didn't need a pressing though, kept its shape, wood hanger instead of wire and the plastic bag never off it, heavy wool on this warm June day, trouser legs might be a bit baggy but his weight's the same, maybe differently distributed but he can't see, as it was some fifteen years ago and he doesn't seem to have shrunk any, shirt is one of the two he wears at work and last night washed and hung-dried, tie he used for a few of his job interviews years before, shaved though he'd shaved at six this morning before going to work, said to himself in the bathroom mirror while shaving "Feel like I'm going to meet this love-of-my-life girlfriend of ten years ago who I'm still crazy about and she's just split up with her husband and I think there's a chance between us—look at yourself, that's how nervous and scared you are," lots of questions while they sit at their table and all have drinks, kid a Shirley Temple but he says, after Glen gives the waitress their drink order, "For a boy it's a Jackie Coogan, I think," and all three of them and the waitress say "Who's he?" or "What's that?" and he says "Abbott and Costello's roommate and sidekick," and Margo laughs and Glen says "What gives— old family joke?" and the waitress says "But same thing as a Shirley Temple, correct—no alcohol, dash of grenadine, a bar cherry?" and goes and he says "Could be I'm wrong and for all I know a Coogan gets club soda instead of ginger ale and maybe even a couple of drops of rye—what do I know about heavy drinking? and also Coogan was probably more Shirley Temple's contemporary than Bud and Lou's," and Glen says "Pardon me again, sir, but who are they?" and he says "What kind of cloaked—what's the word, closeted, closed-off, maybe—family you grow up in that you don't know them?—mine we made sure my kids learned important things like that—only kidding," and Saul says "You said 'my kids,' Grandpa—you have any more children after you and Grandma Lee got a divorce? Because it'd be nice knowing I have another aunt and uncle and cousins some-where, even if only step ones," and he says "You would have an aunt and no doubt the rest but we don't want to go into it now— she was younger than you when she passed away—is that remark-able, Margo, can that be believed, that she was probably younger than your son here?—sweetest kid," he says to Saul, "outside of your mother, of course—they were equals in sweetness—that was ever alive," and starts to cry and Saul says to his parents "Did I do something?" and Margo says *"Dad,"* and to Saul "I'll explain it all later," and Glen says "Maybe one day," Margo a dark beer, two men scotch on the rocks water in back, Glen, when they talked about what they'd have, said it first and he said "Ah, I'll have that too though I hardly ever drink, and not before eight or nine when I do, then I have to admit I mostly just sit there in my armchair with something to read on my lap and maybe some chips or cheese on the side and slowly get sloshed, which is awful, I know, but what it has to do with, anyone but this boy can guess," and Saul said "What does it?" and she said "You shouldn't let it disturb you so, Dad, especially for your health," and he said "But when your mind's running while you're nipping, or the reverse, what else can it end up doing and you thinking and then drinking more and more till you conk out? but I said it was only occasionally and maybe that occasionally only rarely, but because you brought it up, even that little I'll try to stop," what she does an average workday? done the last few years? ex-actly Glen do? he still doesn't understand what that particularly is but that's okay, he gets the gist, schools they went to? where'd they meet, something with every married couple he's always been interested in: he and Lee, as she must know, met coming out of a legitimate theater in New York: "We both, if you can believe it—well, I'm sure your mother you can still tell just by her voice and face or at least recent past photos of it—wanted to be actors, and she, if you can also believe, picked me up: thought I was cute and maybe for a week I was," where Glen was raised? his folks and what they do? "You think now that we know each other better you can reveal his last name?" city they live in, will they also let him in on that? heard it's a good place, safe, slower paced, great for kids, any reason they each married an only child, at least she is to a degree? "Oh, forgot Lee had another kid soon after she dumped me, just as I would have liked to do almost immediately to sort of make up for Julie and we probably would have if we both weren't so messed up right after and later if she had stayed, otherwise we felt two were plenty enough, one for each hand I liked to say and that's how we'd cross streets, remember?" and she says "For me it's too far back and possibly I've a block, but I take your word," and Saul says "You said you wanted to be actors, how come you and Grandma Lee didn't?" and he says "She to raise kids and me because I had no talent from the start and saw that in the first classes I took and I also think I was only in it to meet pretty girls, which I did with Lee so didn't see the need for it anymore, and that happened at the standing-room section behind the orchestra at the Music Box and not leaving a theater: she asked me for the time though I never wore a watch," questions, he has so many questions, do they mind? for instance— "Oh by the way, how did you two meet? and sorry for cutting in on myself like I have," and she says at college in a chem lab: they shared the same Bunsen burner and sink, their other kids are like? ages and how tall they are? interested in sports more than books? that's good, as the Greeks said or something like: the balanced life, color hair and eyes? all three inherited Lee's honey blonde and yellow-green which perplexed the geneticists since Glen's are supposed to be predominantly dark, "Mom said you thought her eyes the best feature of her looks so I guess we should consider the kids lucky, though they're boys," and he says "She

had lots of nice features—I can kick myself to hell for making it
so easy for her to leave, but nothing I could've done—I was
crazed, as they say—'nuts,' " to Saul—"since I knew but couldn't
do anything about it that nothing like finding and knocking off
those guys or beating my head blue against a wall would help,
and after I left my long-term residence . . . how much does he
know?" and Glen says *"Niente,"* and Saul says *"Niente* what?"
and she says "Nothing, it means nothing," ". . . it was too late
for a second wife if she couldn't be another mother and I was in
such ugly shape that none that young could be gotten around,"
their other sons' names again? how come nobody in their family's
got a nickname? his is Nat which he hates for it sounds like a
buggy rat, but at the place he works he can't escape from, what're
they doing this summer for vacation? "Me, I'm staying home for
the two weeks I get and just sleep—I'll be that bushed . . . oops,
sorry again and then for the last time before for not waiting for
your answer but I guess I'm in too much of a rush to let you
know everything about me before dinner's finished and you're
gone," and she says "Don't worry, there'll be other times," and
he says "When, you coming in again?" and Glen says usually they
go to a British Columbian beach for three weeks but this summer
they're driving to Alaska for a month and he says "Boy, what I
wouldn't have given to do either of those with my family but
closer to home in the East—Maine, upper Canada or just Canada,
camping and occasionally stopping off at sort of an inexpensive
sea resort to sleep and eat and wash off, flying into the ocean
with my two kids or if the water's too cold, into a pool or just
stepping into one and splashing and swimming around, worth
almost the other fifty working weeks, why didn't we ever do that?
how come I think of these things always much too late?" and she
says "Maybe we did them and you don't remember, for I think
we once went to Chincoteague for a weekend—I remember the
name and wild ponies or mules by the ocean and that you got
me a plastic figure of one that I slept with I loved so much," and
he says "I don't remember but I'll have to work on it till I do,"

and what did the figure look like? how big? did she give it a
name? did it have a mane? attached straps or any apparatus like
that? saddle and rider? but wouldn't if it was wild, dessert, coffee,
Glen pays and gets up and taps Saul's shoulder to and he says
"Well, guess I ought to be going too," and starts to stand and
she presses his hand to the table and says "Stay for more coffee,
Dad, or another beer—they have a discount record store to go to
the likes of which doesn't exist in our neck of the woods and I'm
sure you've plenty more you want to talk over with me," and
they go, "It's been great, Mr. Frey, and hope to see you again
soon," "Nathan, or Nat if you prefer and which I promise to
answer to without asking if you like your coffee black or with
sugar and milk or cream," "What do you mean?" "Nothing, just
being silly, and I saw and am such a pro that I'll probably never
forget how you like your coffee unless you switch it around from
day to day," "Nice to meet you, Grandpa," and he kisses Saul's
head when Saul sticks out his hand to shake, and she stares at
him while they share another beer and he says "What're you
staring at, do I look that funny, like a big wizened old fart?—
excuse me," and she says "Not at all, for your excuse or your
supposition, this is an event and I'm remembering it and then
remembering that I'm remembering it to help me not to forget,
and what are you saying?—you look fantastic for your age, lean,
one of those going-to-outlive-us-all vigors and physiques, a little
less hair than from the photographs of around the last time I saw
you, or a few years before—you didn't take any in there, did you?
and I'm not being facetious either—in most ways you don't seem
to have aged a day in twenty years," and he says "Which ways
have I, outside of my hair?" and she says "Your elbows, nobody
can do anything to conceal aging elbows," and he says "But I'm
wearing a jacket and long-sleeved shirt," and she says "I know,
so maybe your humor and quick-wittedness have suffered a little
too—I'm not serious," and he says "Listen, don't kid me, I'm just
an old blowhard now, which when you think of it is not too far
from being a loud fart, excuse me, must be the beer and just

seeing you which is making me talk to my daughter so sillily like this, though actually talking to you alone here—before with them, Saul and Glen, I was just feeling better than I have in years—but with you now I feel less stupid, even half intelligent which I almost never feel, than I have since I went to prison, as much as I tried to keep and even advance my mind in there, but here the words, even, that have eluded me—like 'eluded'—or I've simply forgotten, and just speaking them—the fluidity in the way I speak—and 'fluidity,' for christsake—it must be that among other things you're the first really brainy person I've talked to in twenty years, at least one brimming with mental nimbleness and ideas and intelligent intelligible speech, if that's how long it's been since I went in, or that speaking to someone like you, even one's daughter who I'm supposed to, I suppose, posture and lord over, that if this person—me—had something of a mind before, generates or regenerates something like it in him, but you want to know something?—and most of that was confusing, wasn't it?" and she says "Some, but what 'do I want to know something?' " and he says "And cut me off if I'm running on too much, and I am but if you think it's just irritating boring stuff, but you said I should stay if I wanted to say something to you," and she says "I said stay because there may be things, with the implication being it's been so many years, you only want to talk over with me," and he says "Anyway, my darling child, and you're not getting angry with me, are you?" and she says "No, or only a little, but I'm always a bit of a grouch," and he says "Anyway," and takes her hands and rubs them on his cheek and kisses them, "now that I've seen you again—" and starts crying on her hands and she pulls them away and wipes them and says "Dad, please don't, it's not that it's embarrassing for a public place, although it is in a way, or that I hate or disapprove of seeing you cry," and he says "But you don't know what this means to me—no, that's too baloney a thing to say, and when I said it I wasn't talking about just holding and kissing your hands," and she says "I know, but what is it you want to say, because really I can't understand you when you're choking and coughing up tears and phlegm," and he says "I've killed it for ever seeing you again, haven't I, with all my whining and crying and sentimentalizing?" and she says "We'll see each other again, you heard Glen," and he says "But when I asked one or the other of you when, you went into this double- or just avoiding talk," and she says "We'll call, we'll write, this is Convention City now so before you know it we'll be flying in again or Glen will and he'll call and if he can make it or same time you can you'll see him for dinner or lunch and everything you talk about he'll tell me," and he says "But you know what I've been wanting to say to you now so I don't have to, right?" and she says "If it's not that you're very pleased to be with me here and somewhat despondent that we're leaving tomorrow," and he says "Tomorrow?" and she says "The other kids, Dad . . . but that sort of thing, then I don't," and he says "It's more, but that also, but of course, but okay, here: now that I've seen you, and excuse me for blubbering again, even these little tears now, but that's good, isn't it? not bad, for these compared to the bigger ones before for Julie and also your mom leaving me, are radically different tears, but where was I?" and she says " 'Now that you've seen me again,' " and he says "And one of my wonderful grandkids—let's skip the 'wonderful,' he's obviously a good kid but it'd be dumb or just what? presuming to think I really know yet what kind deep down inside—*presumptuous*, or anyone but his parents and later on his wife and maybe much later on his own kids at a later age could, but now that I've seen you, sure, and to a smaller extent, Saul, and that you seem quite happy with Glen and same with him with you and so on and that he seems like a nice guy—sweet to you and kind to the kid and attentive to you both and that sort of thing . . . oh, this is such silly awful straight-from-the-farty-heart crappy shit-stupid talk, and no excuse me's," and she says "No, go on, not so much with the profanities if you prefer, but you started, so get it over with," and he says "Words right out of, for that's essentially what I was going to say—now that I've seen you I feel I've done everything in my life I ever wanted to except maybe—no 'maybe'—except to see my kids grow up before me and maybe get married at their actual marriage, the ceremony I'm saying, and maybe to have stayed married another ten years myself or at least for those years hooked up with someone else; now, as for your little sister," and she says "Let's not go into her again, it affects me too," and he says "Let me just say this about her and that'll be it, not forever, but I swear—that as for her, thinking of how old she'd be now as I did before and all the things that wonderful big brain and person of hers could be and also have done, like the marriage I mentioned and schools—medicine, I thought, since she was always so caring of people, asking them this and that when they were sick and saying she's sorry and so on, maybe a passing phase but it really hit me, and interested in books in just looking at them so much because she was only starting to read and so curious of bugs and leaves and other scientific things—plus the kid or kids she would have had and the side things and ideas and stuff, all still in there to come out, but still knowing me through all this right till today, that it kills me, literally kills me every single day, for that's how often—" and she says "I know, you've said, I don't think of her as often as that, having my own children in a way that you didn't after she died and still don't have me and also that second but much younger sister Mom gave me, but I certainly think of her and miss her or sort of like you when I do, but let me tell you also, Mom says she thinks of her that way too, maybe more like I do and around the same amount or maybe a lot more than I do but not as much as you because I still lived with her and she fairly soon after had that other child, so it was equal in a way for all of us, you can say, or a little to maybe a little more than a little for you than Mom and me or maybe a lot more for you but still a hell of a lot for us too, but you dealt with it differently than us—well, I was too young to deal with it any other way than I did—but you simply handled it differently than practically anyone would and it fucked up your life almost completely, certainly I don't see how you could have done a better

job at fucking things up for yourself and us other than bashing
our brains in too and leaving us for dead when we weren't, for
in most ways what happened to Julie and then what you did to
those men and as a result of that what happened to you fucked
us up pretty well too," and he says "I'm sorry for what I did to
you and your mother, sorrier I swear I don't see how I could be,
but tell me though, aren't you glad, when you think back on it,
that I at least, for all that I screwed up for you two in other ways,
got the fucking, since you're using the word, scum that did it—I
mean, in all honesty, sweetheart, aren't you glad I made them
suffer as much as they did our darling Julie and then us in other
ways because of her?" and she says no and he says "Come on,
the honest truth now," and she says "That is," and he says
"There's got to be more," and she says "I'm telling you, no, or
not really, and if I did feel glad it was only for a day here and
there and really only a half hour of those days and each one ten
years apart and maybe two out of three of those sprung from
some sadness or bitterness about something else, because those
men were nobody to me, nothing, just filthy little pieces of shit
whom I never wanted to think of again," and he says "But they
fucked up my life, as you say, and as a result, yours and Lee's
for a while, besides we won't even say again what they did to
Julie," and she says "But they also should have been nothings and
nobodies to you, that's what I'm saying, and then everything in
time would have almost been evened out and gone on okay," and
he says "Well, I'm glad and for all I know the two of you are
too, especially for killing the one who killed Julie, which was
probably the highlight of my life, losing her the lowest of the all-
time low, the highlight in other ways, you understand, being just
having you kids—I'm talking about the births and you the most
for you were the first—and marrying your mother another, first
knowing we'd mutually fallen in love with each other, also maybe
first meeting her and sort of seeing straight off what she was going
to mean and be to me and the kids she'd give, besides just little
things that are big without you knowing it at the time, like climb-

ing up a park hill with you on my shoulders and at the top just looking out, taking a photo of you both and Mommy in a bathtub and the photo not coming out, first day I drove Julie to preschool, first day I picked you up after regular kindergarten school, driving on the Interstate with you and Julie in back playing cards or whatever you were playing"—"It was a tiny board game where the pieces had magnets, though what particular game I forget, but not checkers or chess"—"Well that trip before those scumbags drove up especially stands out among a few others, for it was so peaceful and cheerful till then, two of you getting along so well, which you did on and off most of the time, and so nice for once to have you both in the car all to myself for a long drive with a couple of rest stops—I can spoil you the way I want at Bob's Big Boy or Roy's, I remember thinking—and that night alone seeing to all your needs and day after next after school the three of us picking your mom up at the train, though maybe that recollection's big only because how it turned out to be so with those two scummy men, anyway, I'm glad what I did to them, never that I can remember had a doubt even for half an hour on a single day, but a bit sorry you haven't been glad at least once or twice or in some way said I did the right or natural thing, though I think I can understand why, but we'll forget it for now for I can tell what the whole conversation and subject and so forth is doing to you and of course what it's done and continues to do to me needs no further going into, am I right?" and she says "Okay," and he says "Want to share another beer?—this is one I'll surely remember: first time not only having but sharing a beer with you," "You used to let me take occasional sips but I guess those don't count, and no, I think I better go and help Glen tuck Saul in," "But he seems a competent man and Saul a big boy," "It was more an excuse, Dad, I'm pooped out, much as I'm enjoying this," "Well, it hasn't been that great for you, I can tell, but it has in doubles for me," "Don't speak or think for me—I have a head and it has, it's been nice," "Nice isn't so okay," "Nice is nice which to me means really good, with Glen and Saul before with you and now just us two, so don't start ruining it," "Ruin it like I do everything, is that right?" "I didn't say that, but you're at it again, making me feel like why am I staying here the extra few minutes?" "I'm sorry, my apologies, I'll try not to—ruin it and stick my thoughts in your head and mouth and that kind of thing—speak and think for you what you're not, but you know what I mean: I'm just, because I think I've ruined it with you now for maybe a long time, confused, so therefore these thoughts, jumbled and so forth," and she says "You haven't ruined it yet so now just stop," and he puts up his hand in the stop sign, says "Will do, madame," laughs, she, he pays for the beer, " 'You're right, I won't try to speak and think for you, period,' is what I wanted to say or all I should have," he thinks, puts down several bills for a tip, she fingers the money and says "Not so much," he says "Ah, we restaurant-bar people, meaning also bartenders and even the cooks who hear the waiters bellyaching and so on, are usually big tippers, since we know how hard we work or at least the long hours and how the feet get to hurt and what it is to be tipped little for it or stiffed, but besides, for me, my sweetie, this has been one very big day, among the best in my life, which maybe doesn't say much but it is," and kisses the top of her head, "Still," she says, "Glen gave a more than adequate tip already," and takes two of the four dollar bills off the table and sticks them into his jacket pocket, "What you just did," he says, "is something waitresses could kill you for, so let's hope she didn't see," "You'd protect me," and he says "I don't know if I'd be able to control her, but I'd try," and walks her to the hotel a few blocks away, " 'Maybe I shouldn't profess to speak or think for you any time of the day,' is all I should have said," he thinks, "but too late, it'd seem like studied afterthought if I said it now," points out some changes in the skyline, new tall pointy all-glass building there he doesn't like, beautiful old full-of-ornate-work smaller one demolished for no doubt something ugly like another cement stickpin or wraparound glass suitcase on its end going up, "Change is so stupid and useless most times, what do you think? and I mean it when I say I'm

only talking about architecture and let's say hairdos and cooking
fads and things," and she says "Why, what else would you be
talking about?" and he says "People and their spur-of-the-moment
sometimes lifetime changing plans for their inner selves, I think,
but what about the architecture?" and she says "It's not my city
anymore and I never felt much for it before and the memories I
have of it are mainly bad, principally because the last ones were
the worst ones so the ones I remember best, so let them change
the city all they want," "Anyway, who cares?" he says, "for none
of it's important but as a place to walk safely through with you
and I guess the new modern tall hotels and such and their eleva-
tors on the outside walls like crawling bugs and the people who
are drawn to it all make it more safe, and let's face it, Glen's
company wouldn't have held its sales meeting here if it hadn't
been for the changes in this part of town, so suddenly I'm going
to have one of those spur-of-the-moment even lifetime changes of
opinion of this place, though I don't know if it's an inner one,
whatever I mean by that, and say the whole change of it is great,
for you wouldn't be here with me now if it wasn't for what they
did to the waterfront and the new convention center and hotels
and restaurants and all sorts of tourist draws, individual pad-
dleboats in the harbor, for christsake, the aquarium with performing fish," sees her to the lobby, "Well, this is it, I guess,"
"We'll see and speak to you, Dad, okay?" and offers her cheek,
he kisses it, takes her hands and kisses them, "What pretty hands,
what a pretty face, what a wonderful girl you are, do you need
any money?" "Dad, Glen and I are working people with more
than decent salaries or certainly one very decent one between us
and we're also not big-time spenders as you loved to call it or
said your dad did—" "My dad," "—so no, but thanks," "Well,
if you ever do need anything on the money end, you'll let me
know, all right? or the boys for school, I mean it—it might sound
silly, on my income, but I've lived cheap since I got out and put
some away only for you," and she says she'll remember and
thanks him again and kisses his cheek and he stays there looking

at her as she gets in the elevator, turns around and blows a kiss at him and doors close and he thinks "What now? what do I do? where do I go? just don't get drunk or too depressed—that's it, call her early tomorrow from work, well, not too early, and maybe she and Saul and even Glen can stop by the place before they leave," and goes home.

Calls the next morning, they're out, "Damn," he thinks, "waited too long," leaves a message for her to call, no phone call back, calls again and they've checked out, "What the hell does that mean?" he thinks, calls her in Oregon a few days later and says seeing her and her family was one of the best things that ever happened to him and he's been thinking about it and would love to come out to see them all for a week or so some summer, even less, not this one though since it'd be so soon after he's just seen her and he knows they have other plans with Alaska and he'd like to give them plenty of leeway to prepare, emotionally you can even say, for his visit, not that he's saying he'd be a hardship on them or burden he means or anything like that—he's independent—"Fiercely so, as they say, though not fierce"—those days are long over if they ever began—and he's the last person in the world to get in the way or upset things or busy- or nosybody around and no problem as to who'll cook him breakfast or cook him anything if she wants and in fact she might even have to fight him as to who'll cook for all of them during his stay, only kidding, and also only kidding about assuming there'll even be a stay and she says what does he mean? she'd love having him but they don't have that much room in their house, comfortable as the place is— each boy has his own bedroom and there's no family room and now no playroom to convert, that room has become Glen's home office and the basement his woodshop and the only other places are an unventilated attic and an airless crawl space, but maybe the two youngest boys can double up and he can stay in one of their bedrooms for a few days. "I don't want to put anyone out— I can sleep on the porch if you have one and the weather's not too damp or cold"—he doesn't know Portland or really any part of the States west of the Shenandoah Ridge he thinks it was and it's called which he visited with a friend and his friend's folks more than fifty years ago, "We slept in pup tents, made bacon over a log fire," but maybe it gets like that there summers—cold—unlike here, and she says they do have a porch in front but it's not screened in and if it's bug season, which all depends, at least on how bad the bugs are, on how much precipitation they had that spring and how chilly the summer's been, they'll feast on him, so porch-sleeping's out because it's either bugs or cold so you just can't win, besides that their house is on a relatively heavily traveled street. Anyway, he says, they have something going here—started, in plans—and he's looking forward to it already, if it works out that is, and if it doesn't work out, no sweat, sweetheart, he'll more than understand, and hangs up and thinks she doesn't want to see him out there or Glen doesn't or them both or it's the kids and they've discussed it with their folks and don't want any old something or another staying there for even a week and the parents or one of them went along with the kids, but it's never going to happen, whatever the reasons he just knows he's never going out there, that's all. Hey, worse comes to worst and he wants to see her that bad, which he knows he will, he can fly out there without telling them, stay at a nearby hotel and call from there and say he's here, always wanted to see the West Coast and for sure shouldn't die without doing it sometime in his life and if they want to see him—no, he won't be that tough—and he wants to see them too and had planned to but if they have something better to do—not "better"; "something more important"—not even that—just something already planned that can't be put off like another Alaskan trip tomorrow or this time the South Pacific or Japan—he'll understand and see Portland himself and then continue his trip south by bus for the rest of his two weeks to San Francisco and places like Mexico and L.A.

Late that fall—he calls his daughter about once a week and they talk a few minutes and then he usually asks to speak to one of the boys—a young man comes into the luncheonette, no more than eighteen—but things with Margo like "How are you?" "We're all fine," "How's the weather?" "Could be worse," "Hear from your mom?" "She's always the same: couldn't be better," "How's work? how's school? what's doing in Portland these days? I've been reading the weather map in the paper lately and it's been saying you're getting tons of rain," sometimes sports talk with the boys which he has to read the paper or talk to some of his customers to know about, for a week a lot about their trip to Alaska: lot of driving around, didn't seem too interesting to him for all those miles, bunch of seals, loose bear or two, some kind of antelope or moose, could have been a modern zoo like even one that's in his city but didn't say that—up to the counter looking around—"You know, I went to Julie's grave a few days ago, try to do it every other week but then sometimes find myself going two or three straight days, lay some flowers, just stand there, listening to the wind whistling and things, everything looks great, same with your grandparents': shipshape," "That's good; I'm so sorry I didn't visit it while I was there, I used to with Mom pretty much before we moved away, it was all very sad, especially because it was so soon after she died"—something's wrong, he almost knows what's coming, he was robbed a few years ago on the street going home from work: "Give me your money," "You got it, baby," for there were two of them with sawed-off shotguns it seemed, little bit of overkill he later liked to joke, "What would you have done if there was just one?" he was asked, "Just what I did: handed it over with a smile, what do you think?"—the guy's eyes: shifty, suspicious, jittery movements, sweaty-faced— never any mention anymore about his trip to Portland some summer so he supposes it's off—he says "Yes sir," no other customers, from where he's standing nobody looking in at the place from the street, boss and his wife out buying meat and deli for the week, Jesus he sometimes wishes he had a handgun under the counter for when his life's at stake, at least some mace—"Anything I can do for you?—you come in for chow or what?" and the man pulls out a gun he doesn't know where from it's out so fast, maybe from inside his coat sleeve—that's what he should have told the detectives for a laugh: "Check all the theatrical agents in town, the thief was a magician, the gun was followed by rabbits and doves"—and says "This is a holdup, keep your fat mouth shut, no stupid moves, hands where I can see them and quick let's have everything you got in your register and pockets and if you got a safe in back then open that or you're going to be one big dead prick," and he says "A holdup? a holdup? in this joint? get out of here," and looks around for something to scare the guy with, something's pumping in him where he swears he can tear off the whole twelve-stool counter with his hands and throw it at the kid, iron skillet's way over there, hammer he uses to nail things up sometimes is at the end of the counter in a shoebox, knives are around but they're short and he doesn't know how to throw them and the big carving ones are in the sink, grabs a long spatula by the grill he's beside and waves it and says "I told you to beat it or I'll brain your fucking brains in, you fucking imbecile, for who the fuck you think you're dealing with?" and when the man doesn't move he swings it at him and the gun goes off, that's all he remembers that happens: he hears, gun, sees, fire out of it, and maybe he doesn't even remember that but just imagined it, and is treated on the floor by the emergency med people and taken to the hospital, no memory of anything in the restaurant or ambulance after he's shot, just went black, no pain, none after that except for a few days later when a nurse is told by mistake by the floor resident who meant another patient that he's to be taken off painkillers and boy for a while did he scream before they put him back on, someone came in he was told, guy with a stack of flyers for a new neighborhood runner's shop, which he probably would have tossed out right after the guy left, no place for them— counter ends and top of cigarette machine crowded as they are— and nobody takes those things except to stick their chewed gum in and anyway who wants them flying to the floor every time the door opens with a little wind behind it or just customers walking past them fast? called out "Anyone here? I'd like to drop off

something if you don't mind," put the flyers on the counter to
leave there, saw him lying behind it on the floor, ran out to the
street screaming "Someone's been hurt, robbery must've been,
help, people, someone's been butchered or shot, man behind the
wall, man behind the wall," is what he kept saying, instead of
"behind the counter" probably, and pointed to the restaurant but
wouldn't go in when some people from the street did, register
emptied, pockets untouched, cheap watch gone, thief had to be
kidding about the safe or else had no idea what a simple place it
was, police said it could have been one of the persons who ran
in to help or see him who took the money and watch or a few
of them because usually when a robber shoots you that bad he
gets out fast and doesn't waste even a few extra seconds looking
for dough and why would he take a cheap watch? "though could
be it was a combo of both: thief and passersby," his boss calls
her and says what happened and that he wants her to know he's
not one who likes giving bad news but Nat told him to if anything
like this happened to him, "for you know he was once robbed
with some guns a few years ago and was concerned he might be
again and not get off so lucky," and she says "No, he never told
me, though of course you must know what happened years ago
with his youngest daughter, my sister, Julie," and the boss says
"Nat once mentioned, that's about it, but not her name, though
someone else told me he served time for something connected to
it, like getting the guys who killed her but where he was completely in the right and like who wouldn't have done the same
thing if he could? so it never stopped me from keeping him on,"
and she says "I'm sure he appreciated you for that, but really, he
only spoke about my sister once in that regard in all the time
he's worked for you?—that's surprising, since it seemed the thing
uppermost and forever in his mind," and the boss says "Twice,
then, even three times, let's call it four, but quickly, like where
he's reading a newspaper at work with a similar article in it where
an innocent kid got killed between street drug dealers—crossfire,
what's in the papers so much today—and it comes back to him

and he says something 'You know, something like this happened to my kid,' and he just touches on it but I can see by his face and so quickly into another subject or news story that he doesn't want to go deeper so I don't . . . but you know, he also told me to call you if other things ever happened to him which he seemed a little worried about, like getting a heart attack, not that he wasn't strong as an old bull before he got shot, or just not answering his phone when he didn't show up for work and it turned out, as he said it's turned out for a couple of old bulls he knew, that he was dead in bed from a stroke the night before in one second flat—anyway, missus, he seems to be doing okay, as I told you from everything that's been told me, probably be in the hospital a few weeks but no complications expected the nurse said who answered the phone in his Intensive Care where I called, so rest easy for now and first chance I'm allowed to see him—Intensive Care won't let me because I'm not family, but he should be out of there soon—I'll tell him I did what he asked me to and that's spoken to you," and she says "Please call me collect any hour of the day if you learn that his condition's deteriorated or just phone me collect after you've seen him, when you have a free moment, and of course give him our love," and she takes his home phone number and number of the I.C. unit her father's in.

His good arm's for the most part paralyzed from the shooting so he can't go back to work, tries getting a cashier's job in other restaurants but no work around or times are tough so some of their jobs they have to double up and excuses like that or else they just don't want him, he thinks, because he doesn't look healthy anymore and not good for customers' appetites or something and his clothes are old and out of date and arm stiff like it is and with everything about him unkempt and with possibly more health and accident insurance for them because of his age and wounds from the shooting and maybe they think a possible medical relapse on the job or they know what he did to those killers years ago and feel he brought the new shooting on somehow and don't want a hothead working for them and then if you're going to hire a cashier or guy who hangs up coats or things like that, even someone who takes care of the men in the restrooms of the higher-class restaurants, better to have one who can chase not-too-threatening unwanteds out of the place or at least look like he can, finds it more economical than working to just retire, maybe for the time being, and take the small union pension he'll get and accident insurance from getting shot at work, which isn't half bad, and in a year full Social Security with the medical cover-age the government gives, -care or -caid, calls her a lot but after five and on weekends because it can cost a great deal, it grieves him is the best he can put it that she still talks to him in the same formal way she has since a few years after he went into prison—it wasn't like that before with her but she was just a girl then and of course things were much different: he lived with Lee, one fam-ily, Julie, had a good job and wasn't a temporary maniac and in fact he was a pretty good father, around average, he thought, fairly relaxed and not at all the browbeating or faultfinding kind—asks to speak to her boys and Glen almost every time after he speaks to her but not much talk there too, Glen kind of quiet and, what's the word? unforthcoming or something and reserved, the boys always acting shy or don't know him enough so don't see why they should have to get on the phone with him so much, which makes some sense and he'd probably feel the same if he was them, tells her how he's really grown close to her family almost solely by phone, isn't that funny? and that he'd still like to come see them if she isn't going to be in his city anytime soon, but come to think of it he can't afford the fare right now—"Though I still have the same money put away only for you or the boys' schools, I want you to know, or even for you and Glen if you both lost your jobs or just one of you did and you were suddenly strapped for cash—not much, you understand, so don't set your hopes when I die on buying a swimming pool with it or building an additional wing to your garage," and she says "I don't harbor macabre or calculating thoughts like that and surely not on what I'll gain monetarily from someone's death, not that you won't live past a hundred, and besides, we've only one car and park it in the street—Glen gladly takes the bus to work—and we don't as a rule go in much for building private pools in our area— only a few days get very hot, the community is kind of artistic or professorial with a flock of doctors mixed in and very ecological-minded, and there are already several fine public pools at minimal costs," and he says "Only kidding, honey, only kidding, about the garage and pool and my death both," and she says "I know but I felt I had to say something as to how and where we live so you wouldn't in the future be put in the position of possibly prejudging or just misunderstanding us, and listen, Dad, if you do want to visit us that much, use your savings for us to fly out here and we'll put you up comfortably for a week at least," and he says "No, I got to leave something to you, it's an absolute must in my mind after all I haven't done—maybe I'll win the lottery or a big part of one, but if I did that'd mean I'd have to play it and I always thought tossing away dough like that a tremendous waste and dumb escape—excuse me, I hope you or Glen don't play them," and she says "*Please*, and I don't even know if we have those games here."

They speak on the phone for two more years, occasionally a letter or postcard between them and always birthday cards and gifts at Christmas from him, a few times she says she thinks she's coming east for a convention or with one or two of her boys to visit him and then perhaps take in New York City and Washington, D.C., but then writes or phones that her plans were canceled or fell through because of personal reasons she doesn't want to go into when he asks what, "Well, I thought it might have been over me—a dispute between you two, for instance, though I wouldn't know why, I'm really a harmless and mean-well guy— or something to do with stopping you, though there also I'm in the dark about, my lousy memory of last week's things," and she says no and for the last time about it that's as far as she'll go, okay? and he says sure, "I was only saying, nothing to it, so I'll be speaking to you, honey, goodbye," and about a month later she gets a call from an official in his city (there were a number of reasons they hadn't spoken since their last conversation when she said her plans had fallen through and he thought it might have been over him: it was midsummer and they were away two weekends in a row at Glen's mother's beach house when he called, another night they were having dinner in a restaurant when he called and then he got tired and took a nap that ended up a six-hour sleep and when he awoke he felt it was too late to call even with the three-hour time difference, another time her son took the message that he'd called but forgot to give it to her, another time Glen took the message after a brief exchange with him, "So how's it going?" "Everything's fine," "Tell her I called?" "You bet," but got into an argument with her when she got home from work and after it was still so mad at her he didn't want to tell her anything and next morning he'd planned to mention her father called but they talked mostly how sleep usually irons over any bad feelings still lingering from the previous day's fight and then he forgot till three days later when he thought "Why bother, he'll probably call today anyway?" she called him that day but he'd pulled the phone jack out of the wall because he had a stomach flu or it was something he ate but anyway was too weak to answer the phone and didn't want to be woken up by or even hear its rings, the boys were in day camp and she yelled from the bedroom "You interested in paying me a visit?" "You bet," and later the phone rang while they were making love and Glen reached for the receiver and she said "Leave it," and he said "What if it's important?" and she said "If it is, they'll call back," they got an answering machine that recorded his message but something malfunctioned that first day or maybe it was the way she'd assembled or connected it into the wall, but the entire day's tape was erased and next day without them doing anything new to it except taking the plug out of the wall socket and putting it back in, it worked fine, she called and he wasn't in, she thought she'd call him back in an hour or so but then a number of things happened—Glen called and they had a long talk, one of her sons was

invited to sleep over at a friend's house and she had to pack his
things and give him an early supper because she knew he wouldn't
get fed much there except for sweets and drive him, she decided
to make a potato salad now instead of tomorrow for a picnic, a
bird feeder fell down and broke and it took some time fixing it
and hanging it back up in a tree, the radio was playing a familiar
Mozart piano sonata and she wanted to hear it to the end to get
the number, she got interested in the last of a series of articles on
welfare and the poor and then went through the newspaper pile
for the papers of the two previous days for articles one and two—
and she never got around to it, he called but their line was busy
for hours and he gave up after almost twenty tries and went to
bed thinking he'd call her at work next day just to hear her voice
again and see how things are going with her and her family after
almost a month or even earlier at home if he can remember to
call, say, between eleven-ten and -fifteen his time but he died
overnight) that he died in his sleep it appears, in no way is there
any indication of foul play, and may have been dead three to four
days—"Excuse me, but if all this is too much for you," the official
says, "though you are the person I really want to talk to, I can
speak to your husband about it," and she says "No, it's okay, it's
been a while since I saw my father, more than a month since I
even spoke to him, and we haven't been close for many years and
I don't want anything decided about him without my immediate
say, so please continue and if it does get too much for me I'll let
you know," and the official says "As I was saying, and if I do get
too blunt please excuse me, it's not the job but my manner . . . three
to four days he might have been there—the police had to break
in his door as the neighbor he kept a spare set of keys with for
emergencies like this one might have been, just as he had a spare
set of hers for the same thing, was out of town all that time and
because no one else in the building saw him for that long, or the
smell—I never got straight which one, but that shouldn't be an
issue now—but that's how he was eventually found"—and though
he laid out sufficient money with instructions that his body be

cremated and for a small ceremony at the cemetery for relatives and close friends where his ashes are to be buried unmarked next to his daughter Julie's grave, does she want anything different done?—"His instructions, along with where his passport is and checking account and union membership number to help with the cost of the funeral and things like that were all in an envelope in his night table drawer but weren't notarized, the instructions, or even properly witnessed, so you can have the final say," and she says "Why would I want to countermand my father's wishes?" and the official says "By the city's health law we have to give you this opportunity, your being, so far as we know—his instructions say you are and we'll look into it further—his only heir, so we even have to get you to sign a release for the cremation or regular interment or whichever kind you finally decided on," and she says "That's what I mean—what else could I possibly want that's different than what he said?" and the official says "You might not want him cremated, for example, as it could be antithetical to your beliefs, religious or otherwise—considerations like that, which you might not have thought about yet because of the suddenness of the news," and she says "No, that's the way I also want to go—it's easier for everybody," and the official says "You're saying cremation," and she says yes and the official says "Okay, and that's what your father wrote in his instructions too— he, quote, don't want to cause anyone a fuss, unquote, but another thing is the ceremony—and I'm only trying to be helpful here, this isn't part of my regular job—he wrote he didn't want any professional religious person officiating—someone, quote, lay and unpaid, unquote, as he says, could easily do it and that way too, quote, my daughter's spared the minister's or rabbi's or whatever officiator's expense, unquote," and she says "There too, it's fine with me, whomever he chose—did he, in these instructions?" and the official says "He has written down here the funeral home taking care of the cremation and graveside service but no one named as speaker or what kind of service he wanted, secular or otherwise, so I assume that's all up to you—maybe, if I can poke my nose in a bit further, this neighbor lady friend of his will know who his closest friends were—*she*, even—and who can speak and be understood and lead a service . . . but the place of burial might be something else for you to consider—the truth is, my dear, though your father kept up and paid for in perpetuity, it says in his instructions, the grave of your sister and several others alongside hers plus some empty burial plots, you might not even want his ashes buried there but flown home with you," and she says "Now that you bring it up, it would be senseless for me to come east for only a ceremony with people I mostly don't know and with not even a casket to look at and really nothing much else to see there except the gravestones of my dead sister and some grandparents I never knew, so perhaps I can have half the ashes buried next to her grave and the rest sent to me and buried unmarked in my husband's family gravesite—it would only occupy a small part of the plot so I'm sure my husband's family won't mind, and that way I'll be able to pay my respects to him whenever I want since I don't see when I'll be flying east again now that he's not there, and he'd be, or his ashes would, half of them at least, buried next to or near me since I'm sure I'll end up buried here too," and the official says "I'm positive all that can be arranged through the funeral home doing the cremation, but one last thing, dear, with your permission: if you don't intend on coming east soon then you better start figuring out what you want done with his apartment, or room, rather," and she says "Can all his belongings, for a price, be junked, the ones that aren't worth anything, and the rest given to charity or some Goodwill place that might take them?" and the official says "That'll have to be arranged between you and his landlord but I don't see why it couldn't be done—as for his private papers, if he has any," and she says "Oh I'm sure he has: letters from my mother dating back before they were married, photos of the family and when he was a kid and no doubt some personal objects of my sister Julie from day one," and the official says "Those, then, plus some more practically important items to you like his bankbook and checkbook and birth certificate perhaps and deed to his cemetery plots and maybe even some tucked-away savings or stocks and bonds certificates or things of that ilk he might have accumulated over the years though we hope paid income tax on," and she says "I doubt he had any of those—not only was he just making it, we'll say, so too poor to buy them, but he frowned on that kind of income like playing the stock market, money made on paper and if it turns out to be real money when cashed in, then money made without doing hard labor for it—he was old-fashioned that way, of that, from the little I spoke to him about gambling and liveli-hood, I'm sure," and the official says "Whatever, but once you sign and return the documents I send you, if you're truly not coming here, then the padlock will be removed from his apartment and you'll be able to designate a surrogate to go through it and send those things of a more practical financial nature to you the surrogate might find—as for the photos and your sister's posses-sions and such your father might have had," and she says "It's not what she possessed but what he might have kept of hers—she died when she was five, you know, murdered by a maniac; we were in the same car at the time—a crazy spray highway shooting," and the official says "I didn't know and I'm very sorry, dear, extremely," and she says "Oh yes, that's what started all my father's problems—marriage breakup, in essence giving me up, certain quirks and obses-sions, losing his job and so on," and the official says "I didn't know that either, dear, I'm sorry—anyway, those things, the ones that are only of possible personal value to you, well, unless you come here and claim them or have them sent to you or keep up his lodgings till the landlord thinks, because no one's living here, that he wants the place vacated so he can raise the rent, then I'm afraid they'll be disposed of as garbage too."

Everything's worked out, papers are sent, signed and returned, half his ashes buried beside Julie's grave but with no ceremony or guests since she didn't see any reason for even a simple service at the cemetery, for the lady-friend neighbor didn't know who else would come or how she'd get there if she was the only one, and what was left of his relatives in the area, Margo remembered him saying, he'd lost all contact with, they never especially liked him in the first place or not since he was a fairly quiet timid kid, and it'd be hypocritical to ask them to attend the ceremony if she wasn't going to be there, other half of his ashes sent to her in a can and buried between two empty plots at her husband's family gravesite after a brief service with only her sons and husband and his parents and the gravedigger there, her husband officiating and saying "He was a good person from everything I heard about him and the few hours I spent with him in a restaurant once and the many phone conversations we had, albeit succinct as a majority of them were—honest and sincere and hardworking and devoted to his daughters, the living Margo, the deceased Julie, surely no man could have loved his children more, and who because of that love perhaps, but anyhow what became a deep misfortune, a disturbing calamity if not tragedy, actually, which perhaps no words can do justice to or describe so why try?"—"Hear, hear," his father says—"seemed to blow it all, to be colloquial but direct, but he came back from, let's be forthright about it and conceal nothing at a location where nothing should be back door, incarceration—paid his debt to society, as the state would put it, and perhaps undeservedly paid that debt but that's not for us, in our inconsiderable power or whatnot, to say, to live a respectable and meaningful life from everything we know of it, and should be forgiven"—"Amen," his father says—"he is forgiven from our standpoint I'm sure, and if there is a higher being, which my parents and perhaps my sons believe there is, and who can say? then we plead that he be forgiven by It too, that's all I can say today and I believe is enough, thank you all for coming, and I don't mean to hog this, although I want you to know I was asked by the deceased's sole survivor to conduct the ceremony, so if anyone else wants to speak about Nathan Frey, please feel free to," and they all shake their heads, his sons look at one another with the expressions "He doesn't mean us, does he?" his father says "What could we say that could add to your words, Glendon?—your eulogy was fine and to the point and summed it up wonderfully, and memorized or off the cuff, no less," "Extemporaneous," Glen says, "I thought it would all just come to me and that that's the way it should," "Well, good job, son," the lady-friend neighbor says she's too feeble to do any work ("Your dad probably never mentioned me or my condition and age but I'm an old shrunken diseased cow he looked after when he could, going out for groceries and pharmaceuticals and squiring me to various doctors and things") so a second cousin of Margo's who lives in a suburb not far from her father's building agrees for a certain fee to search through his room and send her whatever she wants from it, "There's a rocking chair here," the cousin says on the phone, "very old and in good condition, do you want that?—it looks practically like an antique," "He must have found it on the street; I know it's no heirloom, his wasn't that kind of family and everything of worth from the marriage my mom took, so no, keep it or give it away," "There's a fantastic espresso coffee machine, really expensive-looking and with one of those spouts for steamed milk, it could be boxed and UPS'd," "We have one and I'm surprised he did—probably given to him by one of the restaurants he worked at where it was used once—but doesn't sound like my dad the last twenty years: café au lait, espresso, twist of lemon on a demitasse spoon, no; keep it if it's so nice, but without any reduction in what I agreed to give you, you understand," "A stack of letters to your mother and another stack to you—copies, I saw, from a few of them; do you want them and the ones in a third stack that you sent him?" "I don't see the point, as the letters to my mother I'd find uncomfortably amorous or vituperative if plain poisonous sometimes and the ones to me I probably still have the originals of someplace, stuck in whatever book I was reading at the time, habit I have—every so often when I go through a book I've read, one drops out but I can't say I reread it," "The letters to you seem to date back to when he was in prison and you were a young girl," "That's too much of the past, most of which if I haven't remembered or have tried my darndest not to, I want to continue to forget, so thanks but no," "Photos of him, I suppose, and who must be his parents the way they're smiling and cuddling him so close, and one of him, since the face is the same as in the others or a near lookalike, on a donkey or dwarf horse I think commercial photographers used to lead around the streets to take pictures of kids on—how else could the animal have got there? for it's taken in front of an apartment building and with old cars around, but probably new then," "Sure, include it, all the photos, since it'd be wrong just throwing them away or giving them to some junk shop for people to go ho-ho over, and my own kids will get a kick out of them for the resemblances to them, if there are any, at that age and maybe to his father and his father's dad and also for the cultural significance and interest—how city people lived then, these photographers without shops and street musicians he used to tell me, when he was a kid, whole rhythm bands of them going down block after block and horse-drawn carts of ice for the icebox and vegetables and fruits and I even think milk, though the last might have been when his father was a boy," "Lots of pre-'54 coins—a tall jarful, a couple of the pennies are silver and some of the other coins go back to the teens and twenties, from just a quick look, so there might even be better, and I think I saw an Indian-head penny before it got lost amid the others, and I know there was a quarter with a lady with wings, for a second," "Yes, send them all—he once said many years ago that since he was around coins in the restaurant all day he'd started up a collection for me to help send me through school, so if they're of any value I'll use them for my own kids—insure that box for a few hundred, please," "Several bills have come in—phone, utilities, a window washer, and a letter from Honolulu just today," "Send and I'll take care of them, but the window washer's a joke—just that he'd use one with the view he once said he had, other buildings like his, and what's he have, two windows?" "Three, plus the tiny bathroom one but it's smoked," "The letter, who knows what it means?—maybe a customer who passed through and once he got there he got lonely— if I wrote him my father died he probably wouldn't know who I was speaking of—return it to the addresser saying 'addressee de-

ceased' . . . any books? no, I have all I want to read, or the stores
and libraries do, unless one or two look extremely old—in fact,
would it be too much to ask you to hold the books upside down
one by one and flip through and shake them in that position?—
I'll pay you something extra if there are more than a few of
them—for like me he might have kept a few treasures and memen-
tos in them," "A very expensive-looking silk tie, it says, hundred
percent and never used for it's still in its box tissue-wrapped and
from one of our finest stores and of the rest of his clothes the
only thing that still looks good is a leather belt almost brand-
new, size 34," "That's my husband's waistline but I doubt he'd
want to wear my dad's belt—as for the tie, since the one he wore
last time I saw him was stained and old, it must have been given
to him since by a friend—a lady perhaps? I don't think so, he
seemed to have become kind of chaste and at home sort of an
ascetic recluse, so maybe from his boss as a Christmas gift or one
of his steady customers who gives nothing during the year but
something lavish like this as an annual gift, but it was a cheap
luncheonette from the way he described it, so I don't think so
there either—or maybe he bought it for the next time we saw
him, that'd make sense for I can see him splurging for us, but I
don't see my husband Glen or one of my boys walking around in
any of his things—the kids would find it creepy, a dead man's
clothes, so do what you want with the tie, decorate a tree with it
as long as we're on the subject of Christmas, only kidding . . .
oops, that's something, the 'only kidding,' he'd say, so it's funny
why I picked it up and how come now for the first time?" "An
address book with not many names," "No, past life, and what
would those names mean to me if I don't already have them? so
to be disposed of, but of his photos, you never said but were there
any of Julie and me?—little girls, she had bangs from age one and
was exceptionally pretty, like a girl model, and my hair was always combed back long, in a ponytail or braid and I was the
taller but also the homelier of the two, brown hair to her bright
blonde and glasses from age three to her none," "Plenty, and you

both were adorable, but I already assumed you wanted those so
I was going to include them whether you said so or not," "My
mother, another beauty, any of her or the two of them as a couple,
and with us, as a twosome or alone?" "A few, in all the possible
family combinations," "Just wondering, but who do you think
Julie and I resembled at that time?" "Can't tell for sure, at best
parts of the two of you in them both and you also resembled each
other despite the glasses and hair," "There was one of my folks
together I especially remember, in fact I'd take it out of the photograph drawer in their dresser and pore over it when there was
still the four of us, probably because they looked so happy in it,
which is what I wanted, because in truth, okay as their relation-
ship was and seemingly solid, they used to argue a lot and I was
often scared they'd break up—but his arm around her shoulder
and both of them leaning forward, snapping their fingers to some
popular musical number it seemed, something like a rumba but
that one reached its heyday before their time, and standing beside
the new car they'd just bought, in front of a summer bungalow
they were renting," "No, it's not among the ones I found and I
think I've searched all over and your father didn't have much,"
"He was in hiking shorts, striped polo shirt and sandals and
looked lean and weightlifter strong and with a mess of hair and
healthy tan, she, prematernity with me, in a skimpy two-piece
bathing suit, really a gorgeous figure, long smooth legs, teeny
tummy, midget waist and a large perfect top, her hair tumbling
everywhere, and barefoot, and both with these smiles as if they
were having and had just had—maybe even had just climbed or
fallen out of bed, that kind of fun—the time of their lives," "There
are only three photos of them alone, unless the one you're talking
of is stuck to the back of another, and it's not one of them," "My
mother says she doesn't have it either, and why would she unless
she wanted proof of what a great body she once had, but why
would she? and even at her age now, a bit wrinkled in the legs
and such but it's still pretty good, so I wonder what happened to
it—maybe in a rage after she left him—well, he was in prison by

then but he might have brought it with him, she looked so great—
he tore it up, or it could still be in his wallet cut down to wallet
size or maybe he looked at it and handled it so much he used it
up," "It's not in his wallet photo section either, which I'm sending
you the whole thing as is, by the way, meaning even the little
scrap papers and play or movie ticket stubs tucked away, unless
this photo, again, stuck to the back of another photo in one of
the photograph sleeves, but why'd you, if you don't mind my
asking . . . no, I can probably answer it myself," "What?" "Your
not looking at that dresser drawer photograph again once the
family was no longer intact, if I got it right, was because your
sister died, no? and you didn't want to see—" "That's right, I
suppose—whatever a kid goes through at that age over the death
of the person closest to you—to me—same thing my father went
through in a different way, I guess—and the way she died too
perhaps—bang-bang—I mean we slept in side-by-side beds once
she was out of her crib and on vacations sometimes in the same
bed for a week and had our birthday parties together though our
birthdates were a month apart—my God, we used to play together
eight hours a day straight some days, drawing and cutting out
fifty or so paper figures and acting them all out in different voices
till we were hoarse, starting from scratch whole puppet shows,
meaning not only making the papier-mâché characters but the
scenery and stage and thinking up the play—I wouldn't—what'd
I say, five? maybe it wasn't even to you, but she died at six—but
I wouldn't—six years old, of course—I could barely stand sleeping
in our old bedroom but it was the only other one we had—in fact
I had to have not only her bed removed but mine too because
they were twins and a new one put in for me—my dad wasn't
even aware of it he was so into his own world looking for the
avengers—no, he was the avenger, they were . . . oh, they were
this and that, how does it help? scumbags, rats—but I wouldn't,
what I started out saying, even look at the framed photograph
my mother had of her by her bedside—Julie, at a beach in a
bathing suit, bangs being blown back above her head, whopping

smile, fingers entwined beneath her chin, her eyes, I forgot to mention, dark black to my green—'Turn it around first,' I used to say and frequently scream at my mother if she summoned me into her room for something or sent me there to get her necklace from the dresser, let's say, and years later, long after she'd remarried and had another child and I not only had a different house and time zone to live in but another new bed and I was still doing this, she suddenly said 'What're you, crazy?—it's just a picture, a beautiful picture, there for our pleasure, your dearest sister, my darling treasure, get over it already, at least that aspect,' and I swear slapped the photo smack into or maybe just up to my face— must have been up to it or maybe even a foot or two away but facing me face to face, and I could look at it even less after that and maybe I couldn't even look at that one today ... but his kitchen supplies, utensils, you know, for he worked in restaurants and might have taken home some very sturdy professional ones, anything?" "Huh, how's that?" "Carving knives, ladling spoons, chopping board, great pans and pots, kitchen stuff, any there at his place?" "Couple of butter knives and forks and spoons, one table and one tea, and a plastic spatula, bread knife, sieve—that what you call it?" "Colander, strainer?" "—with an unmeant hole in it so of not much use, and that's about it—rolling pin, whatever for, for there are no baking or bread pans," "Maybe to beat off muggers," "I think he had a bat for that, kept under his bed— oh, a paring knife here, I see, and potato masher, and that's really it, can opener, bottle opener, corkscrew, really junky stuff, not worth the price of shipping, cheap as UPS is, and same with the dishes, service for two or one and a couple of beer mugs I guess for everything from beer to water to coffee to tea, since there are no, if you can believe, cups or coffee mugs," "Maybe the carving knife wrapped well so it doesn't slice the shipping box—I have a feeling it's a good one," "Who said anything about a carving knife?—paring, butter and bread, plus the little one with tweezers and toothpick on his key ring," "Prints, paintings, art photographs on the wall or anywhere?" "Only magazine stuff, meaning coming from them or possibly art catalogs, reproductions from paintings or pen-and-ink things in a museum or at an exhibition, looks like, but glossy colorful ones on good paper so looking quite real, fifty of them at least, taped or tacked to the walls all over the place," "But you're sure none are real?" "Picasso, Chagall, Hopper, Matisse, Orozco, Tintoretto, Signorelli, Parmesan Cheese or some Italian name like that of a little angel and his or her little girl-friend—most of the painters' names even I recognize—your father had quite the collection, should go for several mil," "Then thank you, Jane, I think we've covered it all—send what we've settled on UPS and any little last-moment thing you might think to add and also a note on how many hours you've put in, but you've saved me a hell of a lot of expenses and work besides taking a great load off my mind," "And what's that?" "Simply to know nothing was thrown out or given away or left for the landlord to scavenge that was worth anything, emotionally or monetarily or what," "Oh."

For weeks later she has dreams almost every other night concerning her father—in one he says "Save me, I'm drowning in dirt," in another he greets her with a formal handshake while she has her arms out for a hug and kiss, asks her to cup her hands, she does and he spoons a pyramid of earth in each palm and says "One more time?" in another she gets a telegram saying "My dearest child, I am completely in pieces and unmotivatedly scatter-brained, is there no rhyme not to say a season why you're also not distraught, my deepest regards to those authorities above who might be able to do something to redress this, your loving poppy, Nat," in another he's a boy of about six sitting on her lap and she's supposed to be his mother she thinks in the dream "but how's that? since he's this and I'm his," when he says "Mamma grammar, divided we're lame, together we contaminated, do you know that hysterical smote?—who said it second? ah, I could never teach you nuttin'," and dives off into a hole in the sofa and disappears, in another he appears in the distance riding a horse, shouts "Hi-ho, my Margo, hi-ho," and rides closer waving a

sword over his head, stops under her bedroom window still shouting hi-ho, her husband stirs in bed in the dream and says in his
sleep "Largo, heed the drosses, need the worms, give them crosses,
sieve the burns," she says "Glendon, wake up, be up, we've got
to start making some sense," and to her father from bed "Daddy,
hide away, now, bow," and her father says from below, still seated
on the horse but sword sheathed, "Dearest Julie, I mean my darling Margo, I'm so lonesome, separated, throw me a rope, I want
to crawl up and join you," same night in another dream he's
standing talking to her cordially, seems like an art opening at a
gallery, then a cocktail party at her home, he seems to be a friend
of a couple she invited and he clinks her glass with his and says
"So how's the weather up there?" "Am I that tall to you?" "I'm
talking real weather, lady: shrouds, tornadoes, lightning storms,"
"Excuse me but who brought you, the Kahns, the Kanes?" "I'm
still asking weather, missus, weather," "Weather? where? we're
both in the same spot and consanguineous, Father, indoors,"
"Hardly, earthly, cementally, it's as dark as a person can see,
though I love you neverthebestly, I mean beastly," then he suddenly becomes a rat, same size and color as one but with her
father's face, and leaps onto her chest and starts scratching at her
eyes and she swats it off and runs out of the house, her husband
in pajamas, when in her dream she thinks "That's funny, he only
sleeps nude," yelling from their bedroom window "Come back,
he's scampering up the vines, I told you we should've cut them
down, now he's coming through the window, don't leave me be
a solitary speck with him, he still has all his teeth and the rat can
bite," in another her father's a mosquito buzzing around her head
and she says "Stay away, now stay away—okay, don't say I didn't
warn you, for I can get murderously allergic to bugs, having attacks like you've never seen," and slaps at it but keeps missing,
then she doesn't see or hear it and while she's looking around
and listening for it it lands on her arm, she watches it stick its
proboscis in, "Wait till it's drawing blood," she thinks, "even if
there is some pain it'll be worth it," counts to six, whispers

"Time," and slaps it hard and lifts her hand to see what she thinks will be its squished bloody carcass even if it is a male, but nothing's there and she yells "Damn air pockets, damned if they're there, damned if they're not, but I still might have nipped its tip if not flattened it and it's dead or dying on the floor and all I got to do is step on it," when it starts buzzing around her head and she says "I can take it, you don't bother me so don't think you do, I can take much more than this so you'll just have to do your sneaky biting and then buzz away on your own, for I'm not wasting another wave on you," in another she's sleeping alone and he pushes open her bedroom door with his head and crawls into the room and up to her ear and says into it "I miss you, I miss your sis most persistently not to mention you, what dries up isn't a scream, what cries down isn't a dream, I can come up with these long after you're sufficiently sick of them and me, fried, dried, you got it, so make more meaning out of me, my sweet, release me, let me already Margo," and she says in her dream half asleep "But it's you, goddamnit, you, I did everything good I could, cried, dried, so all right, didn't fly, but that's over and done with so now let me sleep," and her eyes close and in her dream-sleep she dreams of hovering butterflies and bees, a flower garden with a deer eating the sweet peas, and a few hundred feet behind it an old barn with several big holes in the roof and its doors off and a buggy in a cow stall showing through and nothing else around but pasture with the tall grass being jerked by the wind, and she thinks "Peaceful, I like it, even the peas, by God, even the sky, blue with downy clouds, and thank goodness, nothing of him," in another she and a grown-up Julie enter an empty cottage she and her family rent for two weeks every summer, wonders where's the ramshackle furniture that practically makes the place in addition to the missing woodstove and the picture postcards of artworks she's tacked to the door frames and the owner till now hasn't taken off, hears tapping under the floor and says "What's that?" "What's up?" Julie says, "I don't hear or see anything," "That tap-tap, tap-tap, it's even louder now and could be a code of some sort, Morse, lost, from under the floorboards," and Julie says "You're seeing things again, hon, for what floor, who boards?" and she says "And pardon me, my nearest miss, but you've either lost all your sensory powers or I don't know what, lower powers, infrapowers," and says to the floor "Tell her in taps or words if there is someone down there for I don't want to appear hard of feeling," and he says "Yeah, it's me, Daddy, to you both though you're so much apart, hidden from you while I'm hiding from one of the Axis, and if they find me, the Nazis particularly, I'll be pitched into an infinite dip like everyone else of my kind, first shot, stabbed or gassed or eaten by dogs or two of those or three," "Maybe Julie can help you, sir, but I've got to inform you I'm not that sort of daughter and don't see how I could ever be, in fact now that I know you're there and wanted, if I don't say anything I'll be risking all our lives for yours—even mine, let me tell ya, which I have to admit is to me of much less significance, feeling deep down that being last on line and kind's the only thing," "Please, enough with heartfeltness and panoplied philosophies, pry open the fucking boards, help me out and to get away for I'm too goddamn weak to, and take me to my mother cunt where there are no such things as axioms and Nazis, then I'll be free and never again need to ask you for anything for me," "No can do," and Julie says "Who you speaking to, hon, me?" and she says "Yup, you, nope, me, maybe, unclear, over, under," in another she draws up a pail from a well and he's cramped into it, chin pinned to his knees, rubbing his knuckles and looking asleep, pail's seams stretched and buckling, in another he says to her in a barrens with no houses or other people around "The weather's been so inclement out here, I can't see any shooting stars this year, there are only another few days till the peak of the shower's over, I wish I could go back to where I started from to see it better, would you buy me a ticket?"

Next morning she says to Glen "Again, another one of those deadly daddy dreams, what gives with them? last night there might have been two, maybe three—you know, I really can't take it anymore, I mean I can probably take it so long as I don't lose a lot of sleep over it, but I don't want to take it anymore, goddamn guy won't leave me alone and I think I know what it all means, not 'goddamn,' that's just what was in my last dream or one I remember as last, the goddamn cursing, but you know what I mean, and it's not, I swear—how do you like that? 'swear,' 'cursing'—but it's not that I believe in spirits or anything like that, and I'm aware that cementarians or something—that's from another dream about graveyards, the made-up word I mean if it is made up—don't stick much of the cremated person's dust into those soup cans, maybe a tenth of it someone in the know once said, so for me perhaps one fifth for two cans, but I almost feel that his ashes are talking to me in their way, or his spirit's doing the talking for his ashes, or it's neither of those, which is probably the case, for things like that can't be, can they? and it's just my mind which I don't think will be normally composed for months unless I get his ashes and dust and bone fragments and eyeballs, for christsake, and whatever back together again, two cans, I don't plan to mix them and put them in one, that'd be too complicated and messy and probably smelly and not something I'd ask anyone to do and I certainly won't, but one on top of the other or side by side but at least as close as two cans can be in the same burying place," and he says "So you have to do something about it, what else can I say?" and she says "Good advertisement for plane travel and what I was thinking myself, you think you can handle the boys for up to two days?" and calls work and says she won't be in today and possibly the next and drives to the cemetery, at the office there asks if she may dig the can up herself, she knows exactly where it is and she brought a garden trowel for the work, and the person in charge says they'd get into all sorts of difficulties with the gravediggers' union if they let her do anything with the trowel but fluff up the earth a little around the privets or dig up some weeds and she says "Good, so a professional digger will have to do it, I don't care what the charge so long as it's done in the next hour though I hope you'll be fair, this isn't a casket I'm asking you to unearth but a small can which is maybe at the most, or was when we put it there, a foot and a half underground," gravedigger's taken off another job and can's dug up and she takes it home in the shoebox she came with, wraps it in several layers of aluminum foil and plastic produce bags, phones her father's cemetery and tells them what she's coming for and they say it's all right though of course there'll have to be some costs, phones her travel agent, arranges for a friend to be home when the kids get there and calls Glen to say she's leaving now, "I've been thinking," he says and she says "My mind's made up so don't try to change it," "It's not that but can't it wait till the weekend when I'll be freer to take care of the kids and your leaving won't be such a shock to them and you also might have had more time to think about it, because for all you know your bad dreams might end for good here tonight," "I've already made all the arrangements, not that anything like that can't be changed, but I don't want to keep the can around the house for that long, it wouldn't be right for the kids or good for me, I also don't see myself bringing it back to the cemetery and asking them to rebury it, so I just want to get the whole thing done with and if all goes well I'll be home tomorrow around midafternoon," drives to the airport, flies east with the wrapped can in her carry-on bag, stays at a hotel near the airport, the can in the bathtub behind the drawn shower curtain while she sleeps, gets up early and doesn't remember having any dreams about her father or Julie or graves or holes or anything alluding to them, breakfasts and cabs to the cemetery and tells one of the owners she doesn't know where the other can's buried except that it's around her sister's grave so if they don't have any record of the exact location, which isn't to say the can couldn't have shifted underground, they'll probably have to go get a gravedigger to search for it, something, she said, they probably would have done anyway what with the possible labor trouble with the gravediggers' union, while two men poke around Julie's grave with poles she thinks of her and closes her eyes and says very low "You know, I don't pray, I mean, never,

I'm telling you, maybe not since I was a little girl and was afraid of God and thought he'd kill me if I didn't pray so I felt forced to, but I'm doing it now for you, my darling sister, so if you're near and you hear me please know I love you and have always loved you more than I can say or can express in any kind of way and feel you got the rawest deal anyone could get in this world and I only hope it never hurt and that things where you are now are all right for you, and I'm sorry I haven't been out to see you since I don't know how many years ago, when I was still a teen, I think, the last time, but I live far away and it isn't easy but that's no excuse for all those years, and I miss you too, meaning I miss you much the way Dad always used to say he did, said it in words and letters to me and also in my dreams since he died how he missed me but especially you, Mom you must know how much she loves you for I know how often she visits you even though she lives a few hundred miles away, and of course you know what I'm doing today and if you don't it's that now all of his remains or what's left of them and I'm hoping his spirit too if there is one will be beside you, and I also think so much of what it might have been for me if you had lived, this I've been thinking since a little after you were killed and have never really stopped thinking it since, been for us both, really, both, so, that's enough, there could be more but I don't think I can go on any further, I hope you heard if you're there or the essence of the message got through to you or just got to you or just eventually does in some way, essence or the whole," cries, someone pats her shoulder but she doesn't see who, breaks down, walks off by herself to be alone, wishes she'd brought flowers for Julie and her father and grandparents whom she never knew, thinks she saw a flower stall about a half-mile down the road from the cemetery but too late for that and she picks some flowers bordering another burial place out of view of Julie's grave, there are lots of them around this plot and they seem like fast-growing and abundant healthy flowers so she doesn't think the grave owners would mind, goes back to her family's gravesite, "Found it," one of the gravediggers says while she's arranging some flowers on her grandmother's grave and he holds up a rusting can, same size and kind as the one she has in her handbag, she says "Think it'd be all right if I do the honors?—it's what I came for," "Your privilege, I guess, I've no objections, and hole's not so wide or deep as for you to fall in," she asks him to make the hole a bit wider, unwraps her can, switches around the cans behind her back till she doesn't know which one is which, doesn't look at them till she sees just their tops in the ground, buries them side by side and touching each other, pushes the dirt over them till the hole's filled, tamps the earth around it till it's flat and says "Okay, Dad, now rest in peace," and goes back to the cemetery office and asks the receptionist there to call a cab to take her to the airport.

INTERSTATE 2

Driving home, thinking of his mother and him when he was little more than a baby, a photo. First only his mother for a moment. Doesn't know where the thought came from or why the picture popped in. But suddenly—forgets what he was thinking of just before her, probably nothing much of anything—there was her face and neck and open-collar top of the summer dress she was wearing in the photo and then the whole photo, backdrop and concrete ground and crossed knees included, her shoes and his bare feet, even the white border or frame or outline with the notched or jagged edges or whatever one calls them when they're by design kind of frayed, the style for years then, which he knows has a name because he recently read it in an article on photography but forgets or never recorded it in his head. Something he saw on the road set off the thought? He was thinking, he now remembers, of the car radio, what the call numbers were, if that's what they're called, of the public radio station of the little state he was driving through, 90.1 or 90.3 or 89.3 or 5, which he somehow thinks is one of them from the trip up a couple of days ago or should he try to find the public station of the much larger state bordering this one, which could also be one of those, when the photo first appeared to him. Bumper sticker "Save the whales, harpoon a fat chick" was the last one he noticed or remembers. Few minutes ago few miles back. But that'd have nothing to do with his mother since she was, till she started dying and became gaunt, slender all her life, even in her child photos, and though "chick" could relate to him in just his age in the photo, he doubts it was that. Said to himself when he saw the sticker "Stupid, how can a guy drive with it on his car? Stamps him as offensively dumb. Or if he's driving someone else's car, how can he without feeling embarrassed unless he also thinks it's funny? But could be he never noticed it or realized, if it was someone else's car or maybe even in all the time he owned the car, if he'd bought it used with the sticker on, what it means." So not that one and no billboards he can recall or signs of any kind along the road and nothing on the radio, because up to about an hour before the thought he only had on solo piano and harpsichord tapes, and nothing about the music or instruments could relate, since his mother didn't like that kind or play. Also no people in passing cars he can remember reminding him of his mother or her sort of pompadour hairstyle in the photo or her clothes or anything like that when she was that age, early thirties, or him as a toddler or just his mother, period, at any age, even when she was home and then in the hospital dying. He thinks "toddler" 's the right word for someone just under or around one. Or anything obvious or just somewhat concealed he saw or thought suggesting that particular photo, so maybe it was something from underneath. But to be a toddler don't you have to be up and sort of walking with short tottering steps? And he wasn't walking or even standing on his own when that picture was taken, his mother said, which was why she was holding him sitting up in her lap. He'd learned to walk and talk late. Maybe his kids playing or squabbling—but you don't learn to talk, maybe not even to walk, and if you're delayed it's only because you started late. Or for a while the youngest angelically sleeping or something they said or did in back of the car or just being there with him acting as both mommy and daddy today and for the next few days had something to do with it in some way, but he doesn't see how one of those would. Doesn't know where the photo is now. Not among the ones he owns. Those he goes through about twice a year, either because he happens to come upon the two toiletry cases they're in in his desk at home—three to four times a year's more like it—when he's searching for something else in the drawer or because he wants to look at his kids when they were younger or babies or just-borns in the hospital that day or next or his wife at their marriage party they gave or a couple of years before that or after, before the kids were born, and especially sometimes the two nude Polaroids of her he took when she was eight months pregnant with their first and had breasts twice the size they usually are and the only shots of her, at least one of them, other's just shadow, with pubic hair. His mother's photographs, if he doesn't have them, are all gone, so it's gone, though he doesn't know how he let that happen. Particularly this one and a number of other old to ancient ones—his parents as children, his father as a lifeguard and in the army, their marriage photo and his mother's first day at work in a bakery when she was fifteen, her parents here and in their original country, her grandparents only there, some with them young and one with her grandmother or grandfather with his or her parents and grandparents, but was photography even born then or that advanced where one could take family portraits? That article he read said something about it but he forgets what, though he thinks the reason he got it out of the library was to find out. But the missing photographs had something to do with a plastic bag they were in in her basement where most got damaged or ruined by the moisture down there along with being in the enclosed bag for so many years, making it even worse. So he threw most of these out, didn't he?—not his infant one, which wasn't among them, but those where there were no faces anymore and the photographs were mostly mold. He was in shorts in the photo, no shirt on, no doubt diapers underneath, the shorts of course. Whenever he had a shirt on, no matter how hot the day, then underneath it an under one, for that's how his mother was right into his teens. Backs of her fingers clinging to him around the chest, short-sleeved summer print dress, she looked so beautiful, even with what to him seemed like too much lipstick and showing too many big teeth and the comical hair. She was a beauty all right, no question of it, dark, hair and skin, small features, high cheeks, gracefully slim, though big breasts in the photo because she was probably still suckling him, or he suckling, she nursing, since hers, unlike his wife's, were any other time pretty small. Less chance of breast cancer he once overheard her say, so of course she dies of it, where even the little ones she had had to be lopped off. "If I hadn't nursed you I bet I would've been spared," she said, "not that I'm blaming anyone. I wanted the experience if I was only going to have this one child and it was also then the rage." He said he thought that nursing gives one a better chance of avoiding breast cancer, but read that ten to twenty years before he said it and wonders if doctors still think it's true. Or was he thinking of prostate cancer and masturbating, but anyway, maybe her breasts could be the "whales" and "fat" and he the "chick," if that's the way the mind works, or just his, but too far-fetched so seriously doubts it. Taken in the narrow backyard of their apartment at the time. First-floor floor-through. Tall green wooden fence behind them, though photo was black and white, painted that color to simulate grass and leaves, she said, couple of clay pots hooked on nails on the fence with some kind of ivy inside. All the vegetation they had back there except for a few plants from grapefruit seeds in coffee and big juice cans and an ailanthus tree from a neighbor's yard covering part of theirs, none of that in the photo. Summer deck chair she's sitting on, the attached foot and leg rest. Lots of curly hair, both, or hers more wavy than curly, his a bit lighter than hers. Who took it? Not his father. No matter how simple the camera, and he thinks the only kind they ever had, and they got a second when the first broke, was where you pressed a button and the front part, looking like a bellows, sprung open. His father didn't make coffee, toast breads, boil eggs, change pillowcases, draw blinds, take pictures, work the TV, line the garbage pail with newspaper, didn't even put in lightbulbs—he said he usually got the screwing-in part caught and was afraid if it shorted he'd have to disconnect and even change a fuse, besides not knowing how to open the stepladder to reach the socket. "I'm inept—how do you like that word?—at everything but my work and getting to and from it," was how he liked to phrase it whenever she asked him to do a chore, and which she said was his alibi for doing nothing around the house as if he thinks his son and she are his slaves. But his light to lighter hair. She in fact used to say he was blond till he was five or six, "what they call a towhead in other religions," but he never saw any evidence of it. No envelopes with hair, or photos, and none of his relatives remembered him that way. Also used to say his eyes were blue, at least a bluish green, till he was three, but his father said that was hooey and just another example of her wanting to think of him as some rich little patrician kid just as she'd like to see herself as a rolling-in-dough old-money lady. "Anyone for Jell-O?" his father liked to joke when he thought she was putting on an aristocratic voice or even an English one and manner. "Crickets, anyone?" was another, hand raised as if he had a tennis racket in it. "Then rickets, rockets?" till she told him to cut it out—her voice and accent, if she had one, were as regular and natural as anyone's and she was a person without airs. "What are some other examples?" he asked his father and remembers him saying—they were sitting in the sand, no blanket or towel under them, maybe their one time at the ocean together like that, meaning actually down at the water and not on a boardwalk or seeing it from a bungalow deck—where he can even remember his father's bathing suit and without summer sandals or shoes or just socks, which means of course how long had his father had that suit before he saw it?—maybe from before their marriage, so twenty to twenty-five years? A suit can stay in style as long as that? Just stay in a drawer without being moth-eaten? Anyway, it's—bathing suit and beach—they're, rather, what made that time in the sand especially memorable, though he forgets what beach it was—if it really was an ocean and not a lake—even what state it was in. Did they take a long car trip one summer, or just a short one, a week, two, a few days? Certainly one to Canada and back or cross-country or tour of the South, let's say, he'd have no problem remembering. And it had to be some time when he was between ten, he'd say, the way he sees it in his head, and his early teens. Just him and his father or with his mother but she wasn't with them on the beach that day, or maybe she was, strolling along it or wading or swimming or going for refreshments or back to their cabana to change if there was one. He tries to remember it, her in a swimsuit, which wasn't so rare, the three of them on the beach or walking back from it to the car or someplace or even looking for seastones or shells along the water, but nothing comes. A trip like that, place to place, lake to lake, ocean to lake or whatever. . . . And it could have been after Labor Day for several days, or Indian summer October be-cause his father couldn't get away sooner and they took him out of school that one time for it, but an event like that he'd remember easily. But one night here and other there, since there were so few trips of any extent with them—he can't right now remember one, so maybe there was none, though does remember summer vaca-tions for two weeks to a month in various rented bungalows and once in the mountains with them with an aunt who rented one— but anyway he wouldn't think he'd forget a fairly to semifairly long car trip like that, especially if it was just his father and him traveling together, when a car pulls up, he looks at it after a while because it stays even with his but is in the passing lane. Man in the passenger seat is staring at him when he turns to it and he nods with no expression and man smiles and he smiles back and goes back to his no-expression and quickly looks front and thinks What gives with this guy? Funny look, even a menacing one, and kind of a sinister smile. Nah, he's being paranoid again. Gets like that a lot, or just sometimes. It's living in the city and reading its papers and occasionally seeing its TV news, or maybe just having been brought up in one and in a rougher city than his now and often in a tough neighborhood or bordering on one. But then it was different, isn't that what they always say? But it really wasn't. There were plenty of violent gangs, kids occasionally mugged you on the street in daylight and tried to bugger you in the boys' room in high school or that's what they said they were going to do, and some of them who you even knew beat the shit out of you if you so much as gave them what they thought was a dirty look. But at least they didn't shoot you on the spot over nothing or at least not with anything more sophisticated than a zip gun, which half the time blew up in their faces instead. But he sees a look like this, he thinks he's being threatened, when a couple of times it turned out the other person thought his look was threatening him. That mean the other person's paranoid too? He'll have to think about that. It could be that because he felt threatened he started to look threatening and that's when the other guy felt threatened, but who knows. But with this one, and why don't they move ahead instead of staying exactly even with him, or fall back and get behind him if they're not going to pass? Maybe this is the speed the driver's settled on as the fastest he can go without being pulled over, sixty-five on a fifty-five-miles-per-hour road, and he like a lot of drivers likes to drive in the passing lane. If another car pulls up behind his and wants to pass, he'll move over to the next middle lane. But that is paranoia, isn't it: someone you think's threatening you when he's not? His wife says it's just a projection of his own hostility, something she thought up or read but those were her exact words, and maybe it is but at the time he told her that was just a lot of Freudian crap, or Jungian or Rankian or whoever he used, without knowing much about Freud and nothing about the others. His kids know the word?

Bets not, or not the youngest. With this man though, and car's still even with his and when he turns to it the man's staring at him kind of creepily again, and he nods and looks front—maybe, but he doubts it, but maybe he's just a character who doesn't know how to smile right or look nicely at anyone he doesn't want to con or get something from or is trying out his creep look on him for someone else he's going to really do in later on and could be driving to now. Or else he's carrying out some sort of grudge on him meant for someone else—maybe even the driver—but is doing it in this car-quick kind of distant or removed or anonymous way. For it's just two cars driving fast next to each other on a major highway for a few miles and then in another minute or two one of them will speed up or drop back or exit and they won't see each other again. Thinks of looking over again, but maybe he shouldn't for if the man really has nothing against him and it's just the unfortunate way he looks or even some facial paralysis making him stare or smile like that, but probably not, then he might start getting angry at him for constantly turning his way, like "Who you looking at, sucker—something you see you don't like?" But looks anyway, almost in hopes of finding the guy minding his own business, and there's that same awful smile and their car is much closer now, might even be straddling the dividing line—it is, he sees, by a little—and the man if he leaned out of it and stretched his arm could almost touch his car. "Hey, watch out, you're too near," he says, but the man's window is up while his is down and the man says "What?" and actually smiles nice and looks pleasant when he says it and indicates with his hand for him to roll his window down. Down? What's he mean? His is up and mine's down. Forget it, guy's a wise guy or stupid or just nuts but more likely just a wise guy and driver doesn't seem any better, nodding at him now but with this look of seriousness and with his right hand, while he holds the wheel with his left, making a rolling-down motion. He nods, looks front and steers the car to the right till it's almost straddling the line, and slows down to around fifty.

Kids in back making too much noise now. Or maybe they have

been for a while but he just hears it now. But too much with that man having looked at him before like that and their car getting so close, though now it's a good two hundred feet in front of him. So maybe he shouldn't say it, leave them alone, they're being all right, but the noise is kind of irritating if just as noise and he says "Kids, come on—Margo, be quiet, enough." She says "Why's it always have to be me just because I'm older? She could be doing something wrong too." "Then Julie, Margo, both of you— anyway, I'm a little nervous, maybe just tired from the drive, and your noise is disturbing me, so please tone it down." "What, Daddy?" Julie says and he says "I said, and come on, you must have heard me, I said to tone it down, be a little less noisy—you both are, so you both." "We're not doing anything. We're playing games together, not hurting each other, and having fun. You want us to have fun, don't you, and not pester you when you're driving like you've said we do?" "Please, don't, you're too young for that, to also start trading cleverness or something with me, using my words for that—what I said I said and so on—to get out of it. I'm trying to concentrate on my driving, which you've got to on a big highway and so many cars and trucks, and I need you two to be a lot less roughhouse than you are." "Be less what?" Julie says. "We're not," Margo says. "We're even being quiet, playing well for a change, so you should be happy." "Okay, nothing, really, fine," he says, "but just try to keep your voices at that level you just spoke, both of you, kind of low. In fact, don't try, just do it; please?" The other car's slowed down to where it's even with his again but back in the middle of its lane and man's staring at him when he turns to it but with this new look of niceness and no sinister smile. He smiles, one of those flash ones which means he's smiling because something isn't nice or funny, and looks front. Probably shouldn't have done that. Just smiled naturally or not at all. But what's with them? Don't they know they're distracting him, which could be dangerous for him driving the car and then for them if he's distracted into them or too near them by losing a little driving control? Well, it won't go that far, but the level of danger is raised a little he'd think by their looks, even if those were nice ones they just gave, for something ugly's obviously underneath, and now coming back and such and what went on before and also raised by their driving fifty in the speed lane which seems to be just to stay even with him—what else could it be for?—and they should know all that. They should just leave him alone. He has kids in the car too, goddamnit, don't the idiots see? Forget it, they're just trying to needle him, for some reason. He's their target or mark on the road for the moment, source of entertainment because they're bored with driving or their own conversation, the music on the radio—they can't locate any station or bring it in clear in this sort of open-land stretch—or they've run out of tape cassettes or have none to play and to each other nothing much ever to say—but having kids' fun in their own big dumb men's way, or they just don't like his face, he reminds them or one of them—the passenger—of someone the guy really hates or maybe the passenger even thinks he's that man. He could speed up but feels they'll only keep up with him. Or go into the next middle lane or even to the slow one and drive slower in either but how slow can you go on this big Interstate without being a danger yourself with all the cars flying by and buses and trailer trucks? Certainly first cop car he spots he'll honk for or pull over if it's on the side of the road or the divider, but he better keep a sharp lookout, and first turnoff or rest stop that comes up, he'll pull off. He rolls his window up all the way. That's at least some protection if he needs it or a signal to them to leave off or just enough of a shield between them where they'll now feel they can't get through to him. Other front window's down a little but that's okay, nothing wrong on that side. Kids' windows are only pushed out a little at the back and clasped. Glances around to them and then in the rearview. They're all right, playing quietly by themselves, Julie, because of her yawn, probably starting to nod off, but no sign they're aware of any uneasiness in him. Senses some arm action from the car and looks and man's smiling nice-like again and saying something like "Your window, your window, roll your window down," and points to his chest and then his mouth and then to him as if he has something to tell him and now with this slightly urgent face, and then to the highway on their side and all the time the driver's nodding agreeingly. "What?" he mouths. "Can't make it out. What? Sorry," and looks front and drives into the next middle lane. He thinks "They're trying to inveigle me into something, that's all, I can see it a mile away." They drive into the lane he just left and stay even with him. He glances over and both are looking at him now and smiling, then the driver laughing, the passenger then laughing, the driver then laughing hysterically it seems like. "Hey, what gives already?" he says through the window. "What the heck you want?" "What's that, Daddy?" Julie says and he says "Nothing, sweetie, go back to your nap." "I wasn't sleeping." "Really, nothing, I was only saying out loud before something I was thinking inside." "You were talking to those men there," Margo says and he says "Those men, in the car beside us? No, but don't pay any attention to them, wave or anything, you hear? Are you both listening to me?" and Julie says "What men?" and Margo says "The car outside my side," and Julie says "I didn't see them, I wasn't waving, maybe Margo," and he says "No fights, both of you, just play or be quiet," and he looks in the rearview a few seconds later, has to shift it around a little, and they're back to what they were doing or something else. He turns to the men. They're still laughing or only started laughing again when he turned to them but not as hysterically and the passenger shaking his head at him as if how could anyone be such a jerk? and he looks front. Why'd he even answer them? They didn't hear, but just with his mouth moving. They're crazy or just bastards. Best to ignore them. They could sideswipe his car or whatever's the word. Sideswipe. That what they're after? Bump or graze his car a little with theirs to give him a scare? Even to send him off the road or into another car for all he knows? They might know how to do it without losing control of theirs, but he could lose control. That could be what they want, for him to crash, but more realistically to just scare him and they might be so stupid as to think everyone can get back control of their car once they lose it for a second, at least any man his age, so they actually might not have any thoughts about making him crash, but he could. He's a good driver but not great. Car spinning on a slick or ice, he never knows what to do. Brake, no brake, left when it goes right, right when it goes right, steering the car where? and it's happened. Then out the side of his eye the passenger's hand out the window, which is all the way down now he sees when he looks straight at him, and pointing it to the front of his car and down, the wheel or somewhere near. "Something is wrong with your car," the man seems to be saying. "Something is wrong where I'm pointing, up front." "Something's wrong with some part of the front of my car?" he mouths, not wanting the kids to hear, and the man nods and the driver, looking back and forth at the road and him, nods vigorously, saying "Yeah, babe, yeah," and the man says with his expression and hand "Roll down your window so I can tell you what it is." Wait wait wait. Something's been wrong with his car and their staying even with him and everything all this time was for that? And the laughing before, even the hysterics, was because they knew he was thinking they were doing something terrible or nuts or intending to when it was only his car and safety and stuff and even his kids they were concerned about? Good intentions all along? So maybe it's that, it seems to be, which he's relieved about but now worried about his car, though it's probably only the air in his left front wheel's low or hubcap there's loose, it's not a flat, he'd feel that, nor his door the man's pointing at and he can see it's shut tight, or maybe something's stuck to his fender or somewhere—the grille—a dead animal, a bird, even, and he rolls his window down and says "What is it—the wheel?" and the passenger says "No, man, it's nothing, but this," and sticks his left hand out beside his right and there's a gun in it. Guy's got a gun, pistol, fingers around the trigger part. "What're you, fucking crazy?" he screams and speeds up and they catch up and he yells "Girls, down, duck, duck," and they say "What's wrong?" "What's the matter, Daddy?" "What's 'duck'?" Julie says and he yells, quickly seeing the guy alongside with the gun out on him, "Down in the seat, away from the windows, now, now, get down," car staying beside his. He takes his hands off the wheel and keeps shaking them over it and says "God, God, what am I going to do? they're trying to kill us," before the car starts hooking right and he grabs the wheel and straightens it, man with the gun out and both men laughing, girls screaming. "Down, keep down," he yells, "are you both down?" and in the rearview sees they're down because he doesn't see them and from below somewhere still screaming, or just one is, scream's so loud. "On the floor, get on the floor if you're not, even if you have to take your seats off, seatbelts, on the floor, now," and floors the gas pedal till the car gets up to as fast as it can get and starts vibrating, men right beside him, arm out with the gun out, driver clutching the wheel but lunging back and forth in the seat and bouncing on it he seems so excited and passenger not laughing now, serious, both hands on the gun, arms resting on the window frame, finger seems to be on the trigger, head cocked and one eye closed, taking aim at him. "Don't," he shouts, looking front, "don't, please don't, I'll crash and kill the kids, they're in back on the floor," and slows down, men's car speeds past, good move, what else? slow down some more, into the slow lane, maybe off the highway, even into a ditch, anything better than getting shot at, slows down, into the slow lane, no cops around, no other cars or trucks except far ahead and in the rearview way back if that's a truck, men's car into the middle lane he was just in and slows down, another car in the passing lane speeds past doing eighty, maybe ninety and he honks and keeps honking and it honks back but never slows, no houses on the road, just fields and trees, way off a farm, dart off and crash if you have to but going slow and where you have some control. He see a good spot? Too many trees or steep inclines. Maybe shoot across the highway and stop in the grassy middle strip or even cross it if he can find an opening in the fence and then north, but some maniac doing eighty or ninety on this side might suddenly appear from nowhere and hit them. Can't keep my eye on everything at once. Some cars and a bus pass in the passing and left middle lane. He honks. Men's car's slowed down till it's almost even with his, gun out on his head again but with some kind of cloth over it and the arms, just the barrel he sees, passenger laughing and driver back into hysterics and slapping the dashboard with one hand. "You down, kids?" he yells, "you still on the floor?" and they just scream, never stop, two of them, blocking out his thoughts, and he yells "Stop, stop, I can't think, speak, tell me where you are, you both on the floor?—I got to know," and Margo says "Why were we—" and he yells "Answer me," and she says "Yes, we're here, but why were we going so fast before and now slow—can we get up?" and Julie says "We stopping, Daddy, those men with the guns away?" and he says "Not stopping, don't get up," and looks for them in the rearview, not there, "Or stopping, yes," and slows down, more cars passing and pass in the two last left lanes and he honks, men alongside him, gun out, guy laughing, and goes off the road, on the shoulder, wants to get as far off the road as he can but tries to keep from getting too near the incline, which is only a couple of feet deep he sees—not even—but car can turn over if he gets only the right wheels in, though comes to that, chance it, they shouldn't get too hurt if it just rolls over once and stops and he gets them out quick, wants to roll down the right window all the way so there won't be any smashed glass but he can't, seat belt, and unbuckles his and rolls the window down while he holds the wheel and yells "Hold on, stay down—kids, you hear? we're going to stop," and brakes hard, expects shots, kids bang into the back of his seat by the sounds of the two slams and his head's thrown forward and bangs into the windshield but doesn't smash it and he's snapped back into his seat, looks up, car's going on and arm's in and in fact seems to be speeding up but still in the same middle lane and then arm's out with the gun and no cloth and aimed back at them, two hands it seems around it and from in back the kids' screams and he yells "Girls, duck, down, duck down," and throws himself to the floor, shots, two, two more and screaming and ripping of metal in his car both. "Oh my God, oh Jesus, oh no, my darlings," and gets up, car's way off, jumps around on the seat on his knees and looks over it and down to the floor. Margo's screaming, Julie, nothing, eyes closed, Margo's opening on him. Blood around and on them both, blood running down his face but he's too alive and alert and no pain so he knows he's not hurt and it must just be some cut on his forehead, but Julie looks dead. She has to be hit. But maybe just her head slamming against the seat before and she's stunned or out cold but she'll be up or she's faking and he says "Julie, you all right?" and there's nothing and he says "Margo, you?" and she says "Daddy, your head," and he says "Hell with my head, but you're all right, right?" and she says "My head really hurts, I think I might've broken it," and he says "No no, you're okay—Julie, you all right? You okay? What is it, dear? Get up. Margo's fine. We're all fine. It's over now. We're safe. Don't stay there. Tell me. Don't pretend if you're not hurt. Margo says she's not pretending. Really hurt, I mean. Julie, lovie, do the same," and Margo says "She's not pretending, Daddy. She's very hurt, look at the blood. It's all over," and jumps away as if suddenly afraid of it and sits up, legs tucked under her, on the seat. "It's mostly from me, that blood there," he says, wiping his head with his sleeves, "not her or that much of it," and gets out on his side, cars passing, a truck, tries opening their door on that side, locked, beats the door with his fists and yells "Stop, stop," then thinks "Quick, do something, save her if she can be saved," and then shakes his head and says "No no, not that thought, never," and gets on his seat and leans over the back to open their door and goes in back through it and sits on their seat, Margo in the corner, and lifts Julie up by her back and head and doesn't want to look but has to and lifts her blouse and pulls down her pants and sees she's shot in the chest near her neck. Blood's coming out of it, has come out, one shot it seems and wipes the blood off her back and doesn't see any place where the bullet could have come out, and presses his chest with his hand while holding her and screams "Oh no, oh my God, not my child, don't do this, don't, make her live, not Julie," and Margo screams. "Shut up," he yells and she says "My head hurts bad, Daddy, I feel sick," and he yells "Fuck your head, your sister's dying or dead," and she starts crying and he says "I'm sorry, I'm going crazy, I don't know what to do, what should I do? but be quiet," and she's quiet and he listens at Julie's mouth for breathing but she isn't. She is. Thinks he heard something, a gurgling, a voice. Then nothing. "What, what? You say something, Julie? Say it again." Ear at her mouth. Nothing. Ear against her chest. The blood, which he feels on his cheek, and looks around for something to stop it, his hanky. Margo's shouting something at him, the words "important, important," and he says, pressing the hanky hard against the hole in Julie, "What's that?" and she says "A hospital, it's important we go to a hospital," and he says "Where is one? You see a sign before for one?" and she shakes her head. "We could be driving around looking for one till she really dies. Right now let me just see. Maybe a police car will come and they'll get an ambulance here quicker," and listens against her chest around where he thinks her heart is. Nothing. Listens to other places where her heart could be. Parts her lips with his fingers, ear on her mouth. Thinks he feels something, breath, wet. Maybe it's the blood again and he isn't feeling anything like breath, or can't hear it and closes his eyes and concentrates but there's nothing, no breath, sound, gurgle. Wipes his ear where it felt wet and looks at it; was blood. Parts her lips and sticks his ear inside her mouth far as he can get it. Cars zip by, what sounds like a big truck. "Shut the noise," he shouts, "shut the fuck up," and Margo says "I'm not saying anything, I'm quiet," and he says "The cars, trucks. Shh, I'm listening, I have to listen," and sticks his ear back in, closes his eyes and holds his breath. Nothing. His ear out, lets her lips close, kisses them. They're not warm, they're not cold. That wasn't why he kissed them but feels them again, kisses them. Same thing but colder than lips usually are he thinks. "Oh my God, help, someone help, we need help." "Breathe into her," Margo says. "What?" "Breathe into her. They do that; it could help." "Oh fuck, I forgot," and pounds his head with his fists and she says "Daddy, please, breathe into her. Down and up like I've seen, down and up," and he says "I know how, I think, but nothing's going to work, I know it," and lays her on the floor and breathes into her mouth, comes up and takes a deeper breath and breathes into her, twice more, listens, nothing. "More, more, those times aren't enough," she says and he breathes into her, takes a deep breath, breathes into her, deep breath, eight more times till it's ten, listens at her mouth and chest. "Go out, I'll continue," he says. "Flag down a car. That's with your arms," waving. "Stop one. Stop a lot. Maybe one will have a doctor." "I still think we should go to a hospital, look for one." "We will but first do what I say. We just need help. Now go." She opens the door to the ditch side, starts to step out, he yells "No, don't, you can get killed, the cars. What am I doing? Stay with your sister. She starts moving, yell for me." He goes out, flags car after car. None stop or slow down. "I have to do this quickly," he yells at the next few cars, "so someone stop. I got to get back to helping her. —Margo, can you breathe into her?" he yells. Her head pops up; what was she doing? "If you can, do." "What?" "Breathe into Julie, into her, you saw me. Anything might help. —Stop," he yells at a car that just passed in the slow lane. "My kid's been shot," pointing to his car, thinking the driver might be looking back in his mirrors. "Stop, stop, she's dying, I need help," running into the middle of the slow lane, looking at a car way off coming in it and then to the one that passed. "She may be dead. Please, please." Other cars and trucks in all four lanes. One that was in the slow lane moves into the nearest middle lane when it gets about two hundred feet from him and the driver points to his own head and then him with the motion "You're nuts." He was going to stay there till it was about fifty feet away. He stays a few feet into the slow lane yelling. Most people look, several honk, some point, a little girl waves back at him, a few seem to say to each other "You see that?" a couple of them signal with their faces and hands "Sorry, can't stop," a motorcyclist goes past in the fast lane but never seems to see or hear him. "My daughter, my little girl, stop, I'm not kidding," pointing to his car, front door open. "She's shot, hurt, maniacs on the road, she was shot by a maniac." Makes his hand into a gun and shoots it at his car. "Like this, a gun, don't you hear?" All the cars in the slow lane go into the middle ones to pass him. "Shot, maybe killed, my kid, over there. Oh fuck it." Starts running back to his car when he sees a car's stopped about a hundred feet past him, now driving in reverse on the shoulder till it's right in front of his. "What's up?" the driver says from the window, "something the matter I can help?" a kid, around eighteen. "My daughter, in there, she's shot. Some guys from another car. I think she's dying or dead. I'm going crazy what to do." "Better get her to a hospital fast. There's one a few miles from here. Next exit. No, exit after that. What the heck's the exit number? I know it, every day, and now I have to forget? But one of the next three exits for sure. They're all one quick after the other, the first about five miles from here. There's a big blue H sign with an arrow on it by the exit sign you're to get off. Follow it to the hospital, there'll be other H's, a mile, no more than two from it." "Please get out and stop other cars. I've got to get back to her. Maybe one will have a doctor. They'll see our two cars here and think something's wrong and stop." "Put your emergency flashers on, that's a signal," putting on his. "And let me see her," getting out. "I don't know anything but I think I can tell if she's too far gone." "No, just go, even to call nine-one-one. Get an ambulance here; you know where we are. My other kid will wave down cars while I keep the shot one breathing. They'll stop for a kid waving." "Daddy," Margo yells, "you have to come here. She's changing colors and didn't feel right when I touched her." He drops to the ground and pounds it and screams "Oh my God, please don't, You got to do something." "You really better get her to the hospital," the man shaking his shoulder.

"That's the quickest. They can pull her back even when she's dead a minute. I'll lead you." "Right," and he jumps up and gets in his car, man runs to his, and he says "Margo, buckle up," looks back, Julie's where he left her, man's honking, wants to go. "She didn't get up, did she?—make a move, a sound, nothing like that?" and Margo says "I don't think so but I wasn't always looking—what about her strange color? She's not dead, is she?" and he says "She's the same, no new colors, alive, only hurt, she'll be fine, fine," but doesn't remember seeing. Just there, that's all he recalls, on the floor, same spot, eyes closed, too peaceful, maybe with some new blood on her. "It's smelling back here, Daddy." Blood; has to go back to help her, stuff it up, get her breathing, keep her, he means. Man's honking and pulls out. "Okay, okay—my keys, oh no," and looks for them above the dashboard, feels his pockets, screams "My keys, where are they, why am I always losing things?" in the ignition, turns the key and there's this ripping sound from it, ignition was still on and he says "Oh my darling, my darling, and I could've killed them both," crying. Man honks and he screams "I can't take it, I want to kill myself," and follows the car into the slow lane and along the highway. "Daddy, you're not going to crash us, are you?" and he thinks, "Oh I wish that was Julie saying that," and says "No no, it's just I feel so bad," and she says "Me too—your lights on like that man's?" and he puts the flashers on and says "How's Julie doing? Some movement, anything with the eyes?" and she says "The same. I can't look at her anymore, Daddy, I can't," and he says "Just tell me if you see any part of her move or breathe. I don't know what to do. What should I? Go back and breathe into her, try and stop her cuts?" and she says "You're doing right, Daddy, the hospital. They'll do it better, they know how." "Faster," he yells out the window to the man, "go faster," for the man's only doing fifty-five, then sixty and then fifty-five again and keeps turning around to see if he's still behind him. "I'm here, what do you think? just use the mirrors, you fucking idiot, don't waste your time turning around to me and cutting your speed," and honks and honks, gets very close as if to say speed up or move over, but the man looks back again and looks alarmed when he sees how close the cars are and waves for him to get farther back and he waves for the man to go faster, faster and yells "Faster, faster," and the man speeds up to sixty and stays there. "Jerk, fucking schmuck, move, move," and sees a sign for the next exit one mile ahead, no H on it, maybe it'll be on the exit sign, but the man isn't signaling right, maybe he never does when he's changing lanes or leaving one for an exit, lots of drivers don't, but it'd be a signal to him that this exit's the one they get off. They approach the exit and the man passes it and soon after it is another sign for an exit a half mile ahead, H on it and he signals left and skirts around the man and speeds up and the man honks and tries keeping up with him and he gets off, doesn't look back to see if the man's behind, maybe he should because maybe the man's trying to tell him that this is the wrong hospital, the next one which might be off one of the next two exits might be the right one for emergencies, looks in the rearview but man's not there, no no, there couldn't be two hospitals so close or the chances of it are very small in what seems like such an unpopulated area and besides that the man would have said something about it before they took off, or even if the man just realized it it's too late and this hospital will have doctors and stuff to help and going fast as he can he follows the H signs and then Hospital signs and sees the hospital, it's a large one so will probably have an Emergency and goes down its road and looks for a sign saying emergency, "Margo, look for a sign that says emergency," he yells, "e-m-e-r—you know how to spell it. Is Julie all right, everything back there okay?" and she says nothing and he sees the sign and then the emergency entrance and parks in front, "There's Emergency," she says and he says "I know," and honks and honks and nobody comes out or is around and he yells "What do I have to do, go in to get you?—this is an emergency, I'm honking emergency," and looks in back, Margo's crying, "Oh this is so tough for you, darling, I know," Julie in the same place,

"Julie, my love, Julie, how are you? Please be well. We're here, getting help, dear, help," and gets out of the car, says into the back "Stay put, both of you, I'll fetch them," and runs in thinking " 'Fetch,' what a dumb word, how could I have used it?" and yells to a man behind a window in Reception "Emergency, emergency, my daughter's been shot, someone, someone, I almost know it's too late but help me, help her," and a nurse charges through the double doors next to the reception window toward him and just as she's about to say something he grabs her arms and shouts "Where were you? Why wasn't someone outside? Get a doctor, breathing equipment, something to stop the blood, she's in the car outside, dark gray one, charcoal," and runs back out and into the backseat and sits her up and breathes into her, comes up, breathes into her, lips are cold but that can be just that she's very hurt, the opposite somehow of a temperature from an infection or cold where the body's doing something he doesn't understand because of the hole in her and loss of blood. Breathes into her, listens, nothing, but he might not be hearing, where's Margo? "Margo," he yells, "Margo." "I'm in front. I couldn't stay. Is that all right? Did I do wrong?" She's so sticky and limp, back, wrist, forehead, cold all over, she's dead, has to be, the purple coloring and film, there'd be some life sign, eyes, he opens one, it looks dead, he didn't act fast enough to save her, just should've kept breathing into her with Margo waving for help on the shoulder till someone came. Or taken her outside the car and breathed into her there so other cars would see and stop. Didn't do what he should've done on the road to get away from the men which would have been what? Swerved more, tried earlier to dart into the median strip and then gone north on it, got off sooner onto the shoulder and immediately driven in reverse. Moment he knew she was shot, without even going in back, should've raced down the highway till he saw a sign for a hospital—just should've believed one would come. If only they'd stopped at the rest stop twenty miles or so back as Julie had asked him to instead of his insisting on getting home soon as they can, eager to get their things away and dinner prepared so he could read the mail and newspaper over a drink. She didn't have to go to the bathroom— he asked her—she just wanted water, maybe a soda, she said, "No soda," he said, "and water you can get at home." Margo wanted something to drink too but also didn't have to make. If only one of them had wanted to go to the bathroom badly, just said that, even lied they did and then got water or asked for soda there, he would have stopped. If only he'd wanted to pee, but really had to, was about to explode or felt it coming, or twenty miles or so back he'd been so tired that he needed a break and cup of coffee, he would have stopped and never have come up against those men or probably not. But don't get sick over it. He can still help, who knows? and breathes into her, listens to her mouth, nose and chest. Stop kidding yourself, there's nothing there and hasn't been for minutes, she's dead, that's all, but you're not a doctor, you don't know, so she might not be, but she's already started what's got to be an impossible-to-change change, he can see and feel it, so she's dead. "Oh God, she's dead," he thinks, and bursts out crying and cries hysterically and Margo leans over the seat and rubs his back and says "This is very sad, Daddy, I don't know what to do either." Hospital people are there now, may have been there awhile, all the doors open, nurses, doctors, aides, equipment, with so many people and stuff they'll be certain to help her, each of them has that competent look and this is the country, not the city, where people are eager to help and do their job well and no one's on the run, and someone says, pulling his arm, "Please come out, sir," and he thinks "That's a good sign," the relaxed voice and calm look and pleasant manner, just by looking at her they can tell things aren't as bad as he thought and maybe not even an emergency and he says "Wait, I have to put her down first," but she's not in his arms, not even in the car now, he must have put her down, or dropped her, God forbid, or handed her to someone or they took her away from him, even out of his arms, without him even knowing it, so what does that say? A bad sign, but he's not sure. And where is she? He's escorted out, Margo's already out, and he's looking around for Julie, best place he bets is on the ground and he looks down and doesn't see her and up and sees a crowd of hospital people whisking a wheeled stretcher toward the emergency doors, her feet sticking out or rather her shoes and little socks and a bit of her legs, then they're through the doors which fly open, second set of doors which fly open and they're gone, he can't see them and he yells "Julie," and a man, probably a doctor because he's in white, says "She's in the treatment room, we're trying to revive her, just tell me quick, is she allergic to anything?" "I don't think so, I don't know, my wife knows all that." "How long ago would you say she was shot?" "Half hour or so, I think, twenty minutes, longer, twenty-five, maybe more." "Was any other harm or blow done to her, knife, head injury in the car?" "No, it was from another car, guy with a gun on the highway, we didn't crash but I did come to a quick stop and she might have hit her head against the back of the front seat, but minor, minor compared to the gunshot." "Anything else about her medical history, can't clot, prone to seizures, any severe recurring illnesses, is she on any drug now, anything to do with the heart, congenital, recent operations, like that?" "Not that I know of, healthy, normal, colds, flu and that thing with the throat, strep, operations I know there's been none of, only one time when she was very young there was a scare, pressure behind the eyes they thought could be a brain tumor, but it turned out to be nothing," and the man says "Stay here, or preferably in the lobby, but somewhere where we can speak to you immediately if we need to, and if we don't then someone will come out to see you after we're done," and runs to the emergency entrance so fast that the doors don't open when he gets there, has to step back and walk forward and they open and then the next ones open and the man's running someplace and then's gone, and he's looking for Julie again, maybe they didn't take her, on the ground, nothing there, I should go to her, he thinks, but what use could I be, since she has pros taking care of her now and they probably won't let me in. But maybe I could get in, "I'm her father," I could say, "I've rights and I could be of some help," to comfort her, from the sides saying "You'll be all right, you'll be all right, dear, do what they say, Daddy's here, your daddy who loves you." Margo's holding his hand and says "This is so awful, Daddy. What will Mommy say if Julie's really dead? Please hold me," and he thinks "That I should do and can use a little of too," and he tries but is too weak to. He knows he should comfort Margo also, say something like "It's going to be okay, you'll see, with so many nice capable people helping and in a treatment room where they can treat her capably, how could it not be?" but he's crying and says "Oh no, I was all wrong and you're right, it really is awful, how could it be worse?" He doesn't want to, more for her sake, but slips his hand out of hers and holds his head, tries to think. There's something I should be thinking of, he thinks, but I don't know what. No, there's something I should be doing— that's it—but what? What is it I should do? I should do something. I should go into the lobby, stay there, waiting to be of help, that's true and I will, but something else. I should wake up. Oh, that's the easiest way out, isn't it? and the least realistic, though wouldn't it be nice. But I should. I should really wake up. This is too terrible a dream, they don't need me in the lobby, everything with her is okay, some would call it a nightmare—it is a nightmare, but why quibble over definitions?—and if I can wake myself up from it I should, for then everything would change, but there I go again, the world's easiest and most desirable cop-out, the dream. But where will I be if I could? Julie will be here, Margo. Lee will be with her folks and I'll call her soon as I can and say "Well, we just got here and everything's fine. How you doing? Kids and I miss you." *Here* is home and wouldn't that be grand. But how do I get from this place to that, with Julie still being worked on in the treatment room, or so it seems like. There's nothing wrong, that's how, no treatment room, everything's fine, or she is there but suddenly jumps up fully recovered, or just needs a little bandage here, some other place, and I sign a couple of papers, even write out a check, and we drive home. But it doesn't even have to go that far—all that *was* a dream and you are home, that's where you are. I'll cook dinner for the kids, make sure they get to bed on time. School's tomorrow, how about that? "We have clean clothes for tomorrow? You know your dresser drawers better than I, but if you need help, even if you want me to do a wash for tomorrow, let me know." I'll read Julie a story while her light's out and they're both in bed, Margo reading in her own room. Lately Julie's been engrossed in Greek myths. Or I'll sit in the hallway between their rooms, lights out for both of them and maybe on in the hallway, or only the hallway bathroom light on but with the door mostly closed, or their night lights which they haven't had on for a week—"I'm too old to still be scared of the dark," Margo had said, so Julie said she didn't want hers on either but she's been waking up and going into their room almost every night since because of it—and I'll tell them a story. Continuation of the Nancy Drew and Ned Nickerson saga after they got married and had a child whom they lug around in a back or chest carrier while solving crimes, or just a story started by the first thing that pops into my head. Moral or folk tale, fantasy, biblical or chivalric story retold mostly with dialog, but better, with my kind of mind, something made up on the spot and new. One incident leading to the next, usually humorous and where most of the characters have accents, and the ones I've had the best success at and with some great endings that even surprised me. Stories where they both said when I kissed them goodnight "That was a good one, you should write it down so you can tell it to us again." I usually said "Don't worry, I'll remember," but I never do. Or I can have one of them choose what kind of story she wants me to tell and even what characters she wants in it. "Who picked the topic last time?" I'll ask, and whoever did it'll be the other's turn tonight. That is if they don't say right away they want the same one. If they want, or Lee says they need a bath before bed, I'll run one and make sure they dry themselves well, especially their poupies and hair, and then that they brush and floss their teeth. In other words, everything they'd do if their mother was here, though maybe not the flossing. If they want their dessert after the bath, then the teeth-brushing after. Maybe they have to brush their hair too before they go to sleep. I'll ask them or Lee when I speak to her, which probably should be after dinner and before the bath but certainly at a time when they can both speak to her. If braids are needed, which I've seen them go to bed with, that I can't do. TV? None, or a half-hour show at the most, preferably a public one. And where would Lee be now? Probably at her parents', maybe helping her mother with supper or having tea with her dad. And the men? Get to where they were going? They think they have to make a detour? Still talking about what happened before, making jokes about it—Fucking great shot, probably got the two snotnoses with one bullet—or they even know how it came out? Maybe the man intentionally shot over their car just to scare them but his aim was bad or the driver made a sharp turn or car went over a bump moment the gun went off and they never saw the bullet or bullets go into the car. It certainly wasn't anything the driver could see in his mirrors, since the windshield was smashed. He should tell the cops about them, give descriptions, but can he even remember what they look like? Clothes, even their hair? One wore a red tie, but who? Color of their car he knows but was it a two-door, four-door, station wagon, even a van? Seemed to be fairly new and the exterior shiny and clean and something seems to stick in his head that says it was a fancy model of some kind, but he's not sure. What good would it do? Well, stop them from doing it to other people on the road or elsewhere, and to get even, of course. He should do that now, or later. Write it down, but who's got a pen? And now, not later. Lots of it should come back, but for now it's a jumble. Margo! and wheels around for her, yells "Margo," sees she's standing beside him, head against his side, frightened now she did something wrong, squeezing his hand. Gets on one knee and hugs her, starts crying and she cries and says "I love you, Daddy," and kisses his head. If Julie were here she'd make a face and say "You kissed his hair; you're not supposed to, it's unsafe." Wants to say "I love you" back, but no way to, not even nod.

Doctor approaches. Doctor comes over. Stands in front of

them. He's sitting with Margo on the curb where the car was, someone must have moved it away; she sprawled across his thighs, though he doesn't remember sitting down or how she got there and if he stroked her head and back, which is what he's done other times when she was so distressed, till she went to sleep or shut her eyes. Someone in white at least, looking seriously at him and as if preparing a speech. Probably a doctor: whole outfit white, even the shoes. "Dr.," tag on her jacket says, and after it— strains to read—"Lynette C. Jones." Millions of Joneses but always a surprise to meet one. "Lynette" to do what: individualize, particularize, set apart or off?—heck, no reason he should be expected to come up with the right word now—like the Harrison Jones he once met, and another: Severen or something, and a Velásquez, that's right. Why's he thinking this? Fool, stupid, and bangs his forehead with his free palm. And who were those people in uniforms before who came over while he was in a stupor, he thinks, or just asleep but feeling drunk, and asked questions? They were told by him or someone else, he thinks, another doctor, male, that he'd see them inside. What color men? they asked, race, they mean. How many in the car? What make, car color, how many doors, did he see the license plate, what color plate then, did he know the men, any distinguishing features other than a red tie on one of them? Then they were gone, as if given strict orders to go, something he'd never do to police. *Police.* Margo answered some of it but they wanted him. Doctor's hands cupped in front of her—clasped, he thinks he means, and at her chest, serious expression unchanged, takes a breath to speak. He looks away and says "I know she's dead, that's what you came over to tell me, let's keep it between us and not the kid, but isn't that so? Don't answer if it is, and notice I'm not looking at your face to see what your expression says. Or maybe she's alive. That you can tell me—no, don't answer that either, for now if you didn't tell me that'd mean she was dead, right? But if you just threw out that she was alive you'd see a man jump or rise but go clear up to the sky and take you and my daughter Margo here with him.

Tell me she's saved," still not looking at her, looking at the curb, road, doctor's shoes, even white eyelets for the white laces, car driving past, Margo still sleeping or resting or pretending to sleep or rest, not at the walk to the entrance where they were working over Julie on the run, or something they might have dumped or dropped on the ground along the way, a towel, tubing, syringe cap, bloody strip of gauze, but he doesn't look. "Or just still alive, that she is, but not out of danger and that I can speak to her, even if for now she wouldn't be able to hear. Too critical, but that can change, and it seems when people are critical, young people particularly, they always rally. Rally, what a word, Let's all rally around, really rally around. If only we could, and prayer helped, and so on. My father, the doctors used to say, was a goner I can't tell you how many times when we took him to the hospital in a coma, but he always, till he died at home in one—our home, a coma, meaning my home as a child, though I was a grownup when he died—managed to survive. I didn't make myself clear then and haven't been, but as I was telling myself before, something personal between me and me, I shouldn't be able to—expected to, is what I told myself. Another bad example. And he was old and she's so young, his body had gone through lots of drink and cigars and all that crap, while she hasn't even started—milk and English muffins are what she loves most to drink and eat, chocolate milk, even better, and the muffins buttered with real butter—so I don't have to believe in miracles regarding her survival. The young always have a greater chance of beating the odds or just surviving a tremendous body trauma, as they say, isn't that true? And they should too, for reasons of living and right and what ought to be and what's due them and also if there's a God in heaven or some place, just because they are young and haven't, so to speak—and not just the cigars and drink—lived, though there's a lot of life in six years, little that it is. You must know what I mean. And six years, that's how old she is; this one's nine, and that's it for my kids, meaning all there are. Anyway, I can believe anything you say so long as it's good and hopeful, and I'm not taking you away from her, am I? and please excuse me that I didn't go into the lobby to make it easier for you to speak to me and not have you come out so far, but there are people and police there I didn't want to see. Keeping you, I mean," looking at her, "I'm not keeping you away from her where you can be an important part of her surviving?" "No." "You are a doctor, yes?" "I'm a doctor. Doctor Jones." "I can see that and I can believe anything you say if it's good or just a little hopeful, but I said that. I should say something I haven't said, but what? I'm obviously in bad shape, that's obvious, and you're obviously a doctor, I can see that as I've said, the tag, but she's dead, right? Don't say it or even give it away with your face, try not to, at least, but she is, isn't she, which is what you came over to tell me and I absolutely don't want to hear. No one wants to die before his kids do more than I." "We probably shouldn't talk about it here, Mr. Fry." "Frey, it's pronounced, Frey, but that's not important, so what is? Not my name." "Mr. Frey, excuse me—but it's probably not a good idea to discuss this in front of your daughter unless you're sure she's asleep and can't hear." "You mean this one." "Yes." "She's asleep. I can tell by her light breathing and easy way she's lying on me. But the other one. Don't say." She bites her lips. "There was no conceivable way," she starts to say. "No conceivable way," he says. She nods, is talking, saying something, something's being said, thought he told her not to say anything, but she did, so what? Won't listen, or can't hear. No insides, nothing inside, so cold inside, no conceivable way she started to say, or said but it was part of something else she started to say that he missed, because nothing to hear with, everything's frozen, all of him's sick but he doesn't want to vomit, can't, if it's coming up, even feel it, though he is faint, so good, let me go. Screens coming down around him, bang-bang. Shields, really, sky to floor. She's talking, saying something, something's still being said, she's still standing, shaking her head now, commiserative look, though he told her not to look, whatever you do don't give it away, windows closing around him, thick, then

door following door following door, slamming shut and closing
him off, voice in his head saying "I've been cut short," but not
his, knows whose it is. He believes in quick spirits? Thinks he
gets what the whole thing means. Hears a bird and there is one,
at first thought, well at first thought, it was just in his head, but
a bird in a tree near them, answered by another in a tree across
from it or one not too far away, same call, back and forth, cheep-
cheep, cheep-cheep-cheep, and so on, like Morse, saying in code
"We're bell-like birds, knelling death." Bellbirds, bell-bell-bell-
birds. Grabs his ears, folds them over the holes and squashes them
closed. It would be nice not to breathe now, not to breathe from
now on in, just to instantly stop or disappear, right now and here
the end, kaput for good. But Margo, his darling Margo, what
would she do if he did and that sort of thing? *Mein licht* in
heaven, huh? And Lee, for then there'd be two gone when she'd
need him for Julie when that time comes, which it will, just wait.
But Margo. Minor light in *nacht*, *nicht* in what, huh? Panic, her
dead or disappeared dada stopped, run out into the driveway,
under a car wheel, if one didn't get her before that: all the way
back to the highway to die. What's he talking about? That plus
the *nicht* what. She'd stay put but would never be the same. Hold
her, stay, best thing, now you're talking. But so fucking co, so
co, can't for the life of him stand it. And what's there? Body all
bare, blank and hollow and wet with icy sweat but why wipe it?
besides: can't. "Yes," she's saying, which he can hear now, her
head bent to one side to show sympathy, and that sympathetic
puss, one of her hands taking his which he shoves off. Don't
show, yes means death, show means no, co means what? can't
she see that? but "Yes, yes," he says, hates them: give life, take
life, work with their picks and drills on life, don't be irrational,
"that's right, no," since she seems to have answered something
he seems to have said and in a way where he'd made sense, but
what, he doesn't know. "Yes, I'm afraid so," she says, "I'm so
sorry. I can't tell you how much. What in the world can be worse?
Doctors know. We haven't seen it all, believe me. We're human

beings first—mothers, fathers, just people. One doesn't have to have children to understand. I wish—we all do—some of them were crying when they were trying to revive her—it could have been otherwise. How much we do, honestly, sir, Mr. Frey. I'd have given anything. We all would have. But she wasn't breathing and her heart had stopped and rigidity was already setting in." Tries closing her off by waving her away with both hands. Wants her to disappear. The whole scene to go except Margo, and Julie, of course, but hears her. "When she got here we couldn't do a thing. There was no conceivable way as I mentioned before. She arrived in an exanimate, unresuscitable, deceased state and we couldn't for anything get her around, what more can I say?" Nothing, none, thank you, he thinks, you've said everything inconceivable, go away. "Nothing, none, inconceivable," he says, "I heard. Amazing, just amazing. I always thought kids were so strong and savable no matter what the obstacles, but of course up to a point. But that point way beyond our point and that they bounced back, like that, or sort of," snapping his fingers or trying to but they don't snap. She's saying no, it's not always the case, that "up to a point" he said, though their reviviscent and recuperative chances are usually enhanced because of their youth, but again up to a point. Then he says "Injuries, not obstacles, and I want the truth. This some kind of ruse? I'm—even my other daughter here—are we being tested for some reason in this way? No of course not, why would anyone? no rest or ruse. Seeing is believing, hey? Feeling is. You feel and her skin's got the feel of slick dried leaves and things are hardening up in her limbs and there's no beat and nothing brings anything back and the rest of it, her breath and brain waves, and that's the reason for your belief? Well why not. Let's not just think of the poor survivors. She was dead coming here, dead down that road and along the way, over the overpass, under the under-something, onto the ramp and across the bridge, that's from an easy-reader book I used to read to her when she was even a littler kid and then she learned by heart and ended up reading on her own, under, over, by the, all prepositions I for some dumb reason only just realized, out of, into, down the path, between the rocks, along the lake, through the woods, up Spook Hill, probably the hardest words for a kid to comprehend the meaning of, wouldn't you say, for what are they? Nouns name things, verbs are active, even adjectives have a little more life or something to them. No," and inside: all a lie. This, that, everything about her today. She wasn't in the car; yes she was. She's home, sleeping peacefully, missed her flight. Huh? There are drawings of hers at home. Oh boy there are. She loved to draw. "I like art best," she used to say, for years. As a very little kid always scribbling pictures and recently subscribing them with titles and dialog. "The owl flies away." ("Daddy, how do you spell 'flies'? Not the flies that are pests but the ones where something flies away?") "Mommy, Daddy, Margo, me and the Iguana I want them to buy for me." ("Does 'guana' start off with *w* or *g*? Do you think I drew him well? It's from memory.") "Leave! Get out!! Help!!!" the princess demanded. "Someone, save me!!!!" All over the place and he knows he's going to worship them every time he stumbles on one which he'll do a lot unless he junks his entire library, for he's put them away in books and between them on bookshelves and in his work drawers at home and work. And what will he do when he finds one, which he's sure to: tear it up or throw it away? And the framed ones above his desk at home and on the walls at work and the big one of Demeter and Persephone in the living room, tear them down and smash the frames and glass and dump them in someone else's trash can or one of the ones in the men's room? There are things to attend to, nothing he looks forward to, and suppose Lee wants things to be left as they are? "No," he yells and Margo's startled and sits up and grabs his arm and says "I think I heard what you were talking about before you screamed. I first heard it in my dreams, I think, or maybe I wasn't, but I've been listening in and out of them a long time, so I know. We have to call Mommy, Dada, we have to. I need her around." "You're right, we have to, I'm not doing right by you or just what I should for you, soon. Because we can't just stay here like this bawling and screaming and acting babbly forever. But it just happened, dear, not even an hour ago. I didn't see the time then and I won't look at my watch now; I don't want to know even what time of the day around any of it took place, but do you really know what this all means?" "With Julie I do." "It means that the worst possible thing that could ever happen, happened. No, it would've been worse if you had died too. And worse yet if Mommy had been in the car with us and she had died with the two of you. It wouldn't have been worse if I had died with all of you. That would have been better. Then I wouldn't know anything that happened, as I now do. It would, in fact, be better, if Julie died, that nobody died with her but me. Of course. But better yet, absolutely best of all, if somebody had to die in that car, though I don't know why anyone would, that only I had, that's true too. If only that had been the case. If only that could be made to be the case. How do we go about doing that? It would be bad for you all but not as bad as just Julie dying. Now that's a tragedy. So in moments like this, can't we all just crack up, or each to his own? Anyway," to the doctor, "what happened is just about the worst thing that could ever possibly happen, don't you agree with me?" "I'm sorry, sir, what? I didn't quite catch all that or realize till late that you were talking to me." He looks up at the sky. Hopes to see the bird from the tree again, cheeping. And then to sort of sweep down and pick him up some way and haul him off somewhere. In other words, death, to replace hers, a miracle, with him the most eager party to it, where she suddenly springs up wherever she now is and acts alive. No, doesn't want to see anything in the sky, and doesn't know why. No, hopes to see Julie in the tree but a little lower in it, waving at him. "Here I am, look at me, peekaboo, hide and seek, fooled you. It was a big trick, with the whole wide world in on it, even the two men on the road. They were actors. The gun was a phony. Mommy hired them. Don't ask us why. We have no answers for we didn't have a reason. Unless just having crazy fun and playing a joke on the old joker and maybe scaring him is

one. Oh Daddy, I'm so sorry, did it upset you that much? We
went too far. Margo, we'll have to tell Mommy. Doctor—for she
is a real doctor, Daddy—do you think he'll be all right?" Keeps
looking at the branches and leaves in the tree for some sign of
her, then thinking if he thinks hard enough, and he'll have to
close his eyes for this, and does, clenched tight, maybe she'll really
appear in them. The power of something. He's become a believer.
By all that's mighty and strong and so on, he means it. A great
one, maybe never one better. He will give anything, he will do
anything, his life, as he said, and how many are willing to give
that? Well, for something like this, probably a lot, almost all
fathers. Or just on the ground for her to appear, moving, even
twitching. One little breath or twitch and he'll pounce on her and
save her, he swears it, he doesn't know how but he will. Give
him a chance. Give him this chance. Give her, give her, he means,
just one, only one, and he also swears by everything he's Yours.
He opens his eyes on the tree. Nothing there and he's not that
surprised: too high for her to climb. Slowly moves his eyes downward to the walk on which they ran her in. "You should come
inside with me," the doctor says. Nothing's where she was; place
has been emptied and cleaned, even the stuff that must have fallen
out of his car when they grabbed her away from him to put her
on that cart. Few people around anywhere, even; thing's over,
other duties, next emergency or just to get the cart cleaned and
equipment they used on Julie ready for one. "Margo and you
both. There's a bit of business to do, I'm afraid, which only you
can take care of, or your daughter's mother if she were here. Some
signing, identification, nothing you'll like. What kind of coverage
you have, for instance. I only want to prepare you. After you see
her she'll be taken to the county medical examiner's office, which
by the nature of the crime she's required to. After that you'll have
to arrange for a funeral home to pick her up from there, of whatever kind you want. But I'll try to make everything as easy as can
be for you here. We won't be asking for organs or parts. We're
not that kind of facility for most of them and the ones we're

usually interested in were mostly lost and it'd be too big a strain on you and also our facilities for her to be brought back here. Incidentally, I've been told to tell you there are several state troopers and other police people who want to speak to you some more. They're in the lobby and I'm sure by now are getting impatient and want to see you and inspect your car." "Where is it? It's not here and I don't ever want to see it again, so good. But could you promise me, as one of the things you can do, to get rid of it for me? Sell it if you want, I'll hand over my registration, and use the money for the hospital." He sticks his hand into his back pants pocket for his wallet. "We can talk about that later, Mr. Frey." "Margo, was there anything you wanted in the car before we give it away?" "I'd have to see." "It's possible they're already looking at it," the doctor says, "but someplace else so they wouldn't have to do it in front of you and maybe they just needed better light. Judging from previous incidents here, they want to help and time's of the essence if they're to get your assailant. But give them only as much time as you wish. They understand what's occurred and the effect on you both." "Me? What's to say? Two men, one drove, the other shot. I don't know their faces anymore. It's funny because that's what I was just telling myself before. Blurs. In a car, I don't know what kind and I'm not even sure if it wasn't one of those small wagon-trucks, a pickup that you always see on the road, sometimes driven by guys in ties. One of them had a red one, and wide." "It was a regular car," Margo says, "no wagon, new and white." "That's right and I think what I already told them, no wagon and white, but you're sure new?" "I don't know." "To me it looked recently washed and waxed. But what make and how many doors? These particulars are essential, dear, they'll need to know for sure. Windows, though, one to stick a gun out of, the right one, if you're standing behind the car and facing front, all the way rolled down. I told you I'm no good," to the doctor. "I can tell you what his hands looked like— Mr. Killer. The fingernails were bitten down—but not the face, though he had big teeth, or at least that's what it seemed. I might

be imagining that part of the horror. I see my youngest daughter's
not around the area any longer, just like my car, any reason for
that? Everything's getting lost. Today's minute is not tomorrow's,
and so on." "Excuse me, sir?" "May I please see her? This is
important. I want to see her before she completely deteriorates."
Glances at Margo, no reaction to what he just said, she's staring
at her arm and pulling up the shirtsleeve. "Daddy, there's a bad
bloodstain here. Lots of them, little and big, and some on my
pants. I don't want to wear them." "I know, it's okay, we'll wash
them out later and change soon as we can." "There's clothes in
the suitcase." "It's in the car; we can't get it now. Please, dear."
"But if we wash out these clothes, they'll be wet. I can't wear wet
clothes." "Please, dear." And to the doctor: "If there is something
you can use of hers—Julie—sure, go on, take, why not? I'm talking about parts. I even like the idea that something of hers is
walking around on or in someone else, and not clothes. Oh, that's
an old thought, thousands must have had it. You look in someone's eyes—I'm being extreme now—and see your wife's corneas,
when of course you couldn't. But what would you do—what
would I if it was Julie's and I somehow knew—swoon? Ask that
person to come home with us and put her up in Julie's room?
Would I tell bedtime stories to just that person's eyes? The person
could say, to make this possibility more plausible, that she got
them from such and such hospital on such a day, today, and even
give the donor's name. I in fact could first say, after meeting this
person at a party, for example, what beautiful or more likely just
clear eyes she has for someone her age, and that's when she could
say 'Well, some of it isn't mine.' But the hospital probably covers
up records like that for insurance purposes or something else—to
avoid the lunatic reactions I just gave, taking that person home
for her eyes—and corneas don't have to be immediately trans-
planted to someone else, but you know what I mean." Hears
Margo crying, he went too far, and puts his arms around her
head and presses her into him and says "I'm sorry, dear, so sorry.
Is it still the bloodstains?" "No." "So, I'm getting carried away,

I know, forgive me, but what can we expect? This is what happens. If it happens to you, let it—shriek, crazy, cry—it's probably good. To us both, I don't know, let them straitjacket us. No, I'll come down, you go ahead, and I'll take care of you, I swear. But something else," to the doctor. "I'd like a phone and a private room to call from, if you have one." "For Mommy?" Margo says. "Oh, I don't know if I really want one. And we have time, dear, don't we?" to Margo. "Why rush her? She may just be sitting down now for dinner. Wouldn't that be nice if all were right. But we have to think about this hard. You and I and our brains and some advisors, like this doctor and maybe the police. They've been in situations like this or close to it and will know what to do and how to, what's the best time and so on. But I don't know if she has to know, ever. Really. No, that can't be. But why go so fast and how could we do it? Not when she just goes to sleep, not when she just gets up, and she'll call tonight if we don't, so we'll have to tell her then if we don't before and we're home, and think up what and how and words and then words after we tell her if they're needed. Can't just be on the phone, can we? Better she see it on our faces first, faces only, and then together we can all just die. But then how do we get there, and by the time we do you'll be asleep and she might be too, which could be good, and we're not going to wake her up, or I won't, because you'll be asleep. No, nothing will work and I'm in no shape to speak or help and don't know when I'll ever be and I don't want anyone else doing it for me but me. She'll need someone there when she hears. She has your grandparents but someone like me, I think, around, when we tell her, when we do. Or just I will, of course, but you beside me, if you don't mind." "I don't." "You don't mind, dear—you'd do it?" "It's not what I want but I will if you want me and it helps and to stay near you." "Good, what a doll you are. But here I am, still doing nothing much good for you, isn't that true? It's awful," and kisses her hand and heads inside holding it. "I'm going the right way, aren't I?" to the doctor as the first automatic door opens. "Though I don't know for what.

My stomach's shriveling. Am I going in here to see her? She's in here, just wasn't a guess, right?" and the doctor nods, looks at her watch, says "If you could give us twenty minutes more, sir, I'll take you to her. Meanwhile, I've asked for the priest, who usually makes his rounds about now, to come down here, and also the resident psychiatrist, just in case you need them." "Religion, the mind, what about a general?" "I don't understand." "I'm not sure myself. What did I say? Something about war. Alluding to it, though I don't see where. Law of the jungle? Maybe I just meant law, and instead of a general I meant a judge. No, that can't be: mind, religion, law or war." "Daddy, please stop it. You're making things worse." "But why can't I go right now to see my younger one, Julie?" he says to the doctor. "What're you doing to her?" "Don't you want to continue, Mr. Frey?" for they've stopped in the entryway between the doors. "I only want to just touch her when she's not—you know . . ." "It's your privilege, I'm talking about seeing her, if you want to do that now." "I do. And whatever you want to do, Margo." "No, sir, I don't think it's a good idea for the girl," the doctor says, "at least not now." "Then I won't," Margo says. "If you don't," he says to her, "maybe then I shouldn't too. I don't know what to do. And there's so much to. I think I should stay with you, for your sake and mine." "Give us the twenty minutes or even a bit more," the doctor says. "Then maybe decision-making will come a little easier, and there are the police who want to see you right away." "I don't know. What am I going to do about my wife? That's something I'll never be able to know, though I know I'll have to do something." "As you said before, you have time to think about it and decide, and I and several other people on the staff will be more than glad to assist you."

He's supposed to say that's nice, thanks? Can't say anything. As they pass through the second automatic door police get out of seats in the waiting area and go to them. In uniform, out of, different colors, beige, blue, maybe some from some city, others troopers, starched bright white shirts and dark ties, union or federation pins in their lapels, anyway, some fellowship or order, but all officials or police official-like-looking, even those in plain-clothes, and two take their hats off and hold them at their sides. Respect, he thinks, I don't want it. Give me back Julie; take all the other shit and jam it. He says "Police, police, where were you? I know you tried speaking to me outside but I'm talking about way before when I was looking all over, this is my other daughter, for miles on the highway while we were being stalked by those two dogs. If you had been there and I had pulled over to you, which I would've risked our lives doing across the road for I almost knew they would shoot, what a break it would've been if I'd've made it. Everything now would be the opposite. We wouldn't be here, you wouldn't be with us, she wouldn't be there," pointing past them to double doors some hospital people are going in and out of, "no coroner would be waiting. It's amazing, beyond the beyond and into the unthinkable." *"Daddy,"* Margo says. He squeezes her hand. "It's all right, sweetie, they understand my rant and anger, for what was I saying?" "We do," a uniformed man says, brass on his shoulders like an army captain, "and we're extremely sorry, sir, young lady, for everything, and especially your youngest. She is that? You have others?" "No. By three. Listen, I'm in no condition." People around when they walked in, now, maybe waiting for treatment, others their relatives or friends with them, or just waiting for others inside undergoing treatment, through those doors he saw, looked at him and Margo, look now. He looked at them then, glimpsed, glanced, they stared, looked sad, word had passed fast, then looked away. Doesn't want to see what they're seeing. Sympathy, wants none of it. Give back Julie, stash all the other shit. It doesn't mean or help anything, though people got to react to something like this; or it works for most people, words, gestures, hand on the back he's getting now from the captain, but not him. Shuts his eyes. So they see him crying. This big hand lifts him up and sits him in a tree. Trees again, but she's not in it with him, and no birds. Tries to make her appear but can't. Is this what he's going to do rest of his life? He's worthless in every respect now, will be for years. Then a voice but it's somebody saying something from outside his eyes, he thinks to him, but doesn't hear what? Not Margo's, it's deep. Then he's back on land and this big hand, maybe the same, lifts him through the hospital roof into space. Stars shoot by but no shots. Lots of police around, so of course not. He reaches down to pick up Margo, other hand up to reach Julie, good thing for years he hasn't lessened his stretches and push-ups, together when he gets them he'll carry them in his arms to any place but down there. He has Margo and Julie's saying "Only two more inches, Daddy, two more," when it all stops, freezes, blanks. Tries to bring it back but can't. Squeezing his eyes tight as he can doesn't work. What other tricks could he use? Be nice to be a Bible reader and have that faith. For other than seeing to Margo now he'd just pore and pore. The answers to how to tell his wife and when might be in it, capital *I*? chapter two, patriarch three. His wife too, he'd hope, a Bible reader and quasi-religious zealot; then their madness would be justified or rerouted or decontaminated or whatever the word, none of those but on their knees, and things might begin to look good or just pick up. "Nathan?" and he opens his eyes, heard that, a man's, the captain. "Nathan, listen, we're losing a lot of valuable time. We sympathized, outside, that you weren't in terrific shape, but now—" "I gave info outside?" "Not enough of it, which is why we stayed. You mentioned two men and we want to get these guys, for you, for everybody." "What'd I say?" "You said too little. Car and a gun and these men and a red tie. Most was mumbled. Let's face it, you were incoherent. We can respond to that, then. But now—" "Look, I can't see or talk to anyone now. My kid's just been killed. Maybe to you an hour ago isn't 'just being killed.' But to me it's *just, just*; in an hour it'll be *just, just*. In three hours, four, tomorrow, next days. I'm a nut case from it, so what could I possibly do for you—I'm sorry, Margo," patting her hand; "I won't be this way forever. But one of you be nice and get me a Bible?" he says to the police. "You'd like a Bible?" the doctor says. "We have a priest here, he's supposed to be down any moment, I don't know what's delaying him, but any particular kind? I believe we have the King James, Good News, Holy Scriptures if that's what the Jewish one is called, the one without the end." "I don't want a priest. I don't read those things except for the poetry and plots, which I haven't for years and aren't interested in now. But say, wouldn't it be great if I was. If I just had time, as at home, you know, my two kids finished with their dinner, reading their own books or playing quietly with each other—loudly, savagely, anything, for after a while I'd know how to tone them down and bring them around—and I got out the house Bible, glass of wine by my side on the arm of my armchair, Tanakh, whatever that means, once looked it up but it wasn't there and I've a good dictionary, and red, and just turned to some of my favorite stuff in it or what I remember was, not the brutal, revengeful parts of God's or the Israelites, Solomon, songs of his or was it Ezra's or Samuel's? Saul hunting down David in the cave and that spider, Joseph when he sees his father again after so many years, if Joseph wasn't the father and it was his son who saw him after so long, something about Ruth, search for a couple of proverbs and psalms that once struck me but will be hard to find. See how bad I am at it? but wouldn't that be a scene. And then I'd call my wife and wouldn't have any trouble how or when. 'Dearest dear, miss you. Kids are fine and fed and asleep, what a relief.' " "Daddy, you're talking that way again, I'm sorry," Margo says. "Am I? I am. It's embarrassing you?" "It's not that so much. But these people are wanting to speak to you and I can tell by some things that they're just being nice in waiting." "Okay, I'll stop. I'll try." "Please, Nathan, down this hall, if you would," the captain says, extending his arm, doing something like a headwaiter or restaurant hostess, table this way, sir, miss, nonsmoking, an upside-down wave, to show where he wants them to go, of course. Hey, I'm beginning to catch on to things, he thinks; I'm not so bad off as before. Maybe a help, maybe a hindrance. "Maybe we should follow," to Margo, "what do you say? Give

them what they want in a few minutes and then we can be alone
to forgive and forget, I mean to figure out what I now can't, like
what to say to Mommy, like I must see poor Julie." Starts crying,
someone has his arm, it's that damn word poor, he thinks, Margo
the hand of his other arm, doesn't want to look at her, she'll start
crying if she isn't, down the hall, through doors, up Spook Hill,
left, right, left, right, cadence count, another hall, and what's with
this 'cadence count'? he was never in the army, will he ever find
his way out of here if he has to make a dash? Has to pee, badly,
he thinks when he sees a sign on a door Men, and says "Do you
have to go to the bathroom, sweetheart? We probably should
while we have the chance." "I'm okay." "Go, sweetheart, so you
won't have to later, that's what I'm going to do." "If I have to
later, I will, Daddy. Please don't force me." "I'm sorry, but why
not go now? Later, I don't know, there might not be—we could—
anything—stuck in some room, but do what you want." "Okay,
I'll go if it means that much to you, and also to wash my face
from crying." "Me too." A policewoman goes in with her, ladies'
room next to the men's. An officer follows him in. "I don't need
company or assistance." "You're not the only one who's got to
piss," the officer says. "Of course," and he does, officer beside
him pissing. "I used to say, though I don't know why because I
was never in the service, that as they say in the infantry, you
never want to pass up a latrine. Maybe they said it because of
the long marches with no breaks, or sudden sentry duty or something where you couldn't budge from your post for several hours
straight. I don't know why I brought it up. Of course, all those
uniforms." "I was in four goddamn years and I never heard that
line, but I get it," the officer says. First piss since Julie was killed,
he thinks, looking at the tile wall in front of him, smelling his or
the officer's piss. Maybe both, a real stink. And is it the first piss?
Yes. First time too looking at a tile wall and smelling piss since
she was killed. That's not true. Thinks he smelled her when he
held her, piss and shit. So no doubt lots of firsts. First night to
come, day to go, evening breezes, but not thoughts of poetry,

without her. First time he stopped at a hospital in this state. First time he stopped anywhere around here with them that wasn't connected to the Interstate. First time shaking his prick after a piss, shoving it back in, feeling a few drops on his thigh, zippering down, up, flushing a toilet, and he flushes. First time flushing one twice, and he flushes. First time this, that, what other thing? Doesn't want to look into the urinal as a first. Look at it! Ugly. No butts, but always ugly. Life is ugly, pissing is, shitting, butts, men's rooms, the works. Throwing up. When will be the first time he does that since? Maybe when he next sees her. What hands have touched the handle of this urinal? Why think of it, where'd it come from, and why'd he think he had to look? Crazy, man, I'm crazy. Why not stick your prick in it, your face, nose, lick it? And if you wash your hands after touching the handle, what's the problem? though wash them well. Hasn't washed anything since she was killed, and looks at them. "You all right?" the policeman says from the sinks. "Yeah, fine, just thinking. I'll be over. Everything's going slow." Blood on a shirtsleeve, blood on the other, what seems like blood on a few nails. So, blood on his hands or close, and probably if he looked close, blood on those. Oh that's rich, rich. Doesn't want to think of it, hers of all bloods. But maybe later he'll cut out a piece of the sleeve of it, put it in a little plastic box, carry it around with him for whenever he wants to look at it, or just leave it on his night table, kiss it or the box before he goes to sleep. He'd do it. The box, for the blood might run. Anyway, has to remember to cut out part of the sleeve, maybe two pieces in case he loses one. Maybe three pieces if there are three, and so on, though has to be some cutoff point. Sees her face, down on the car floor, sleeping, oh my darling, and shoves his fists into his sockets and grinds hard. Stars instead. "You still all right?" and he says "Sure, sure, just thinking." "How about if you stop for now so we can get out of here and do our business?" "In a sec. Sometimes pissing comes hard for me." There was a joke. Should he tell it to him? He'll think he's stupid and nuts, coming here and now. Good, inject him, put him away, keep his mind off it forever, and he won't have to call. Something about after a woman kisses the narrator's lips he says he's not going to wash them for a week. Or was it the cheek? And was it something his father used to occasionally say to him when he was a kid and kissed his cheek? So just an affectionate remark, not a joke. But how does it relate? Well, to the blood. If Julie kissed his lips now and that was it, last kiss, he wouldn't wash them for a week. Whenever, a month, a year, but probably his cheek, and he'd stay out of the rain and wouldn't swim and so forth. But he'd have to shave, wouldn't he? and if he didn't the spot would be covered and he'd forget where it was. Don't be silly. But when did she kiss him last? That's an earnest question. He knows she came into his in-laws' living room this morning when he was reading the paper and having coffee, but did she kiss him or he her? Is there a difference? She'd just got out of bed, first one up after him, and he was disappointed when she came in for he wanted to read some more and have another cup, had pajamas on, the orange-and-yellow-striped ones, bare feet, because soon after that Lee said "Get some socks on." No: "Please get your socks on, Julie, there's a draft." Her little feet. He liked to grab one around the arch and squeeze it, can feel it in his hand now. Forgets what socks she had on when she came back in. And she must have seen how he felt when he first came into the room, for she said "I'm sorry," and he said "For what?" though he knew and felt lousy about it right after. Isn't it strange, what could be more odd? when he thinks what later happened to her. Why, if she came into the room now, it was morning, he was reading and having coffee, same place or any place and he wanted to continue to read in peace, he'd put down the paper, make sure the coffee was out of the way so it wouldn't spill on her, and hold out his arms and say "Good morning, my dearest, how lovely to see you so bright and early and you so beautiful, or you so bright and early and everything so beautiful, because everything's so bright and early which makes everything so beautiful, but you know how Daddy likes to go on," and so on. Anyway, not the white socks she had on in the car, for this morning's were last night's and would have been put in the dirty laundry bag he threw into the car trunk. He knows he kissed her goodnight several times last night, never just one kiss for his kids unless he's sick with a possible contagious illness, so she must have kissed him, for they both always do except when they're angry at him or they've suddenly fallen asleep when he's talking or reading to them, let's say, and neither of those happened last night. He pictures it: she's holding out her arms from bed, is on her back, room's dark, he leans over her and she says, this is almost exactly what she said, "Me want hug, no go sleep without hug, won't stop baby talk which you hate without hug," and he let her hug him and he put his cheek against hers, she said "You scratch," and he said "I only shave in the morning," and she said "How does it work then?—the shave-hairs only grow at night like people?" and he said "Too complicated a subject to go into now, I'll tell you at breakfast, now go to sleep," and he probably kissed the air beside her ear or even her ear, forgets. Then she released him and grabbed his wrists and said, and this is almost exactly what she said, he just knows it, "Now you're handcuffed and can't get out unless I let you." He has to remember this. It was the last night; has to, and he'll write it down at the sink if he didn't leave his pen in the car and if the policeman asks what he's writing, he'll show him. He said okay and sat on her bed. Margo was saying "Now me, my turn for goodnight," and he said "I'm coming, sweetie," and Julie said "He can't go because I have him in handcuffs and he can't get out of them for all of tonight," and he said "You mean I have to sleep here?" and stayed there another minute, maybe he was finding it relaxing, resting in the dark with his eyes closed and her hands around his wrists, and she said, maybe she was tired now and wanted to get it over with so she could go to sleep, "I bet you can't get out if you really tried," and he said "Bet I can," and pretended to wrench free. She was laughing, he liked it that she was enjoying him but he also had Margo to say goodnight to now and she'd probably want equal time, so he pretended to wrench some more, gritting his teeth and making straining noises and arching back as if he were trying to pull free and then pushed her hands till they couldn't go any farther over his fists and her grip snapped. "Goodnight, darling, no more noise," and quickly kissed her forehead. "More, more," reaching for his wrists but staying flat in bed and he said no and sat on Margo's bed and let her hug him, kissed the air or her ear, she grabbed his wrists and said "You're locked forever," Julie said "Copycat," and Margo said "No way, J. I did the lock-forever trick, but around Daddy's neck mostly, long before you were even born," and he said "It's sort of true, Julie, though maybe not that long before and maybe even a bit after, though nobody can pattern it," and she said "What's pattern?" and he broke Margo's grip the same way and said "No definitions, no more delays, goodnight, all," and left the room. "Don't forget to keep the light on in the bathroom outside" were Julie's last words. What were her last words today? Can't think of them. This is important. Tries harder to, eyes squeezed tight, nothing comes. But did she kiss him, can he picture her kissing him last night? Must have, on the lips and cheek, one after the other which is how she usually did it, cheek first, then the lips, sometimes both cheeks, oh so French without knowing it—no, he's told her: "Whoo-whoo, so Frenchie," and then having to explain it—Margo just a lip peck. But the door handle going out, he thinks at the sink. Lots of people don't wash after they shit and pee. Policeman's right beside him, looking at himself in the mirror but probably at him. Half, he bets, and what did he once say he discovered about toilet seats in public restrooms and even in his home with guests—say to whom? to his wife—maybe ninety percent of them by men are left up. Which might mean ninety-five percent by men who just pee standing up, since he has to account for those who sit down to shit and pee. And first time washing his hands anywhere since, but he thought that. Then turning cold water on, any water on, splashing some on his face, taking his glasses off first to wash them and splash his face. Is it the first time he's taken his glasses

off since? No, lots. Also, pulling a paper towel out of the dispenser, drying the glasses and then another towel out for his face,
but not the first time looking at himself in a mirror, though certainly this mirror or a bathroom mirror. Did that, just the mirror,
when he was looking in the rearview at them on the highway
when she was alive. Thinks he saw her, maybe he didn't. Right
after he told them to duck. No, they were down then, so last time
he saw her alive was in a mirror sometime before when it was all
innocent, driving on a road, no worries about maniacs in nearby
cars, and they were playing, he thinks: cards, smaller magnetic
board versions of checkers and Clue, or a mind one with their
own rules, or just into their books. Books are now in back of the
car, probably a fucking red, unless the police took them away to
inspect them. Some outdoor clothes, dolls and their clothes for
the outdoors, car and bed, stuffed animals for tonight, those little
things Julie always brings with her for the car trip, tiny dinosaurs,
miniature rabbits and cats, markers and a memo pad to draw and
write on and small balls from the Giant store vending machine
for a dime each and her lucky polished stone and magic necklace,
also a red mess on the seat and floor unless the police took most
of these too. Pieces of her flesh, did he think of that? embedded
in the car seat perhaps or just lying around or stuck to the car's
walls. Oh dear, oh God, oh my darling, why you? why you? it's
not so, it can't be true. If he found a piece would he cut it out
of the seat with part of the cloth it's in or on, somehow get some
substance to preserve it and seal it to the cloth, stain it with
colorless shellac perhaps and put it in a plastic box and set it on
his night table or desk? Doesn't think so. For some reason her
blood on a cut-out piece of his sleeve doesn't seem so bad, but
the other would be gruesome and too sad. And her little shoulder
bag, he forgot, that holds all those little things she brings for the
trip and which she empties out almost first thing on the seat
between Margo and her. But all those firsts, each breath another
first added to the next, every goddamn step, new rooms, familiar
corridors and stalls, first piss after the last one and so on, first

fart, belch, what'll be his first cup of coffee sometime when and
no doubt pretty soon, first shot of scotch, beer, slice of toast, he's
got to eat and drink, doesn't he? and certainly get drunk and sick
and drunk until he stops, first glass of water and hangover, old
and new people he'll see, friends, family, first piece of meat, first
celery, carrot, aspirin, aspirins after that aspirin, will he still take
his daily brewer's yeast tablets and vitamin C? first tranquilizer
he's ever taken, also first sleeping pill and doctor's exam, first
tooth worked on or just a simple cleaning and checkup, will he
do it when the reminder card comes he addressed at the dentist's
months ago? will he also do the funeral which'll be the first sharing of grief like that for his wife and him? first mail, first time he
opens something from their mail, first time he listens to music
again or will that be at the funeral if he has nothing to do with
it or if he just mechanically turns on the car radio? first time again
behind a wheel, seated at a typewriter, shopping in a supermarket,
looking for a coffin and choosing a funeral home if there's to be
one, there has to be to retrieve her from wherever she goes after
here, first coffin he chose was for his father, first walk out of his
house if there's to be one, no he means first walk out after he
first comes back, first time he'll speak to his wife since, first time
he'll see her since, first time both of them break down or crack
up together like they're sure, at least the first one, to do, first time
sleeping with her and so forth, no more good sleeps, no more sex,
pleasure, amusement of any kind and so on, first time he sweeps
the kitchen floor, does the family wash, on his knees cleaning the
toilet pedestal, first time he squashes an ant with his thumb, gets
enraged at seeing another one on the kitchen counter and smashes
it with the side of his fist. Margo's birthday and their anniversary
and so on. Days Julie's come up. Shouldn't they get away, maybe
leave the country, take Margo with them but go if only for those
times, but where can they? In a hole, on a transoceanic ship, but
he'd probably feel like jumping off. First time he sharpens a pencil
or fills a pen. And what if he comes across the safe scissors she
told him yesterday she lost at home and needs tomorrow for

school? School, what does he do, simply call or drop in and say she's not coming in anymore, she's dead? Same with her after-school ceramics class and what if the teacher wants to give him the things Julie made that were baked in a kiln last week and were supposed to be distributed this? But when will he stop thinking about it and let the subject rest? First things first but he thinks never. He'll look at Margo; they looked something alike. He'll look at his wife; Julie resembled her much more than she did him. Photos of his wife and her at four and five and six and you can't tell one from the other except for the setting and certain clothes. He'll look in the mirror and perhaps see the little there was of her in him, the narrow eyes, big lobes, somewhat pointed chin. First little girl tossing up a ball the way Julie did or learning to rollerskate, which he'd been helping her do with Margo. Piano. She just started to learn, so first kid's lesson-playing he'll hear out of someone's window or if he goes to a friend's house where there's a girl or even a boy around that age who plays that way or just uses the same series of lesson books. First time he sees their piano, even. First time after that time and every time after that and so on. Will he move the piano out? Then every time he sees a piano or space where the piano was in their house or hears one played even by a pro and even on radio, record or tape. It's possible. It could happen. Fathers who cross the street holding their kids' hands, every single one. Any kid, any age, either sex, mothers and nannies too. It's what he always liked but she didn't always like to do. "You're too young to cross the street by yourself," and what would she say? He forgets. "I know what to do. I've watched how. I'm old enough. I'm five. I'm six." "Okay, now that you're almost seven, and maybe I have been too protective, look both ways, then look again, then make sure nobody's in the parked cars and just about to pull out, and even if you hear a car coming but don't see it"—this just last week—"don't go, wait till it passes or till you don't hear it, even if that takes a few minutes, then look both ways again and at the parked cars, and only the not-too-traveled street in front of our house and when Mommy

or I am looking, or the one by the school with the crossing guard."
Home, her room, all the rooms, bathroom where she washed up
and brushed her teeth before going to sleep. He was thinking
about firsts before but now he's talking about everything. His
clothes which she's seen, every plate and cup and such in the
house, all the furniture, carpeted floors, woodpile on the porch,
streets she's been on with him and so forth. Jungle Jim he erected
and put in with hundreds of pounds of cement, how's he going
to take that out? Neighborhood trees they've passed and huge one
in the backyard she's run around. Sky where he's often pointed
out to her a cloud. What's he talking about? Wash your face, put
soap in your mouth. Bang your head against the mirror till it
breaks or you're knocked out. "By the way—excuse me, sir, Mr.
Frey," the policeman says. "But by the way, I never said it so far
but I couldn't be sorrier over what happened to you and your
family and I know I'm talking for every law officer in the county
and state." "Yeah, yeah," looking in the sink. Somebody else's
black hair there, he hates it, why didn't the guy pick it up and
get rid of it or wash it away before he left? "If there was anything
we could do, but what possibly could we? But we'd do it in a
flash, without question, but even apprehending the rotten fuckers
and executing them by injection, what's it in the end mean as
help? Damn, it's the pits. There's no comeback from it. I put
myself in your position each time." "You mean," not looking at
him; turning the cold water on and with his finger pressed to the
spout spraying the hair to the drain and then down it. "You're
saying, killing a kid like this, it's happened with others and maybe
in the same way?" Turns off the water, looks down the drain,
doesn't see the hair but lets the water run some more to get it all
the way to the sewer, or to the river and then the ocean or wherever it winds up but away from here. "Jesus," to the man's reflec-
tion in the mirror, "just saying it I feel like I'm being killed myself
right here. But I suppose I shouldn't think we're the first. She is.
I am. We all are. Ah, I don't know what the hell I'm talking
about." There are other hairs in the sink; just noticed them. How

come he didn't before and how'd they escape the spray? Gray, that's why, two of them, and one white, so they blended in, plus five or six little black nappy ones which probably have a way of sticking to the porcelain more than what might be the lighter straight ones, but he's not going to do anything about them. To get all the hairs in all the sinks he sees into the ocean or wherever they go from here, something he never thought of before, and all the sinks he sees into the seas he could see, the shining sinks and shrinking stinks and seas he could mean, though he doesn't know how, well—well what? He's lost his train. He's lost it all. Oh, don't get so self-pitying, please. And why not get that? And the objective, not the correlative—for he doesn't know what's a correlative, it's just a word he's heard in attachment to that—would be absurd, wouldn't it? sinking all the hairs in all the sinks, sort of like going around flushing all the toilets in the world that need to be flushed. Slobs don't. Absolute slobs. Who let their shit and stuff stay there to swim and stink so the next stiff can see it and wonder about seas and shifting sinks, though they don't do it for that reason he doesn't think. They do it because they're egotists. "I've actually seen only one child killed," the policeman says, who's actually been talking about that or its correlative for a minute perhaps but he hasn't heard him till now or not words or not exact. "Oh yeah?" still to the mirror but the policeman to him. I want to get out of here, he thinks. I want to get home with my kids. That's absolutely what I want, out of this pool of siss, no small thing. "By a bullet, crossfire, druggies shooting up each other over some territory dispute from across a street." "Druggies, that's what they were or could have been. Of course," slapping his head. "What are you saying, something essential you only now remembered about them?" taking out a pen and pad. "No, I don't know. But who else could kill kids like that but them? They're out of it. Mind a freaking forest. They've lost consciousness or conscience or both or something like that. They're egotists, aren't they?—people who kill people like that. And kids, imagine. Even if you're aiming at me, to know kids are behind. Their lives over them. Meaning, that they think they can, it might even be their right, that someone else's life is so much shit to them and that they can go on, laughing, even joking about it. 'Hey,' " nudging the policeman's arm with his elbow and looking directly at him, " 'we just blew those two halfpints away, what a gas.' 'Halfpints.' That's from Wilder, once the older girl's favorite, never hers though she tried, always wanting to catch up. Or they're just not thinking of it anymore, those men. Imagine. Who else but egotists, drugged out or straight, that's who killed her." "You'd be able to recognize them?" "I don't know. Men, around my age or younger. My dead kid—shouldn't I go to her?" "You've time. I don't think they're ready for you yet." "What're they doing?" "Still examining, cleaning, other things, probably—I'm not a doc." "What're they, pulling out pieces from her, putting them back? I didn't give permission." "Nothing like that. That's for the medical examiner's office across the ridge." "How could they, not the examiners, but those men? And the alive one, Margo—she must miss me now too." "She'll be okay. We're taking real especial care of her, treating her royally. We're always prepared for something like this, if usually it's normal car accidents. But those men— around your age, you say?" "You got me. All I can see of their faces is laughing, and the only thing of that is wide grins." "Laughing, huh—when they drove away? I got to hear this. This really makes me burn." "Well, they could have, but I didn't see them do that when the guy in the passenger seat shot at us, for by then they were hundreds of feet ahead. But they laughed when they were alongside us. Druggies, who else but them—like the ones who killed the kid you saw. Maybe even the same ones. You should check on that. Did you catch those guys? You've pictures and a file on them?" "If we did you'd be able to identify them?" "Right now I can't even remember what color they were. Of course I'm not really trying. But white, black, a mix, maybe, but definitely not Oriental, but I shouldn't be so sure on that." The policeman's writing this down. "See? it's a blur. Or maybe I'm all wrong and one was one and the other one of the others. But druggies I'm almost sure of, just by the crazy wildness in their eyes, or the one who aimed the gun, and the driver going on hysterically as if this, this scaring the shit out of me and my kids, was the funniest thing there ever was." "Actually, by calling my men druggies I'm possibly giving them a better name than they deserve. Sellers, who ought to have their eyes gouged through. Monsters, when one of them shot her, or maybe two of them did—right, two different-caliber bullets in her from both sides of the street. Though that they shoot up each other, great, for lowers all our tax rates." "How do you mean?" "From execution, incarceration, hundreds of thousands of dollars per prisoner for the last one—it's the public that pays. But this poor kid got caught in, is how. Same age as yours around, though actually it was a boy. Yours was what, eight?" "Six." "Six, my goodness. But the same, correct? Six, sixteen, twenty-six, even thirty-six—who cares, to the parents, if they're good kids and they're yours. If they're the sellers and gunmen though, you want them dead and I'm sure the parents do too, for they're just a plain nuisance, often stealing you blind, shaming your home. And I didn't see this other kid get hit, just after, which was bad enough. What a nice-looking boy. I don't have kids myself but what it must do to you. I'm, as you see, a police officer, no problem with that. I like my job and I've been doing it well for almost ten years. But I know what I'd do to the monsters who did it to my kid if I had one and one ever did. If we caught them. And I'd work my ass off at catching them. I'd, well, they wouldn't live long if it was up to me. Worst beasts there are. And I wouldn't care—I shouldn't be saying this and I'm not trying to give you ideas, but I'd ruin everything I've worked for, in fact ruin my whole life and throw away any chances of getting married soon, which in time I want to do—well, I'd be married, if I had a kid, I'm not one of that set, so that doesn't figure—but to get even and one above with them. I'd probably gun them down—both of them—that's getting 'one above': two for one, the hyena who drove, as well as the actual killer. Though in something like this you can never get even, never—but right in

the station house I'd even do it if they were, and I knew it down
to my teeth, the killers of my kid and I felt this was the last or
best chance I'd have of getting them anywhere. And in the head,
both of them, smack in the gray matter—I'd see to that so they
wouldn't live and if they did it'd be as all-out cripples. But with
me—I target-shoot twice a week at our armory—there'd be slim
chance they'd be anything but dead." "I understand. I'd probably
do that too, for my little one, if I had a gun and knew how to
use it and had the chance to. But tell me. This has nothing to do
with what you were saying, but you've been straight with me so
maybe you know something about this. How would you phone
your wife, if you had one, that your kid's just been killed? I
haven't done it yet and it's killing me to know how and when
and even what words to use and just what's the right thing." "I'd
have to think about it." "It's okay, I shouldn't have asked." "No,
let me. We've been instructed on this so maybe I'll have for you
some guidelines or an even better idea." The man shuts his eyes,
puts his head back and his hand on his forehead, seems to be
thinking hard. "Really, it's okay, forget it, I said. I'll find a way
how." "No, it's coming to me. All right, I know," opening his
eyes. "They tell us"—Nat covers his eyes, doesn't want to hear—
"to advise you one thing, which is to wait till morning if the
murder or car accident where someone's killed is in the nighttime,
and not to do it anytime when you're overcome. If you have to
do it then, for some reason—like you got to reach her at the
airport right away before she flies to Germany or France, and
you're way too overcome—then to get someone to do it for you,
but no total stranger. A police officer who's a stranger would be
okay, but one who identifies himself to her as such. Or if there's
a doctor around to do it, and again the identity—'Hello, I'm Dr.
So-and-So at such and such hospital'—this one—even better, because he can explain all the medical things involved in it and also
why you're too overcome to tell her the news yourself, for you
know she's going to ask why you're not there. Now if it's by
phone you're telling her and you're reasonably together with your-

self and calm, to make sure, by calling close friends and relatives before, that she has a barrage of support like that around her when you call—and this is to mothers and fathers and husbands and wives, if let's say the husband dies, and the like. Well, I don't know what else there could be. Children, about their moms and dads getting killed. Or their sisters and brothers and so on. Fiancés. But I'll tell you also what I'd personally do. Of course my wife, the one I hope to get and will when I get her, might not be like yours. She might be stronger for something like this, maybe even a police officer herself, but then again, maybe yours is a rock." Takes his hands from his face. "She isn't. She's normal, not hardened. Even if she was, it's her kid, so she'll suffer, just as I'm sure a police officer woman whose kid died and she suddenly learned of it, would suffer, whether she loves it or not." "Maybe. No matter what, unless she falls apart at everything, which you're not saying she does, and by shaking your head now I don't think you're saying. So I'd say to call, and when she answers, and since she doesn't know how things are she's saying how are things and such with you and the kids, I'd say 'Honey, hold on to yourself. I'm about to tell you the worst news you'll ever hear. Our daughter's been killed.' What's her name?" "No, that can't be the way." "What's her name though?" "Who?" "Your daughter." "Julie, I don't want to say it, but that." " 'Julie's been shot, killed, murdered, it's a nightmare to me. I'm half insane over it, absolutely out of my mind, hurting like nobody, feeling I want to kill myself. I didn't know how to tell you but I knew you should know soon as I could tell you, so I'm telling you this way. Forgive me a hundred times for it. For telling you. Monsters did it. Monsters in another car on the highway. I'm with the police in the hospital now. I was told not to tell you this way, to sort of do it some way else for you to learn of it, not to tell you when I was so overcome, but I didn't think that the right way to do it.' And I'd do it now. I wouldn't wait. I'd let her know soon as I could as I said in that pitch so she'd start adjusting to it soon as she could too. And that's what I'd also tell her, my reasons for just shoving it onto her like a ton of bricks. Because whatever you're going to say to her and whenever you say it and no matter which way she's going to hear it from you or anyone else, it's going to hurt like hell, so sooner you do it, sooner it's done with. Is anyone there with her, or can there be?" "She's at her parents' place now." "Even better. They'll take care of her, though they've got their own big loss now, since they probably loved their grandchild too. But she has people who looked after her when she was a girl and I'm sure they'll do their duty and put back their own sadness for the time being to see to her, since hers has got to be so much worse. You're lucky, I mean she is, for that piece of good fortune, though relative, relative, for it couldn't be one more horrible lousier day. So that's the way I'd do it; no other way. But if you think the way the professional crisis experts suggest you do it is better, go ahead. But all those people surrounding her, accumulating where she is, she'd know something was wrong before she was told. And that'd take lots of calls and time and you'd be a wreck by the end of it before you even got up the nerve to tell her. My way, it's rough and maybe even brutal but it's right out, done, and then you start the bandaging and healing process. Then I'd have her parents drive her here, if they still drive and have a car, or a sister or someone— she have a sister or brother around?" "Nowhere near." "Then a good friend. Or her parents can hire a private car if they're too emotionally worked up over it themselves and have the money, or rent a rented one—for something like this, if it's the private car, you beg, borrow or steal for it, or you give them your credit card number and pay for it yourself. And then you two can go through what you have to, face to face at this hospital even if your little girl by then, Julie, is with the medical examiner ten miles from here. She's not that far away, is she?" "My wife? About three hours by car. Maybe longer because of the trouble in finding this place." "So. There'd be doctors and nurses and medicines to help if it ever got that bad, which it probably will and should. I say tell it quick and get it out—here, from inside.

And with those three to four hours in between your telling her and her getting here, a lot will already have been started in her getting to accept it, though the real crash won't come till she sees you and the deceased. And in it taking place here—in fact, they probably won't remove her to the examiner's till your wife gets here. They definitely want to determine the angle the bullet came in and caliber of it but I'm almost sure, if you ask, they'll hold out till your wife comes; it'd only be right. You don't want her seeing the little girl after she's been examined really bad, which they sometimes have to do. But I was saying that in that too, in it all taking place in the hospital with your wife, you're in, well, not luck but something like it. Just that you're here at the worst time of it, where people who can help, can help you." "No, I don't think so but thank you." "No to what?" "To a lot, and maybe yes to some of it too, but I don't want to go into it this moment." "Boy is this tough. You poor guy," and pats his shoulder and then leaves his hand there. "We're also told to do this, to make physical contact with pats and holding hands and looking in the eyes, when someone's really emotionally hurt, but that's not why I'm doing it I want you to know. When you do it that way, because you have to, it's bullshit. Am I being too frank?" "No. I'm not sure. Thank you. I think—you're all through with me, aren't you?" "Hey, I only came in here to pee and then we got caught in conversation. Sure, if you had said something important to the crime while we were talking about other things, like a vivid description of the hyenas who did it or you suddenly remembered their license plate number, naturally I would have been interested and reported it back to my superiors." "Then I'll get out of here, see my older daughter, maybe also see the younger one all cleaned. I've got to sometime." "Fine. I know what room the other cops took your older girl to, so I'll lead you," and holds the door open for him, takes him by the arm and they leave.

INTERSTATE 3

Guy in the next car's looking at him. Why's he staring like that, what's he think's so interesting to look at? Some people just like to bug you out, especially from cars and especially from ones going fast on the highway, and this guy, oh God what a mug, mean as hell, written all over it. Pay him no attention, next thing you know he'll be gone. "Daddy, do you know that man?" Margo says behind him and he says "Why, which man, what're you talking about?" and she says "Not the driver but the man over there in the next car sitting next to him and looking at us," and he says "Sitting next to whom, what do you mean?" and she says "Next to the driver of the car beside us, you can see it if you look," and he says "Pay no attention to him, don't even look another second at their car, both of you. Maybe he thinks we're someone he knows and he can't exactly place us. But we're not who he thinks we might be, that I'm almost sure of, and I don't like his face," and she says "What's wrong, it's ugly?" and he says "It's not that. I'd never not like someone just because he or she was homely or had a physical disfigurement," and she says "What's—" and he says "Deformity, and I know you're going to ask what's that, so, uh, Jesus—I'm sorry—but gosh almighty sometimes the easiest words come the hardest. Malformation. No. Something wrong with the face, let's say, if the deformity or disfigurement's there—a scar here, but a bad one, or a couple of lumps there. A person's lost an eye, for instance, and just has a socket in his face for one—an eye socket, that's where the space for the eye is. Or a—" "Oooh," she says and Julie says "What, Daddy said something disgusting?" and she says "The way he was describing," and Julie says "What's describing?" "Saying things. Eye spaces without the eyes. Lumps on faces like big pimples like I once had," and he says "Describing's more to make clear by saying what the thing is in a more detailed way, or something, and you never had a big pimple. Harriet—Doctor Harriet said, well, that you were too young for pimples and it had something to do with—and she's a dermatologist, a skin doctor, besides being a pediatrician, but what'd she say it had something to do with? You often remember those things better than I do, Margo. But not pimples or acne, which you kept insisting your one pimplelike blemish was . . . blemish, in a way, that's what disfigurement or deformity, et cetera, is to some extent. A flaw or mark, like a pimple or scar, but on a much grander scale—a big scale, a huge one. Instead of a mark it's a scar, instead of a blemish or pimple or boil, it's a huge lamp—lump—where'd I get lamp from? on your cheek or neck—goiters, for instance, which people used to have for ages and when I was younger and maybe some still do." "It was a pimple I had and I got rid of it with Mommy's skin cream." "It wasn't a pimple and you got rid of it by it just going away." "What are they, goyas?" she says and he says "Goiters, in the gland, thyroid, the enlargement of that gland—a swelling caused by an iodine deficiency—you know, the lack of this iodine in that gland," and she says "But iodine's a poison, Mommy says," and he says "But you need a small amount of it from natural means—you know, produced in the body, that thyroid gland. If you don't have it then you get it from artificial—fake, Julie, fake—sources, prescribed by a doctor, or you can get it from using iodinized salt, I think's the word. Or ionized. No, iondized— one of them, maybe not even that. Iodized, that's it. I haven't seen any people around lately with goiters but there was, when I was much younger, this goiter lady where I worked as a waiter. It was at a Schrafft's—that's like a, well, it's not like any restaurant today. In New York. For tea and tiny lunches and mostly frequented by women, but that was during the day. At night, simple dinners—lamb chops with mint jelly, and creamed spinach and apple pie, and known for its ice cream." "I want to go there next time we're in New York," Julie says. "I don't think there are any more of them, but the ice cream's still around. It was in my first year of college. Eight to midnight shift. And she came after the dinner crowd left, where we served mostly sodas and sandwiches and snacks. She and her husband, this tall, bald, skinny guy who always wore a suit and vest, came in every night, I'm saying every single night, and took the same four-table. If you're a couple you're supposed to take a two-table, one much smaller and for two people, but they always sat at one for four. And sometimes, if that table was taken and all the other fours were, they joined together two two-tables to make a four or added another two-table to the four-table they already had because they were expecting friends, who usually never came but when they did, ordered just as little and stayed as long and were as cheap as the goiter lady and her husband. You have to understand that the manager only assigned the waiter four to five tables for his station, and only one of those was usually a four." "What's a four?" Julie says. "Not *for* something?" "I didn't tell you? It's a table for four people, and with four equal sides usually, like a square." "And what's a station?" Margo says. "Not like a radio's?" "Good question, as really what the 'four' was. For it's an unusual word for it, 'four' for four-table. And even 'four-table' is unusual for what it stands for. But a station's the total number of tables you get to wait on, and they're all usually close together so you can wait on one while bussing or cleaning another." "Bussing?" Julie says. "To clear off the dirty dishes or get fresh water for it—you know, *that* job. But the point is you didn't want, if you were a waiter, a single couple at your only four-table sitting there from eight-thirty till closing and only ordering a Sanka or Postum, I think it was called—a vegetable coffee made out of grain. Wait a minute, does that make sense? A grain coffee, for people who didn't drink regular coffee or Sanka but wanted something like the taste and look of them, and also maybe sharing between them a slice of peach pie for the night, 'two forks, please.' That's what they always asked for if you didn't already have the silver on the table. I mean, I couldn't believe those people." "Grain coffee?" Margo says. "Like *grain*?" "Yuh. Like wheat, barley, rice, but barley I think it was made of—he, I remember, always had tea in a glass. They were Europeans, refugees from World War Two where they had fled Nazi Germany or even survived the war there. And where I suppose they drank tea in a glass and which was just another chore for the waiter, getting the hot water in the glass without breaking it. You first put in a spoon to conduct the heat—I don't want to go into now explaining what that is—but you had to know that about the spoon. And then the glass, if you picked it up right away, like to put it on his table if you first didn't put it on a saucer—well, what's the difference? You burned your fingers either way—by first putting it on a saucer on your tray or no saucer and taking the glass off the tray and putting it on his table—but his fingers never burned. I don't know what protection he had on them but he just picked it up and drank from it, so even his mouth and tongue should have been burned." "What's Nazi Germany?" Margo asks. "You mean with Hitler?" "Right. Adolf Hitler, she means, Julie. And these people were probably from Austria or Hungary or Poland and barely survived the war. And they were also Jewish, I'm sure, which I don't know if you know but they were persecuted then over there. Persecuted: hunted down, killed because of their beliefs or just because they were born Jewish, so they probably also fled to America to escape all that, the goiter lady and her husband, which is what being a refugee is—fleeing—or just because they couldn't ever go back to it for various reasons. For that time must've been something; beyond words; that old saw, a living hell." "Hungary's a country?" Julie says. "Hungary's a country. Very good. How'd you know that, sweetheart, for it's not the most known one?" "I just know." "Though I was only saying Hungary was one of the countries they could've been from. Even Germany they could've been from, but I don't think they drink tea in a glass there. I don't know what they drink when it's not wine or beer. Probably coffee. And I remember they spoke German and when their friends were there, a couple of other languages, which meant they could've come from any number of countries. But she had her coffee every night, that's for sure, and very often she asked for hot water when she was down to a quarter of a cup. We couldn't charge for the extra water, you see, and it meant she could sit with her cup in front of her awhile longer. I suppose she had the grain one—they didn't have then the kind of decaffeinated coffee we have now, I don't think—because of her goiter condition. Doctor might've said no, but who knows? But then their leaving me a single quarter tip for the night. They'd leave around eleven-thirty when it was of course late and near closing time and nobody else was coming in. And if anyone was coming in, you didn't want them because that'd mean they'd be sitting at your table till way past closing time, when what you really wanted was just to clean up your station and go home, got it? Okay." "A quarter's not so little money." "Daddy's talking about *then*, dummy, *then*," Margo says. "Margo, don't talk to her that way. And right," he says to Julie. "It was worth a dollar by today's quarter, meaning you could buy for a quarter then what you can for a dollar today. Do I have that right? I think so. But imagine one dollar tops in tips or so for one of your four- or five-tables for an entire night, and your biggest most productive table too, meaning the one you stand to make the most money from, and you can see what I mean. You were losing money as a waiter." "You lost the dollar?" Julie says. "Every night from those people?" "No, I mean—oh gee, why'd I go into this? What started it? Good passing-the-highway-time talk, right? Right. But what I'm saying, and this isn't your fault if you don't understand it, sweetie, is that they were incredibly stingy and inconsiderate, sitting at my table or any waiter's table for that long for so small an order and tip, and the manager shouldn't have put up with it." "What should he do?" Margo says. " 'Have done.' Well, his policy was let them sit where they want, customer's always right, blah blah—you've heard that one before—" "What?" Julie says. "It's a saying, an expression. Honor thy customer and so on, because he's got the money." "And *she's*," Margo says. "She's got. True. Especially there. So long as there are other empty tables at the time. And since the restaurant was generally quiet between eight and nine, when they came in—lamb chop and jelly crowd having left, soda and snack crowd not in yet—they usually got the four-table they wanted. Besides, he couldn't give a—he didn't care how well we did. He was paid his salary, got no cut of our tips, so he didn't rely on them the way we did, and that guy had been there forever, Mr. Feeny or Reilly or something—I forget his name. Art. That's right, Art. We used to call him Art the—well, whatever we used to call him. Art the something—I forget. 'Mister,' though, that's what he insisted we had to say before his name. But this customer, she had the most enormous goiter I ever saw and that's why I and the other waiters—it wasn't nice, I know that now and wouldn't behave that way today. In fact, I didn't like to say it then, but you know, they all did it and it was a rotten job, running around like mad for little dough and when you were really tired, for I had college and studying all day, so to make the job better you did little bad things for laughs. But we called her—that isn't excusing it, you understand, for nothing really makes it right—but we called her the goiter lady, and the man, 'the goiter lady's husband.' But her goiter was about the size of a football. Or maybe like a softball, the kind you hit with a bat, but bigger than my big fist," and he makes a fist and holds it up, "and was on the right side of her neck, or the left one, but anyway was a deformity. That's why I brought it up, to explain the word," and Julie says "The poor old lady. It must have been sad to walk around with that big thing on her. Why didn't she have it taken off? Couldn't she? Would it be too big a scar?" and he says "I don't know about cutting it out, that's a good question, and it is *out*, you know, not hanging on her to take off but pressed to her neck and chin and inside her skin. Today I'd have much more sympathy for her and, ironically, would ask—'ironically' meaning the reverse, or almost, to what I was saying; that it's odd having that feeling now and you asking that question before, but—where was I? I'd ask the same question you did, Julie, and maybe even find out from a doctor why she couldn't have it removed—I had two uncles who were ones—or what she could do if she could get it removed and then tell her while I was serving her, even. Or more likely—certainly more likely this—call her husband aside and tell him in private, for maybe they didn't know. Maybe they thought 'You have it, you live with it, you die with it, or if it happens to get smaller in time or disappear, even better,' or were just not aware of what we can do in America with illnesses like that, deformities, et cetera. But if I was still a waiter today I'd still be a lot put off, even with my sympathy for her goiter, that they chose my four-table and that it'd be occupied by them for the next three hours. She was a nice lady, though, I'm not saying that. Nice smile, always okay to me. But sometimes the nicest customers, I found, were also the stingiest, and vice versa. Vice versa?" and Margo says "You mean the opposite, the other way around, vice for verse, verse for vice, I mean, versa," and he says "That's right, what it means, but that was more a question for me, that vice versa, for what I was about to say was that sometimes the worst customers—most demanding, gruffiest—were also the stingiest, which isn't vice versa. And sometimes the worst and nicest were also the most generous—in fact in most cases the nicest gave the best tips—but anyway, enough of that," and looks around and sees the car from before is beside him again, for a while it wasn't or maybe it was for longer than he knew but he got so caught up in the conversation, talking, remembering—the goiter lady, where'd that memory come from after more than thirty years?—that he forgot about it or didn't see it, and it stays even with his, drops back, then quickly comes even again and gets even a little closer, so close that he wonders if it's crossing the lane line and he looks and it isn't but he doesn't feel comfortable with it so close and moves a couple of feet to the right. Guy with the same creepy look of before, smile, combo of both, staring at him, and he doesn't like it and thinks when he's looking at him "What're you looking at, schmuck, you got a problem?" but gives the face of just the opposite, "Hey, how are you, nice day, see ya," and looks front, and not to start anything with him, meaning give the idea he's doing this out of some grievance or fear, he stays in the lane for about half a mile and then signals right, looks in the rearview and right side mirrors, giving more time to these than he usually does and just pushing up the directional signal the slow way he did, though no other cars are anywhere around his, and with what he thinks is a casual could-care-less look, so if the guy's still looking at him he'll think he's in no great rush to get away from him, and then pulls into the next slower lane, depresses the directional manually before it clicks off by itself, and the guy's car—the passenger; driver next to him looked a lot like him, almost like his older brother but his face doughier—goes into the lane he just left and stays alongside him. What the hell? he thinks, not looking at them. What're they doing? They're scaring him and scaring him can make his driving shaky and that guy's creepy look can also scare his kids too. Doesn't he know that and doesn't the driver know it too if he's encouraging the creep? Just driving that close to him and sort of stalking him so many miles, makes the driver just as bad. God, the stupid things guys can do when they got nothing better going, or what? Listen, he's nervous at the wheel to begin with sometimes, especially when his kids are with him without his wife and they're going at a fast clip on a long drive, so it's never a good idea to act like this, it shouldn't be done—scaring and grinning or just looking plain peculiar at other cars is something an overgrown kid does and not a smart one. Or maybe there's something wrong with his car they're trying to tell him about. If that was so the guy would've pointed right away or made some kind of signal and not given him the spooky look and ugly grin. But they're beside him and the guy still grinning and staring and the driver with this hey-what-a-howl look, and when he slows, they slow, and when he picks up speed, they do, so nothing to do but find a cop if he can find one or signal to pull off at the next exit and if they do beside or behind him then to stick on this one for he doesn't want to get on any smaller even more deserted road with them, or just slow down all the way on this road and stop, but if they stop on the shoulder with him he doesn't want to have anything to do with them, it could be a robbery, that's what he now thinks they might be after, maybe not just his wallet but his car too and even his oldest girl, so he'd just zip away and maybe the whole thing would start again, slow, fast, shifting lanes, same stupid smirks and grins, looking for the next exit or a cop or some other car or truck on the road to somehow signal to that these guys are menacing him, or maybe he should just face up to the guys straight off. Maybe that's all he needs to stop it. A look that he's not taking their shit or just that he's hip to it, and then they'd fly off. The wrong thing to do?—maybe not. But no angry or put-down look, just one that says, well what should it say? With his voice and face, something like "Hey, what gives already, fella, what the hell gives?" So he looks at the guy but no casual could-care-less look, a look with his face serious and eyebrows raised saying "So, what's up?" and with his index finger making a whole bunch of little quick circles to the guy, he doesn't know why or what it means, probably just nerves, and the guy raises his eyebrows same way but grins and then with his lips mimics almost a stripteaser's or showbiz kiss and with his hand closed makes several circles in the air for him to roll his window down. He shakes his head "Sorry, I don't understand, what's that you're saying and what was all that with the kiss?" because he's at a loss now what to do and feels he made a big mistake looking at the guy like that and doing whatever he did with his finger, for who knows what the guy took it as, and is suddenly afraid of them again, doesn't want to rile the guy more than he thinks he has, make him think he's a wiseass, he for sure doesn't want to say what he really thinks and that's that the guy's acting, well, not "say" or also "say" but to gesture and look at the guy to give the impression, well, not "impression" either for that sounds too much like "suggestion" but to sink definitely into the guy that he's acting like a complete asshole, driver too, that in fact their actions are wicked or something, no, wicked, when you consider the kids, wrong, totally wrong in every way and that they're imbeciles, if they want to know, imbeciles and pigs and probably always have been for as long as anyone can remember, that he's a punk, this guy, a tried and proven punk and no doubt the one responsible of the two for what's going on, and the driver's his stupid stooge but almost no less to blame, that's how he sees it and what he'd like to get across and with his finger this time pointing right at him as if he'd like to stick it through his chest and then to wave for the guy to have the car pull over to the shoulder and if the guy says "What?" not to back off but to point and wave and say "Come on, come on, you know what I mean, pull over to the damn side," and after they both stop there for him to get out and go over to their car and when the guy opens the door to grab him out and slap his head against the car and punch his face a couple of times and pick him up and throw or roll him over the hood and then grab the driver out and if he locked his door, to go through the passenger's side and if he's locked that too to just smash a window with a rock nearby and open the door and grab the driver and say "You want some of the same too? Then leave us alone. Leave everybody on the road alone. You got problems, go work them out for yourself some other way but terrorizing, or trying to, people on the road. It's the stupidest thing to do and also one of the rottenest, don't you know that? Couldn't you see it in my face? Haven't you any idea how you made my kids feel? Don't you have any concern for anyone but your goddamn selves?" and then to throw the driver back into his seat and go back to his car and get in and even if the kids are screaming for an explanation or just hysterical, even hysterical, to just start the car up and go.

They're still beside him. He took his mind off them a minute but there they are, probably never left. Doesn't look to see if the guy's staring or anything, just sees the front of their car even with his. Looks for a trooper car. Been looking on and off since he first felt those guys were menacing him and if one's around he'll pull over if it's on this side but first try to get their license plate number for he wants the cops to go after them or when this is over, even if the plate's probably stolen or the car is for all he knows. But to get it he has to get behind them so he slows down, they slow down, maybe figuring what he wants to do, probably not. Oh yes, they know, they're old pros at all this stuff, he doesn't know anything about it or not much. But if a cop's across the road in the median what'll he do then? Car's got him blocked. Honk, that's what, honk like hell and open his window and wave and yell and slow down and stop on the shoulder and then back up on it if he's by that time far away from the cop or if he's near to get out fast and scream and wave for the cop, but get their plate number or as much of it as he can and the state. Hasn't looked at them in a while now, feels weak at the wheel, for his kids not him, and wants to keep his eyes on the road and also on the front of their car in case he thinks they're going to bump or ram his, turns around quickly to the kids to see if they're all right and once through the rearview to and that time doesn't see either of them. When a car or truck passes on the left in the speed lane he honks and honks but not once does the driver or passengers look at him when they're near, though the guy goes between facing front with a blank look as if innocent as hell or looking at him with a concerned one and once even saying or mouthing "Anything wrong?" but a couple of passengers do look when they're way past and in one car two young boys in back point and he thinks look alarmed at him. He wants to roll down the window and yell out "Help, stay near, help" while he continues honking, but by then they're way out of hearing range and he's also afraid of taking his hand off the wheel to roll down the window with the car next to him so close. Looks at the passenger window when no other cars are around and they've moved left a couple of feet and the guy's just staring at him with his fist holding up his chin as if he's studying his face hard and then he smiles almost politely and nicely and with his finger beckons to him. But to what, get his car even closer? Guy wants to say something to him? He crazy? And what's with the smile after all they've done and those hideous looks before? "Girls, you all right?" "Yes, we're all right, Daddy," Margo says. "We're playing by ourselves, why?" and he says "Nothing, everything's fine. Still buckled up, though, right?" and she says "Sure, us both. Why's that same car still there?" and he says "Oh, nothing, they like our company I suppose or my good looks," guy smiling pleasantly at him, and she says "They gay?" and he says "Only kidding, honey, I know nothing about them." Then looks at the man again and he's beckoning with his finger but with this peculiar expression now, as if "Come into my dark chamber" or something, and moves the rearview around and sees both kids are busy with what they're doing with their eyes down and he looks at the man and he has that same peculiar expression but even more sinister or demonish, and turns front: this guy means trouble, they do, they're not letting up, they're sticking to him, slowing and speeding with him, getting their car even closer. Or maybe the guy's just a joker, that's all, driver the joker's friend, in on the joke and both just having fun playing with him, and any accident that happens to the jokee or whatever you want to call him that goes along with the fun they couldn't give a hoot about. A car passes in the speed lane and he honks and honks and it goes even faster while he keeps his hand on the horn, guy looking front again, an angel. "Hey, you bastard," he wants to yell, "hey, stop, slow down, look over here," and open the window to yell it and wave but doesn't want to cause any thoughts that might upset the kids. Maybe what these guys want is to get him all the way into the slow lane and then force him off the shoulder into something, a ditch, or over it and down some hill, but why? Kicks. Kicks. Now they're in part of his lane and he has to move to the extreme right of it almost to the lane line. Doesn't want to get in the slow lane because then some more muscling by them and he's on the shoulder and whatever's there. Car behind him on the right honks, he hadn't seen it, driver probably thinking he's switching lanes without signaling, and he honks and honks and the driver looks at him as she passes and he points to his left and mouths "They're crazy, killers, they're nuts, maniacs, I need help, get help," and leans back so she can see through the front side windows and he doesn't look at the guy but figures he's doing what he did when the speeding car passed, facing front angelically, learned it sitting in church or school for when he did some lousy thing someone else got blamed for, and she scrunches up her face to a "Huh?" and shakes her head she doesn't get it and he points and mouths "Those men, those men," and slits his throat with his finger several times and she signals left and cuts in front of him while he's honking like mad and more signaling to get in front of the men and then the speed lane, maybe because she's afraid of him, maybe she even gives the men a look she is when she's on the other side of them and the three cars are even. "What's wrong, Daddy?" Margo says and he says "Why, my honking?" stopping now and Julie says "Why were you?" and he says "That stupid woman—that driver there, I mean, on the other side of the car next to us—well, now she's away—but cutting in front of me without signaling, she could've killed us. All right, she wasn't that close, but it's the wrong thing to do," and Julie says "Why, she should warn you, how?" and he says "Lights, not lights but these signals," flicking the directionals up and down—the emergency lights, he thinks, turning them on—"but let's forget it, it upsets me but I'm okay," hoping that just with the emergency lights and his honking whenever he sees a truck or car, they'll drive away. Guy back to staring sinisterly at him. No other cars around, sees in the rearview and side mirrors. Nothing in front but that woman who's got to be doing eighty now. He speeds up but so does the car alongside, slows to sixty and they slow, looks at them and they're both laughing, looking at each other and him and back and forth like that and laughing and he thinks What's so fucking funny? and mouths to the guy "What's so funny?" and the guy points to him and he thinks Me, huh, me, huh?—I'd like to shove your fucking laughs and smiles and teeth right down your dirty throats, you fucking idiots, get lost, get lost, and mouths "I'm going to tell the police, do you hear me? the police," and guy raises his shoulders *so-o-o?* and he slows down some more, thinks he might pull into the slow lane, looks at the right sideview, no car there anywhere, guys' car slows down and driver honks and he looks and the guy opens his window and motions for him to open his and he thinks What? and the guy mouths or says "Open your window, open it," and again motions with his hand to and now his face isn't so bad, as if he only wants to tell him something like his door's open, wheel's low, and he says "What?" and Julie says "What, Dada?" and he says "Not talking to you," and to the man "What?" and the guy smiles nicely and drops his hand below the window and still smiling at him shouts "You . . . dumb . . . prick," and hand comes up but with a gun in it and points it at him. "Holy shit," he yells, "holy God, kids, duck, get below," and to the man "Don't, don't," and to the kids "There's a guy with a gun in that car, duck, duck," and speeds and they speed and looks in the rearview and kids are shouting "What, Daddy, what gun?" Margo, Julie, both, and he says "Get below, the floor, on the floor, *floor!*" and swivels around, kids still on the seat, looking bewildered, scared, looks front and steering with his right hand, left reaches around his seat and gropes till it touches Margo's ankle and grabs it and jerks it down and shouts "Unbuckle, get on the floor, both of you," jerking her leg down now, "maniacs in the next car, fucking maniacs, they'll kill us," and they start screaming and he yells "Stop it, screaming, get down," and looks at the guys' car, he's too close to it and clamps both hands to the wheel and without signaling or looking pulls into the slow lane and they into the lane he left, and yells "You hear me, down, I'm saying, are you?—Margo!" and she says yes and he yells "Julie?" and Margo says yes and several cars in the speed lanes now and he slows down and honks and the guys' car slows and honks and he speeds up and they do, honking, blocking him from any car's view and he shouts "Oh no, what're we going to do? keep down, down," and they're screaming and he thinks Think, come on, what should you do? oh my poor children, and they're shouting "Daddy" and some other things, maybe not words but they sound like them, "mudder foam, doll bait, pip feed, call a thong, radiator so," and looks right, shoulder seems fine to go on, thinks maybe with all the cars around the guy's gun's gone, looks, barrel of it on the window bottom and aimed at him, only the tip of it but enough to blow him to shit, same crazy two-faced face and the guy saying or mouthing "Hi, how ya doing, great day, wouldn't you say?" driver busting a gut at all this and pounding the dashboard while he steers with his left hand and then no hands when he rips his hat off and whacks it against the wheel, still plenty of room on the shoulder and he drives onto it, try not to stop too suddenly and if the guys stop in front of him, go in reverse fast as you can, and in back, the reverse, go front and then try to shoot across the road without getting clipped and onto the median if one's there, looks and one's there, and then tear north and if they chase him, well, later, if it happens, later but now stop, does, too suddenly, kids pitched into his seat and he's thrown forward and back, guys go on but then the crazy sticks his arm all the way out with the gun and with his face behind it seems to be taking aim at them, and he yells "Kids, down, stay down," and dives to the seat and there's gunshots, windshield shatters but doesn't break, screams in back just before or just when the shots are fired and then, which one? just Margo screaming. "Julie," he yells, "Julie, you okay? Margo, you too? They're gone but both you stay down

till I look." Nothing from Julie. "Margo, tell me if you're all right."
But the men, and lifts his head just enough to see their car's not
in front, and turns around, they might've, but they couldn't've, but
they might've gone on the median and around and then from behind and on the shoulder in back, and lifts his head above the seat
but they're not there and unbuckles and jumps up on the seat and
looks down and Margo's screaming and he yells "Shush, tell me,
come on, are you all right?" and she says "Just my knees hurt from
bumping the seat, but I think so," and he says "You think you're
otherwise okay?" quickly looking through all but the passenger-
side windows to see that the men didn't come back and she says
yes, rubbing her knees, and he says "Julie," looking at her, on her
side, no look back, "Julie, what about Julie?" and reaches down,
can't reach her, that eye's closed and he thinks maybe she's unconscious, just her head hurt from hitting the seat, it's facing in that
direction for that to happen, but otherwise okay, a cut and concus-
sion but nothing else much, and Margo shrieks and says "Daddy,
there's blood," Julie doesn't stir, and he says "Yours?" and she
says "I don't think so, it doesn't seem like I'm bleeding," and he
says "Check, check," and she feels herself all around and says "I'm
sure I'm not, not even my knees, they don't feel wet," and he leans
over some more and stretches down to Julie, doesn't want to move
her but has to to find out, should he get out of the car and go in
the door where she is and do it that way? no, do it now, touches
her but almost falls over and gets on the passenger seat and reaches
down and lifts her up by an armpit till he can grab under both
arms and lift her up straight, her legs stay on the floor, head flops
around before settling, she doesn't seem to be breathing, there's
blood on her neck and chin and coming through her sweater, and
holding her around the back with one hand, unbuttons the top of
her sweater and then her shirt and pulls down her undershirt
soaked with blood, all the time saying "Oh no, oh no," and thinking I know what it is, I don't want to know what it is, and screams
when he sees blood running out of a bullet hole.

INTERSTATE 4

⟨⟿⟩

*H*appens during the drive back home. He's with the kids on the main highway south, his wife's with her folks for a couple of days in New York. He said goodbye to her about three hours earlier. Last saw her at the front door. They'd all gone to the city to visit her folks and do some things there. While she went with a friend to a matinee one day, for lunch and a long talk with another friend and then alone to some bookstores and an acupuncture session the next day, he took the kids to several museums: Natural History, the Modern, Met. He also wanted to take them to the Frick, which he hadn't been to in years and the kids had never seen—he thought they'd like the courtyard pool with the lily pads in it, he thinks, and also the Limoges—they had at the Walters in Baltimore—and he wanted to sit on the couch with them across from the Rembrandt self-portrait in that long room and talk about how the face, expression and body bulk always reminded him of his father. He used to go there a lot just to look at it, no other painting, or maybe the two Vermeers in one of the front hallways, how could he just go past those? so something else to show the kids they might like, sit on the same couch and jot down whatever came to mind about him and some of the incidents between them and sketch and draw the painting, usually in different colored ballpoint, and sometimes the painting and the huge vase of flowers or leaves on the table between him and it, though he wasn't an artist. What happened to those drawings and notes he doesn't know. But they said too many museums in two days so choose any three of the four so long as one was the Natural History. They also wanted to go to the Central Park merry-go-round and zoo and F.A.O. Schwarz after all the museums, "have a day on the town just for kids, hamburger restaurant for lunch but not a fast-food—stuff like that," Margo said. He said they went to Schwarz's—"it sounds funny calling it that, but anyway, the last time, and the zoo and merry-go-round the two times before that. But if you want to go and we're all not too pooped by then, okay—at least it isn't Christmas or Easter seasons at F.A.O.'s with wall-to-wall shoppers but mostly sightseers like us." Merry-go-round was closed with no sign on it saying why, on a day it was supposed to be open. They went to the zoo, had lunch at its cafeteria because it was convenient and the food looked pretty good, then F.A.O.'s where Julie cried almost the second they got inside when he wouldn't give her money to buy anything. "I thought the understanding we'd agreed to at home was that we'd come only to look, not buy—window-shop, they call it, though in this case outside-in window-shopping—come on, sweetheart, don't make a scene, you're embarrassing me, people are going to think I really did something wrong like beat you and then the police will come and I'll be arrested and you'll have to save up all your next year's allowance to bail me out," but words weren't working so he tried taking her aside but she pushed his hand off her waist and said "Get off me. And you are doing something wrong. You can't take us here every time and expect us not to buy something; it's unfair," and Margo said "It is, Daddy." "All I want is ten dollars for if I see something I like. That's not much." "Ten dollars? What do you think, I'm made of money? which is what my father used to say whenever I asked him for ten cents for a comic book, and he had much more dough than I. In comparison, he was practically rich, but he knew I shouldn't ask for money when anyone was around, which doesn't apply here since we don't know any of these people, but especially when the agreement beforehand was not to ask for any money at all. But look, I'll give you each, something my father never would have done, two bucks to spend as you please." "Two dollars is nothing here," Margo said. "That's what I'm saying—this is a place just to get ideas for things to buy in cheaper toy stores." "Ten," Julie said. "I'll pay you back tomorrow." "With what?" People passing were looking, some smiling or raising their eyebrows as if they knew what he was going through with the kids and he said "Come on, both of you, over here where we can discuss this without the world bonking into us," and they did. "Now, with what money you going to pay me back?" to Julie. "And I give you ten, I have to give Margo ten—that's twenty dollars and we're not even talking tax, and New York's got something like eight percent now, maybe even nine." "What about the money Grandma gave Margo and me for summer? That adds to thirty, which is way more than twenty." "Oh, fifteen plus fifteen; this kid can count; very good. Mommy and I bought you things with that money, and I don't want to argue anymore. I'll give you each three dollars, buy what you want. If it's not enough for whatever you pick out, put a down payment on it, what do I care? I'll also give you enough for the tax, so up to three-fifty apiece, but that's my last offer." "Ten." He said "Why do you have to be so stubborn?" and she said "You owe us thirty dollars: Grandma's. You didn't spend it on us. Mommy was holding it and I remember when you didn't have enough and you asked her for it; you bought gas." "You have five seconds to accept my offer, Julie," looking at his watch, and she said "I want the money that's mine, or just ten dollars of it." "Okay, that's it, agreement's over, I'm sorry you have to lose out on this too, Margo, but she won't compromise, so we're going," and when he took Julie's hand and she pulled it away, he said, which he knew was a threat she wouldn't take seriously, so why'd he make it?—it just came out, he'd done it several times before and she always reacted the same way and after the last time he told himself he'd never do it again—"You don't want to go? Fine, stay, but we're going," and took Margo's arm and they went through the revolving door. Looked back, she was staring angrily at him and then turned around and headed for the escalator. "That goddamn kid, I'm so goddamn sick of her," to no one, and to Margo "Stay here," and she said "Don't hit her," people going in and out bumped into him or skipped around him and he said "Excuse me, sorry," and to Margo "What do you mean? When have I ever?" and went back in. Have I ever hit them? he thought. I don't think so. She was at the escalator, her back to him—once, if any time, and not hard, but he forgets when and which one and just a slap on the back of her hand and probably for something important, like she was about to dart into the street or just after she did it or started to and he caught her—pressed a button on a panel beneath a large bear and it started talking, mouth moving, "Hi, I'm Teddy Ruxpin" or something, and gave directions to the Barbie shop. "Up the escalator, turn left, keep going straight till you pass the Talking Tree, then right till you come to the Barbie dolls, they're real pretty and say hi from me, Teddy." Another button; he said "Julie!" Same intro, then how to get to the stuffed animals, "and when you get there, check out my friends and me, Teddy Ruxpin." "What do you think you're doing?" Another button: board games. She said "I'm staying in the store till I find something I like. With my money Grandma gave me, which you should give back or it's stealing." "Stealing, hey? Wait till Christmas and I'll go ho-ho-ho." "You're not funny." "I'm not funny? And why do I answer every utterance of yours with a question? But then who's funny,

you?" "I'm serious, Daddy." "And I'm not? Listen, you're not
getting any money. I have to be decisive. I shouldn't tell you what
I have to be, for you might think I haven't made up my mind and
that you can change it—" "I don't know what your word 'decisive' means." "So we're leaving, right? My threatening to leave
you here before was stupid, since I would never do that, but now
I'm serious, so," which he didn't want to say, it'll only make
things worse, and he knew he'd never carry it out, "if you insist
on embarrassing not just me but you too, by staying when I'm
saying we have to go, then I'll be forced to drag you out of here
or lift you up, rather, and carry you out bodily, meaning with my
body, on my shoulder if I have to, one way or the other or even
something else, under my arm, I'm still strong enough to, so are
you coming?" and she said no. "No?" and she said no. Another
child pushed a panel button: puppets and magic tricks. A trick,
he thought, and said "Who's Teddy Ruxton or Ruxpin—this
guy?" and she said "You can see: a bear." "But from where:
television, movies?" and she said "I don't know; you don't let us
see them." "When? I'd let you see a movie or some public TV if
it was good." She just looks at him. "Listen, my sweetheart, isn't
this a bad place to discuss all this? Let's all go for a snack, cool
off, maybe we'll come back. We can if your attitude's better." "I
don't want to eat and you won't come back even if I acted like
an angel." "How do you know? No, I almost swear I will, if
we're still close by and not tired, and same deal, three-fifty apiece
to spend here, even four. But that's my last offer and last time
I'm offering it. And if you don't leave with me now, and nicely,
this will also be the last time you'll ever be allowed in here again
so long as I live," which he knew, he knew, it was the kids'
favorite place in New York, which was the point, but a ridiculous
dumb threat, one that'd absolutely have no impact, though maybe
a combination of all those offers and threats and just that she
might be hungry and tired of arguing with him would change her
mind or mood. "I don't want three or four; I want my ten dollars
you owe me." This time an adult: Legos. I know how, he thought,

and said "My God, where's Margo?" and looked to the front of
the store, too many things blocked his view of the doors, said
"Wait, I'm going to see," ran around some people to the doors,
Margo was right outside, facing the street, she was fine, nine, very
self-sufficient, if anything went wrong she'd come in and stand by
the door and look around for him and if she didn't see him she'd
stay there till he came, ran back, said "Come on, let's go outside,
I didn't see her and I don't want to leave her alone. This is New
York." "So?" "So people steal little children, your age and
Margo's, and prettier they are, quicker they go. I don't mean to
scare you, and not every day of course and it could happen anywhere and is probably the rare instance when it does, but you
don't want to leave your child alone here, smart as Margo and
you are." "You go; she could be inside already and I'll tell her to
wait for you here." "Listen, this is important; no fooling around
from you now. And tell you what. Next time we come here—not
today, so another day; today's just three-fifty to four dollars if
you cooperate—I'll give you each five bucks. And that's not between you either, which is a fair compromise. Altogether, ten."
"You just say that," and he said "Whatever I said, we got to get
outside to find Margo, but I swear by anything that I'll keep my
word—ten. We'll tell Margo, so she'll be a witness. But let's get
out there, I'm worried," and took her hand, she jerked it back
but followed him to the revolving door. He got in a section first
and slowed the door, for other people were entering from the
street, so she wouldn't get caught getting inside or have to get
out too fast. They stayed at his in-laws' three nights. They couldn't
leave for New York till late Saturday afternoon because his kids
had swimming lessons that morning and Julie a piano lesson at
noon and Margo a painting class at two. They'd only miss one
school day for Monday was a special teachers' day off for an
education conference, and he took two days off from his job so
he could go to New York and his wife worked at her own stuff
at home. Margo said "Where were you? I was looking all over"
and he said "But you're all right, right, everything okay?" and

she said "Sure, why not?" "Well, I looked and didn't see you before and got worried," and she said "I don't see how. I was standing here all the time, watching the crowds passing. So many people. I even saw a fight between two men. A policeman broke it up. I think I got a good idea for an art project from it." "What of?" he wanted to say but she said "You were so long, Daddy, I thought you were lost," and he said "Me, in my old city? But what would you have done if I hadn't come in another fifteen minutes?" and she said "Stay here and wait and then go in to look from around the bottom of the escalator and finally call Mommy." "How do you know the number?" and she said "I'd ask for Grandpa's name from Information and give the street." "You know how to get Information?" and she said "Four-one-one, or I'd go to the store's office for help. They'd give it, wouldn't they, if I told them I was all alone?" "Sure. Probably happens all the time. I didn't think of it. Besides, maybe they have a public address system for lost children. They have to, so why not use it for fathers? They probably even have a special pickup area for lost parents and kids. But what if a man came up to you before you went into the store, or a woman, and said—you know, nice voice and face and nicely dressed—'Young lady, your father's suddenly not well—' " "I'd ask what your name is, for this is a creepy person who's doing something bad, right?" and he said "Okay, then he knows my name, for some reason, or he tricks it out of you—kidnappers can be clever—but he said, or she does, that I was suddenly stricken with something—he even knows my birthdate and what I do in life and was wearing today, so he's convincing. And to be even more convincing, there could be a man and woman working together, pretending they're a sweet married couple. But that I had a heart attack, or stroke, whatever story, and was taken to a hospital and that I asked them to take you there to me, what would you do?" and she said "But your story's crazy. You were inside; how can you get out without me seeing you or some kind of crowd around you or the ambulance?" and he said "I cabbed to the hospital, felt I had to get there fast, and there's a back entrance to the store on Madison," and she said "Your story's still all wrong. I don't want to hurt your feelings, Daddy, but you couldn't have been heart-attacked and taken to a hospital or gone there alone by cab in so short a time." "Not true. We're talking of twenty minutes. I could be on my way to the hospital while this man's talking to you. But before I went out that back entrance I told this man, and I wouldn't have done any of that, of course. I'm also as healthy as a horse, so I'm not about to get any heart attacks or strokes. But if I was too sick to get you, in actual life, because of a sudden stomach flu, for instance, which knocked me cold and kept me on the ground groaning for half an hour or in your store office where some store people took me, then I'd in some way communicate to these people to send a guard outside to get you, and also to keep Julie safely beside me. But this is the man's lying story to you I'm telling you, not mine, so what would you do?" "What you told me to lots of times in things like this, so why are you asking?" and he said "Let's say for Julie's sake. I haven't really talked about it with her yet and when I was in the store and didn't see her for a minute I started thinking of it for her." "I know what to do," Julie said. "I remember you told Margo once. I say to the man 'Let me'—no, 'Let a policeman take me to the hospital for my father.' Then when I get one I say 'Let me speak to my mother,' but I wouldn't know how to call her in New York." "In the store's office, dummy," Margo said. "You can't expect her to know that," he said. "But close, Julie, very good—and why are you talking to her like that?" to Margo. "What'd she do to deserve it? —But you'd go to a guard, if you couldn't find a real policeman—someone in a uniform in the store, or you'd just ask a salesperson to get you one. Salesperson: someone who sells the stuff behind the counter. And sometimes the guards have plain clothes, no uniforms, to catch, let's say, the shoplifters better, but the salespeople would know who they are. But if they didn't, for the plainclothes guards are probably also there to stop the salespeople from stealing, then they could make a call for one in uniform. And you'd tell this guard that you're alone, your sister and daddy are suddenly gone and some man's said your father's been taken to the hospital and he asked this man to take you there and your parents have always warned you against strangers taking you anyplace, and you want to speak to your mommy. They'd find her eventually. They could do this from the office. Actually, you don't want to go with the guard—a real policeman's okay—but not a guard, plainclothes or not, to the office alone either. Sometimes these businesses aren't careful about who they get as guards, so these guys can be crazies too. If it's a woman guard, uniformed or not, I'm sure she's all right. So when you go with a male guard you also want to go with, and you have to insist on this—not easy for a kid but you got to do it, you say your parents told you you have to—with a salesperson to the office and not alone, and that's where you call Mommy. You'd only have to give there, as Margo said, in New York, your grandfather's name—he's the only Horace Cole in the Manhattan book. And—the phone book, I mean, the directory, and Manhattan being New York, of course—and my name, or Mommy's with the Cole last name, in our phone book where we live, but you know that number." "Eight-three-five . . . but do you want me to give the area code too?" Julie said. "No, where we are you don't need the area code when you call home. Oh, this is so complicated. You just don't go with strangers, that's all, the one rule you have to remember in this. One comes and is pretty aggressive in wanting to take you someplace—forceful, won't take no, you see?—yell for a cop. Really, yell, both of you, 'police, police,' but much louder—I only whispered so the people around us wouldn't wonder—but that's all you say, and also if you're together and a stranger wants you to go with him or her somewhere. Or you see what seems like a nice person passing—certainly someone passing you know is even better. But if not, then a nice person while this awful stranger's trying to convince you to go with him, tell that person—man or woman, just that the person looks nice—the problem with the stranger and have that person get a cop. But stay with that person, don't leave yourself with the stranger. Though don't go with that nice person either—alone, you know, into a house or car or cab or anyplace in a store except straight to its office where lots of people would probably be and you can call the police and us from. No, forget that, just stick with that nice person till a guard comes, if it's a store, and then you go to the office with the guard and this nice person or a store clerk, but always two people unless the guard's a woman. If it's a lot smaller store than this one with probably not much of an office anywhere, then you have them call Mommy or me and the police from the selling part of it. Of course if it's just that you're lost or we're separated, you don't need the police if you can reach one of us. If it's a street and you're now with the nice person and the threatening stranger goes or even stays, call the police and then me from a phone booth or go into a store to call and tell the nice person or store owner or somebody that we'll pay for whatever the phone costs and any other expenses, though I don't know what those others might be. If there is no nice person but there is a store and you're lost or being threatened, then you go into it and tell them what's the matter, though if you can, make sure it's a nice store. This rule about strangers goes for anyplace, you understand—street, in front of the house, walking home from school, playgrounds, malls, cars stopping and the driver or passenger talking to you; same thing. You just don't go with them, get it? You in fact—look, we're talking about it frankly now—open—and I'm going to go even further than I ever did with Margo. But if you're being dragged or coaxed too hard by a stranger into a car or something like that—basement, house, backyard—and I don't mean to scare you. Chances of anything like this happening are small, slight, small. But you yell—and when I say 'coaxed too hard' I mean ordered, bullied, or offered things to get in the car, for instance. Bribed—money, gifts, candy, you know—well you yell like hell, kick, put up a tremendous fuss, bite if you have to, the hand, the ear. Fight with your fists and nails. Scratch, punch, even your head—butt them. Believe me, kids can hurt. I know, from when you've hit me by accident. One good kick—a hard one, all your might—in a man's groin—where the penis and testicles are—can knock a man flat on his behind." The kids laughed. "No, it's true, listen to me, I'm serious. It might sound funny but that's where a man can hurt most. Or poke him right over here in the middle under the rib cage," and took Julie's finger to show where on him; "that'll knock the air out a moment, but enough time for you to get away. Or punch him in what, well, to illustrate my example—make it more real and remembered—in the balls." They seemed shocked, then looked at each other and laughed. "It's not a dirty word when you use it that way, as a teaching aid, believe me. And same with a woman too, I think, in hitting them down there, kicking, you know. But we'll have to ask Mommy what her most sensitive spots are that hurt. I heard the breasts. Certainly the eyes are one. Even just one eye, finger in it, deep and hard, but they're the most sensitive for everyone and also probably the most difficult to stick your fingers in because of our own squeamish feelings about eyes. But you do it, you have to. And you don't have to just use your fingers and hands and feet. You see a stick on the ground, a branch, brick, rock, some stones or even pebbles or sand, you throw it at their face or head or club them with it, the branch or maybe a bat or bottle that was lying around. If you're carrying books, throw that at their faces too. Of course, if you can—meaning you're not being held, you can run away—first thing you do is run, preferably home or to someone you know—a teacher or school parent if it's near your school, the house of a friend of yours on our street. But if nobody or nothing like that's around, then to that person I've mentioned who just looks protecting and nice if you see one. Which means that that person should look like a nice teacher or school parent or crossing guard. This also goes even if the coaxers or strangers who want to do these things to you are neighbors or say they are and they want to take you someplace, but we don't really know them. Even if they live a few doors down and you've seen them but have never really talked to them and you know Mommy and I haven't. Or you have talked to them, just as

Mommy and I have. A hello, a hi, a wave or nice talk beyond just greeting talk between you and them and even between them and Mommy and me, which you've seen. And they've acted nice to you up till now but suddenly are acting peculiar or asking you to do peculiar things or just things you know you're not supposed to, like going alone with them to places I've told you not to go, a basement, park, car, garage, someone's home or their own. Now, if you hit these neighbors in defending yourself or trying to get away and it's by chance a mistake, they'll have to understand that it was done because I'd told you to protect yourself this way and that there was a misinterpretation—an error in understanding—just a problem in what they were giving off with their words or actions or looks and what you took in and that perhaps I also might've been too strong in my warnings to you and what to do. Still, you've got to do what I say. This is how things have become today, I'm afraid, I'm almost sure of it. In being extra cautious you might occasionally go too far, but better that way than not going far enough where you didn't defend yourself when you could have and got hurt or didn't do enough to get away. I'm sure Mommy will agree with me on this but we'll ask her. If she doesn't then that's going to cause some conflict because I'm going to insist you do everything you can to protect and defend yourselves against people who might want to hurt you and in fact I'm going to spend a little time with you soon teaching you how. Just kicks and where to hit and stuff but more than I just did. Let's hope, of course, this'll never happen, and chances of it happening have got to be one in a few thousand, a hundred thousand—most people are good and wouldn't touch you—so one in a million, or maybe less. But we also have to hope that a neighbor or anyone doesn't get a heart attack or stroke or fall and break a limb as a result of a blow from one of you, that is if he or she didn't mean anything awful toward you and it was a mistake, on their part or yours, in judgment or perception—how you see things—or whatever. If it wasn't a mistake then truthfully I wouldn't care if they tripped and fell in front of a passing car. I shouldn't say that perhaps, but I think people who do things like that to kids are among the worst and deserve what they get. Okay, maybe that's too harsh, so something also that shouldn't have been said, but in a nutshell, you don't go with anyone anyplace, child or adult, without our permission. And 'nutshell' meaning 'in a few words,' so as not to confuse things with more of them and also so you can remember what I'm saying better. Anyone, that is, except really close friends—our very best, like the Kaplitzes, though maybe not with Rick, their oldest boy. Kids that age can suddenly change in ways and act funny. I don't want to go into it or maybe I will but another time, at least to Margo." "Why not now?" Margo said and he looked at her and Julie said "Why not me?" and he said "Because you're too young, quite truthfully. And of course relatives—but not any long-lost cousins or cousins of cousins you've only seen once—and our next-door neighbors, the Troys. They're obviously very decent people and their boy's much younger than both of you, so if they say we're not home and we've asked them to pick you up at school or meet you in front of the house and that we can't for some reason get to a phone to explain it all to you in the next hour or so and they're to look after you till we get home, you believe them. They'd never lie like that or do anything to you that's not in your best interest and which we wouldn't approve of, I know it. We're lucky to have them as neighbors; some people get nothing close to that. Or even if we haven't told them anything or called and you come home and neither of us is there and the door's locked, which it would be if we were both out, then you go straight to their place and ask them to check around to see where we might be. They know where I work—you do too, Margo, so you can do this as well as them. But they can also help you locate some of our good friends, whose names you know and maybe their addresses or just their streets and who might know where we are, or one of us. Actually, the Troys could let you into the house—they have our keys. That's how much we trust them, you see, and they trust us, for we have theirs. But when you do get in, though it'd probably be best for

you to stay with the Troys till we get home, especially if it's
getting late—let me double-check with Mommy on that. And certainly you stay with them if there's only one of you," and Margo
said "Maybe her," and he said "No, you both. But if the two of
you do get in and nobody's with you, like the Troys or Aunt
Bea—I can't think of anyone else; the Kaplitzes are too far away.
But you lock the door and wait for our call or for one of us to
get home, though all the time trying to find out by phone with
the Troys or whoever where the heck we are. None of this will
happen, you know. Chances of our not being home for you with
no word or warning to anyone about it are maybe a little better
than the others I mentioned, but still not great, but all this is just
in case. So, everything clear? Or did I go into too many things
and do what I didn't want to, confusing things by overdosing you
with possible situations and how to get out of them?" and Julie
said "About what?" and he said "Strangers, wrongdoers, or just
people who bug you, but a little to a lot worse than just kidding,
and if we're not home and so on," and she said "I'd know what
to do, I promise," and Margo said "It was a bit overmuch but I
think I'd know what to do too with all three of those people,"
and he said "All right, then what would you do if . . . nah, let's
drop it. But, good girls, both of you. Wonderful, great, so smart.
I realize it's difficult to digest all of it—to take it in—but just that
some of it got through and maybe even some of the most important parts, fine. Anyway, Margo, to get back to before, why I
was so long in the store when you were out here was that I
couldn't find Julie for actually a lot more than a minute," and
winked at Julie; she shut her eyes and turned away. Okay, won't
play, he thought, but he's sure she's not still mad at him. That
last long discussion or instruction got her off it. Then she bright-
ened and opened her eyes and said "Daddy said next time he'll
give us ten dollars for us both in the store. Or we can go in now
and he'll give us each four." He said "Is that what I said? I
forget," and she said yes and he said "Anyway, not now, let's go
for a snack first," and Margo said to her "We can pool our

money." Julie asked what that was and Margo explained and they convinced him to give two more dollars between them, they promise they won't ask him for more, they won't even go for a snack if he doesn't want, "that'll save you money," and they went in and he gave them a ten and told them to stay together even if they decide to split the ten and buy what they each want at separate departments and that they should come back to him right after they bought their purchase or purchases and with no more browsing around and the spot where he'd be waiting for them, "Right here outside the men's room. Just say, if you forget where it is, 'the men's room in the doll section on the second floor,' and anybody working in the store would know; it's right by the ladies'. By the way, I'm only letting you go off alone together because in this store there are plenty of guards and the salespeople and customers seem safer or trustworthier and nobody's going to run off with you. Other stores I might not feel so good about it in." "That's racist," Margo said and he said "What do you know about the word?" and she said "I know it and it is," and he said "It's not. Whatever the people are here, race and other things, they all just seem more law-abiding. Not *more,* which would be racist, just law-abiding; virtuous, even. Simply not interested in crime—in committing it. I'm not a sociologist—how society works, what goes on between people and when they're in certain places; you know, behavior. Maybe it's that the store's so expensive, so poorer people don't even think to come here. Or they think it but feel uncomfortable here or something—the grandeur or showiness of it and the street, and it's also out of their neighborhoods. Well, it's out of ours too where we are. But you also have to associate poverty—being poor—" "I know what the word means," Margo said. "She might not." "Do too," Julie said. "Well, poverty with higher crime and stuff, they often go together, not that somebody who'd steal a kid or do harm to one couldn't be rich or middle-rich or above-poor. They probably are, in fact, the majority of them—not down-deep or average poor—something tells me that, though I don't know from where. Probably the newspapers. And then maybe it's only that there are more guards here, why there'd be less crime like that—snatching kids, walking out with unpaid-for dolls—real dolls—and also the surveillance cameras watching and recording everyone's moves. They help, but anyway, go on, the two of you, go." About twenty minutes later, while he was leaning against a wall reading a book he brought along in his pocket for this purpose, waiting or on the bus, they rushed up to him with that look and no package or bag and he said "Uh-oh, don't tell me; well, it's going to have to be no," and Julie said "Please, just listen," and Margo "It's a board game but one for the mind and also creative and to have fun with and it's on sale and only 11.99 plus tax and was 22.99 plus tax before, so you save more than ten dollars," and he said "As my father used to say 'So I guess I can put that money you saved me into the bank, right?' And what do you mean 'plus tax'? That with it, meaning including?" and she said "I don't know about those things." He gave her a five, calculated how much tax would be on twelve dollars and said he wanted at least two dollars in change back. "If it comes to a few pennies less than that, nickels, even, fine. Your mommy's going to kill me for giving in to you like this. She'd probably do the same thing I'm doing if she was in my place, but my head, she's gonna have my ox-dumb head." "You're the best daddy," Julie said and kissed his hand and they went to buy it, played with it about two hours that night once he'd explained most of the rules and set up the board and shuffled the various stacks of cards. "Usually I have the toughest time reading board game directions, but I got this. My interpretational or figuring-out skills must be improving. Maybe it comes from owning a home and family and all the unreadymade things that come in that the paterfamilias in me—I've told you that word plenty of times but have never checked to pronounce it right— says I have to put together or they just won't be set up, though your mom's much better at unriddling and building things." Played with it an hour this morning, said they liked the game so much "and we're not just saying that," Margo said, "because you bought it and we want you to feel we didn't waste your money," that they wanted to play with it in the car ride home. He said better not, pieces and board aren't magnetized so they might lose some of them, "and in this game, lose one of the more important ones and the whole thing could be spoiled." So, they were out of the way a good part of the previous night and an hour this morning, not that his wife wouldn't have taken them for a walk to a store or done something with them alone or one of his in-laws if he'd asked them to, and he was able to get some work done he'd promised his boss he'd do during his two days off.

His wife had planned to go back with them but he'd convinced her to stay because he knew she wanted to do a little more shopping, possibly see a foreign movie with her mother that would never come to their area, be with her folks another two days, "and I can handle it and I love being with my girls," putting his arms around them, kissing the top of their heads, "my little darlings, and I mean it; that you are; and that I love being with you alone. It gets me closer, though I love having you around too, of course," to his wife, "all of us together, et cetera. That didn't come out right but you know what I mean," and she nodded. She was her parents' oldest and closest child, hadn't seen them in months, spoke to them on the phone almost every night and sometimes to her mother two or three times a day. When her folks called together, which they usually did, so one probably said to the other "I'm calling Lee," and the other would pick up the phone in a different room, they invariably asked how her day went—not "invariably"; it was always what they said after they said hello and how was her family: "So how did your day go, darling?" If he answered the phone only one would say hello, other would stay silent, and "How are you?" and he'd say "Fine, everything's good," or something, "Just fine, everything's grand, really," "Fine, thank you, kids and Lee too," "Fine, thanks, and you and Horace" or "Frieda?" and the one who called would say something like "We're well, nice of you to ask" or "thank you," and he'd say "Good, I'll get you Lee," and if he didn't ask how they were he'd say something like "Fine, thanks, I'll get you Lee," and the one who called would say "Thank you." After Lee told them how her day went and frequently things about the kids and him, she'd ask how their day went. If her father or mother called alone, the other, if she or he were home, would often get on in about a minute, though her father only would if he hadn't talked to her that day, and listen to how her day went if she was still on that and then say something like "It's me, Mommy" or "Daddy, I'm on the extension" or "other phone" or "line," or "Hello, dearest, I'm listening, continue" or "don't mind me," and then answer how his or her day went. Quick-kissed his wife on the lips when he was leaving today with the kids and then said "Well, bye, my love." " 'Bye, my love,' " she said. "You never call me things like that anymore, how come?" and he said "Wha, 'love'?" and she said "Occasionally 'dear' or 'my dear,' but that's not very personal or deep but about all there's been the last few years except 'sweetie.' " " 'Sweetheart. Sweetmeat. Pookyface. Dipsitz. Scrabble. Bedhogger.' " "Come on. And . . . no, nothing else that I can think of. Hearing it is nearly reason enough for me to stay here again next time and have you go. Anyhow, I like it, more, more. Do you think I'm fooling?" "Who knew it meant so much?" Looked around: was thinking of giving her a bigger deeper kiss. Not as a response to her "more, more," or maybe a little or just encouraged by it, but mostly because he really wanted to: lips-lips, some tongue, eyes tight, moving the bottom of his body in but subtly so it wouldn't be seen, kiss that left him a bit dizzy after it and her too she's said, partly because of the length of it and just breathing through the nose and the nose bent against the other's face in a way or just a single nostril closed by it, but one like their first kiss night of their first date in her little apartment's little foyer as she leaned against the closet door: "God, I nearly thought I'd die," she said, "everything knocked out of me. One more, okay? though I'm not insisting on exact replication and if you think I'm acting too managerially, so be it, for this is nice. But probably we should go inside, the doorknob's killing

me, or just sit on the floor here, it's carpeted." Kids were in the
elevator, her mother with them, father in the hallway with his
finger on the outside elevator button and other hand over the
door and part it slides into, in case it started to close. Wouldn't
if he kept his finger on the button, though maybe he knew better;
he lived there, but it didn't in any other building when the button
wasn't the heat-sensor kind. One last one for the trip too. Some
kind of reminder and also because of the way she looked. Reason
she didn't go down to the street with them. Just out of the shower.
Face still flushed, body smelling of her mother's perfumed soap
and her own herbal shampoo, so that too; barefoot, in a bathrobe,
no doubt nothing on underneath. Knew there wasn't, so what's
he talking about? and robe tied in a loose half-knot. Saw her in
the bathroom drying herself and putting on the robe. As she slid
her arm through a sleeve he went "Ummm. Dopey, huh?" She
smiled and said "If only conditions were different and there was
time." "Why, your period, suddenly?" and she said "No, I'm still
good—in fact, perfect, just two or three days away." "Where
would we do it anyway?" and she said "On the toilet, standing
up, there's the mat, too wet perhaps, but we could put plenty of
towels down, so also on the floor. But, wrong time," and he said
"Ah, if only, be a nice going-away presence," but didn't think she
meant it, or maybe she did. Even so, so what? Parents there, kids
and he leaving momentarily, so just a throwaway line with a bit
of truth and mischievousness to it but no probability. Well, that's
what she meant about if conditions were different, or maybe she
generally felt like it more after a shower and maybe also after a
shampoo. The water, soap, soap smells, body rubbed and
scrubbed, so skin stimulated, touching her genitals, breasts and
thighs while she cleaned and dried, and asshole. And she has to
know he always feels like kissing and licking her body more after
it's washed and soaked and smells so, the tiny hairs there curled
into kinks and still damp if not too long after the shower or bath.
Gets an erection. "Could you hand me my robe, please?" since
he was at the sink having come in to wash something off his

fingers and other bathroom was occupied: ink. Driving, erection stays. "I can still get dressed and come down," she said at the front door, "do you want me to?" and he said "No, yes, nah, stay, it'll take too much time and effort, and what the hell for? And so soon after the shower you'd be more prone to a cold or chill, since you're still a little wet, isn't that how they come? not that I believe in that if-then." "Dada," Julie called from the elevator, "we have to go." "Nathan, please," his father-in-law said, "we're holding up the elevator. Other people want to use it; the inside panel says so. Want us to wait for you downstairs?" Good idea, he could give a little squeeze into her, quick feel of her ass or something and that longer deeper kiss. But she was shaking her head, indicating better go. "Coming. —So, bye, my dear," to his wife. "Have a nice day—oh, I hate that expression. Just I hope everything goes okay," and she said "Like what?" and he said "You know, train trip back, movie's good, all that. And call when—oh, that's ridiculous, I'll speak to you before; tonight, right after we get there. But find out before when your train gets in so I can pick you up. But you've time, since I'll call tomorrow night too and also probably during the day." "Departs three twenty-two, regular Amtrak, so should get in around six, but you don't have to. I'll take a cab." "I'll come, I'll come, the kids love that station and I love picking you up. We can get another good kiss in." "Daddy," Margo said, "people living here will get mad." "My car and train awaits me—*await, await,* we're talking about two," and kissed her quickly, said "See ya," and went into the elevator, his father-in-law following him in and pressing "1," his mother-in-law and Julie not there. "Oh my goodness, where's Frieda and Julie?" and his father-in-law said "They couldn't take it any longer and walked downstairs."

In-laws were waving to them as the car drove off. Tooted the horn twice; if he didn't, well, they might think he was snubbing them, didn't appreciate all they did for him the last two days; probably not. Happy to have their daughter and grandkids and that he brought them, did all the driving and bringing up the luggage and stuff and now leaving Lee there and taking care of the kids the next two days, so would tolerate a number of slights, if they thought the no-tooting or non-waving one was one, though doubted they even understood what the horn signal meant. Kids waved lollipops back. "Where'd you get those—the lollies?" he said at the corner. "Grandpa," Margo said. "I don't know why he gives them without my permission. He knows how I feel about sweets and teeth and they'll just stick up the car and I hate the fake-flavor smell. What are they, purple, for grape?" "Mine's orange, Julie's is lemon. Mommy said it was all right to have them and you always give them to us for long trips." "Three and a half to four hours isn't long." "Four hours is so," Julie said. "Oh, standing up for your lollipop, hey? And four hours for a kid, okay, maybe, but we'll be stopping for snacks and pee-pee breaks, at least one. But all right, open them and suck and lick to your heart's content but don't bite—not with your teeth sealant on. Your dentist said—I can never get his name straight from the other, your eye doctor, both in the same complex, one's Lanker, other's Larkin . . ." "Dr. Larkin," Margo said. "Larkin said for things like gummy bears and sour balls, not to bite, and a lollipop is as close to a sour ball as you can get. They crack the sealant and cost plenty to replace." "You're always concerned about money," Julie said. "You never think about people or your children." "Children aren't people? Anyway, not true. You heard that someplace on TV or from one of your friends. But it cost mucho, kid . . . or maybe in a book your whole class read. This Good Citizenship Week or Be Tolerant and Generous to the Homeless Month or something?" "That isn't funny, Daddy," Margo said. "The homeless are as good as you." "I know; I'm not saying. You're both right; it was a bad joke." "It was a remark, not a joke." "Well, I wanted it to be a joke but it didn't make anyone laugh so turned out to be a remark. But you're so smart. Look how you took me up on that and you were right, and won." "He's just saying that," Julie said, "to get on your good." "I'm not. But it does cost a lot, the teeth thing, and is supposed to serve a purpose—no pain with your teeth because you won't have cavities, or far fewer—so why go in for another application? You'd like that, strapped to the dentist's chair having that cement or plastic swabbed on?" "What?" "I like it," Margo said. "You get to see videos in the ceiling and switch it with these chair controls if you don't like what they've on. They have three: cartoons, nature and old TV comedies." "Fine. What argument I got against that? But I'm still maintaining control over your sweets intake. And also the garbage in the car. For instance, where are the lollipop wrappers? I bet on the floor." "They're in our hands. What do you want we should do with them?" "What do you think? Don't play dumb. Roll them up, but sticky side in, and then keep them on the seat, or just hand them to me, because they'll end up on the floor with everything else. I can't stand the mess here sometimes," and stuck his hand back and soon got two wrappers, which he crumpled up and put on the seat next to him. First rest stop, he thought, he'll take them and whatever other pieces of crap he can find in the car and dump in the nearest trash can. Newspapers too, he saw on the floor in front of the passenger seat, from when they drove to New York and Lee just left them there, maybe two or three days' worth. "Peace Talks Proposed," upper right headline read; fitting, he supposed; he should talk peacefully, peaceably. *Peacefully.* Later he will, he will. He's ruining their lives and way they'll look at and respond to various future things by talking hard and rough with them. In fact, setting the example or groundwork, laying it, whatever, of how they'll talk to men and maybe also what to expect from them, by acting grouchy, unnegotiable, overcritical, sometimes deranged, just saying the first hot things off his head. Years from now, what? They won't be so small and eager to please and quick to forgive and resilient after one of his harsher remarks or lousy moods or tirades and they also won't sit on his lap because they'd be too big to or hold his hand because you just don't do that with your dad when you reach a certain age and they'll mostly be with friends or their own interests and more schoolwork and they'll have their own problems much deeper and longer-lasting than the ones now and his will seem like what to them? like the same they do now, nothing compared to theirs and he won't be able to do much with or for them but produce money for lessons and schools and things like that, clothes, camps, drop them here, there, pick them up and pray they have good friends and don't do wrong things, and he'll regret the way he acted now just as he's regretted the way he's acted before and that he didn't take advantage of these years. So, he's got to change in the way he is to them. He's not that bad, but be better. Said it to himself a lot but this time he means it or at least means he'll give it an even bigger shot. Little while later when he heard them sucking their lollipops: "Hey, will ya don't make so much noise with those things?" "What things?" Margo said. "The lollipops, what else?" Snapped it out; jeez, already forgot. "You have your radio music on, so our sounds shouldn't sound so loud." "Just each of you, please deal with it more quietly, that's all I'm asking. No reason for any disagreement about it. In fact there is none. It's just a lollipop, and I'm glad you're enjoying them, but please, you know, eat it by licking and sucking more quietly. If you can't, but you've tried, so be it." "Okay." "Fine, thanks, good. I thank you for your cooperation. My mudduh thanks you, my foddah thanks you, my brudduh—" "Are you being insulting?" "Me? To my two dollcakes? No. I'm being serious though maybe throwing in that other stuff just for laughs, which again didn't work, right? But I won't if you don't like." "We don't mind." "Great." Julie slept part of the way. Good, he thought after he looked back and saw her; she can use it. Got to sleep way too late last night, Lee said. He knew she'd make it up in the car and now he can tell Lee that on the phone tonight. New York classical music station till it began to fade. Stayed with it another ten minutes of increasing distortion and fading because he liked the piece and wasn't listening before when the announcer said what it was and who wrote it—modern, for voice and chamber symphony he thought and the words sounded Russian or Polish but the music in parts Brazilian like that Bachianos whatever number it is, so maybe the language was Portuguese, and unbearably sad but uplifting in a way, he can't explain it, and then it was gone. Tried the other two New York classical stations, both commercial; wouldn't it be something if one of them had that same piece on, a musical miracle or just a one-in-a-million situation, but couldn't find them or they were gone too. Dialed to the Philadelphia station, had the number for it in his head and the one in Delaware further on the way, but couldn't bring it in yet. Tried the Delaware one; just maybe some fluke and it got through because there was no interference from there to here and its transmission was that strong; country-and-western music or something. "I like it, keep it on," Margo said and he said "Oh really, sweetie, and it might wake Julie, so do you mind very much if we don't?" and she said "It's okay, you're right." Good, this is the attitude. Patience patience patience. Respect thy youngsters, and so on. "Daddy, could you help me with my numbers, then, if we do it softly? I'm good at them but I want to be better and we did miss a school day." "That sounds like something, well, it's amazing, but something what I was thinking just before, but I won't go into it." "What was it?" "No, I'm sorry—okay, why not, and you're older so you won't misinterpret it. That I should behave much better to you kids. That's it. And that I suppose I'm okay sometimes but I definitely could be better, more patience, less stridence and anger—you know, hotheadedness, mad, sharp, knocking you down with words, even insulting you like you said, which I don't think I did then—I didn't—but every time I do do it I can kill myself for." "You're all right." "As Julie said, and let's speak just a teeny weeny lower, you're just saying that, aren't ya?—ever notice how many times I use the word 'just'?" "No. And you do yell too much but when you don't you're mostly nice." "And not just because I give you things, bribe you, because I don't do that too much, do I? Mommy thinks I do." "No, you're nice, like now, except when you get too rough with us." "When the heck do I do that may I ask?" and she said "Like today when you punched me." "I punched you? You mean when I asked you to get dressed so you can have lunch and we could get going? I just grabbed your arms—didn't grab but simply held them—I didn't even clutch or hold hard— and I said we got to get moving and eat and our things together or we'll never get out of here and if you do it, Julie will too, that's all I did and said, don't you remember?" and she said "You held me hard, you pressed my arms above till they hurt and left marks," and he said "What marks?" and she said "They were there when I undressed but are gone now and I started crying and you let me go when you saw it, I'm sure, my eyes," and he said "I didn't see your eyes, sweetheart, were they crying?" and she said "Almost, because you don't think one or two tears is crying," and he said "I'm sorry, I swear I only held you—you know, that kind of holding to give the other person time to get some sense into his head, or hers, meaning just to think about things when she's a little out of control—but I didn't grab or clutch or squeeze. Or maybe I squeezed a little without knowing it, and your skin's very fair and sensitive so I might've left some red marks, while on a darker skin I probably wouldn't have, but I'm sorry. I'll try not to be even as rough as that again, if that's what I was, rough, okay?" "Okay." "We've ironed it out—you know, worked it—" and she said "I know what that kind of ironing is. Yes, it's worked out. It's all better. Really, Daddy, thank you, now that we've talked. And I love it when we talk like this, personally. Want to do it some more?" and he said "Now? It's difficult without seeing you, or constantly turning around to see you because, you know, some things ought to be said right to the face, and straining my neck, so maybe later. We'll talk some more personally later." "Without Julie." "Sure. Though I'll also talk personally alone with her, but sometime later. You want me to do your numbers now, something I can do with the back of my head. But quietly so she can sleep." "She looks like a doll, doesn't she, Daddy? She can be so sweet when she sleeps," and he said "You're the same." "But look the way her arm's around the top of her head and hand under her chin. I never do that," and he said "How do you know?

And I'm driving, so can't look." "Use the mirror. She might never be scrunched up like that again and you should see it." "She probably formed that position in the womb sometime, like one does thumb-sucking, I think, and sleeping with your knees and whole body squashed into itself because eventually you get so jammed in there, and things. So I picture it; I've in fact seen it. And both of you dolls, believe me. F.A.O. Schwarz would say 'priceless, out of sight, just for display.' Really." "No, I'm ugly, she's pretty," and he said "What a thing to say about yourself, and so untrue. Self-abuse. We'll have to call the cops in on this to arrest you. You have your toothbrush and a complete change of clothes packed?" "Mommy put them in—" "No, I meant—ah, what about what you want with your numbers?" "I am ugly, and really tough multiplications that I can do in my head. The teacher's quizzing us on this, minute each and no paper or pen, and I want to get a hundred on it." "Two hundred sixty-two times sixteen." "Okay. You take the zero from the ten in sixteen, add it to two hundred sixty-two, get two thousand six hundred twenty, and now six times two hundred sixty-two. Well, there you make it easy for yourself. —Why'd you think up those times' numbers?" "First in my head, I guess, though they could mean something more. Social Security for women, for instance—the sixty-two— when they can first collect it, I think, the full amount, which I wouldn't mind after working straight almost thirty-five years. And two hundred—nice and even and not the hundred percent you mentioned wanting to get on the test, though maybe influenced by it. Sixteen? How old are you two altogether? Fifteen, so doesn't count, but maybe deep in my subconscious I added up your ages to that. Bad in math down there, still doing it like an average five-year-old. Or good, better than up here," knocking on his head without turning around. "Because with your added months, yours almost three, hers more than seven, it's almost another year, which could be considered a year, since you don't say when you're nine years and ten months, let's say, that you're nine, do you, or even nine and three quarters? You'd say 'almost ten.' " "That's right.

Or 'about ten.' That's what I'd say." "So there." "Six times two
hundred fifty, or six times two hundred and then six times fifty,
and you get with either . . . fifteen hundred. This problem's too
easy. Now six times ten and six times two—what was the first
number I had, two thousand six hundred twenty?" "I believe so."
"Three one nine two." "What's that?" "The answer to everything.
Three thousand one hundred—" "Good, you got it, great," he
said, "you're a whiz." "Fooled you. It's four one nine two. How
can it be three one nine two if the first part of the answer was
two thousand six hundred and twenty? Six is more than half of
ten, and one thousand and three hundred is at least half of two
thousand six—" "I don't get you. But maybe we should check the
first part of your answer." "Why? Zero added to two six two is
two six twenty." "So? I still don't get your point. Anyway, let's
say you're right and I'm slow today. When I was a kid though—
" "Give me some even tougher ones. A hundreds number times
one in the thousands." Did. "Another." Did and several others.
She got them all right or some she got before he did and he just
assumed they were right, for while he was still doing one she'd
ask for another and he'd give it. "Now some minuses in the thousands," and he said "Those you need paper for. And even if you
of all quiz-whizzers don't, no no no, I just want to be quiet and
think." She started talking and he said "Pleez, sweetie." Her lips
poufed and he said "All right, but whisperingly, and last gab from
you for a while, what?" and she said "I wanted to ask what you
were thinking of or planning to," and he said "I haven't given a
thought to it yet, okay? Now finished, and don't tell me you're
bored. You've books, paper, pencils, markers, imagination, introspection, fanciful inventiveness, memories and so on and you're
also musical and can hum a sweet soft tune, besides those ole
standbys, passing scenery, dreams and do-nothing sleep." He
drove and thought she's not talking and what should he think
about? Work, but hell with that, wants to be rapt or entertained.
Turned the radio on, woman on the Philadelphia public station
was gushing about a group called The Jazz Messengers and he

thought he doesn't know these guys but he hates jazz or most of what he's heard for forty years, same thing and shallowness and no talk's going to make it more interesting, and turned it off. If not deep music or just about anything by Vivaldi, Poulenc or Bach then why couldn't it be, and in a car preferably, something to think about and maybe even stir him up, a good talk, debate or discussion about ideas and stimulating people and things, not crime, drugs, health, business, politics, finance or another international or cultural report—alligator hunting in the Everglades, icebound Aleuts going potty or getting juiced—but art, philosophy, ethics and if art not opera, films, musicals, crafts or dance and where it'd go on for an hour and had only now begun. Maybe once every three years he catches something like that on the road, and really almost any poet or playwright who talks about his life and work on the radio's okay, novelists are always pushing their books or beating their chests or he can hardly understand. Should he get up to seventy? No other cars around, it's legal on the Interstates in Maine and New Hampshire and places, so why not here? It'd be fifteen over the limit and if he's stopped it wouldn't so much be the cost, though that'd hurt, but getting delayed. What's, he crazy?—it'd be about a day's wage. Hadn't seen, and then he saw one, between some trees in the median strip, car facing his way and trooper watching him as he passed, so good thing he was thinking of the should or shouldn't he while doing sixty for he's sure he would have been nabbed, no other cars near him for half a mile now it seemed. Then Julie awoke, knuckled her eyes and he said "Good, you napped almost an hour," and she said "I wasn't asleep, I only had my eyes closed and was thinking," and Margo said "What about?" and she said "None of your business," and that she was thirsty and had to pee and Margo me-tooed and that she was also hungry, so they stopped at the next rest area for gas and bathrooms and a snack, coffee to go for him, curly French fries between the girls for the car and fruit punch he had them drink in the Roy Rogers because he didn't want them to make a mess and if the car suddenly had to slow or stop, the straws to cut their palates, "but if you're good the rest of the trip, real hamburgers in warm hamburger buns and all the trimmins for dinner and ginger ale in champagne glasses"— took no more than twenty minutes. Wanted to get home fast, get the mail, unpack quickly and put everything away, garbage and two weeks of plastic, bottles and cans on the walk for tomorrow's pickup, get the kids' dinner ready, while things are cooking have a scotch on rocks as he sits in his Morris chair and goes through the newspapers and mail that had collected past two days and dump the catalogs and advertising circulars and inserts that had come before Lee gets ahold of them. Then after dinner make a couple of calls and finish his work work. No calls. Tomorrow the kids can talk to Lee before they go to school, or she might not be up, so that evening, and he'll see his associate soon enough and work he'll do after the kids are asleep. Read them a story when their lights are out and they're in bed, or tell them one from his head, maybe about a car, the trip, New York City, the road. Comical incident in the tunnel or at a rest stop. Or they're being followed in an unmarked car by Goofy—loves him as a character, as he gets to talk in a stupid voice and say funny dumb things— and Nancy Drew, since Margo says she's getting too old for just Goofy and Minnie and the gang. Goofy and Nancy are an item, he'll say, and explain what "item" here is. They think the car he and the kids are in is stolen and while they're tailing them they put in a check on their license plate. They pull them over and Goofy asks all sorts of dumb questions. He's much better at dialog than description or that thing that moves the action along and has all the filler and fill-in, like what the setting is and surroundings look like and why the characters do this and that and so on. "Is this a car you're in?" Goofy can say. "You mean," Nancy can correct him, "is this their car they're in." "Um-m-m, I think that's what I said, didn't I? Is this a their car they're in?" "Excuse me, Goofy, but what's a their car?" and Goofy can say "Um-m-m, wha'd'ya think? A their car is their car just as an our car is ours. Gosh, Nancy, you goofy or something? No, you can't be, since you're Nancy, I just said, and I'm Goofy, I think, and the captain would never put two Goofys in one patrol car, would he? 'cause how could we be able to figure out the more harder police things?" "Oh, I give up on you already, Goofy. Our engagement's off and I don't want to be your police partner anymore either. And now that he's out of the picture," she can say to the girls, "you two want to be my sidekicks? Even if our engagement's kaput, police work's got to go on." Not that but something like and Goofy can say "Hey, don't blame me for getting out of your picture, for who wants their sides kicked?" The girls love when he brings them into the stories. But he'll forget this one by the time he decides to tell it tonight and he might even forget he was planning to tell them about Nancy and Goofy. Knows his memory. He'll come up with something though. Always does even if most as stories with satisfying endings that relate to what came before it and tie it all up, fail. Maybe one with his wife and kids in the car. Taking a vacation or the highway suddenly opens up and they drive spirally down an Alice-like hole. Or where the kids and he drive straight home, no Goofy and Nancy stop, open the door and she's there, house warm, fire going, dinner ready, table set, drink waiting for him with the ice just plopped in, while he's sitting reading the paper and having the drink, his wife and kids unload the car and put everything away and the garbage, plastic, bottles and cans on the walk, lots of good mail to go through, correspondence and checks, no ads or bills. "But how'd you get here?" he can say and she can say "Flew." "Plane, and then you cabbed over?" and she can say "No, this time with my arms," and demonstrates around the house, up the stairs, down to the basement, then opens the front door while hovering above it like a hummingbird and holding the knob and flies outside. "We too," the kids can shout, "teach us," and he can say "Not Daddy, he's afr-fr-fraid of heights when his f-f-feet aren't on something," but they convince him it'll be a great unforgettable family event and they all, after the kids and he ask her how and she says "Just hold your arms out, no trick to it, and say the magic blessing,

'gefilte fish,' " fly someplace. Out the window, or door, for windows are too Peter Pannish and he tries with these to be original
as he can, so to Inner Mongolia, outer Bessarabia, Central Chile,
interior Australia, soar with condors and wine and dine with abo-
rigines who are swinging on vines while the four of them glide.
"Whee, whee," it could all be pretty happy and the right kind of
dream-generating stuff for the girls before they go to sleep. So
something with Lee, and it'll be nice for them too if he includes
her, Mommy with them if only in this way. Actually, he thought,
wishes she were in the car with him; talking with her passes the
time better and he likes putting his hand on her thigh while he
drives and rubbing and squeezing it or under her knee and maybe
her backside. If he were doing it now with the thigh, he thought,
kids in back, she'd probably smile for him not to go further and
maybe even say as she's done a number of times for something
like this "Can I take a raincheck on it?" If one of the kids said
"For what?" he or she has always said "Conversation." Alone
with her on a big empty road or just a car now and then flitting
past, he's stuck his hand on her crotch, even unzipped her fly a
couple of times in broad daylight and tight as her jeans still were
was able to push her panties down enough to stroke her hair there
and once got the tip of his middle finger to the top of her crack
but not far enough to touch the bump. Never got that far with
any girl in a car, he thought. Once, though, forgets who, though
she was very pretty, long dark hair, and slim and always smelling
of some intoxicating rose perfume or cologne, Fanny or Franny
her name was, they were in high school, rich kid who at the time
said she wanted to be a medical missionary while he wanted to
be a dentist—called her several times after that and then lost track
of her—on the way back on a date where they danced and illegally
drank in a Long Island nightclub, and she stuck her hand in his
fly, or he steered it in for her. He'd unzipped it, she had to have
heard the zip and probably the couple in the front seat too, and
he put her hand in under his coat and she jerked it around a little.
Tried to get his hand in her underpants under her skirt but she

wouldn't let him. Then tried sticking his finger in her vagina through the underpants and she put her lips to his ear and said "No, that hurts. I'll do this for you," jerking him some more, "but do you have a clean cloth?—that stuff can gush." "How do you know?" and she whispered "Don't be immature or I'll stop." He got out a hanky, forgets how far he got or if she had to stop because of the couple in front or something. Once, though, maybe this was the first time, he met a girl at a party who after he danced and necked with for a while, did it to him till he came. Her name he remembers: Honey and that she had lots of wavy honey-colored hair on top and that when they sat on a radiator cover in the dark she took out some pins and let it drop to her butt. Never even phoned her after that though she gave him her number and said she'd really like to see him. When he was going back to the subway with his friends—party was in the Bronx, they lived in Manhattan—he told them they'd never believe what happened with that girl he was with and one said "She gave you a handjob," and he said "You saw? It was almost pitch black in the room and I had my jacket over me," and his friend said "No, but she did?— what a triumph. Nat got jerked off by a chickie he just met, Nat got jerked off, the fucking lucky." They all said for him to call her and she'll bang him the next time or the time after and then every time after that and he said he probably will but she's so homely and they said "So what, her cunt isn't; they're all the same, a big juicy slit." What complete schmucks they all were. Winced in the car when he thought of himself then, vulgar, ugly, stupid, and the girl: she liked him and was nice to him, how could he have been such a creep? His father once said, when he told him he was going on a date with a girl he liked, "Don't tell me: when you're your age all a girl's good for is for whatever you can get. That's what it was for me and don't tell me it isn't for you. But be smart like I was though; you get her in trouble, deny everything or your goose is cooked for keeps." He said "Wrong, this girl is sweet and from a good family and a real brain and I like her and would be satisfied with just lots of talk and being with her on more dates and at the end of them and only if she wanted, a goodnight kiss," and his father said "Who do you think you're fooling? Ah, you're already on the road to being a patsy with that attitude and ruining your whole dumb life." Honey didn't seem very bright and had been too eager to do him, he didn't understand that since they'd only just met and he never said he liked her, and her dress was too loud and she wore these sparkly dangling ear things and clunky bracelets and had on pancake makeup and her mouth was very wide with a ton of smelly lipstick on it and when she smiled, too much of her gums showed and he wondered if she was doing something to keep a lot more of it hid. She got his number from the girl who gave the party who got it from a friend of his and she said "So, were you serious about wanting to have a date or was that just a line?" and he said she lived too far away for him to subway back and forth to her all the time and she said she could meet him in Manhattan every other date, she loves the city, and he said okay, when he didn't mean it, "but not this weekend, I got all this studying to do plus my deliveryboy job," and she said "Maybe I should've gone slower with you, but that I didn't says something about how I felt, doesn't it?" and he said "Sure, no complaints, I appreciate it," and didn't call back. Then Lenore when he was sixteen, girl who did it to lots of guys he'd heard and first to do it to him more than once. That was how he'd heard of her: "She does it to you first date sometimes and to some guys, once she gets to know you, she sticks your prick between her tits and squeezes them into it till you get off. All you do is introduce yourself to her at a dance or on the street, even, if she's walking with some girls and then you call her up and say you're the guy who said hello to her or something and is she doing anything now, can you come over? and if she isn't doing anything, like whacking off another guy, she usually invites you up if she liked your looks and style and she isn't sick." Her parents or one of them were always there but they left her alone with him in her bedroom. Amazing, he thought, and with the door shut and lights off except for a bedlamp of such low wattage that it couldn't have been there for reading or anything but lying back listening to music or having sex. He'll never permit that with his kids when they reach that age or even twenty and they're still living home, and it's probably more accepted now than then so might even be more accepted ten years from now. Knows it's more accepted: some parents thinking better the kids do it in your home where you can give them a condom than on a beach or in back of a car without one and where they can get mugged or the girl gang-raped. Door will always have to be open, main lights on and music not so loud to drown out every sound. Eight years from now with Margo it might begin, though he hopes not after what they've subtly instilled in her so far and he expects to openly impress on her later on: do young youthful things while you're young, save the older fake reveling and rebelling stuff for when you're over twenty-one and have half a brain what's right in those goings-on, and he's sure Lee will go along with him on that, though who knows? She might say "I had my first all-the-way when I was sixteen with a boy several years older who I loved so why not her when she's a year or two older than I was if she truly wants to and is prepared for it and the boy's nice and they've been seeing each other awhile and are genuinely fond of each other and absolutely safe about the act?" On his first date with Lenore, and he can't really call it that and he never saw her outside her apartment, she answered the door and said "Come in, hello, these are my folks, Martha and Mo" or something, "this is Nat," as they passed the living room, parents were seated reading the papers and waved, sometimes he went into the living room if they were there to say hello and shake their hands, "Now I want to show you my room," and they went in and she said "Close the door, it's okay, they hate me and I hate them, they're demented old assholes but they're cool." "Jeez, what a way to talk about your parents," and she said "Why, something wrong with it? I live with them, you don't, but if my talk's not up to your standards, split," and he said "No, I don't mind." She had her own little refrigerator in her room with sodas and snacks inside, double electric burner for making hot chocolate and mint tea, she said, though she never once offered him anything but a cigarette every time he was there when she knew he didn't smoke, record player, shortwave radio, TV set when lots of homes didn't even have one, all sorts of things, even a toaster and table cigarette lighter and a carton of cigarettes on her night table and a type-writer on a desk and two walls of tall bookcases filled with books. She said when he was staring at them "Do you like to read?" and he said "Oh, I love it," and she said "Good, we got something in common—who are your favorite authors?" and he mentioned a few and she said "They stink—maybe I can loan you some of my books; I got too many," and he said "Sure, I'll give them a closer look after," and she said "After what?" and wasn't smiling and for a moment he didn't know what to say because he didn't want to ruin it and he said "When I'm going, now let's just talk . . . where do I sit?" and she said "I guess the bed, there's no good chair for sitting here," and they sat together on the bed and talked about people they knew and movies they've liked or they want to see and what clothes she thinks boys his age look good in and he said he wouldn't mind owning some of those but it'd take every dime he earns—"My parents have the money, I suppose, but I want to be independent and I think it's good," and she said "I should be more that way too with money but Martha and Mo won't let me—they give me more things than I need and always leave plenty of money in a kitchen drawer for me for whenever I want it—even enough to buy you a restaurant dinner with me if you'd like to one night," and he said "Sure, that'd be nice, I've hardly ever gone except with my parents for lunch, but I wouldn't want you to pay and I don't think I could pay for myself unless it was a kind of cheap place," and she said "Don't be silly, it's an invitation, and I hope you like French food, I do," and he said "Sure, probably, what do they have?" and she said "Snails, atmosphere, cloth napkins, who cares?" and moved closer and he did and they kissed and did that for a while, kissing,

rubbing each other's backs and necks and he thought this is probably a good time and reached for the night table light, wanted to
get it over with and go home and maybe call one of his friends
and tell him, and she said "Wait, listen at the door," and he said
"For what?" and she said "Do what I say, tell me if you hear
anything, or I'm not turning off the light," and he got up and put
his ear to the door and heard nothing and said "Your parents?"
and she said "Lock the door, they can be snoopy even if they are
cool—I think they'd like to burst in here sometimes and see me
naked, not with boys so much but when I'm undressing for bed
or drying after showering—I have my own shower, by the way,
with these needlelike side sprays from Sweden if you ever feel like
taking one when you're here," and he thought "With you? I
shouldn't say," and said "Thanks, but about your parents barging
in here, come on now, they wouldn't do that," and she said angrily "You don't believe me?" and he said "Hey, if you say it,
it's got to be true, but you can still see how someone could find
it hard to believe, parents doing that," and locked the door and
got back on the bed and she turned the light off and they kissed
and he said "Could you put out your cigarette, please, it's the
smoke, it gets in my nose," and she said "If you insist, sir, though
I hope you're not going to next complain about my breath; I try
to be mindful of others with what I smoke; they're mentholated,"
and he said "No, I don't mind cigarette smell even if it doesn't
have that," and they lay, as they always did, on the bed—this
probably happened five or six times before he said "Do you think
you could put my thing between your boobs and rub and stuff
and do it that way?" and she said "Where'd you ever get that
idea? You've got to be sick, sonny, thinking I'd ever do that to a
boy. Better you get the heck out of here and pronto," and got off
the bed and buttoned herself up and shooed him out and told
him not to call her anymore, he did and she said "I was serious;
leave me alone or I'm calling the police"—and she'd grab his penis
through the pants after he touched her breasts through her shirt
and then he'd unzip his fly or she would and she'd jerk him up

and down and he'd stick his finger in her vagina and poke and probe and wiggle it around inside and they'd go on like that and continue kissing till he'd come into a bunch of tissues she'd quickly pop out of a box by her bed and hand him or cover his penis tip with. She never came but maybe she did. He didn't think about those things then for girls and didn't talk about it with her and for all he knew he had probably hurt her with his finger. He just didn't know what to do in there or around it and he's not so sure he does now. Several women before Lee tried at times to improve his fingering technique and even Lee now and then says he's not doing it right or he could be doing it better, though Lenore never complained about it and she was the sort of person who would have or at least said when he hurt. Maybe she didn't even know what she was supposed to get out of it. Or she had somehow come to believe that a boy scratching deep inside her was about the gentlest and most skillful fingering she should expect to get. But she had to have done it to herself lots of times and there must have been a couple of guys before him who had done it well, so who knows what she thought when he did it. Anyway, the poor parents, he thought in the car before. Lenore was a little homely too. Big nose, nothing that would bother him today, he found ugly then. He didn't want to be seen outside with her, and she was also a little heavy. His friends would have said, which they did when he told them what they were doing to each other in the room, "Take a peek at Nat with Miss Beak" or "L'Amour Schnoz" or "the blimp." Maybe her folks thought this was the only way she was going to get a guy. That's what he thought then. But they didn't look or seem dumb. Father was a doctor, mother an interior designer and both were always reading something when he went into the living room to say hello or waved when he left: news magazines, books, professional journals, big thick newspapers, *Times* or the *Tribune*. He should have taken her out. She would have felt better about him and her folks would have thought he liked their girl. To a movie, not to a party, or the dark neighborhood hotel bar he and his friends occasionally went to with fake ID's and eventually she might have put out for him more than she did. He always had bags on him and they could have done it in the bedroom with the door locked and it would have been the first time with anyone but a paid whore. Though she told him a couple of times when she was jacking him off and he made some motion with his body that he wanted to stick it in her and started pulling off her panties or with his hand pushing her face close to his penis, "I want you to know the only guy I'm ever going to give head to or screw is my husband, if maybe a short time before with him when all the marriage arrangements have been worked out, and I'm not planning on getting married till after college. So don't expect even a lick from me and don't ever think I'll let you do it with your mouth to me either. That's also only for my husband or when he's my bona fide fiancé." Then another girl. Renee, about three years later. She only wore black and her short hair was dyed black and she had black eye makeup and liner on and sometimes an inch-wide strip of black makeup or paint under her eyes and black lipstick when she wore lipstick or it looked like it. He was at a table in the college cafeteria when she put her tray down beside his and said "So how you like your soup?" smelling of incense and sweat and even her mesh hose and shoulder bag black and he said "I don't know; hot, I guess," and she said "That a man; how's it taste?" and he said "It's something called mulligatawny and it tastes odd, not like soup," and she said "That's the curry in it, Mr. Green-horn, from India where they know how to make exotic sculptures and food. But who's dragooning you to eat it? You don't like, push it away. Tell me, you a bonebrain or do you have the force of the raw nerve and divine breath in you plus a bit of sybaritic responsibility?" and he said "I don't get what you're saying," and she said "I didn't ask if you have a boner—you can't keep your freaking eyes off my voluminous bust, that I can say; you like, right?" or something like; anyway, he thought in the car, she said things like this in this way, "but I was saying, do you only think of lucubrating and calibrating and slide-ruling and laboratory-tooling and scoring in your chosen boredom and becoming chairman of the Sanitation Department one day?" and he said "No, I like to read for enjoyment too and do other things, movies, run around; I'm not an engineering major and I haven't stared at what you said I did; I'm just eating here, my crackers and soup," and she said "Tell me, if there was a contest in this sonofabitch dreary collitch for future statistics for the chick with the pinchiest waist and biggest tits, you think I'd have a chance and would you vote for me and shove your ballot in the box—I need every vote I can get," and he said "Why do you want to think of that? You've other things going for you; you're obviously articulate, got brains, words at your command, et cetera," and she said "Oh, come on with the line, Harold, come on, give it to me, give it to me, you fucking square—I want the truth; do you like chicks with big tits or not?" and he said "Big, small, they're all nice, I don't like you cursing at me, whatever they have," and she said "Pigshit liar; maybe mine are so heroical they border on the grotesque, I'll accept that, like the David paintings with the French flags and rafts, but tell me, you'd take a no-tit chick over an above-average-size one, all other things being equal?" and he said "I haven't thought of it," and she said "What fugging excrement," and he looked around, people at their long table were looking, and he got up, "Excuse me," and took his tray to another table and she sat down beside him with her tray and said "So I'm sorry, so I was crudely rude to you, oh poo-poo me and boo-hoo, so do you accept my apologonorrhea? and you're still eating your green soup you said you didn't like, you must be hungry and poor. Listen, Arthur, or whoever you art, I'll be straight with you. You look good, you don't smell, you're no dumbbell, you've a cute ass and lots of curly hair locks and a dimple in your chin like my favorite Jewish movie star and are no know-it-all or psycho blowhard, you've some dignity and ingenuity and a trace of guilelessness which I like and yet you're still complex and like sex preferably with chicks, that's obvious, and are artistically but not ostentatiously dressed and you didn't tell me to fuck off, which a sliver of me would've preferred—I detest noblesse politesse—so we should talk some more, for I believe we're mutually putting the make on each other. Come to my dump tonight—it's in the city and near a subway stop and then if you like, sit across the room and ogle at these all you want," swelling her chest, "I don't care, even my derriere and legs, they're I swear not grotesque, so long as you yak a blue streak with me and do everything I want. If you turn out to be taciturn and uninteresting and half of what I thought, out you go, a deal?" and he said "After my last class I work in the Garment Center till seven, but you have your own place?—I don't know anyone who does," and she said "Own john, own bed, own radiator, own linen closet, own electric coffeepot, own toilet paper rolls, own night light, I got it all," and gave her address and subway directions to it and said to bring a creamy cake dessert and two India Pale Ales. Her mother answered the door; they lived in the same apartment on the top floor of a six-story walkup but once in the entrance hall there were two other doors with front door locks and peepholes on them. Never saw anything like it. Her mother, very small, almost a dwarf, maybe a couple of feet shorter than her daughter who was tall, yelled out "Renee, a gentleman visitor," and she opened the door, said "Thanks, Mom, and how's it going today?" and her mother said "You know, the same, I'm dying, but am I going to complain, and if I do, who to?" and Renee said "Good, for it's a pain in the tush when you do," and to him "Did you meet my *madre?*" and he said "I said hello," and her mother said "I said good evening too, that's what she's told me I'm supposed to do," and went into her place and they went into Renee's. "Strange setup," he said or something like, probably looking out the peephole and she said "Mom pays for the rent for both of us; it was that and turning this into two flats or my moving out and probably starving on the streets till I got my degree and with not only no comforts but few pleasures. For she knows I like reefers and strong beer and this here with plenty of men," her big toe poking his penis through the pants, "so it's what we came up with where

she also wouldn't have to live and die alone. You smoke 'em?"
and he said he never had and she said "Then let's light up; I love
virgins, they'll always remember me," and he said "I'm not a
virgin," and she said "I know that, dummy, I was talking about
tea—gosh, and I had you pegged as a semisophisticate who I could
make whole but you're too far behind," and they smoked and
had the cake and ale and she said "Let's go straight to bed, no
staring till after; I love the feel of feasting on some rooster's cox-
comb while I'm naked and high and he's also supping me. You
do do that, I hope, or else out you go. And that foreplay's my
final play, you know. I never want to get pregnant from something
I don't especially like doing and ruin my body while also bringing
some piglet into this hideous world with people like you and me,
and I'm also not one for postcoital snoozes and snores and morn-
ing-mate coffee and toast," and he said "Fine for now, but we'll
see," and she said "Oh, I'm telling you, Bernard, that's the law.
Don't so much as unzip your fly now if you think we're going
any further than what I said. To me, it's the only thing, not simply
out of necessity but choice." In bed he said how come no black
pillowcases and sheets, for she had black window curtains and
towels and washrags, and she said "Those they don't make yet
but they will. It's one of my life assignments to put them in every
bedding department and store." Saw her in her flat about a dozen
times over three or four years and it never went further than she'd
said. She screamed a lot during it and yanked his hair and pulled
back his ears and dug her black fingernails into his rear till he
snarled for her to stop and later he said "Don't you think your
mother will mind about the noise?" and she said "Let her install
soundproofing in my room, for there's no other way I can do
this." Doing it in her room and the business about the noise and
how she acted to her mom and stuff made him think of Lenore
just as thinking of Lenore before had made him think of Renee.
"Had"? Just "made"? There were others. Renee became a window
dresser for New York department stores and could have been the
designer behind black bed linen a number of years ago when it

was the rage, and maybe it still is or has come back. Of course he never could have remembered exactly what happened with those three, Honey, Lenore and Renee, but what they did and said and the circumstances and some of his thoughts then went something like the way he put it. Women he'd only call to have sex. If they wanted to go out to a restaurant or bar or movie first, fine, if he had the money or could borrow it from them, and he always insisted on paying and paid back, just so long as they knew how the evening would end up. Wasn't nice, he knew, but if they didn't like it they could have said no, and none of the women he went with saw themselves as easy playthings. And he used to call some of them at one or two in the morning if he was a little high and lonely and wanted to have sex and a few would let him come over at that hour or would cab to his place if he paid for it and met them in front of his building. He'd look out one of his street windows or lie in bed usually playing with himself while listening for a cab to pull up and then jump up and throw on a bathrobe or pants and shirt and run down the three flights of stairs. If they lived close and said they were on their way, he'd say "When you say 'on my way,' does that mean in two minutes or ten or fifteen or what?" and if they said in two, he'd wait in the building's vestibule, usually reading a magazine or book, or if it was a nice night, sit on the wrought-iron fence on the little garden wall bordering the sidewalk. But most after a while called him a horny bastard and said not to phone again if all he was looking for was to make it with them, but he still called and gradually there was just about no one to have sex or go out with. Sure, lots of dates and encounters over the years and several one- or two-night flings and a few brief romances which he thought might turn into something more but for years nothing that lasted till he met Lee. Doesn't know why it was different with her. Used to call her at one or two in the morning sometimes too, even when he wasn't drunk, just wanted to get laid, and most of those times she said to come over or phone her at work the next day if he wanted to see her tomorrow night. A few times she called him around those hours, or maybe no later than twelve, asking if she could drop by for the night or if he wanted instead to cab to her place. If he said it was late or he was tired, she'd say something like "Listen, sweetie, it's no problem; I suddenly felt like I needed your company and that even a little sexual release would be nice, but we can see each other at a more sensible hour tomorrow or whenever," and he always ended up saying he'll come by or she can. Talking to her, he got excited, and she probably even intended him to, or he just didn't think it a good thing—manlihood, something—not giving in, and that if he could ask it of her, why not she of him? Maybe it was that, her calling him to come over those few times, and that she put up with his late-calling crap, or only gave him a slight scolding for it because it was two o'clock, three and she was sleeping, but never said never call again if it was just to get laid. Next day if he had come over she usually even said she was glad he did. So she was different in that way, more accommodating and less reproachful than other women he'd known or just not as harsh in the way she carped and blamed, and as pretty and sweet in other ways and well-built and intelligent and quick-witted and good-humored and lots of other good things and better in bed than most of the others but not as good as one or two for a short time, though almost anybody can be hot stuff for a couple of nights with someone new, but over the long run, the best. Dozen-plus years and they still go at it almost every day and lots of times twice in an hour or so, something when it happens now often surprises him that he's still able to. Second's never as good as the first anymore when it's done so soon after, and maybe never was—he forgets—but that he's still up to it with the same woman after so long and finishes more than half the times he starts and never any other woman since they met, is something. Maybe also it was just time to marry and have kids if he was ever going to, for he'd always said he wanted them, and there were no serious disagreements between them when they were seeing each other and he was actually making an okay living then when he never had before. Glad he did marry, and especially the kids. And continuing to go out on dates at that time and trudging around to different apartments and too often being rejected on the phone after a couple of dinners or in their living rooms or foyers after they'd been kissing and fondling awhile and he had most of the woman's clothes off, just wasn't in him anymore. But some of the others? Vicki, last one or maybe the one before the last before Lee, in Boulder when he was there being interviewed for a job he didn't get, woman around twenty years younger than he but that didn't stop her from inviting him to her place and it for sure didn't stop him from accepting, "Breakfast," she said, "nothing fancy: orange juice and health bread and scrambled eggs and then I'll get you to your plane," flat-chested he thought when he first saw her when she picked him up at the airport to drive him to her boss, but when she took off her shirt it turned out she'd been self-conscious of her large breasts and did everything she could to conceal them, like loose-fitting clothes and a special bra that seemed to strap half her breasts to her sides, in fact she almost put her shirt back on when he said "My goodness, your breasts." Wait. He's lost his train again. He was thinking of women just jerking him off years ago, though how the thought started he doesn't know, and who was the last woman he slept with before Lee? when Margo said she was starving and wanted to stop. "We can't while Julie's sleeping." "She's not, are you, Julie?" Margo said, probably shaking or pinching her for Julie said "What, what?—get off me, that hurt." "Margo, leave her alone, she needs her sleep." "I wasn't sleeping," Julie said groggily. "I was only resting with my eyes shut." "Boy, I've heard that before," he said. "It's true. It gives me as much rest as sleep does and later makes my eyes see better too which sleep doesn't do." "That's foolish," Margo said and he said "Who knows, maybe she has a point. It might've even, that later-see-better stuff, been something studied and proven by scientists, only we haven't read it in the papers yet. I'm sure some major experiments start like that, from what people said they'd experienced, and maybe just one person. Have any scientists been eavesdropping on your conversations, Julie?" and she said no. "Daddy's only kidding you," Margo said and he said "I am, somewhat, but I'm not discounting—making little of what she said. We might have a great budding scientist in our midst and one principally interested in the differences between deep rest and light sleep and the benefits and limits of each," and Julie said "I don't want to be a scientist. I want to be a poet, do you think that's a good thing to be?" and he said "Poetry? Fits your wistfulness and sensitivity. And what could be better doing and more beneficial to everyone? So sure, if it comes to you, become one—meet my daughter the poet—though you'll have to do other things for a living, like marrying a doctor or best-selling author—only kidding. And you don't marry for a living; you do it out of love, like poetry, because someone's been called to you, right? In fact, for our driving pleasure today do one in your head now and recite it to us, I'd love hearing it," and she said "I'll try, I've never made up one in a car," and he said "Take a few minutes, make it a special one," and turned the radio on. A reverend, or preacher or Christian healer, anyway, obvious by the snake-oily voice and every other sentence with the word "Christ" in it or reference to Him—He'll move things, stand by Him, He's with us, believe in His ways and words and your luck and fortune, spiritual and otherwise, will rise, as He did—that it was, oh, lost the train there too and anyway not interested in what he was thinking about this hustler, "Come my little pretty," pulling the girl's pants down, they used to joke as kids, "and let me put "Christ" in you," for that's what he sounds like, asking for dough now in that universal reverend-rabbi-probably-imam voice, since he's never heard one, the whole thing for dough—money and sex, and don't forget power, so like just about everyone else when they have the chance and no different than selling soda and cars on TV, right? though being a man of God—but what's he going on about?—this might be the one decent preacher of them all, just as to my kids most times or let's say lots I'm the best daddy that ever lived, and moved the dial up the band and back—wait, do those two con-

nect? some other time, but what do they all do, go to a special
religious speech school to talk that way? how can people fall for
it? or maybe it's just if enough do it's worth the air time—and
all he could find was another preacher or healer, must be the area
they're driving through and also the scarcity of stations or low or
short frequencies of them if that's the word, and then some
hillybilly music as one of his professors said it, another fake, for
though corrected by students with their laughs—he was German—
he said it that semester a half-dozen times more—20th Century
Intellectual History, Part One, maybe his favorite college course
overall, though Two, and he never looked forward to a course
more, was a dud, forgets why, maybe became a strain to make
out his speech in that huge lecture hall and also got tired of his
crowd-pleasing ways, and dropped it—"Love will get you down,"
singer was singing, "but love will get you up too, so risk it, for
life's" something, incomprehensible, followed by a plucking instrument and backup caterwauls from a group. Double entendre?
Why not, simple enough, and nobody's got gonads like these guys,
and just another kind of preaching for dough, no? and turned it
off. "Daddy, I liked that," Margo said, "you finally had something
good," and he said "So okay, listen to it on your own radio at
home with your door closed and the sound low," and she said
"We won't get it, we'll be too far away and the program will be
off," and he said "So what can I say? Rough. No, that wasn't
nice, I'm sorry," and she said "It's all right, at least you admitted
it. But if I can't listen to the music, there's nothing to do, so we
have to stop," and he said "I'm not going to ask this, for if I do
you'll say yes even if the real answer's no, but do you have to go
to the bathroom?—be honest," and she said "Not yet," and he
said "Then if a rest stop doesn't come up soon, we'll stop," and
she said "What's that mean?" and he said "If there's one in the
next two to three miles, or make that three to four or even five,
but no more than that—the odometer here says 22-0-8-7 point 6,
so we'll say anything past 0-9-3, no, 9-2, which is less than five
miles but I want to be fair and take in the half-mile or so we've

done since I started talking about the rules of how we'll stop. In fact why don't I set the trip odometer," and he did, "this even littler mile measurer thing here for car trips and when it hits 4-0, to be really fair, for we've gone about a mile since I first started up about all this, then the first rest stop that comes after that number will be the one we stop at, okay?" and she said "I don't understand, you make it too complicated," and Julie said "I have a poem. It's not one of the same ones I've said to you before and it's not good because I didn't take long in making it up, but here goes. 'The radio's playing and went off. My daddy was saying and then became grorph.' " "Grorph?" Margo said and Julie said "For gruff. 'The music was swaying and then got lost.' That didn't happen but I didn't want another rhyme with 'off.' And I first had 'and then like sounds got lost,' but then thought it sounded better without it. 'Night isn't near and the stars aren't out yet. But I see clear. I see clear. For passing the time in a car, poetry's the best bet.' The end." "God, that's something," he said. "Even down to the contractions and the repeat line and that throwaway 'lost' for 'off,' and rhyming 'best bet' with 'yet'? Why'd you say it wasn't good?" and Margo said "May I say something?" and Julie said "I know you hated it," and Margo said "No, it was fantastic. Recite it again though, I want to hear it whole," and Julie leaned over, he saw in the rearview, and kissed Margo's shoulder and said "You're so nice," and Margo shut her eyes as if touched and he thought "That's what I love to see, almost nothing better, more than their looking up with that look at me, wouldn't it have been great to have had an older brother to worship or a younger one I loved who worshiped me," and said "I wish I had a pen around to jot the poem down," and Julie said "Down and around, whole and though. Jot the dots. The pen and the ... the ..." "Men," Margo said and she said "Doesn't fit with what I'm thinking. I got it. 'Pen in my own den, when I'll write this down, all words all around, till then say it again and again.' Den is my room, you see; I'll remember it by then," and he said "Good also, sweetheart, and do write them down, especially the first one, but second one if you can do it too, when we get home or at the rest stop where I'll borrow or buy a pencil or pen. I want to read them to Mommy on the phone tonight and also keep copies of them to show later on what a wonderful poet you were even back when," and she said "When's that?" and he said "When you were a kid, now; for I'm talking about for when you get older," and she said "Maybe you can help me type them on your machine—I have so many I can even make a book of them and Margo can draw the cover," and he said "And Mommy can do the music—okay, will do or I'll even type them myself." They drove. She recited the first poem whole. Margo said if Julie didn't mind she had some very small criticism; she didn't like that " 'best bet'—it sounds like something you buy in the supermarket," and then to him she was starving even more than before, couldn't they take the next exit and go somewhere on that road and then back on?—they must have gone more than four miles and they wouldn't lose, by going off and back on, more than a few minutes, and he remembered the bagels he'd bought for the trip early that morning and slapped his forehead and said "Stupid Dada, I have bagels, plain and sesame, from Bagel Cottage in New York, anyone interested?" and Margo said "Plain, me," and he pulled the bag out from under his seat, "Oh lucky bag," he said, "saved the day, made a girl happy," passed a plain back, Margo split it and gave Julie a piece and they ate. Then they played together and by themselves. Then what happened happened.

INTERSTATE 5

Notices the car on his left. Nothing unusual. Car driving along-side his, two guys in it. Looks at it, passenger in front smiles at him, he smiles back, looks front, car stays even with his, looks over, no particular reason, just something to do on the road, passenger talking to the driver, he accelerates a little to get ahead of them, for he doesn't like driving alongside another car on the highway or really anyplace at the speed they're going, sixty, sixty-five. It's dangerous or could be. One wrong move and their cars might touch. Then he's thinking about other things, what mail might be waiting for him at home, drink he'd like to have some-time soon after he gets home, kids are quiet in back, maybe sleep-ing or looking out the windows, and that's that. Then the car's on the other side of his. How'd it get there? Could it be the same car, for it was just over here. Looks more closely and it is. Same men, driver with the same two fingers from each hand, ones to the left and right of the thumbs, hooked under the top of the steering wheel same way as before as if he doesn't really have that much control over it or wouldn't in the slightest kind of ticklish driving situation. Couple of years later he thought maybe that's what first gave me the impression it was a bad idea driving so close beside them. That if anything was unusual at first *that* was, driver holding the wheel with just four fingers and from under rather than over so opposite from the way he should if he was going to do it that way and loosely it seemed, though he had a strong face and the confident look of someone who was competent and experienced behind a wheel. And maybe he was holding the bottom of the wheel straight with his thighs or even his belly— he seemed heavyset—but that still wouldn't have given him much control over it in an emergency situation. What he also should have done, he thought, was drop back instead of move ahead, for moving ahead of a car you've been even with awhile and which is being driven by a man and certainly when there's nothing but men in it is a challenge of sorts to some guys, especially when you're doing it from a slower lane. The guy might have looked like a good driver but not very bright, and neither did the guy with him, so that should have been another tip-off not to move ahead of them, for neither of them looked the type to say to the other "Hey, leave the guy alone." Maybe in fact that's when they thought "Let's get on the other side of this guy as a joke, and without him even knowing we're there till he suddenly sees us, which should freak him out good, for who's he think he's speeding ahead of? Hey, he wants a race, we'll give him one and something more. We'll give him a piece of my fucking fist if that's what he wants," they looked like they could also have said. He at least, if he was going to move ahead of them, he also thought, should have done it slowly, inconspicuously, so they wouldn't think he was trying to show them up in any way, for he did at first sort of dart out, wanting to get away from them fast. Driver looks at him. He smiles, driver smiles and takes the left two of those four fingers off the wheel and waves them at him, as if he knows he's concerned about them, and then speeds up and in a minute or so is about half a mile in front of him and then he loses sight of them or just stopped looking or caring about them, when he thought about it years later. He goes back to thinking about the first things he should do when he gets home. Go to the basement and turn the hot water heater dial from Vacation to Normal just in case the kids want a bath or his wife, when he later talks to her on the phone, tells him they should have one or one of them should. He might want a shower right away too. Driving a distance of around two hundred miles makes him feel clammy and a shower always feels good after the trip. Saved about fifty cents the past three days by putting the dial on Vacation, or maybe a dollar, who knows? But what the hell, it's just a few seconds out of his time and he doesn't like the idea of water staying piping hot while nobody's home for days. He'll also probably have to go to the basement to do a wash, for there are the kids' clothes and his for the last few days and maybe some dirty clothes in their rooms. So the water will have to be hot for that too, or what does he usually set the washing machine at?—warm, not hot, so as not to stretch the clothes or run the colors, or something; forgets. Get the mail, of course, and put the trash cans out for tomorrow morning's pickup and maybe raise the heat thermostat a few degrees if the house feels cold. Raise it something, that's for sure, for he lowered it to sixty when he left to save a dollar or two on gas, or maybe for the time they were away, three or four. Open the curtains downstairs if it's still light when they get home, which it should be unless there's a major tie-up somewhere between here and there, and disconnect the automatic light control or whatever it's called that turned the living room floor lamp on at six every night and shut it off next morning at two. Why two? Why didn't he adjust the dial to shut off at one, or midnight, which would have been a lot closer to when he normally shuts off all the house lights? But first thing to do—that's right, he chose two because he'd read where most burglaries occur between eight and one in the evening and as a safety margin he extended it to six and two—but first thing to do before he does anything, or maybe right after he switches the water heater dial to Normal, is feed Brad. And replace his water and clean his cage, for the bird's gone almost three days with the same seeds, water and floor liner, and lettuce and apple slices stuck between the wires. Water probably has his shit in it and apple slices might have ants on them, even covered with them, which happened the last two- or three-day trip they took to New York, which he hates though he loves spraying the bastards out of the cage till they're all down the kitchen sink drain and then turning the garbage disposal unit on, something he doesn't like but has to do to finish them off. In fact, maybe with Lee away for two days he'll spray the house for ants, outside and in, which she won't permit because of the spray smell and what she says are dangerous poisons. The house has a serious ant problem, where they sometimes swarm around the bathtub and sink on the second floor, even on the toothpaste tube and toothbrushes, but she won't let him deal with it except with boric acid in cupboard corners and places. He bought the ant spray months ago and never used it, but he will, maybe tonight when the kids are asleep. He'll shut their doors, open all the windows downstairs, put the bird in the basement and all the exposed food, dishes and utensils away. She'll never know, or he'll lie if she says she can still smell some of the ant killer and say the oven pilot light was out for a day without him knowing it and he just relit it today: he must be coming down with another head cold. Also rub Brad's chest a little, talk to him awhile, maybe lift him on his finger inside the cage if he lets him—does about one time out of five—for he must have been lonely last couple of days. Maybe also cold, for is sixty really high enough for him, and at night when it's chillier and nobody to cover his cage? Hopes he doesn't come home to find him dead and with ants on him. If he did he'd just chuck the whole thing into a plastic trash bag and put it out with the garbage inside a can and say never again a bird, though the kids would probably insist on a burial in the backyard. If they did he'd give it but just the bird dumped out of the cage into a shoebox into a hole and no words after he kicked the dirt in. Wonders if he sang while they were away. Would if he heard birds singing outside or some rattling truck noises from the street, which often set him off. Does having the family around inhibit or encourage him to sing? Should have brought him with them as he wanted to, but his in-laws don't like pets, especially noisy ones—"Singing isn't noise," he told them, but that didn't do it; "What's music to you," his father-in-law said, "could be noise to me, and same thing reversed"—and thought he might get out of the cage and mess up their place and worse yet get lost where he wouldn't be found till after Lee left. "What would you do then?" he asked them and his mother-in-law said "Let him out the window and tell him to fly home, what else?" "He'd probably hook up with some outdoor birds in the park and wouldn't live through the next winter," he said and she said "Birds like that have a short life anyway so one half-year free with friends would be worth another year or two alone in prison, I'd think. Naturally, I'd hold him for you if you wanted to drive up to get him and he'd flown back into his cage, but for no more than a day; I couldn't take the squawking and I wouldn't know how to take care of him." "It's simple; what is this, run in the family? He was originally Margo and Julie's but they also say it's too difficult looking after him. You change the water—that takes ten seconds; you dump the top of the old seeds and put in some new ones— that's another thirty seconds. And as sort of a treat for him, if you want, you squeeze a lettuce leaf and fruit slice between the wires someplace where he can reach. Then you put a fresh paper towel on the liner and maybe clean any kaka that might have stuck to the wires, which you do with a damp paper towel, and comes to all told about three minutes, and for someone new at it, four. I do this once a day because I think every caged animal deserves a clean roost and fresh food and I feel it's the least I can do till I train him to fly out of the cage and then back when I want him to, but if you did it every other day that'd also be okay." Then he notices a car on his left, same one, how'd it get there from where it was way up front before? Well, he hasn't been following it, but it could have slowed down and got around him somehow. Passenger looks at him, snaps his fingers and points to him as if he wants to say something pretty important, rolls his window down, smiles as if he recognizes him, "Oh you, how ya doing, buddy?" passenger seems to say and he nods and says through his window "Fine, thanks," but also doesn't like quick chats with cars alongside, feels they're even more dangerous than just driving beside them and close, and looks front and picks up speed and their car speeds up too and stays even with his. What's with them? he thinks. Years later he thought I should have known something was wrong right off and not looked at them or rolled down my window or smiled and said "Fine, thanks" or just not looked after my first look, rather, or played around or anything. I didn't play around, but just not bothered at all with them after my first look. Or maybe "Fine, thanks" was enough, for saying nothing, ignoring them completely, might have triggered them too. I should have switched to the slow lane after my "Fine, thanks" and when I saw they were staying even with me, and if they started switching lanes to stay next to me I should have stopped on the shoulder first place I could and I'm sure that would have been that. I also should have started looking for a state trooper, for maybe there was one on the road or median strip then or in one of the opposite lanes going north and I could have flashed my headlights that something was wrong and maybe it would have worked and he'd have slowed down and crossed the median and eventually pulled me over to see what's up. But by staying in the next lane to them, having an exchange of sorts with them, maintaining some contact with them, in other words by not doing more right away to get away from them other than speeding up some, it started things—familiarity, whatever—where they thought they got to know me in a way, something, but enough time had gone by where they'd decided I was going to be their target of the day, of the week, the year, even if there were kids in back—

just their target, period, and maybe for some peculiar reason they even liked the idea better that there were kids with me; more to scare; more targets if they knew all along they were going to shoot at our car. It could even have been that enough time had gone by where they had begun to dislike me for some reason, though I didn't do anything I know to encourage that. It could have been my face all along and only my face that they didn't like, an expression I'm unaware I give to people in passing cars when I quickly look at them, or to people in general—unaware of till even today. No, today my expression's different than it was then, I just know that. I'm sure it's almost never been the same anytime since that day—since that moment when the guy started shooting—when he first stuck the gun out the window, even—except maybe when I sleep. When I'm driving, for instance, I rarely look at people in other cars and when I do, and it's almost always because I think their car's getting too close, it's with a dead expressionless look I'm conscious of giving—I'm not even giving it, it's just there. Or at least I think it's dead and expressionless—again, I might not know my own look—but anyway the feeling is that every time I look at another car and especially on an Interstate or any main highway, I bring back to myself that particular day. It also could be those guys didn't like my look from the moment they saw it when they were on my left the first time; in the end, who the hell knows? But what I'm getting at is that if I'd acted sooner—got on the shoulder sooner, let's say—things would have been different. Much different. Altogether different. They would have passed us, I feel, and disappeared. Maybe. Or maybe nothing I did would have changed things except maybe if I'd had a gun and shot them first, and they would have followed our car to the shoulder, if I'd gone there sooner, and pulled alongside instead of shooting from a few hundred feet in front and opened up on us broadside with two guns instead of one, the passenger with two guns, the driver still driving or maybe getting in on the gun fun and shooting past the passenger at us too, with a semiautomatic rather than just a pistol or something like a machine gun and sprayed our car with bullets and killed all three of us but definitely one or two of us and wounded badly the third. Did I ever once think I would have preferred dying with Julie that day? Sure, thought of it before, plenty. And of course I would have wanted Margo to stay alive and unhurt, of course both of them alive and unhurt and me dead if anybody had to take Julie's place. Thought all that before. But it probably would have been, if I'd gone to the shoulder sooner, different in a much better way. They would have driven on, never seen again. Wouldn't that have been something. I would have then started up the car on the shoulder—but I actually never would have turned the ignition off. I'd have kept the car running in case they got on the shoulder in front or behind us and I had to go forward or reverse. Or maybe I would have turned it off unconsciously, doing what I usually do when I make a complete stop like that, even shifted into Park and pulled the key out and done what with it—put it in my pocket, thrown it on the dashboard?— but what did I do with the key that day? I forget. And if the key was out and they had stopped on the shoulder, what would I have done then? Stuck it in the ignition fast, but why my thinking that? And then driven off the shoulder—if they had gone on—and taken the next exit, reported the incident to the state police perhaps. Maybe I would have remembered better what they looked like if they hadn't shot at us and what happened to Julie from it. I would have looked for a trooper station, at least, or probably just stopped at a gas station to find out where one was and gone to it and then gone home another route to reduce the chances of coming up against them again on the same Interstate. There are a few alternative routes, though longer, but so what? They're probably more traveled, possibly because there are no tolls on them and there's cheaper gas because there are more gas stations, and a wider variety of restaurants, and probably also because of their greater activity they're more patrolled. And then, once home, done all the things I said. Fed the bird and cleaned his cage. Turned the water heater dial to Normal, house heat to sixty-eight. Got the mail, put out the garbage. Had a drink and started the kids' dinner. Opened the living room curtains if there was still daylight, maybe taken a shower. But by then, having come home the long way and stopping to report the incident to the state police or at least phoned them about it and so forth—probably driving slower and more cautiously after what happened with those men, and forced to drive more slowly because I'd be on slower roads and some of the alternative routes have stoplights—it would have been dark. Sat down with the kids at dinner, had a glass of wine while they had juice, read the mail or glanced at it and the front pages of the newspapers, and so on. The automatic light switch. Gathered laundry from around the house and out of the bag of dirty clothes they brought back from New York and started a wash. Called Lee to tell her what happened that afternoon—just to speak to her and maybe as part of that conversation, what happened, or maybe I wouldn't say anything till she got home, not wanting to alarm her or send her to sleep that night with bad thoughts. And maybe because of what happened on the road that day or because I was still keyed up from the long drive, or a combo of both, another scotch after dinner, maybe a third or just more wine. Cleared the table with the kids' help, washed the dishes, got the kids in pajamas and washed up for bed, the story, from a book or my head, kisses, hugs and final words before they went to sleep. Next day, school for them and work for me. I'd set the table for them the night before, make their school lunches the night before too, put the washed laundry in the dryer. Day after next we'd all go to the train station to pick Lee up. Maybe during the drive home I'd tell her. I certainly by then wouldn't have forgotten about it or thought it too small to talk about. In a few years Julie would be fifteen, he thought, five years after that, twenty, and so on. Twenty-five, thirty. Twenty-six, thirty-one, thirty-two, what's the difference? Life isn't divided by fives. They used to celebrate the kids' half birthdays but stopped when she was killed. Just, was never brought up again by Margo, who started it when she was around six. "What're you going to get me for my half birthday?" Margo and Julie would say and I'd

say "I don't believe in half birthdays," but would always get them
something but nothing expensive or big. She would have done
well in grade school, I bet, gone to a good college, probably on
scholarship. She was that smart and there probably would have
been a financial need. Like Margo, tops in her grade-school classes
in reading and math—probably grad school after. Become a scientist of some sort as I predicted she would when she was four, or a
doctor or scholar or done something with the piano—performing,
composing. She was that good and precocious at it too, her piano
teachers said. Married, worked, had kids, continued to work or
even while she was having kids, all of that. She would have been
a great daughter, I just know it, he thought, and I would have
been a better father, though her dying so young and no doubt the
way she died and that I was there and perhaps could have done
something to prevent it, though if she'd died slowly or quickly of
a disease, let's say, and at any age, it might have been the same,
killed off a lot of it for me. I'd pass her room or go into it for
something, suddenly go crazy. Go crazy sometimes when I was
mowing the backyard grass, for instance, and looked up at what
had been her bedroom window on the second floor; was tired,
taking a break of a minute or so from mowing, looked around
just to do something and happened to catch her window, one time
remembered her looking out of it at me and waving and rapping
the glass; depression, would just break down and cry. Sometimes
in her room, fall across her old bed and bang the mattress and
walls with my fists, burrow my face into the pillow, kick the head-
or footboard, wouldn't speak to anyone for hours after that even
when they pleaded for me to, would go to the linen closet for her
old comforter to lie under, would get drunk that night, usually,
and eventually pass out and maybe stay that way for days, drunk,
depressed, out of it, doing odd things, and it still happens occasionally but doesn't stay for days. Anything reminding me of her
can start it off. When I noticed a pimple on my nose in the bathroom mirror while I was shaving I suddenly heard her saying what
she said once when I was in the bathroom brushing my hair: "I

know I'm going to have ugly pimples and lots of scars from it when I grow up; it's in our blood," for I had a row of acne scars on each cheek and at the corners of my jaw. Saw on TV her favorite actress on a kids' show from a few years back presenting an award—like that. Suddenly couldn't make it, would crash. Someone else had to turn the TV off; my wife took the shaving brush out of my hand. Became overprotective of Margo; that's one place where I meant I could have been a better father. When we crossed the street sometimes, even when she was twelve and thirteen: "Hold my hand, I said *hold my hand*, a car can come out of nowhere and knock you down. Do you know how I'd feel if that happened and you were really hurt, do you know what I'd go through? I'd kill myself; with Julie I almost did, but both of you, I'd be dead." She'd be at his funeral most likely—odd how thoughts connect, unintentionally, subconsciously, whatever goes on down deep or just below the brim—but anyway, attend with her husband and kids and maybe her in-laws. We had her about twenty years after most men father their last child and her in-laws would probably be a lot younger than I. She'd cry, say we were very tight her entire life, were so much alike temperamentally, intellectually, physically, our long legs, slim frames, joined eyebrows, big lips and dimple in the chin. That I read or told her and Margo stories almost every night and how that gave her a love of literature or contributed to it, things like that or one would hope. Went out of my way for them on special holidays and their birthdays, even celebrated their half birthdays after Margo made the day up, and then might explain what they are. Was a wonderful grandfather, devoted, delighted, indulgent, extravagant to a fault, and so forth. Maybe mention the pimple incident and how it ended where she never got them or at most only a few and no scars. Nah, people don't speak about such things at funerals in front of guests, but it might be a lighter one than usual since she could preface her remarks by saying "He had a weird sense of humor and irreverent and idiosyncratic view of life and no feeling for religion or any particular philosophy or belief and a cavalier acceptance of his own death. 'What will be will be be will be be be and so on,' he used to say. And 'The only things I'll miss are your mom and an occasional hot H and H plain bagel from the Broadway place where they make it and you two kids, and maybe some other things.' " How overprotective I was of their doing things like crossing the street when they were kids: Maybe she could say "Maybe we weren't ever hit by cars because he had overprotected us so much, but who could ever know?" "Taught us to ride a bike, dive and swim and swing a bat and was always kissing and hugging us, our heads and hands. There were some bad things too, when I hated him for an hour or two to overnight or at least till I fell asleep, but these were outweighed by the good." He looks at the car and passenger's smiling and making a motion with his hand for him to roll his window down. Why, he thinks, something wrong? Looks at his door and one by Margo right in back of him. Everything seems okay, both flush with the frame and locked. "Margo, yours I know, but Julie, your door closed tight and locked?—I can't see from here, the seat," patting the one next to him and she says yes. Instrument panel hasn't lit up that anything's wrong. Maybe one of his tires is low—doesn't feel it or that he's got a flat. His seatbelt or some other thing could be hanging out of one of their doors—that's happened. No, both seatbelts on his side are all right, he sees by checking his and quickly swiveling around to Margo. Julie's he can't see and it'd be too complicated to get her to check, though it could still be something hanging outside—coat sleeve, doll leg—well, last one not out of his—but like that. Passenger's still looking at him and when he sees him looking back he motions to roll his window down. What is it, he mouths, something wrong? "No, nothing, I only want to say something to you." Years later, but certainly not before the first or second year after it'd happened, since during that time he didn't speak to anyone about it, he said to someone "So why the fuck did I roll my window down? Guy had said nothing was wrong so why didn't I ignore him and go on or drop back or do anything to get away from them? I knew I didn't like their faces. They weren't nice faces. And this feeling about their faces didn't come from after what happened that day either. They were sort of hard-boiled almost mean and kind of sly faces, especially the passenger's. No, his was definitely mean and sly and much worse. It was disgusting, evil, thoroughly repulsive. Putrid. I didn't read into his face well then because I wasn't really looking at first and my feeling about people when I first met or saw them then was, well, everybody's all right till they prove or someone else has proven it otherwise, but I can see it now. Evil also because he was trying to pass off that mean, sly, repulsive, putrid face as kind and helpful and nice, your gentlemanly next-door car passenger, and for a few seconds, after I'd had this much better instinctive bad reaction to or at least was skeptical about his face, I fell for it. The driver's face was just go-along-with-anything-no-matter-how-evil-or-wrong, and look what that pig went along with. Die, you dirty bastard, die, die, and I hope by now he is dead from a knife or gun somehow and not just brain-damaged let's say from some guy's beating or clubbing, for what pain's that if you don't know it? But even better, some other evil bastard slowly and painfully clubbing his head and face at whatever prison he probably ended up in, till it killed him. The passenger was hopeless, bent or geared for the kill from the outset—something—for mayhem, rottenness, destruction, the game, intent upon it, which sounds fancy that 'intent upon' and 'mayhem' and 'outset' and 'geared' and 'bent' and so forth, or maybe that's all of them, but that's what he was. But the driver could have stopped him or just stopped it. He had control over the wheel. Unless the passenger took the gun off me and put it on him, or first put it on him and then me, or had two guns, one for him and other for me, and ordered him to stay close to our car, which he never would have done. They were buddies, for Christ's sake, not that anything like friendship or that sort of thing would have had any hold on him. But he still wouldn't have pulled a gun on the driver, for to do it means he might have to use it and if he did where would that have left the car? Off the road, smashed into one of those median barriers or a bus or truck on the other side. But I'm losing it, I'm losing it here. What I was saying was that the driver could have gone on, dropped back, done anything to pull his pal away from alongside us. So to me—nah, what's in it to say that one was as bad as the other, et cetera. One killed, one could have dropped back or charged forward, either could have done something not to kill my kid, neither did. Life's slime, they can't be seen inside of or explained. But when the passenger asked me to roll my window down, to get back to before, I sensed something was wrong with his asking, for everything seemed okay with the car and us. Yet I still rolled it down—you figure it. Actually, I thought I'd maybe misinterpreted what he'd said that nothing was wrong and he only wanted to speak to me, and thought maybe he's saying something's wrong but nothing that important now but what I'd definitely want to know about for later. A brake light not working, for instance. Well, that I'd want to know about right now, though if one works maybe it's not so immediately bad if the other doesn't, but anyway it wouldn't be something you'd signal or want to speak to a guy on the road for, is it? or maybe I'm wrong. But something—I just don't know now what. Back directional signal not working or just that I didn't signal when I changed lanes. Or better, as an example, that my exhaust pipe was hanging by a thread or one of my hubcaps was ready to come off—those would be things to know about right away. My mistake was an honest one, I'm saying, though where's that get me today? Sly and slippery as they both looked, passenger more than driver, to be very honest I was thinking more of the safety of my kids and driveability of my car and also what it might cost if something like a hubcap flew off and got lost or the exhaust pipe hit the ground and smashed. And how else do you find out if your brake light and back directional signal light or one of those other things isn't working—forget that I wasn't signaling, for I always do—except through someone behind you on the road who sees it or when you take your car in for a tune-up or service and with the oil change they give you a twenty-point checkup as part of it as they often do. Or if you think to check the brake lights and so forth yourself because you're taking a long trip—halfway across the country to Des Moines or whatever's halfway across, which I of course wasn't doing—or up to Canada as we've done. For those trips, to Nova Scotia and so forth, I always give the car a thorough check-through if I haven't taken it in for a lube job recently, or even get a tune-up if it's around that time for one or a few thousand miles before, and they do it. So, I thought this guy might know something I didn't about my car and should find out, and rolled my window down. I never should have, I don't know what I should have, but that for sure isn't what I should have done. Which of course goes so much without saying, that it's one of the dumbest things to have said, even if the same thing that happened to us could have happened if I hadn't rolled the window down." The passenger already has his window down and says "Hiya, Harry," and he says "I'm not Harry, you must have the wrong person, is that all it was?" slowing down and looking at him and the road back and forth, and starts rolling the window up, thinking it was a mistake and this guy could mean trouble. Their car slowed down with his, maybe doing fifty now, and the guy's smiling and says "You're not Harry the hairy monster, or is it Hairy the harried monster? Is 'harried' a word?—tell me, I'm a little thick," and he says, window half rolled up, "I think it is and I'm neither of those guys." The girls are laughing; must have heard some of it about Harry and hairy and thought it funny. "Quiet down, kids," he says and the man yells to them "Yeah, kids, cool it, pipe down, do what your hairy Uncle Harry tells you to or you're in deep hot water with me." "I'm their father, not their uncle, and if you don't mind, please don't threaten them. And really, it's dangerous talking to another car while driving and staying so close like this, so I'll see ya, okay?" and speeds up even if he thinks they'll speed up with him, but he has to try it, and maybe they won't or maybe they'll shoot past him, the guy giving him the bird as he passes, and be on their way. They stick with him and he has his hand on the handle about to roll the window rest of the way up when the guy yells out, their cars just a few inches apart, "Oh it is now, Harry, oh is it, dangerous you say, talking to not a person but to another car, right? Well, my fucking Harry or hairy, and you are hairy, very faggot-fucking hairy, it's as simple as all this, so *touché*. I don't like hairy or harried or married heavy Harrys or anything like them and never did. Always with their oh-poo-poo-poo polite warnings and words to the wise and bigshot goodbyes and put-downs, and this is what I do about these I'm-better-than-you attitudes and noses in the air, plain as simple, simple as plain peach pie," driver behind him laughing like mad and walloping the steering wheel with his hand. Later—years later—couple of years at least, he thought what could Julie have been thinking of at that particular time and a short time before? Margo he could always find out, and did ask her about a year after he thought this and she said "I think I was thinking—no, I don't want to talk about it, the whole subject is too sad." "Please, just a little, if it gets too terrible for you or even starts to, stop. But I really think it'll help me get over everything somewhat. For maybe with the complete picture of what everybody was thinking and saying in the car that time or as close to it as I can get, it'll just be too much for my head, filling it way beyond where it can hold that much till it all just blows up and then blows away, or at least what's left I can live with. No, that doesn't make any sense, does it? or just some." "Not that I can see," she said. "But I think I was thinking, and naturally I'm unclear about it since everything then seemed to fly out of me because of the screaming and shots and our car quickly stopping and my being thrown against the front seat and then the shock of after. But that the man was all of a sudden acting strange after he'd been kind of nice and funny, and his smiling face changing with it, which I liked up till then and I think Julie did too—" and he said "Why, how could you tell?" and she said "She gave me a look that she thought him funny because of the things he was saying, like 'hairy Harry' and 'homely hippie'—" and he said "I didn't hear any 'homely hippie,' " and she said "I did, almost all *H*'s, but for those things I thought she gave me a look for and also his funny face, which like me I bet she thought he was making just for us. But when the sudden change came I got scared, for his face also went from funny to ugly." "So you immediately knew something horrible was about to happen, that it, and you think Julie did too?" and she said "For me, not till he took out the gun. And even then for a few seconds, till I saw how scared you suddenly got, I thought the gun was fake and he might still only be having some fun with us but now with a scary mean face." "And Julie, our dear little Julie ... you know, it's still difficult, after three years is it?—did I mention this to you before?" and she said "What?" and he said "Talking or even thinking of her without crying—yes, I'm sure I did, or might have, and I think I even remember asking you another time about a year back if I'd mentioned this before—but what do you think she was thinking right before the guy showed the gun and after he stopped acting kind of funny and started acting very strange?" and she said "Probably the same as me if she was looking and catching everything I was," and he said "Do you think she was?" and she said "I can't remember—for a while, like I said, she did have the look that she was; but then my eyes got drawn only to the man, so it's not possible to say for sure for her and that's the way it'll always be." "Try a little harder to remember, sweetie," and she said "Oh, all right," and shut her eyes and seemed to try and then said "I can't, that's all, I can't see anything after that but the man and the gun and your being scared of it and lots of shouting and shrieking and the car swerving and then us pulling over to the side and you yelling for us to duck, or maybe that was before or both before and after we stopped, and the shots." Julie might have been thinking, he thought, "The man was funny, but now Daddy doesn't seem all right. He seems worried and the man doesn't seem funny anymore either. He seems crazy and angry, shouting like he did so loud and now some more. And he cursed. Bad words too. The *f* one; I think I also heard the *p* one. Daddy hates when people curse in front of Margo and me, even if he does it sometimes when we're around and he's mad at something or us, which he gets a lot, and even curses at us sometimes too, and once the *f* word." She had a little memo book in which she jotted things down: pictures, thoughts, math problems she made up, poems. Once: "What day is it, Daddy?" "You mean today's date? April twelfth." "Well, I wrote down here 'Daddy used the *s* word, twice, April twelfth.' " Other times when he thought about what she might have been thinking at a particular time, incidents or moments that for some reason stand out. Like when he went into her room to say goodnight, lights in it were out, and got on his knees by her bed, thought she might be sleeping, a little light was on her face from the hallway and eyes closed and expression quiescent, and then her eyes flipped open and he said "Oh hi, I came in to say goodnight, thought you were asleep," and she sat up and slowly moved her face to his and then just stared deadpan at him a few seconds, so close he was looking at her cross-eyed, and after he pulled back, for his eyes were hurting, and said goodnight, she did and turned around, patted her pillow and rested her doll on it and covered it up to its neck and lay down and put her arm around it and he said "No kiss?" and she said "Not tonight," and he said "How come?" and she said nothing. So what was on her mind when she stuck her face next to his, he'd thought at first to kiss his lips, and those few seconds she stared at him and also when she hugged the doll while facing the wall and he said a couple of times "You're not going to say anything?" Time they were sitting in a movie theater, just the two of them and her only time in one, picture kind of loud and fast like a toy commercial, and she nudged him, he looked at her and she just stared up at him and he whispered "What? What is it?" and she stared for what must have been a minute and then turned back to the screen. He never asked her again what it was; should have, later. Time he was serving the kids dinner and she said "Can I have something to drink?" and he said "This isn't a restaurant. You know where the juice is and how to pour it and your pouring arm isn't lame, so go in and get it yourself," and she said "I only wish it was," and he said "Wish what was?" and she said "This was a restaurant. Then we could get another waiter." "Oh ho ho ho, so sophisticated untongue-in-cheek siss-boom-bah ridiculing humor," and she put her fork down, elbow on the table and palm holding up her chin and she seemed to be studying him and he said "So what's so interesting, tell me—my stupid rejoinder, saying words and phrases way over your head?" and Margo said "Yeah, tell Daddy," and she shook her head and continued to stare. That he was crazy to make these requests, use those words, that he's always getting excited or irritated over nothing, that he can ask nicely for once if he wants her to do something—"Please isn't a dirty word, you know," as she once said and he said then "I know, I'm sorry, I'm setting a bad example, adults should be, well, role models when it comes to behavior in front of children, and for other things, so please, please, and I mean it, triple and quadruplicate please—no, that doesn't seem as if I mean it, so just *please*," followed by whatever he was asking her to do, or was she just looking his way but lost in some thought that had nothing to do with him? She got that way lots and he always loved looking at her when she did. Time she was sitting on the couch, book she'd been reading on her lap, legs under her, fingers pulling at her bottom lip and letting it spring back, eyes off somewhere contemplatively. Must have been the book she was thinking of, or—she did this—she'd heard a bird or some other sound from outside and was wondering about it, listening for it again, something, but picture of her sitting there stayed with him, including the light—it was night—this time from the floor lamp, slit across her face. Time she was on the merry-go-round at her school fair and he called out "Julie, Julie, Daddy here, give me a look" every time she came around where he was behind the railing separating him from the ride, for he wanted to wave and take a picture, but she kept looking straight ahead, big smile, perfect for a picture but not at him though he should have snapped it but he was waiting for her to look his way for a full-face shot till it was too late and the ride had stopped—imagining she was on a real horse? Exhilaration of the whole thing—tinny calliope music, breeze on her face and through her loose hair, other kids' squeals, different sounds from the fair melding and changing around her as she rode? As he lifted her off the horse he said "What were you thinking of when you were riding round and round?" and she said "Something," and he said "But what?" and she said "I'm not sure, maybe nothing, why's it important?" and he said "It isn't, just thought I'd ask, but your face—staring out and looking so happy and smiling into space," and she said "What's the matter with that?" and he said "Nothing, it was beautiful, let's forget it." Time she snuck quietly up to him at home with fluorescent pink–framed sunglasses and headphones on, attached cassette player in her hands, tapped his back, after he jumped and turned to her and said "Oh my goodness, look at you," she did a quick dance to the music he faintly heard from the phones, and smiled— knowing the joke? Knowing he knew? What? Pleased he liked it and that she'd also startled him but where he didn't get mad over it and it in fact made him laugh? But how'd she know he'd appreciate it or did she only guess or was trying it out if he would? He knew she'd like him doing this so he said "Hey, yeah, cool, babe," and held his hand open for her to give him five, which she did and he said "Looks great; Elvis, right?" and she said "Who else could it be?" and he said "But Elvis Barry Schwartz, no?" and she said "Oh really, Daddy," and he said "But how'd you know who he was?" and she said "On TV, and Margo told me about him and has this tape," and he said "You know, and don't tell anybody because I can be shot for saying this, but I always thought he was way overrated, in fact that he was practically talentless and grue-some, and I grew up when he was thriving and alive, but who am I, right?—and his movies, phooey," and she said "Well I like him and so does Margo and all her friends," and took the phones, cassette player and sunglasses off and set them aside—he'd later have to say "Could you bring these Elvis relics back to their rightful places?" but she ignored him so he did it which she probably thought he would, for they all knew how compulsive he was at trying to keep the house neat and clean. Time she was reclining on the couch in her pajamas and he'd come back from a run that had ended up at a couple of stores—had to be a Sunday or national holiday for them all to be home, since it was within a half-year of when she died and there was no lazing around early Saturdays then, the kids had to be at swimming lessons by 8:50 and it was a twenty-minute drive there—and tapped her knee, she was up, he saw before, looking dreamily at the ceiling or again maybe through it, and said "I got you a chocolate croissant and Margo a plain one, freshly baked from Natural Pastry," and she stared at him, said nothing, he'd expected a big grateful smile and thanks, for a chocolate croissant was maybe the best thing she liked for breakfast, but got a mysterious little enigmatic one. What's she thinking of? he thought. And years later: Do I know any more than before what she might have been thinking of that morning or what her face was trying to say? Waved his hand in front of her eyes to make sure she was looking at him and she continued to stare and smile that way and he said "Everything okay, you have a good night?" and she nodded when he thought she'd say what she usually did, "Sure, why?" "And your dreams," he might have said, for this was how he usually pursued things when she was very quiet or irritable after she awoke, "no bad ones or anything in them you want to tell me?" and if he said that and she didn't want to answer, she probably just shook her head. So? So most of those times when he thought of what she might be thinking, she was smiling one way or another. So? So there were other times not smiling. Time she said in the car when he was driving them to school "Would you be very sad if I died?" That was months before she did. "Why, you expecting to kick the bucket soon?" quickly looking around and seeing she was serious about it, so "No, that's the wrong thing to say. 'No jokes now, Daddy,' right? and you'd be right, because this is serious subject matter you're talking now, very serious. So of course I'd be sad, deeply sad. So deeply sad that it's probably beyond the deep. It's into something I don't know what it is. Total feeling-death, like. Meaning where I don't feel anything. I'm a zombie, walking around like one or not even walking but comatose. Paralyzed, on my back, can't get up, can't eat or drink, can only think about my zombiehood, or not even do that. Can only feel what I don't know I can, or not even that. No, I can't feel anything, as I said, and all that's not a definition of being comatose, but something like it. A person who's nothing anymore, who can't react or respond to anything. Who doesn't know he's alive so might as well be dead himself, though shouldn't be because they often come out of it. Listen, do you know what a coma is, either of you?" and they both said yes and he said "Well that's what it is, comatose—a coma, but in this case in sadness or what that beyond-the-deep sadness brings you to. I don't know, I really can't think straight today. But don't think such terrible thoughts as would I be sad or not of what you said, because it's never going to come to anything like that. Though why'd you ask, if I can ask—I'm curious?" and she said "I had a dream last night you died and I didn't show any sadness to it. No, it was Margo who died and you didn't show it," and Margo said "Oh thanks a lot, that's special. It must mean you want me to be dead so you can have Daddy all to yourself," and she said "No it doesn't, does it, Daddy?" and he said "It doesn't have to, Margo, really. Who knows what she was thinking of in the dream, but we'll forget it, okay? I shouldn't have continued the discussion. I don't mind talking about most subjects with you if they're appropriate for your age—on your level, you know. Where they can be dealt with and aren't disturbing, but not that subject even if you think you can handle it. You aren't going to die—she isn't—neither of you. Who was I talking to?—I was talking to Margo, but I mean this to you both. It's in fact so far away it's going to seem like forever. And maybe it will be forever, for by the time you're my age, they—scientists—may have discovered something to keep people alive for as long as anyone wants to stay alive that way," and Julie said "But that means you'd die if it's so far away, and I'd hate that. It's too sad, you or Mommy," and he said "Well, we're healthy, aren't we? Exercise, we eat the right foods, keep a slim stomach, don't drink much, at least Mommy doesn't if at all—beer here, beer a week later—and I've come down a lot the last couple of years too, maybe one shot every other night's the extent of my heavier booze, and only to relax me. Vitamins, and we don't smoke and I never have, sufficient sleep, things like that. Have a good attitude or good enough, I think, especially Mommy, who never lets the nuisance things annoy her as they sometimes do me. And I've never really been sick yet with anything worse than a bad flu a few hundred times—exaggerating; Mommy once had her appendix out but that's all, other than for a mole or beauty mark she tore on her back and which had to be removed. Ooh, I'm sorry. So, I might live, and Mommy for certain, and also because she's eight years younger than I, long enough to take advantage of this live-forever-if-you-want drug or discovery too." "Good, we'll all live forever together," Julie said and he said "No, you and Margo will have to get out of the house after a while—we'd want you to, you would too, to do things, have homes of your own. But there'll always be room for you with us, always, I promise. But you gotta give me some peace sometime, sweethearts, you gotta. Only kidding," when he looked in the rearview and then quickly around and did see her face, "stay with us forever. We'd love for you to, me no more than Mommy, I mean 'no less,' meaning a whole lot, I mean it," and he drove. Time when she was seated beside him in the car and the street they were on was blocked by a tree that had fallen across it, firemen in helmets cutting it apart with power saws, crowds in this normally quiet neighborhood where maybe the most you see when you drive is another car and occasionally someone jogging or walking a dog or two women together pushing strollers, local TV remote team, policemen, one pointing angrily at him to turn around as if, like his father used to say, "What're you, a dumbbell, it's right in front of your face," and she asked what happened and he said "What you see—did you see it? This huge tree must have lost its roots or gotten hollow inside by termites or some other thing, a tree disease, without anyone knowing it till this happened, and fallen," and after about a minute, when he was looking for another side street to get to the avenue he wanted, she said "What if someone put me in front of that tree and I ran away?" and he said "You mean what would I do with the guy who put you there, for of course I'd be deliriously happy you ran away," and she said yes and he said "And put you there before the tree fell, right? for you got to know when to use 'had' in a sentence or to put in helpful phrases like 'before the tree fell,' and when not to," and she said "What would you do though?" and he said "I'd try to catch him and then hold him for the police," and she said "That's what I thought you'd say," and looked front and continued to be serious awhile, he was glancing back and forth at her, trying to figure out why she'd asked that and did she mean he should have said something else? and what was on her mind now, when she said "What if a tree fell on a house—it would make the rain come in but would it kill somebody inside?" and he said "It would make a big hole in the roof and if it was a direct hit, meaning right through the center and someone was directly underneath, and the house was only one story, yes, it could kill someone inside," and she said "What if it's a brick house?" and he said "But the roof wouldn't be brick; at best it'd be made of slate which is probably just a little stronger than the shingles we have on our roof, so again, direct hit and only one story?—maybe somebody would get killed, but the brick walls might stop the tree from going all the way to the floor where the person is," and she said "If the person is lying under a table would it help any if it wasn't a brick house?" and he said "Maybe by a tiny amount. But a tree falling down would be gaining speed fast, even if it was slightly stopped by the roof, so I think a direct hit on the table in a one-story house would still kill him," and she said "We have two stories, right?" and he said "Two and a crawl space, so we're much safer from a tree falling than a one-story person is if we're on the first floor," and she said "And if we were in the basement?" and he said "If we're in our basement and a tree falls, nothing would happen to us except maybe a little soundproof ceiling tile breaking on our heads and making our hair dusty," and she said "Would we be dead if the tree fell on our car?" and he said "A tree that size? Did you see how big and round it was? Six of my arms couldn't have got around it, and it stretched across the entire street into the house-across-the-street's front yard. And it looked like an oak, a very heavy tree—I got a quick look at its leaves, tree must have been at least a hundred years old—so yes, I think we would, even with a steel or whatever metal's used for the car roof instead of a house's shingle or slate, much as I hate the thought of anything like that for you. I also think I'm wrong about a slate roof being even a bit stronger than our shingle," and she said "What if we're in the front seat and the tree falls in the back?" and he was about to say "This isn't a city bus, know what I mean?" but looked at her, she didn't seem scared, was serious, just wanted to know his answer and he said "Then I think we'd be saved, though maybe bounced out of our seats but probably onto someone's cushioned front lawn," and she said "No, we'd still be in our seats buckled in, but I think we'd be out of the way of the tree, so saved too," and he said "So we agree, good," and wondered "What brings all of this stuff up?" but didn't want to ask because didn't want to continue it, and she took from that little well in the door to hold things like change or a pen or just to hold on to or whatever it's for, two figures Margo had made for her out of pipe cleaners, or made for herself and Julie had taken from the house before she left, and started walking them together up opposite arms till they met on her chest and then held them high and said "This one's Millicent, other's Magnificent, say hello," and he said "Hello, girls, how's it going? nice names, twins I suppose," and she said "No, they're different colors," and he said "Oh," and drove. Time they were in the Aquarium on line for the second floor, kids up front, he several people behind and they were standing by the escalator entrance just looking at the ground and he wondered why they were staying there with so many people behind them wanting to get on. Maybe looking at the flat steps sliding out of the opening and slowly popping up, and after a while when there was a long line behind him he said "Girls, what're you doing? stop fooling, people want to get on," and Margo scowled at him, Julie was hidden behind some people now, a man near them said to him "There's a lady here trying to get her stroller on, it's not them," and he said "Sorry, thought it was my girls, sorry," and the man cocked an eyebrow and faced front and the woman and man behind her holding the front of the stroller with the kid in it and the girls and the man from before got on, and when he got off the escalator and looked for his kids he saw the woman un-snapping her boy from the stroller and he said "Excuse me, you must have been bent over taking care of him when I yelled and I didn't see you, so I thought it was my girls holding up the line," she didn't say anything, shook her head as if he was terrible in some way—way he treated his girls, way he just shouted out like that without knowing what was going on, that he was lying and had seen her but used the girls-excuse as a way to get her to get the stroller on the escalator faster and which might have turned it over and hurt her child—more people are hurt on escalators, he once read, than in proportion—in ratio—how do you say it?— to people hurt on any other moving conveyance including cars— and he said "Anyway, I'm sorry," and went to his girls, Julie seemed embarrassed by him, Margo gave him a dirty look and he said "I know, you both, I done wrong, I thought it was you two holding up the works downstairs, and don't say it, I shouldn't have yelled out, but I apologized to the woman with the stroller and she said she understood, she'd done it once herself but not at the Aquarium," and Margo said "Yelled? You screamed like a hyena, making everybody wonder," and he said "Who screamed? And after I explained, nobody wondered. I spoke loud, loudly— maybe not even a yell—to reach over the heads of the people in front of me, that's why. Anyway, it's crowded here, there really should be more space for people, with all these exhibits on both sides, so stay close," and took Julie's hand and she pulled it away. Why? he thought, looking at her, and she looked away. Because Margo's mad and she thinks she's got to side with her? She'll cut you out of her will if you don't? Ah, okay, better he keeps his trap shut when she gets like this—hey, he's learned that much— and in a few minutes, so long as he doesn't touch her or make any signs to try and reconcile her or look at her searching for some clues to her mood—if he did she'd say "What, what're you looking at me like that?"—it'll be over; usually. Half an hour later or so—nothing more was said about the escalator incident, he didn't stare at her, acted as if nothing was wrong and everything was normal, and it really did seem things were back to being okay between him and them—they were in the basement cafeteria waiting for the dolphin show to begin, and first they didn't want anything when he said he was getting himself a coffee, they wanted to look in the gift shop a few minutes, so he said okay, "but you know I'm not buying you anything in there, if you want something it's with your own money if you brought any with you, for I'm not loaning you any either—I mean, that junk, once we get home, just gets lost, is wasted," "We said we only want to look," Margo said, "and they have some very good things, even Mommy said so, ecology things, and I still have that shark mobile you bought me when Julie was just a baby," and he said "Yeah, ecology—you mean the ecology market, come on, go," and he sat with his coffee at a table, they came out of the shop and Margo said they were hungry now and wanted a hotdog and soda, "No soda, your teeth," he said, "and you'll eat a hotdog each?—they're two bucks here, I don't want to waste any more money," and Julie said "When did we waste any of yours today, Daddy?—we have membership cards, so that's already paid for, and we haven't asked you for anything so far," and he said "Please, first split a hotdog, and also a juice or iced tea or something good but with two cups, and if you finish those you can have more," and they got a hotdog, he cut it in half with the penknife he keeps on his key ring, they didn't want anything to drink if they couldn't get soda, "That's all right," he said, "you get too much sweet stuff as it is—I'm not blaming you but I've been too easy with you on that," Margo took a bite, grimaced, put her hotdog down, Julie put hers down right after without taking a bite, Margo had that guilty look, Julie's a bit bewildered, he said "What's wrong?—no, I bet if I asked Julie she wouldn't know, for she's just following you," "I am not," Julie said, he said "I won't test you, sweetie, I'm not here to even old scores," "What's that mean?—something nasty I bet," "It means nothing, it means I'm saying the wrong things—what's the matter, Margo, suddenly stuffed?" and she said "I'm sorry but it tastes awful, full of ugly fat-juices," he said "That's the water it's cooked in probably, so a tiny bit greasy, so what?" and she said "I don't like grease, I'm not eating it," and Julie said "That's what's wrong with mine too and I'm not saying it because Margo did—it looks greasy," and he said "But we paid two bucks plus tax for it—why do you two always ask for things—not 'always' but often enough for things if you know you're not going to eat them?—just think if I had let you have two," "You'd be crazy with anger now," Margo said and he said "A little angry, sure, maybe, for the waste," "Well, the second one might have been a good one and we'd split it, for this one isn't—taste it yourself," and he said "I don't like hotdogs, at least this kind, full of pork and junk," and she said "Then you shouldn't have let us get it if it's that," and he said "You wanted it, I didn't think half of one would be bad for you, you have them so infrequently," and she said "I wouldn't have wanted it either if I'd known what was inside, but it also just doesn't taste good, Daddy, it tastes spoiled and I've lost my whole appetite," and Julie said "I did too," and he said "Oh boy, you two are a real pair," and bit into Julie's half—it looked more palatable, cleanly cut, not chewed, for he has no compunction about eating food his kids had their mouths on, in fact they're the only ones he'd do that with, he doesn't even do it with his wife except maybe if she wants to give him a spoonful of her soup because she thinks he has to taste it it's so good, he doesn't know why, maybe something that goes way back to when older people talked to him about diseases and germs and he thinks at least he and the kids have the same kind—and chewed and swallowed and said "It's fine, not poisonous, an overcooked pork hotdog like all the rest but less spicy than the ballpark kind, but if I was going to have it with anything, then mustard, not ketchup, which you kids slopped on—here, eat it," and held it out to Margo, she pushed his hand away and said "I told you, I'm no longer hungry," "Come on," he said, "eat, eat, my child, have some, but at least you tried it—but you too, Julie, you haven't touched it and this half was yours," and put it up to her mouth, she shut her eyes, mouth was open and he pushed the hotdog against her teeth, some of the ketchup got on, tears were coming, the chest starting its heaving, he took his hand away and said, didn't want to but did, wanted to placate them in some way but didn't, "What a goddamn waste my family is, a waste, from top to bottom, the worst, I wish I was through with you all," and looked away, knew he was hurting Julie more than Margo because Margo stood right up to him while Julie cringed and probably now felt humiliated, that ketchup taste in her mouth, that in front of everyone he'd jammed that ugly hotdog against her clenched teeth, tears were probably dribbling down her cheeks or about to explode out of her eyes, probably a what-did-I-do-for-you-to-hurt-me-like-this? look, so he didn't look at her, either of them, didn't want to see Margo looking reproachfully at him for what he did to Julie, closed his eyes, opened them on the balcony-mezzanine above them and the railing around, people up there, for the time being happy families, boy on his mother's shoulders, father on one knee pointing something out to his daughter on the huge model whale hanging from the ceiling, his fingers, always back to his fingers, nails needed clipping and cleaning—that white stuff—wished he had one of his nail clippers he was always buying and losing or Margo and his wife were always borrowing and not returning, he'd maybe not clip—made too ugly a noise, that sharp ping and you could almost see from the sound the clipped nail piece flying off—but he'd clean his nails under the table, does that now, nails of one hand doing the nails of the other, after about a minute Margo said "Julie, let's go to the gift shop again—that okay, for a few minutes, Daddy?" he nodded without looking at her and said "No longer," and later, finishing his coffee—not bad for a big public cafeteria like this, richer roast or something like chicory in it—looked at his watch and thought Where the hell are they?—it's four, show begins at four and doors opened ten minutes before that, and looked around—place was almost deserted, Julie was on the balcony-mezzanine looking through a bolted-down telescope at some part of the whale—the barnacles under an eye if he remembered right from one of his last times here with them when she told him to take a look—and he yelled "Julie, what're you doing?—the show's starting; Jesus, what's with you two kids?" and she seemed frightened, confused, something, hand shot up to her mouth, looked around for Margo, maybe, to explain or help or just be with her—she think he was going to go crazy on them again, maybe even hit them, drag them out of here without seeing the show? he felt like leaving because of their actions but wasn't going to, wanted to see the show himself, got a kick out of the way the two dolphins together plunged and jumped and flipped and dived and at the end slid into the wading area and waved their tails to the audience, and why was he getting so angry so many times today? she could be thinking—he didn't know, it happened sometimes, maybe it was chemical, the brain, a couple of times or more he thought maybe he has some pressure like a blood clot or tumor or another kind of clot on it that makes him act that way, but he did get like this about once a month for a few hours a day, unexplained anger and losing control and sometimes total rage, kicking over chairs, sweeping things off tables, at the top of his lungs yelling "shit" to no one in particular, sending the kids running into their rooms or outside and provoking his wife to come in if she was outside or into the room he was in if she was in another, for he never did any of these things in front of her, and say "What is wrong with you today? It's horrible for the girls and not so pretty for me. Maybe you should see a therapist about it—if it were me I would," and thirty seconds after he'd told himself to control himself there'd be a similar rage—"Julie," he yelled, "where's your sister?—we're late, the announcement just said the thing's starting, get Margo," and she leaned on the railing and said "She's probably still in the gift shop," "So go get her, now, now," and she said "But the show's on this floor and I'll have to walk up again to see it—it's closer to you, Daddy, right over there," and she gave him an opening and her gestures and look said she was ready to put it all behind her but he said "No arguments, I said to get her," and she ran around the balcony and downstairs and into the shop and quickly came out with Margo who had a look-for-angry-look look, her defense, offense, meeting him halfway, whatever, well okay, he can understand that, he's been acting insanely, or just some way—testily, irritably, disagreeably, belligerently, tyrannically—but at least he wasn't shouting and snapping now, his face might still be a petulant mess but he was, he felt, calming down some, and he had embarrassed them, don't forget that, they hate it when he lashes out at them in front of others or just anytime, any criticism when people are around, really any criticism anytime, though at least here it wasn't in front of anyone they knew, and he said to himself as he walked upstairs with them "Now keep calm, go easy, be gentle and understanding," and said under his breath a few seconds later "Damn freaking kids," and Margo said "What?" and he said "Nothing," and she said "You still angry at us?" and he said "No, why should I be, it's over with," and Julie said "You are too angry, your eyebrows are down," and he said "I said I'm not, so I'm not, do you hear? I'm not, not, though don't bloody hell tell me I've no reason to be, two of you disappearing like that when you knew, Margo the most because she's the oldest, that we had a show to go to in a few minutes," and Margo said "You should have reminded us better," and he said "What did you want me to do, stick a sticker on you with the reminder and an alarm on it that went off ten minutes to four and also with some recorded voice equipment attached that

said 'You should be with your daddy, find your daddy, you have
to go to the dolphin show with your daddy,' " and Julie was laughing and he said "What's so goddamn funny?" and she shut up and
looked scared again and he said "Ah, nothing would have stopped
Margo from staying in that stupid shop and having a fifth and
sixth look at those chintzy knickknacks and assorted trash," and
walked ahead of them, telling himself "Why didn't you stop when
you had the chance?—not because you can't, you could have, that
stuff about brain chemistry and clots is pure crud, and when she
laughed that was when you could have relaxed things, said ha-ha to
yourself, 'What a dumb bunny I am,' " and looked back, they were
several feet behind and he went back and said "Okay, I'm acting
wrong, I know, but so what?—we'll work it out later but now we
really have to move if we want to be let in—you don't want to see it,
fine, we'll go home," and Margo said "No!" and moved faster but
Julie, downcast, dragged even slower behind and he said to her
"Come on, come on, what is it, you got to give me a fight with everything I ask?—move, move," and shoved her shoulder forward to get
her to walk faster and right away knew what it would do, "Oh,
you're impossible," and walked fast to the nearest entrance, gave the
man their tickets and said "Other two are for the little slowpokes behind me if they're still there, I really don't care," and went through,
what the guy must be thinking now, he thought, and knew if he
turned around he'd see Julie crying, Margo comforting her, turned
around, they were past the turnstiles, man was taking a few more
tickets, she was holding Margo's hand, staring at the ground and
about to cry, and he looked around: place is packed, show hadn't
begun, window curtains have already been closed, "Come on, girls,
hasn't started yet, we're lucky, but no seats except at the side sections
way on top—knew we should have got here earlier," and went up the
stairs—did he have to add that about "earlier"?—and into one of the
left-side aisles with three to four spaces together on the bench, and
sat, "Damn," he thought, "ruined everything for the day when it
could have been so nice, sitting here with them, talking about what's
to come, seeing their excitement, and then for hours after, ruined it

for them, himself, who knows what else?"—kids were standing in the aisle, not wanting to sit with him?—"Come on in, water's fine, everything's okay, really—sit before someone takes your seats," and Margo pushed Julie in first, and when they were seated he said to Julie "Listen, my dearest, I'm so sorry, I got excited, it wasn't your fault and I didn't mean to hit your arm and I apologize, deeply I do," and she looked at the two women and men in wet suits hustling from opposite sides to the center of the bridge behind the main pool, and he touched her hand, she pulled it back and he said "Please speak to me—I'm not so bad, and like everyone else, I have my off days, and I truly hate being mean to you, which I admit I was, I was, and seeing you sad and I want to apologize and I'll do my best not to act like that again—I am apologizing, in fact," and she said while looking at the huge monitor above them showing the trainers patting the heads of the two dolphins and sticking fish in their mouths "It wasn't my arm, it was my shoulder—I'm sure it's sprained it hurts so much," and he said "It's not, believe me, and I'm sorry, your shoulder, not your arm, I forgot," and one of the women said into what must have been a portable mike attached to her suit "Hello, everyone," and a few people in the audience said hello and she said "Say, where am I?—there's no response out there—is there human life in this big beautiful space?—hello, all you bipeds, welcome to the"—"What's a biped?" Margo asked him and he said "Two feet, walking," and she said "Like a person?" and he said "Only," and she said "Ostriches walk with their two feet and don't fly," and he said "But they've wings, even if they're not working— I don't know, maybe you're right"—"National Aquarium's Marine Mammal Pavilion show"—"Or maybe an ostrich's feet don't count as that-kind-of-feet bipedal," he said, "for they're two- or three-toed, aren't they? and penguins and other flightless birds like that neither because their feet are webbed, I think—we'll look it up when we get home. . . . Margo asked me what's a biped," he said to Julie, "—do you know?" and she said "I don't care"—"Now this time let's hear a rousing boisterous hello so I know you're out there," and hundreds of people including Margo and he shouted hello—he never had before at any kind of event like this, just thought it might do something to get Julie more interested in the show and away from her hurt, Daddy as one of the excited guys instead of his usual just watching things quietly—"Say, now that's a lot better, because for a moment there I thought you folks had fallen asleep into the arms of Morpheus on me just when our wonderfully charming dolphins are about to do their superextraordinary things," and he said into Julie's ear "I swear, my darling, I only meant to give you a tiny push to move faster and I accidentally must have done it harder—I was afraid there'd be no seats left and we did get here just in time for these—you saw," and she said "You pushed me hard because you were angry and wanted to hurt someone—you get like that; Mommy and Margo even say it," and he said "When do I? and what an accusation, and saying the family agrees with you—it's totally untrue, I'm not like that, or only a little, which is no more than anybody, but let's talk about it later and watch the show, it should be good." Later: kept sneaking looks at her to see if she was still angry at him or just if she was starting to enjoy the show, which would mean she'd taken her mind off the shoving incident and his other blowups, and she seemed to— laughed, slapped her hands, said "Oh my gosh" to something the dolphins were doing, slipped some Aquarium brochure into the book he was holding, and near the end of it—they'd seen the same show three or four times this year, or it was a little changed from the first one they saw when there was a third dolphin who'd since died—she got up and sat on his lap with her back to him, not once looking at him when she was on it—maybe her way of making him feel better or saying she felt better and had accepted his apology and even now believed his excuse for the shove or maybe just to see the show better, though couldn't be that since they were up too high already and no one had been blocking her view, or because the wood bench was getting uncomfortable or she was cold or tired or scared of something in the show, or something. Anyway, after about a minute of her being up there he kissed the back of her head and she didn't turn around or say or do anything.

INTERSTATE 6

Guy pulls out a gun. What do you do when someone does that? You can't duck; you're driving in the center lane of a huge highway and there's nobody in the front seat with you to grab the wheel. You've kids in back. They're the first things you think of, right?—first ones, but you think of yourself too almost at the same time because of whatever's self-preserving in you or something but more important that if he gets you he gets the kids. He shoots at you and hits, car could go off the road left or right and at the speed you're going and if he hits you good, there'd be a terrific crash. Car could go across the median strip and into traffic coming the other way, if it first didn't hit the guy's car or another one in that lane, or go across both roads, if it missed all the cars on them, and hit some trees in the woods on the other side. Or it could turn over on the strip because there's a little dip in it, or on the right side past the shoulder because there seems to be a trench there, or just turn over without any trench or dip because of your car's speed and that you lost all control of the wheel. One way or the other, if you get shot so bad where you immediately lose control of the car, kids won't have a chance, and guy's so close, his arm straight out and gun maybe three feet from your face, there's almost no chance he'll miss. So what do you do, for christsake, what do you? You yell, your first reaction, at the man "What the hell you doing, please don't, put it back, the gun," and to the kids right after that "Duck, kids, duck, guy in the next car's got a live gun on us." They scream, you're screaming, guy's laughing, driver's laughing so hard he's choking, and slapping the dashboard with his hand and steering with the other and gun's pointed at you and then slowly back to the kids and their car's still beside yours and keeping up with anything you're doing to get away from it, dashing forward, braking and fading back, and you're yelling "Don't, you can't shoot," your window's open, sonofabitch tricked you into it, signaled something amiss with your car and wanted to tell you what, "please get away, there are kids there, don't aim that at them, have a heart, oh my God," and then you think, what do you think? "Think, think," you think, "think quick," and you think "Off the road fast as you can, off, off, don't cut across to the strip as you can get killed doing it, get on the right shoulder right now," and quickly check the rearview and right side mirrors, no cars anywhere near but theirs, swerve into the slow lane and they get in the lane you just left, onto the shoulder and they get in the slow lane and stay close beside you, gun still held straight out but now back at your head, and you're screaming and kids are screaming and their car keeps going when you start stopping and just when you think they're gone for good and you've come to a complete sudden stop and say "Kids, stay down," gunman starts shooting. Youngest kid's dead, that's it. You know right away when you hear no sounds from her but plenty from the oldest. All your shouts for her to say something don't produce anything but more screaming from your other girl. Know when you then jump around and look back and down and see her on the floor in her blood, looking as if she were playing dead. Whatever you might have done it could have ended up same way or worse, right? What could you have done, and what could have been worse? You know what. Not you getting killed. Your own life for years has been just so much shit and will be infinitely worse after this. Nah it hasn't been that bad but for years you have been feeling frazzled and short of breath, there's been just brief stretches of pleasure and leisure and fun every now and then and some every-now-and-then semiserious satisfying rumination and work but for the most part it's been pressures and stresses and a lot of disjointed to coordinated running around at your job and for your wife but mostly for your kids, and now there's this, essentially ending it. What would have been worse is if both kids had been shot dead instead of one. Better than that but much worse than what happened, one dead and the other maimed for life. Both maimed like that? Better than one dead and the other maimed or okay, so better than the rest. Easy to say what would have been the best. You've thought lots of times before this about both kids dying at the same time, usually after you went through a new near disaster with them. Most of it regarding cars: couple of near collisions; also the time your car spun around on an oil slick on a narrow bridge and wound up facing a car bearing down on it. Driving them down the hill to school just after starting out but with the antitheft steering-wheel bar still locked to the brake pedal and you thought you were all going to die and screamed it out before you came to your senses in about five seconds and switched the ignition off and stepped on the emergency brake and turned the wheel to the right far as it would go and guided the car as best you could to a stop against the curb. Street corner where a truck climbed onto the sidewalk where the three of you were and came within inches of clipping them. When the three of you were on a plane to Europe to hook up with your wife—not a near disaster but a thought as the plane took off. In a rowboat when it capsized about a hundred feet out in a sound and for a while when it was getting dark you didn't know how you were going to get to shore without dragging them there. Opened windows in your in-laws' apartment—again, just a thought till you closed or lowered them all. Times you pulled out of a parking spot without first checking the left side mirror or turning around and looking at the street and though no cars had ever shot past at that moment, at least when the kids were with you, you wondered what if one had and crashed into you? Better, with those men, to have rammed their car with yours—this is what you could have done— and then veered right into the slow lane or, if that was the lane you were already in, onto the shoulder, but what good would that have done? Maybe sent their car out of control and where it might have gone into a ditch and rolled over or just scared the shit out of them, making them think "This prick means business, let's get the fuck away," or maybe it only would have knocked the gun from the guy's hand when the two cars suddenly hit. Or maybe you could have slammed their car exactly where the gunman was, one sharp left into it that smashed the guy's hand, and then sped right to get off the road, or dropped back and, after checking your mirrors, cut across the road to the median strip and over it to the part of the highway going north or just stayed on the strip honking and your emergency lights flashing and you outside the car shouting for passing cars and trucks or a state trooper to stop and your free hand flagging them down, and if the men came back for you on the road going north or just across the strip, you could have got off it one road or the other and tried to do something else to escape them—made straight for a state police station if there was a road sign saying one was coming up. You don't remember seeing one when you drove south but maybe you missed it or there's one further on or is north on the highway a few miles or so but on the other side of it, like the station. But it could have ended up worse than what happened or you imagined so far. The guy could have shot you in the eye when he saw you making a sharp left at their car and yours could have gone off the road with you already dead and it could have been hit by their car or another one coming from behind or just crashed on its own because you were no longer controlling it, rolled over and exploded or caught fire, kids dead before the car stopped rolling or before it exploded, or dead in the explosion, or worse, trapped in the car and burned alive.

What do you do the moment you know your kid's dead? You say to yourself you don't know, she isn't dead, she might look it but she's not, all that blood around her and the expression she has and no signs of life anywhere can possibly be, can only mean, they have to be just that she's deeply unconscious, hit hard on the head when the car suddenly stopped and she was thrown against the front seat, cut in the head too, gashed, torn, scalp bleeds like hell, but not dead, in no way is she. So you think you should do everything you can quick as you can to help her if she's hurt and save her if she's close to being dead. That's what you should do, that's what you do, even if you think when you look at her again on the floor in back with all that blood around her and her expression the way it is and still no signs of life anywhere, that she's probably dead, could be, no, isn't. So you rush her to a hospital in your car. Before that you breathe into her mouth and pound her chest to get her lungs and heart going again if they've stopped. You don't pound her chest. You wouldn't know how. You'd hurt her before you helped her or chances of hurting her and maybe finishing her off, if she has any life yet, by pounding her chest are greater than not. And her chest has a bullet hole in it, or what you think looks like one—and that was a gun the guy shot—and probably a bullet inside. There's blood coming out of the hole and has to be the reason for all the blood around her, for she has no other cuts, gashes or tears you see after quickly scanning her from head to foot, and you press your hanky on the hole and when the hanky's soaked through you pull your shirt off and press it on the hole and then, when that doesn't stop the bleeding, a little into it, while you breathe into her mouth. Things you don't think will work but one chance in a thousand or tens of thousands or a million they might. You once heard—you don't think this then but it probably influences your actions in some underlaid way to do everything you can to help and save her, to do both at once, help-save, help-save, for you don't know how badly off she is but feel she has to be very badly off since she still isn't moving and doesn't seem to be breathing and still hasn't given a single sign of being alive. Anyway, to do everything you can for her right away and not just give up because she looks dead and start screaming and wailing and beating your head or think the only thing you can do for her is drive her to a hospital, if you can find one or in time. For where are you on this road? What exit was last, which one's coming up? Are you a mile or ten or even twenty miles from one? And you didn't hear this but got it from a friend in a letter he sent you more than twenty years ago, or a phone call. He'd settled on the other coast and was in a van with his son around Julie's age at the time and was high or drunk, he said, when the van got stuck and then stalled on the tracks at a railway crossing when a train was coming—no. He was going too fast around a sharp turn, he said, and the van went out of control and slammed into a wall. It was in fact a motorcycle they were on, boy holding on to him in back, neither in helmets— they weren't compulsory in that state then, not that he would have worn one himself if it had been the law, he later said, though he would have put one on his son if only because his wife would have made him or she wouldn't have let the kid on the bike, as he called it—and he hasn't ridden one since because of that acci- dent and can't even get himself to be a passenger on one—when he lost control while trying to take an almost ninety-degree curve about thirty miles over the posted speed limit—"I was young, dumb, cocky and sloshed and thought I could make it with mph's to spare and give the kid one of life's biggest kicks and make him think his dad was great"—and flipped over a highway barricade and landed in some bushes though the kid hit a tree. The railway- crossing accident was a few years later when he was alone. He leaped out of the front seat when he heard the train whistling at

him and the van was demolished. The boy had a hole in his head
the size of a lacrosse ball, he said, and he could see the brains
and bones it was so deep. There was no breath, wiggling or heartbeat and he blew air into the hole after he gave up trying to revive
him by breathing into his mouth and pressing down on his chest.
When people tried tearing him off the boy he yelled "Don't touch
me or him, I'll kill anybody who tries," and blew and blew into
his son's head and after about a half hour of this the boy opened
his eyes and, his friend swore, smiled and said "Hi." It was a
miracle, he said, or a million-to-one shot defying all laws of science and biology and everything any expert knows about them
and he only thought to do it because after he stopped trying to
resuscitate him in normal ways a fingernail scratched through his
shirt into his back and he said "Ouch, whoever, get the fuck
away," and then turned around furiously to see who was still
scratching him and there wasn't anyone even near but he heard
the voice of his dead mother say "My dear, the trick's not to lick
or quit but to freshen his intellect with your breath without letup."
So what's your point? The point's that though your friend didn't
think this then he went against all odds and didn't give up when
everything seemed hopeless for his son and people were even trying to pull him away—but you've said that, so what's next?
What's next is you do it too, not into the bullet hole but her
mouth, not thinking what your friend did but only remembering
it weeks later and thinking it must have had an influence. Thinking
now that it's a million-to-one shot she'll survive but chances of
getting her to a hospital in time are even less, so if anything's
going to save her it'll be this, though you don't know why. So
you breathe into her mouth almost nonstop for about fifteen minutes while Margo, not close to the road because you don't want
her getting hit by anything or the air suck of a truck or bus to
pull her onto it, tries to wave cars down though maybe most of
them think she's waving them away or just waving hello at them,
when a car pulls over and driver asks what's up, anything he can
do? and takes you in your car, for you don't want to stop your

mouth-to-mouth breathing into her, to what he thinks is the nearest hospital though you have to know, he says, he's not from
around here but has driven through it a number of times. Says he
sees an H sign, follows it, no hospital or other H signs after a
few miles, stops at a gas station for directions, parks at the hospital emergency entrance, you run in shouting for someone, help,
your daughter, shot in the chest, maybe dying, please, anybody,
it's an emergency-emergency, come quick, doctors and emergency
equipment to your car outside, feeling by now they won't be able
to do anything for her and maybe you should have tried finding
a hospital yourself right after she was shot instead of spending so
much time trying to revive her with your breathing but also that
there just may still be a chance they will.

What do you do when two doctors or a woman and man in
white hospital coats who look like doctors or hospital officials
approach you with what you know, by their expressions and slow
walk and shoulder slump of the man that you know's unnatural
for him except in situations like this, is the worst news possible?
Not "news," just the worst information—not that, either. Just
with the worst thing that's ever happened to you, could happen
to you unless they were about to tell you that both your children
died or couldn't be saved. Seeing your kid shot and then being
told she's dead by someone in a position to know, are two of
the—the two worst things that can happen to you, or hearing she
was shot or in a terrible car crash or a fire, for instance, and hurt
very bad and might not survive and then later that she couldn't
be saved and died. Those two; those are the worst. Or that she's
got an incurable disease and has only two weeks to live, three, a
month but no more—two, but that's all: those might be better to
hear, compared to the others, but maybe not. You haven't experienced those so you don't know. You say to them "Don't say
anything, I can tell it's the worst news possible. Not 'news'—not
'information,' either. Just the worst thing, period. I don't want to
hear. See my ears, see my eyes?" You clamp your eyes shut, cup
your ears. "For it can't be, right? Please, for God's sake say any-

thing to me but what you're about to, if you have to say anything." "Well, we . . ." the man begins. "Look at me in a different way too. That she's okay—that kind of look and words. Or she's going to be or chances are still okay to good for her surviving or some other things from you like that," and the woman says "We wish we could, sir, all of us," and the man says "We did everything humanly and technically possible for her, Mr. Frey, and with the best medical equipment and professional expertise available in any hospital in the state. And there exists no better equipment and staff anywhere, and they all just happened to be here for a staff meeting at this particular time. But when it comes down to it"—"Didn't you hear me? What'd I just say?"—"we got her much too late, I'm sorry." "Much too, much too," the woman says. "We all share your grief." You raise your hands—you want to pound the walls with your fists, get down on the floor and bang it, throw things, push people around, scream some meaningless sound loud and long till your breath gives out—wiggle your fingers and keep wiggling them faster and faster in front of you while saying "Oh, what am I going to do, what am I going to do?" They look at your wiggling as if they've never seen this kind of reaction to what they've just told you. Your daughter, you think. Where's the other one? "Where is she?" and the woman says "She? The one who succumbed? Still in the room down the hall but we seriously advise you not to go to her just yet. Things need to be done with her, and you're not—" and you say "Not she, not Julie, but my other daughter, the older one. Why can't I remember her name all of a sudden? Starts with a what?—I can't even remember that, the first letter. I've never forever—I've never forgotten it ever. I've called her 'Julie' by mistake lots of times when I was intending to call her by her own name. And 'Lee,' I've called her, which is my wife's, just as I've done to Julie and Lee with Margo's name and Julie's for Lee's and vice versa— 'Margo,' that's who. So where is she?" Then "Oh no, I can't take this, it's the worst truth imaginable, possible, portable, execrable, inexcusable, none of those, call it quits," and your head's dizzy and stomach feels sick as if you've got to shit, bowels hot and knees weak and your legs, arms, fingertips, every part of you hurtles and whirls and you want to collapse and spill, when you hear someone yell—your eyes are closed now and you're going— "Guy's absolutely green, catch him," and you're grabbed as you fall, hit the ground anyway and black out and next thing you're lying on a soft bench, head up into a metal dish, you've made in your pants, kaka, vomit, piss, you don't care but the mix stinks, smelling salts held close to your nose, your head bolts and chin clips the bottle, "Get it away," you think and slap at the hand holding it. "Leave me be. I'm all right. I just want to stay passed out for good," and a man says, not the doc, "Sir, Mr. Gray? Listen to me if you can. Your daughter Margo's fine, being attentively looked after by the staff. The police, who think this urgent, would like you to answer some very important questions about the crime. I'm only doing what they ask, sir, so may I help you up?" and you say "Get me pants, get me pants, I can't see people like this."

How do you sit and answer questions from the police? How do you just listen to them when they're talking, know what they're saying, understand what to answer, provide them with details, descriptions, an account of, facts? What the fuck stops you from jumping up and running out the room and beating your head against a wall? Pulling at your hair till it comes out, smashing your nose with your fist, scratching your scalp till it tears, breaking some mirror or glass—just running through a glass door or hurling yourself through a window or just at one and slashing your neck and wrists with a sliver the shattering makes? They've brought you to a room—"This is a doctors' conference room," a police detective says, "but it's all right for us to use it long as we like, though we want to be brief, faster we get after the bastards the better—have a seat, sir—is that one comfortable enough?—would you prefer mine? But we're wasting time. Let's get right to business." You wondered when they escorted you here "Is the room she's in anywhere near? Could it be right next door and I don't know it? Is someone with her? She shouldn't be left alone. Suppose she awakes? Don't be ridiculous." The doctor from before had pointed at a hall when he talked about her but you're all turned around in this hospital, this corridor might only be for conferences and offices and a common staff room for breaks, that corridor for surgery and dissections. "Autopsies" is the word. You sat. Big as she is, they wanted her there for what she could offer, and she sat on your lap. You mean, big as Margo is, and she's also big for her age, second-tallest girl in her class—Julie was small in both categories—she sat on your lap. But how do you just sit there without wailing, talking to yourself, going crazy? Because it's too soon for you, right? Too soon to say "Yes, no, that'd be an accurate assumption, they were this feet tall, weighed in about six-eighty." But you're expected to answer, aren't you? You agreed to come in here to, didn't you? They . . . you . . . they made it seem essential, you felt you had to. You've always been obedient to the police. This goes way back when you were a boy, afraid of them, and you know what you're here for—to answer things that'll help catch the bastards, as the detective who's asking keeps calling them. "I'm sorry, young lady, but it's hard to keep back what I feel about them, and it's not such a dirty word." And to you: "We want, as you must, to catch those filthy bastards and roast them, fry their behinds good, which we can now do in this state, thank goodness, unfortunately only with lethal drugs." Margo asks what's "lethal" and you say "Later." "So, we need your help, sir, young lady," when just about all you can do right now is think of Julie and important things you haven't done yet. Like what? Like call your wife about your girl being shot dead. So, so, what're you going to do, call soon? Right after this? Before you see Julie? For another thing you must do is see her before she's taken away to be examined by the police doctors and perhaps changed irresomethingly. No, they'll do a clean job and there's no reason for them to touch her face and you won't see the incisions they make for they'll be under her burial clothes. But you don't want to see her again after you see her today, do you? No, no open casket, but at the last minute you probably will ask for it to be opened, even if your wife doesn't want to look, so you can take one last quick one, or a long one, so long that the funeral people will tell you they have to close it now so they can start the ceremony. "Please, Mr. Frey, your daughter Margo's answering us just fine, but can you concentrate a bit more on our questions, we want to go after those hyenas tonight." Possible height and weight or let's say, since you never saw them not seated, size and shape of the men and definitely their skin color and complexions and shades and any particular marks, scars, smudges, tattoos on their faces and hands and arms or anywhere and distinguishing features like big ears and fat lips and slanty eyes and large Adam's apples and anything around their necks or on their chests, crosses, stars, ankhs, jewelry of any kind and on their fingers and wrists like watches, rings, bracelets and ID's, cuffs up or down and with cufflinks, and their ages, hair, voices, facial fuzz of any sort including sideburns, eyeglasses, sunglasses, mannerisms, gestures, whatever seemed even minutely unusual to you or the norm, clothes, color, style, design, buttoned, zippered, tight, loose, good condition or bad, hats, ties, gloves, even—suspenders, epaulets, earrings or studs, maybe something through their noses, bandages anywhere or adhesive strips, patches on their clothes, hair curling out of or above their shirts, big foreheads or like pushed in, what kind of smiles and laughs, any obvious dental work or tooth gaps or decay, some of these creeps have front teeth with diamonds in them and platinum- or gold-trimmed which if they had smiled right at you you would have seen, any chance of recalling the color of their eyes? They want them to remember everything about the men and their car, the make, shape, if raised like dune buggies, logos and stripes, how many doors, were the windows clean, rolled up electronically or by hand, radio music or just boppy patter from a radio or tape, overhear any station's call letters, you never know but that can pinpoint where they were heading or coming from, anything hanging from the front mirror like baby shoes or oversized dice or lying on top of the dashboard like a Mary or Christ statue or even a paperback and if so, title or what the cover looked like, tires: white-rimmed, fancy hubcaps, license plate of course, anything on the roof or attached in back, their car hauling a trailer, you wouldn't believe it but some people have even forgotten to tell us that, scratches, dents, horn sound, and the gun: color, shape, report the shot made, did it look like this, or this, this, showing photos of hand-guns, then of cars, none of them is it though the car's color is like this one, as if just painted a bright white, was the muffler noisy or any other parts of the car not seem all right, the men's or just the gunman's accent, any speech impediments or problems and any special phrases and foreign words and obscenities re-peatedly used? While you periodically drift to ways of dealing with those guys if they're caught. "And they will be," the detec-tive said, "make no mistake about it. I mean, I can't give you my word on that, but they have to be, don't they, but not with-out your full help." You'll get them during the trial. First day of it before you have to testify yourself about what happened, but how will you be able to do that? "There they are, I recognize both of them, they killed my little girl, I could never forget their faces, except when they were driving alongside us they had sinis-ter grins or big smiles," though who knows if they won't have them at the trial? In other words, you'll deal with them soon after they're brought into the courtroom. How? You'll wear a fake mustache or by then grow a real one and maybe a beard and comb your hair in a different way or let it grow long or cut it very short or maybe get a wig or just a hairpiece to cover your bald spots. In other words, disguise, so you won't be recognized, by reporters, for instance, for there's sure to be a news story or item about Julie today and they may want to follow it up, and people in the prosecutor's office who will have probably inter-viewed you by then or at least seen you for various reasons a couple of times, and any of the police here who might be at the trial. You'll sit in the spectators' section, but fairly close to the front, and then, right after the judge's call for a recess or a five- or ten-minute break for some legal question to be settled, when a lot of people will be milling around—in other words, when there's a little confusion or commotion or just movement and everyone doesn't have to be in his seat—you'll walk up front with a hidden gun, if you can get one, and you should be able to with so many illegal guns around and your willing to pay ten times the street price for one, or just legally in another state if you have to, and shoot them both in the head. Bing bing, like that, one shot each through the middle of the skull if you can do it or inside the ear and then, when they're on the ground or staggering, though one in the head should knock them flat down, and if the gun hasn't been wrestled away from you, more shots into them but only if you're sure, as you should be when you first shoot them, that nobody else will get hit, and closer to the head or heart the better. If a guard or someone else approaches you when you're walking down the aisle or tries to stop you by saying something like "That's as far as you're permitted to go, sir," you'll run to the front, dodge the guard or whomever and maybe several others some way and jump over the barrier sepa- rating the trial area from the spectators' section, if there's one, and the men will probably be turned around by now to the uproar, and you'll shoot them in the head if you can or the face. If you can't get a gun on the street and there's no time to go out of state and wait the mandatory period for a legal gun, or you get one one way or another but metal detectors prevent you from bringing it in the courtroom or courthouse, and you'll check all that out before, you'll get two icepicks or something long, spikelike and needle-sharp and do the same thing during the recess or break and quickly stick them into their necks or backs or one after the other into their skulls or anywhere you think would be the best place to kill them with one jab or if that doesn't work out then at least to maim them for life, killer first, driver next, for you hate the killer most and want to make

sure to get him if you've only time to get one. Or you'll wait
for them outside the courthouse after the first day of the trial,
if you get a gun but can't get inside with it and know they'll be
coming out at a certain place—you'll check on that too, pay
someone for the information if it can be done without raising
any suspicion to you—you'll say you're an amateur or art photographer who specializes in candid crime photographs—and
when the men come out with their police escorts you'll go up
close as you can to them, but in disguise, and say "Hey, Joe,"
or whatever the killer's name is—"Sly" or "Zippo" or something
if he's got a street name—to get him to stop for a few moments
and maybe turn all of his body to you so you can get a clearer
shot, or "Hello, I'm a reporter"—of the *New York Times,* of
the *Wall Street Journal*—and if you can you'll pay for some kind
of phony press credentials and display them on your jacket or
better yet, since a reporter from one of those papers may be
there or from any other you got credentials for, wave them—
"and I'd like to ask these gentlemen some quick questions if the
police don't mind." Or you won't say anything. You'll just stroll
up to them and their police escorts as if you're a curious ob-
server, with a "Hey, what's happening?" kind of face, or just as
some idiot who gets a kick out of gawking at celebrities, even
murderers, and shoot them in the chest or head. If they're
brought out separately you'll wait for the killer, if he's not the
first to emerge, and aim the gun at his head, or at his heart and
downward if someone's behind him, since if the bullet goes
through him you don't want it hitting anyone else but his friend,
and shoot several times till you're sure you got a couple of good
shots in. Then when he's on the ground and if you're not over-
powered by the police yet, you'll fall on top of him and shove
the gun barrel into his mouth or against his ear or into it far as
it'll go and shoot again. If you can't get them inside the courthouse or right outside it that first time you try, you know you'll
never have another crack at them again. Bumper stickers you
can remember, the police say, decals on the windows or anything

else like that you saw? Special beaded seat pads that some people use for back comfort on long drives. Scratches, dents, paint discolorations, but they've said that. Then they show you a book with many more car pictures and you identify what you're almost sure's the right one. Margo says it's not and you say "If this one's not it then it comes as close to looking like the car those guys were in as I can get. Just that ought to be of some help."

Police say they have all the information they need for the time being and you can see your daughter now if you like, what do you do? When they say that your stomach and limbs get all sick and weak again and you feel as if you're going to pass out. "Margo, please, get off me, I feel ill," for she's still sitting on your lap. She jumps off and you put your hands over your face and try to think what to do. Police have said "So long, lots of luck, we're very sorry, we'll be speaking some more to you, I'm sure," and it's just you and Margo in the room with a doctor who'll accompany you to where Julie is if you want to go now and a nurse to look after Margo till you get back. "If you'd rather not see her this minute," the doctor says, "we've a private room you can rest in and we can also get a cot for Margo." You haven't told your wife yet and you don't know how you're going to. Margo may want to go in with you to see her dear sister and you don't know if you won't let her. It might be easier for you if she were there and it might be right for her to be there. Your wife would know what to do about it but that would mean you'd have to tell her about Julie. Then after you told her, the question whether should Margo go in with you to see Julie wouldn't ever come up. You'd be dealing just with Lee's despair and she with yours. Despair, that's the word, you don't think there's another one that gets it as well. The feeling: it's utter dejection, total disconsolateness, out-and-out grief. Maybe "grief" gets it as well, so maybe there are two. But what's that got to do with it, just part of the stall. So what do you do? Or maybe Margo will think she should go in but say something like, or not say it, just look it, that she's too sad and scared and sensitive to. She is, you don't want her in, not till your wife's with you. You haven't seen Julie since they rolled her away from you in front of the hospital when you first got here. "Out of the way," they screamed, and maybe at you, and they could, they were right, for what's your grief and despair compared to them having a second or two more to save her? And they did, what are you talking about, they didn't. How do you see her without cracking up? Going mad and getting as sad as anybody can get—complete grief, that kind of cracking up. Both, all. They no doubt have her all cleaned up and everything like that by now, presentable, and she'll be looking—oh stop it, but you're only trying to give yourself reasons—not "reasons" but some word that means you'll be able to face going in to see her— like a sleeping child. What like a sleeping child? She, she'll be, that's how she'll look. But that's how she looked on the car floor so she'll look, they'll make her look with all that cleaning her up and setting her on the bed in a just-so certain correct way, or whatever she'll be on and whatever way, even more like a sleeping child. And you'll look at her and remember her sleeping peacefully at home other nights or just recently when you went into her room at your in-laws' or fitfully, even, like a week ago when she had fever from an ear infection till your wife gave her some junior Tylenol and you'll want to kiss and hold her and breathe into her mouth which is probably not now like her mouth was or any live mouth is and kiss her skin which won't feel like skin either, you don't know how it'll feel but not like live skin or even like her skin when she was dead in the car. It'll be hard, you think, it'll be greasy, sticky, pasty, scaly, something like that, one of those, two, three. And you'll want to kiss, not kiss but talk to her quietly as if she's asleep or just coming out of sleep—yes, kiss, kiss, no matter what her skin and lips feel like—and tell her to lie still, don't get up, no need to, she's weak, you'll do everything for her, you'll sit her up and get her dressed and other things, you'll carry her and get her out of here, into the car, home. You'll go crazy, that's what, face it, out-and-out completely crazy, so how do you go in and see her, how, you're asking, what the hell do you do, do you know, do you? If you got Margo to go in with you and you held her hand when you went in and throughout it, even when you were touching Julie with your other hand, leaning over, kissing her, always one hand holding Margo's, it'd be easier for you, you know that, but you can't do that to Margo. It'll be bad for her, maybe devastating, more chance it'll be devastating than bad, something she might never recover from, nightmares for weeks at least, a great chance of that you're saying, later in life: "Why'd you force me to go in there with you, even allowed it if I'd asked you to? You should've known what it would do to me, do to anybody my age. It was cruel, stupid, I don't care what state of mind you were in then." She shouldn't go in, you know that now, but you have to see Julie, don't you? They want you to positively identify her—their words—but you're afraid to see her. Seeing her like that not breathing, and you'll immediately check to see if she's not—her mouth, heart, wrists, temple, neck, ankles, you'll feel, listen, look—will mean she's definitely dead, not coming back. Of course not coming back, you don't believe in that, you mean she can't ever be revived, resuscitated, she's dead, just dead, something you know now but it'll hit you worse then and drive you crazy with despair, crazy with grief, you'll go crazy in there, crazier than you are out here, fall to your knees, fall to the floor, bang your head with your fists, your chest, dig your nails into your skin, your face, claw into it, you'll feel sick, faint, you'll scream scream after scream, you won't be able to talk to your wife on the phone after about what happened to Julie, just that it happened, you won't, you won't even be able to say "Julie's dead, our daughter, murdered, I can't speak anymore," you won't, they'll put you under some sedation, they'll have to, you won't be able to look after Margo, take care of her for she's going to feel as bad as you, you know that. She feels it now, it just hasn't come out. She loves her sister, adores her, if they're on the street or in a mall or someplace and Julie suddenly can't be seen she says "Where's Julie?" and if you both don't know she runs around shouting her name and looking frantically for her even when you say "Don't worry, she can't be far, she's probably wandered into one of the stores, or she's hiding." She'll go crazy over it too, you know that and it'll probably be soon. Will you let them sedate her? Yes, you will, but little, little, just enough to tire her so she can fall asleep on her own, but you you'll want them to put out. No good, she'll probably wake up before you and then who'll deal with her? And you'll also have to deal with your wife soon, not "deal" and not "deal" with anything to do with Margo either, but "speak" to her, your wife, and then deal with what comes after from her and between you two and also what to do about Margo and the possibility of sedating her when she starts going crazy over Julie, but you don't know how you'll be able to tell your wife and just deal with it all. For instance, when, what's the best time, what words, so on? Before you see Julie?—you mean "after" you do, so you can say "Yes, she's dead, I've just seen her," or "I saw her just before in the exam room after the doctors were through with her, absolutely dead"—not like that. No "absolutely" or "doctors through with her," but problems, questions like that. You say to Margo "Margo, listen to me, this is absolutely important, I know how you feel about Julie—how you felt about her before and how you feel now, 'before' meaning all those years before and 'now' meaning now about her and just before—and you know how I do too with all those." She's standing, you're sitting, and you hug her from behind—you can't see her face, she might be crying—kiss her shoulder and head, press your nose into her back. She's not heaving, but heaving might only be a sign of heavy sobs, and it wasn't why you nuzzled her. You want to turn her around but don't want to because looking at her, even if she's not crying now, you both might crack up. Well, maybe that's good, what you need, but you don't know if it is right now, or for her right now too, especially for you when you have so many things to do including looking after her, and cracking up like that you might not come back from it for hours. So you'll let her turn around when she wants and you shouldn't talk about Julie anymore to her now either, you're too confused to, you might say the wrong thing and make her feel even worse than you're sure she's eventually going to, but you will say more, it's that craziness pushing you. "But, you know," to her back, still holding her, "I think I'm doing—I'm going—I don't think I want to—I know I don't but I think I'm going absolutely crazy over this, sweetheart, that's it, crazy with sadness and everything else that's the worst about it, and if I do go completely that way, well, I don't think there's anything to stop me from it, much as I want not to, as I don't want to, no words or cures, no person, nothing, not even my deepest strongest feelings to stay well and sane long enough or just sane and well enough to take care of you now." You didn't say this. There was no response from her, but that's not why. You are holding her, nose to her back, and have been for minutes, but you didn't say any of that. For a few moments, minute or two at the most, you were sitting here thinking you did. Rather, you saw yourself talking, heard yourself too, but you didn't, not a word, you think, maybe another sign of your craziness over Julie or whatever it is. How do you know you didn't speak? It just came to you, sort of like waking up and after a brief bit of befuddlement you suddenly know where you are. "Margo," you say, you actually say, you think, for her head moves around so she can hear better, or that's what it looks like, "I'm speaking to you now, sweetheart, aren't I?" and she nods. "Just say 'Yes you are,' or just a 'yes' so I know for sure, it's important to me," and she says "What do you mean, Daddy?" "Good, now I'm convinced. You see, before I only thought I was saying, but now I really am, that I think I'm going crazy over this whole thing with Julie, and I can't help it, it's the last thing I want to do right now, but it's killing me, for what happened to her's the worst thing in the world that could possibly happen except if it had happened to you and then it also would have been the worst. The two of you, if it had happened to, would have even been worse, but that didn't happen. In other words . . . in other words, I'm not making much sense, you can see that—hear it, I mean, which is just an example of my state of mind now, this state of mine. Listen to me: 'state of mind.' Oh no, this is too awful, I don't want to be alive for it, at least not awake," and she says "Daddy, you're hurting me, you're hugging too hard," and you say "Am I? I'm sorry, I didn't know, dear," and release her and the doctor says "Mr. Frey, is there anything I can do? I'm here to help you both as well as take you to your other daughter when you decide to go, and it'd be better if it were soon," and you break down and she pats your shoulder while you bawl and the doctor, you don't know what he does, and the nurse who was here for Margo, is she still in the room? Is the doctor just looking at you, at his watch, nurse too? That's no rebuke of them; they've been through these things a lot, in various versions, kids going from brain tumors, kids cut down on bikes, pieces ripped, parts split, parents wailing in the hallways, and they're both probably tired as all hell and they have their jobs to do, right? their jobs, and they want to get them done but do well at them and then go home. This isn't all there is, right? So what are you saying? Ask yourself, what? You don't know. No no, you do, what? No, you don't. You forget where you started off from, and it doesn't matter that you don't know, does it? At this time? What are you, kidding? Of course no. You feel a hand on your wrist. Maybe it's Margo's, maybe it's the doctor taking your pulse or just feeling your wrist. No, they just don't feel it, they take. Or the nurse, maybe he's instructed her with some gestures to go feel the guy's pulse, see if it's too fast, slow, whatever that's bad or shows a sign that he should be watched for something worse. But after this, you think, after this, while Margo's patting your back—you should be patting hers, shouldn't you? Hugging her softly too, but you don't—after this, what do you do? There's got to be a next step. It all doesn't become blank after this. This thing happened, this damn no-words-or-curses-for-it thing happened, and you've got to deal with it—yes, deal, deal, so start. For even if it's blank for a few days right after this, there's got to be a next step soon as the blank ends. You making sense? You don't care if you're not. You have to do something, that you know, and

around now, but what? Your wife to know, but when? There is
no best time, a doctor said, or one of the cops, but so what? In
fact now might be the best time for whatever you say and however
you say it, for it's all going to be bad or close to it, right? But
this way, in the state you're in or will be for the phone talk, you
can blame your terrible way of saying it on that: you're distraught,
out of your head, altogether crazed over it, you can say. But that's
fake, and the best time has to be when you're in better control,
for she's sure to be in worse shape than you on the phone for
this'll be the first she's heard it, so she's going to need you somehow. You don't know what you'll be able to do but just to be
there for whatever you might be able to, even to say "I know,
I'm insane over it, want to die myself," might be enough. Forget
it, there is no right or better way, you're in control or out of it,
there's no way of saying how you're going to say it or react to
what she does, you can feel you're in control one moment and
then suddenly blow it, you know she's going to be out of control
and that if you start off without any yourself you're not going to
suddenly get it. Anyway, it's all whatever's the word or words for
whatever the worst's going to be. Thing to do is get it over with,
and who says it has to come from you? It can come from the
doctor here, or the woman doctor from before or someone new,
or a police officer trained in this or the minister who tends to the
patients. One of them can say you're simply in no shape to tell
her what you and they think should be told her and then he can
tell her and deal with what comes best as he can. Is that the best
way? No, just another. If you had years to just think about it you
wouldn't know. So what do you do? Maybe the best thing is to
see Julie first. That again, but to get it done. That way, well,
you've gone over it. Because if you plan to tell your wife before
you see Julie, she might say "Why you so sure she's dead? You
haven't seen her since they took her away from you. Even if they
say she's dead, they could be mistaken. There was that case in
the papers not long ago where the paramedics pronounced this
man dead and then a few hours later the hearse people sticking

him into the hearse to go to the funeral home heard him gurgling. The doctors might have Julie mixed up with another girl, one around her age and who has the same hair color and is her race. Even one from a car accident or a shooting, all of which made them make the mistake. She might be on breathing equipment now, our girl, and getting better even while I speak to you, and perhaps even looking around for you now, wondering why you aren't there. Just your not being there now might be enough to sink her if she's barely holding on. So you have to go to her. I won't believe anything till you say you went in with a doctor to see her and he checked her again and she's dead." "Best to have a doctor beside you when you call your wife," a doctor said, "so he can answer any questions she may raise. And better if you tell her everything in that phone conversation." "I can't speak to her," you said, "you do it," and he said "I will if you wish but I feel strongly it's best it come from you, hard as that will be. One of us will be close to support you in every way in addition to treating you immediately if you collapse or anything like that." So what do you do? "What should I do?" you say to Margo, "about telling Mommy about dear Julie or my seeing Julie before I tell her?" and she says "Seeing Julie dead?" and you say yes and she says "How should I know? You decide, Daddy; don't bring me in it. I have my own problems, you know," and you say "I know, I know." So, what? You look at your watch: no time, just tick tick tick; you turn it around so the face is at the underside of your wrist. The nurse says to you "If you'd like, Mr. Frey, I can take Margo for some dinner now." Margo says she is hungry and would you mind? and you say "No, please go with her, my darling, it's right. We'll meet back here in a half hour," and the nurse says "We'll look for you in the lobby," and you say "Even better, I guess; easier to find." So Margo leaves with the nurse, looks back as she goes out the door and you think "Should I have offered the nurse money for Margo's food? Even for both of them, since she's taking my kid." The doctor says "So, Nathan?" and you say "Should I have given Margo money for dinner? I don't want that nice nurse spending all her hard-earned money," and he says "Not to worry. She'll get it back, if she wants, from petty cash. So, Mr. Frey?" and you say "So, you want me to choose what I'm going to do, right? See Julie, that's probably the best thing, the right one, right? See her right away, then call my wife. And I'll try not to collapse. Just, if you can come with me, or another doctor or a nurse, and wait outside her room."

So you go with the doctor to the room Julie's in and the doctor says, right outside it—door closed, no little window in it, legs so weak while you walked that the doctor had to hold your arm, you said "I think I'm going to fall, grab me," and he did, while you walked you thought "It's like an execution I'm going to, mine, hanging, shooting, injection, gas; fear, weakness, feeling you want to heave," sign on the door saying "Do Not Enter, Medical Staff Only, Permission Required"—"She's in there on the bed. It's not really a bed, we call it something else, but for our purposes we'll call it that." "What do you call it normally, meaning the technical calling—the word, you know?" and he says " 'Bed' will do." "But I'd like to know, if you don't mind. I'm not sure why, peculiar reasons probably, but just, could you?" "An examination table, that's all it is, but now it's made up to look like a bed—sheets, a pillow." "For under her head." "Under her head, yes." "You're giving me a lot of your time, I'm sorry." "It's okay, what I do." "I've been thinking of her head, only before, I think, on a pillow when she was alive. Everybody's sure she's dead?" He nods. "Then I'll see her in there. I mean, I would, of course, if she were alive, but I'm saying for now." You put your hand on the door. It has no knob or bar, only needs a push. Which side of the room will the bed be? The left, you guess. But it's a table, so may be in the middle. "Yell for me, 'Dr. Wilkie,' if all of a sudden you need assistance. Or if you want, I'll come in with you." "You've seen her?" "Uh-huh." "No, I want to see her alone." "I can go in and leave when you want. Or with a flick of your finger, if you can't speak, or point to the door." "Nah, I want it to be now just me and her. 'Me and she' sounds better but it's 'me and her, me and her.' Meaning, they go together, correctly, though in that case it could be 'she and I' for all I know. Why do I bring these things up? Delaying." "No matter what, I won't budge from here unless there's an emergency I'm absolutely needed for. Chances of that are minimal, and I've asked another doctor to fill in for me. But you never know." "You never know," you say. "And I suppose I should go in now, get it over with. Somehow I imagine her in the middle of the room on that table-bed, head on the left side of it, so, perpendicular to us," and you show with your hands in a T what you mean. "I believe that's the way it is." "So there. And all my life, you know, I've been getting things over with— no window in the room, probably." "None." "Lots of lights, some side tables with instruments and things on them, and so on. In fact, there's a standard joke, a running one, rather, around my household—no, it's no time for lines or jokes. This isn't one, what I was about to say, but might sound like it. I haven't told you it yet?" "If you mean now or before, not that I know of." "I think I've told everyone else in the world. I have so few things to say. Of interest. Though it always had a serious degree to it. *Side.* It borders. *Straddles.*" "Go on, tell me if it'll help relax and prepare you for going inside. Remember, here and now, anything you do or say is okay." "Right, better I feel that way, relaxed, prepared, so I don't crash first thing on seeing her, my dear kid, truly the dearest little girl-child-kid there ever was," and you start crying and you cry and say "Everybody says 'ever was,' I bet, everybody, in a situation like this, and I should stop all this kind of talk. Just saying it, of course I know what it'll do, so I have to wonder if I didn't say it just to go to pieces and delay some more my going in. There," patting yourself under the eyes, tears, "these goddamn these. Stop, stop, stop," slapping your cheeks. "But my nonjoke. Nonintended for one, the something I was going to say and will probably say it that I said might sound like a joke, and other times it could be. Now it's just a fact. An insight into me. So I'm telling it as an illustration of my always wanting to get things over with—trips, books, days, work, housecleaning, even sex sometimes. Cooking, quick, quick, quick. A joke to everyone I know, I can tell you, as if work to get rid of to clear yourself for the real or more important work, stuff that's killing you for you to do and which turns out to be the same thing, get rid of it, clear yourself for something else, and so on. So say it. Or do it. My hand's on the door again but I'm not pushing it even a quarter-inch. I can't seem to get in there. Whyever why? The example's this. That I want on my tombstone for it to read— Rather, that I want my epitaph to say on my tombstone, chiseled in— Rather, for 'tombstone' sounds so Western western—in other words, fake—that I want my head- or footstone—my gravestone epitaph to say, you know, under my name, birth and death dates—anywhere on the stone— 'So, I got it over with.' Just that. You see the point; message is clear, isn't it? It's not funny now. Of course, nothing is, goes without saying, and long way I told the story, end of it was dead before I got there," dropping your head, crying again, hand off the door. "This is too hard. Impossible. Why does it have to be? Her, I mean. I know, old question, but couldn't this all somehow be a wake-up dream? All that's done-before crap too, everybody must say it in a situation like this, and especially to you, true?" "But any other time your epitaph line would be humorous. I understand that. You got it over with—you're a man who likes getting things over with, and the big thing, the biggest, life, you're saying in this fictitious epitaph, you did." "Maybe it was 'Well, I finally got it over with' what I told my wife and friends countless—endless amounts—countless times. Or no 'well,' but a 'finally.' So just 'I finally'—and no 'so' either, so just 'I finally got it over with.' I think that's it. It is. Anyway, what's the damn difference? One of those. And I should get it over with, finally. I know I have to see her, I want to." "You're right when you imply I know how difficult it is," he says. "I've been through this with plenty of other people." "Other fathers? But ones who adore their kids? Love them, adore them, worship them; if there was one word for those three, then that?" "Fathers, mothers, husbands, children for their sisters or brothers—everyone close." "Okay. You close your eyes, you hold your breath, you push open the door and walk in. That's all you have to do, just those." You do them, push the door shut behind you without turning around, let your breath out and smell; nothing unusual, something medicinal; and open your eyes. She's as you imagined; on her back, sheet up to a little below her shoulders. Okay, you imagined it'd be up to her neck. Everything, whole room, sheet, her hair, neat. Eyes closed; of course, so nothing unusual to imagine; if they were open you'd leap at her and say "You're alive, you've opened your eyes, don't do anything, say anything, stay still, I'll get help. *I knew,* I *knew.* My God, this is the happiest moment of my life." Arms by her sides. Someone put them there. Imagine, arms were somewhere else, they almost had to be, across her, above her, twisted in some dead position, kept out of the way somewhere so they could examine her, and someone straightened them out and put them by her sides. This is all done for me, you think, has to be, and anyone else who comes to see her but not to work on her or take official notes. And then when I'm gone, what will they do? They'll have to lift her arms up, maybe one at a time, there might be some resistance, to pull the sheet down to do what they'll be doing to her later on. And under the sheet, what? Little skimpy hospital gown, you can see, and you're sure not tied or fastened in back, and holes, some exploratory, one from the gun, maybe some stitched or just pinned or taped closed for the time being so the medical examiners from the hospital or county can resume looking into her later on. Ah what do you know? You know this, that she's there in this very white room with you, a room for sure not for sleeping or recovering, palms up. But you're not feeling, you thought by now you'd break down and drop. You'll feel, plenty, after this; for now, you want a good look first. They place the palms that way too? They were able to? That resistance. Put the arms down, turn the hands up if they weren't, even separated

the fingers so they'd look natural and not gnarled? Pinky so
much distance from the second finger and so on? What do you
think, nature did it on its own? Please, these are experts you're
talking about here, every big hospital has to have them, a series
of them on duty or call twenty-four hours a day seven days a
week, must be hundreds of them in the state, maybe tens of
thousands in the country, a hundred thousand in the world,
trained to do these things, think of it, and like the doctor said
they've been through it plenty of times. Hell, if he has, so have
they. So? So, she doesn't look as though she's sleeping. Isn't that
what she's supposed to be? Maybe they were in too much of a
rush to fix her up for you or that's a job the funeral people do,
not the hospital's. Here, just make her presentable for the hospital viewing. And you, what are you doing? You're not feeling,
you don't even look as if you are, you can feel that in your face
and the way your body's so straight, not bent from suffering,
also your legs not weak or knees buckling. I told you, this is
how I'm approaching it now. I want to take in everything while
I have the chance, not miss a trick. And all for myself, to steep
myself in it after, for I won't tell anyone else. Later I'll have
plenty of time to fall to pieces and I'll be doing it every way,
body, head and face. She looks as if she's about to nod off to
sleep and was only waiting for your kiss goodnight. Oh, all the
stories you've read and made up for her then. A fairy tale come
true? What do you mean? There's something in that thought that
means something and seems intriguing and you're not getting it.
It can't be the prince kissing his future princess out of death or
interminable sleep, for you're the king in this parallel and he
usually dies from despair when he sees his daughter like this.
Then a fairy tale in reverse? Again, seems intriguing but you
can't come up with a meaning. Listen, this is all coming too fast
and think of it, you're in here at last, and you're in mourning,
so you've a right to be incompetent, stupid and confused. "Oh
my darling dearest," you say, "dearest" because she's dead, for
both your daughters were your dearest—*are, were,* you want to

punch the interloping verb, stick it in your mitt and mash it, dash it, grind it to air—and you go to her and take her hand. You think the regardful part's going; something tells you. But don't goof, left hand will feel left out and unloved and you take that one and lean over and say to it "Don't worry, I love you too," and hold and kiss them both. Now the flood will come or soon. "Now come alive," you say; "anything the king says, goes. This is that kind of kingdom. This room's my reign. You're my obedient subject. Do you know your king? Try to sit up when he speaks. The one who told you tales in bed, you and your sis, and got you into this fucking mess. No he didn't. Excuse the language. He did the best he could even if it came to nothing. None of us is great. Put in a predicament like the one we were in, what could any king have done if he also didn't have magical powers—'Away car, guy's gun to suddenly become gum, vanish, road home now clear!' " You think: If you were alive, my darling, you'd laugh; any pun with "gum." "But the king's wish. This is it. Hear me, I'm speaking for the king. If I only have one, here it is. I only have one and this is it. If we have to trade places to get it granted, so be it, he'll do it eagerly, immediately, me. Come alive! I'm and he and all of us are ordering you to. But slowly, you don't have to jump right up. Go easy on yourself, my little princess, you've had an unbelievably tough time. Or no fooling around. It's not working besides. Julie, you are—no princess or king or plenipotentiary, the minister who stands in for him—just come alive." You can't believe your eyes are still dry. Must be something physiological, brain-body, you were an inch away from it, now you're rock bottom, a place where tear ducts don't produce. You also don't shit there, piss or sweat. You certainly don't get hungry, thirsty or hard-ons. It's a place like death but where you're breathing and can still fart. It's the next step over from not. In fact, you just laid one. "Oh my gosh, my darling, I'm so sorry if what you're smelling now is foul." Where your skin continues to shed and hair and nails grow, but so slowly—as in death, so in life—that you don't see their ongo-

ingness. You've no clue as to what you're talking of or alluding
to but you do know why. And your eyes, they're still dry. Of
course her hands are cold, not to your mouth as much as to
your hands, and they don't get warmer the longer you hold them.
Should you now say aye, is it finally time to face up and snuff
out the royal blather and brain-body stuff, enough of all this
wishing-fishing-blaming-talking-to-the-dead such malarkey: cold
hands, in a heated draft-free room, that can't even get a touch
warmer when you keep them folded over in yours for so long,
proof she's dead? But never said out loud. Good God, she might
hear, be once again on the edge between life and death—bordering it; rather, straddling—and one line like that might be all it'd
take for her to give up and die. Her quick last thought: "If
Daddy doesn't believe I'm living, I'm dead." Daddies have that
sway. This one perhaps with this kid in this situation anyway,
so you don't say a thing. You hold, enclose, rub her knuckles,
you look, you can barely see her now because of the water in
your eyes, she does seem so peaceful, she does look as though
she's sleeping, that's a bad sign, at least people in comas, you've
heard or at least you saw with your father nights before he died,
seem fidgety or in pain or get that way every so often, so it's
coming, ducts functioning, entire head's sweating, you might
even end up shitting and pissing in your pants, the whole works
of you might go. It's possible you might just fall into many
pieces, no center hold. But you want to see your little baby so
you wipe the water away. What else do you do now? These little
fingers, a little puffy now, same with her little face. That little
long neck, slim like a slim kid's before, now blotchy and purple
or red. Those shoulders, her big brainy forehead. You can't stand
it. There are altogether too many signs. Probably same with her
whole body, the clotting and swelling and slime. But come on,
what more do you do when you've been standing by your dead
daughter's bed for so many if not way past the maximum allow-
able minutes and sense the doctor's getting impatient waiting and
they want to come in and take her out so they can do what they

have to with her or just to the room with her out of it so it can be reused? It's just that something tells you there's something you can do for her that you haven't done and you don't want to leave her till you've found out and tried and you also don't want to go because if you do it'll really be as if she's gone. So you stay, but what do you do while you're here? You hope that whatever that something is comes to you. And you look, you hold, you enfold, you bend down again and kiss her big forehead. Where do all the thoughts and stuff go? Just puff, cut? So you also think dopey, not dopey but preposterous hard-up thoughts. And you speak. You say "My little darling"—or does some of it stay in her head or around her awhile or even around you in the air, maybe trying to reach you some way with a last message or word or just anything in the little time it might have and feeling, like you trying to reach her or bring her back from wherever she is, that it can when it knows it can't?—"what more can I actually say, I mean do for you now but say 'my little darling'? If I knew, about what I could do, I'd do it, you know so, and if you could tell me—tell me if you can, make a noise, give some sign—I'd do it faster somehow, I swear," water all over your face till you can't see her, so even if there is some visible sign now you'll miss it—is there? can there be? just one and then it's gone for all time?—your lips touching her face in different places till they find what feels like her mouth and with your fingers you touch it and your lips on it and it is. Then someone's behind you. You jump up; must be the doctor. Does he think what I was doing peculiar? you think. Well if he does, so what? I'm allowed, he said, I'm allowed, but maybe it's a different doctor or an aide or even with the same doctor you're only allowed to go so far. Door opened so quietly you didn't hear the person come in. Or it opened normally but you were so absorbed in what you were doing and thinking that you didn't hear it. Or it opened loudly. Loudly for the doctor or this other person, by accident perhaps—he pushed the door harder than he wanted and it slammed the wall. Or he pushed it harder than he normally does because he was angry or impatient or just tired of waiting outside and he wanted you to hear, but you still didn't or hear even other things he might have said trying to get your attention. You turn around, she'll be okay for a second, wipe your eyes, same doctor, doesn't seem to be in any of the moods you thought he might if he'd slammed the door, and he says "Excuse me, Dr. Frey, but don't you feel it's around the time you should come away from here?" "What makes you think I'm a doctor? Wish I was; bet she would've got twice the activity on her if I'd announced straight off she was an M.D.'s daughter, not that it would've . . . well, it wouldn't've hurt. I should do that next time—why didn't I think of it for this? I could kill myself for not," and he says "I thought you were a Ph.D. doctor at a university; I thought somebody told me that, excuse me. And as we said before regarding our efforts for her—" and you say " 'If you were a doctor or a plowman'—where'd I turn up 'plowman,' how, why?—'she would have got the same rigid'— not 'rigid' but . . . but something, oh fuck it—excuse me, my darling," turning to her, she's still the same, such a darling, as if cold-capped, cold-cocked, knocked out cold, but warm, lying, sleeping, and then to him " 'care,' just 'attention and care.' No, I work in a grade school, or did, years, years ago. Not her age but junior high. I was called 'teacher,' most times 'teach.' Now I don't know what I do or am going to. Wait!" and he says "Anyway, sir—" and you say "No, wait, one more thing. Don't push me out of here. Maybe something you said or what we were talking of set it off. But it's what I was looking for before to try when I was by myself, with her, here, I mean. And maybe I already found and tried it but I don't think so." "I don't know what you—" and you say "But not here in this room with her do I remember trying and finding it after everything else had failed or just didn't take place, and with a feeling—listen, I have to be quick about it so you have to go—as deeply as I have now. Not 'fervently,' I don't want to use stupid words to something my argument, but that it could be possible, work. So I have to,"

and he says "Excuse me, you're talking so fast, I'm confused—
you have to what?" and you say "Out, please get out, just another few minutes, you have to let me and leave me alone," and
push him out the door, you don't actually push him but put your
hands on his chest and by walking forward you make him move
back a step and then he looks at your hands flat on his hard
chest—maybe he's even flexing his pects to warn you to back
off—with this, ironical's the word, expression where you don't
know if he's not going to surprise you and suddenly haul off
and sock your face, and then at his watch and says "Fine, a few
minutes, but only a few—*please,* sir—I'll wait outside, but you
know there are many other important things other than seeing
to you that I have to do," and walks backward out the door
with his hand on it and shuts it. You run to her bed and drop
to your knees facing her, cup your hands and say "Dear—" and
then "No, another direction, not to her but to You," and swivel
around on your knees till you face the bare wall between the
bed and door and say "Dear God, dear God, please make her
alive again, please, please. I've never been religious, to my knowl-
edge not since I was a boy. And then only because one of my
parents wanted me to and I fell for it, you can say, a little bit—
I don't think I truly believed in it but was just scared if I didn't.
Nor have I ever asked You for anything and I don't think I did
even then. If I did, only for boy things and that Mommy and
Daddy never die at least not while I was alive, and so forth, and
also myself, to never die, for like everyone that age I must have
been afraid of death. But now it's father things I'm asking—
father, as in dada, daddy, me, and *a* father thing. The deepest
most deep most asking thing I've ever asked for or could and
ever will, unless the same thing happened to her again or to my
other child. And if I'm only allowed to ask it once then this is
that time. If You give it, this little girl here, my daughter Julie
alive, I'll do whatever You want. I'll become a believer again, a
believer in You but this time as an adult, not out of fear and
not knowing anything but from this experience here and belief.

I will believe and believe in You, tell others what You've done, I'll work for You in ways I'll find out about, through religion if that's the way or one of them and every day or any way and anything You want from me for the rest of my life. And by doing anything for You I mean even to killing myself if that's what You'd want, though I'm not saying it is. I'm in fact saying it probably isn't—it isn't, I know it, and I know You know everything I'm saying and I mean before I even say or think it. Or I will know that and never have any doubts about it or You again if You give back her life and make her well again or well enough, full of life enough, for the doctors here or anywhere to make her normal again. Or well enough for her just to continue to live and if this is what has to be, then disabled and sickly, but I would hope to the way she was before those men killed her today. If we can make this arrangement, whatever the word for it is—please excuse me—and I go back on my word to You, dear God, please strike me dead. But give me this and I'll not only become a believer in You and work for You for the rest of my life but I'll be devoted, devotional, devout—please don't be disturbed or put off, set me aside, not listen to me, brush me off as ridiculous and no consequence, my plea for her of no consequence, feel I'm not saying what I most deeply believe and feel, because of my trouble with words now, for especially at this time You can understand why. All that goes without saying, as I said before, if You exist, and up till this time from the time I was a kid You mostly didn't for me. But You will forever if You give me—give her—us both—do this. I'll go to whatever kind of church or synagogue or mosque or place of worship You want me to or just be this way without that, but never be anything but a believer in You. I know I'm repeating myself, excuse me for that too. Repeated myself repeatedly but I don't know what else to say to You when everything I'm talking about is aimed at the same thing: that all I want is for her to be alive and what I'll do for it. In other words—and more repetition, I think, so excuse me again—but besides becoming and being a believer in

You for life, whatever else You want from me or that I can see will show my belief in You, I'll do, and 'want of me,' not 'from.' So what more can I say or do, dear God, what more to get this, tell me? Or maybe I should just think about it myself—think quietly, let me think," and you close your eyes and think, you think "This is very good, I truly believe in what I'm saying. If He's here I can only hope He's hearing me, for I swear I mean every word I'm thinking and I've said so far. I do, I'm not just thinking and saying it to get what I want; I mean it as deeply and unspuriously as anything I've ever thought, said or done. And now I've thought some more about it and I'll be silent in my head awhile and see if anything else comes," and you're silent awhile and nothing else comes, "so there doesn't seem to be anything more now I can think to say to show how deeply and sincerely I mean it and what I can do for Him." "So please, please, dear God," you say, opening your eyes on the wall and keeping them there, "if You give me this and after You do I never hear from You again, or there's no other sign from You, like giving her life back now, from that life-giving moment on, I'll still never stop being this, doing it, being a strong and deep-as-conceivable-and-possible believer in You. I just need, want and am asking for this one thing from You and that's it, all I'll ever ask of You again, so I'm making that promise to You too. So give back—give her back her life, dear God. Make a miracle for her, please. I didn't think anything like that was possible till I started saying this to You—till before when I dropped to my knees to You, or really from the time the doctor left and shut the door and I ran to her side and dropped to my knees to You, and I know You know I didn't believe it before, but if it is possible, and I believe it is, there is no better, sweeter, more wonderful, good-natured, intelligent child in the world, I swear to You, no one who loves life as much and who has as much to live for and who is as loved by her parents and sis as much and who deserves her life back more and You can see, You can see, by everything she's done and said and just the way she's acted so far, that she's going to be the most giving and loving kid and adult there is. If that displeases You, my going on about her like that, giving an argument for her which You already know whether it's so or even close to what I said, as if all those things were reason for her to be chosen for this miracle, and they're probably not. But putting her up before let's say another dead child her age who this moment, and this probably happens around the world to some family every single second of the day, one of her parents might be praying as deeply to You to make her alive, and a parent who had always been a believer, no less, then I'm sorry, I very deeply apologize. And now there is nothing—but it's just, what I said about her, an example of how I feel about her—not an example but just how I do, which You of course also know. But now there is nothing, I was going to say, and You must know that too, nothing else I can say now. Her being alive to me—I mean just her being alive is everything to me, everything. So I beg You, I love You, I will worship You, I will truly believe in You, I will continue and continue to be a believer in You, I will do anything and everything for You, again and again and again I'm saying it, but make her live. Thank You. . . . Oh, those were terrible words or at least many of them were and inept and almost all of it terribly spoken though I swear to You none of it previously thought up or planned, but please hear me and do what I ask. Thank You again, dear God, thank You. There's nothing more I can say but that there isn't and You know that and what I mean and how I feel about her and all this, so thank You again. Yes, that's it, finished." You shut your eyes and cup your hands tight. You know nothing's happening to her and you don't look. Nothing but normal slow decomposing that comes when, well, that comes. But you don't open your eyes because you don't want to break the spell or whatever it is and by looking at her before it happens, this is what you mean, maybe that'll stop it from happening. Or maybe these things take time. The miracle doesn't have to happen or even begin to the moment you stop asking for it. So don't move,

keep your hands cupped, eyes don't have to be shut so long, for
you're looking at the wall and not her, but keep them shut anyway to be safe. But you mean it, you meant every word of it,
you will become a believer, you will. If it happened, everything
for you from that moment on or from the time you got the
doctors in to work on her to keep her alive and you were told
to wait outside, would be for God. Of course also for your family
and day-to-day things too. You wouldn't become a zealot or an
ascetic but you would go along with anything else that came
from deeply believing in Him. What do you mean by that? It
means—well, He knows what it means and this is what you'll
do for Him and you will never stop believing as you said, which
should be enough. But nothing's happened, you know nothing
has or ever will. You mean by that "which should be enough"
that He wouldn't want you to give everything up and do nothing
else but work and think of Him from then on. But you never
know, about that and that nothing can ever happen. For if that's
what He wants from you for Him to bring her back, you'll do
that too. And there are recorded miracles, ones comparable to
what you asked for and more, but recorded—looked into and
authenticated, you mean—by the church or group the people
these miracles happened to were members of, so in a way ques-
tionable because these miracles ended up benefiting that church
or group. But miracles today, yesterday, since people began believing in God, or even before so they would believe in Him. So
many miracles that it'd seem some of them would have to have
taken place. For could there be ten thousand church-validated
miracles in the last five hundred years, let's say, and not one of
them was true? And millions, billions of people believe in God,
so you'd think He'd probably have to exist. It can't be this gigan-
tic sham for centuries on end, millenniums, and if He exists it's
also possible He can make miracles as all or almost all the religions have said and He heard you and did or will do soon what
you asked. You don't know why she should be chosen for this
miracle nor why it should happen because of your pleading. But

if it can happen to someone, why not her? Who could be as worthy of it, as you said? Thousands, perhaps, millions, but nobody more worthy, is what you're saying. That without question has to be true, for how can one really compare the worthiness of children her age when you're talking about goodness and virtues and such? She's as good and virtuous and so on as any kid—how can she not be?—which is why you think, when you stick it in with all the other things about God's existence and the possibility of miracles and that praying to Him for one can work, that she has a chance. A minute, two have passed since you stopped praying. Maybe you shouldn't wait any longer to look. It might turn out to be dangerous for her. She may already have been brought back and have only two minutes for you to rush out and get the doctors to come in and work on her, before she dies again. That could be what God gives you without saying so—some kind of rule regarding miracles like this—two minutes, at the most three. Just think how you'd feel if you opened your eyes in a minute and saw her giving her last breath. No, you're being crazy. It can't work, this whole thing; she's dead forever, you dumb fool. Yes it can work, it's possible, you've shown how it can. You open your eyes and look at her. She looks the same. You stand up and put your ear by her mouth, you feel her head, cheeks, you put your ear by her nose and don't breathe, just listen. You feel her wrist for a pulse, then the other one. You put your hand on the sheet where you think her heart is, your ear to that part and then several places around it where you think the heart can be if it's not there and don't breathe, listen. Then because you think that ear maybe doesn't hear as well as the other one, the other one at several places on her chest. You would pull the sheet down and put your ear and hand on her chest and feel around and listen for a heartbeat but you know nothing's happened, nothing could. No, you don't do that because you don't want to feel and see her there. It'll be ugly, bloody; it'll show gouging, probing, big holes. But you did do everything you could for her, you did try for her, you did, nobody could say you didn't, from start to finish you tried, you did, you tried. No, it's still possible, still. It has to be. You don't know about God and time, you don't know about God, period, or very little, but her life can't be taken, that's all, she has to become alive, goddamnit, and that's final. You cover your eyes, bend your head forward and think "Fuck the cupping-of-hands crap, this should be enough," and say to yourself "Dear God, I'm sorry, for cursing, for whatever. Maybe You do exist, I am hoping You do and You hear me and help her and in some way make this whole thing a fantastic mistake. Maybe it takes longer than three minutes—You know what I'm talking about—longer than five, ten. Do it when You choose to, I beg You. If there's something I left out, didn't do, forgot to promise or didn't know to promise or offer You, please forgive me for that too, all of which I've said and said. But You have to know by now that anything You want of me I'll do and everything I already said I'd do for You and become, I will. Maybe You weren't listening before, maybe You are now; my daughter here, make her alive, please." You look; nothing. You pull the sheet up above her feet and feel around an ankle where the pulse would be. You feel the other ankle there, then re-cover the feet. You shut your eyes. Yes, do it, you think. You pull the sheet down and see a long incision down her chest, two short slices across the incision, dried blood around them, no bullet hole, piece of clean gauze on her stomach over her belly button. You lift the gauze and it's just clear skin and the button underneath, so you don't know why it was left there. You put your ear where you think her heart is and then around there, feel around your chest till you feel your heartbeat and then put your hand on the same part of her chest, then your ear on it and don't breathe, just listen. You hear the door close with your other ear. Doctor's in the room again, you know it without looking. Or maybe someone else, sent by that doctor to get you out of here, for he could have been called elsewhere, an emergency someplace or his workday's over, and you say without looking up "Shh, don't move or speak, I'm listening," and stick a finger in your free ear and listen some more. You put your ear to her mouth, part her lips with your fingers and listen at it some more, feel both her temples at the same time this time. He takes the gauze off her, drops it in the waste can by the bed, covers her up, straightens her arms, takes your arm and pats your hand he's holding and leads you out. Last thing you did wasn't to kiss her. You want to. But you can do it at the funeral chapel a few minutes before the funeral or in some crematory room if she's going to be cremated or at the funeral home in some room they keep her if the only ceremony for her is going to be at the cemetery.

You call your wife. You first asked the doctor if he knew a good place to. "You want privacy, naturally," and you said "That, a door I can close, place that doesn't look out on anything and have people coming through and no one can look in." He said his office, "cubicle's more like it, where I do my more complicated paperwork and phoning and can catnap sitting up," and that he'd leave you alone in it. Margo wanted to speak to her mommy but you said "After, another time, when I call next and I'll be calling a lot, I promise. But you see, I'll be talking to her for the first time since New York," and she said "So?" and you said "So, I have to be more unmistakable?" and she said "I don't know what you mean. It's just I have to speak to her." You said "After I tell her some things I'll see if she wants to talk to you. She might not. Or she probably will want to but not be able to, so don't be offended if she says no. But I will ask her for you, if I'm able to, since by that time I'll probably be in terrible shape too, but she may be too broken up—let's say she will—to talk to anyone after that including me." The doctor unlocks the cubicle door, says "I can't give you the key, it's my only one and I have to go through all sorts of bureaucratic rigmarole to get another one, and the door locks automatically when you close it and there's no way to keep it unlocked if you leave the room. That is, if the door's firmly shut. Please don't, if you leave the room and want to return, keep the door ajar with a chair or shoe or anything. There's been thievery in the hospital, some we think by staff, and I have important papers and possessions in the room, though they even take thermoses and telephones." "A shoe?" and he said "Why would I have one in there? It's one of two. I keep a pair handy for jogging—running shoes. If you get locked out, ask the nurses' station to summon me over the public address system and I'll come fast as I can to unlock it." Margo was taken to a room with a TV. The doctor suggested it. "We have several spare private patient rooms. We can move in a TV if one isn't there, get her soda and snacks, she can sit in the chair or even on the bed—it's okay, we'll remake it, plenty of linen here—and she can watch her favorite shows with a remote control. Of course, all this depending on how long you'll be." "I'll need some time to prepare, to think; you know, and then to get over it after I call. And Margo doesn't know how to use one of those control things, that I know of. And I don't think she has any favorite shows or watches any TV except for some popular two-hour one on Friday nights and maybe a nature film and occasionally, it doesn't count though, a video movie with us or for them if it's gentle and clean." "Strict about it, that it? Feel it'll hurt their intellectual and moral development?" and you said "In a way. But she doesn't especially like TV and I think even those two Friday-night hours and nature film are for our benefit, to show she's so-called normal, one of the kids. And because she didn't, the other didn't, or at least that's the way it worked." "Oh, she likes it all right but I bet is only trying to please you, your obviously being book- and high-minded people, to think she doesn't. But she'll change soon, or would have if this thing didn't happen today— now for a while everything will be out of whack—and go at it avidly, I was going to say," and you said "Maybe. But I hate TV for them; hated, hate. All that violence and emphasis on money and beauty and body and the commercials one-two-three and in all of it kittenish to what I now hear, even in the ads, is semiexplicit sex. Suppose she sees a show now with violence in it, what'll I do? The sex and stupid stuff I don't mind for her at this moment, but the violence? Suppose it's about one or two deranged men who kill a person cavalierly, or even a kid or even a kid in a car and even from a car this kid's killed? But a random smiling crime on the run, even if the killers get it at the end or repent. She'll fall apart. I will too at hearing she saw it. Maybe someone can watch the TV with her. To clear the programs and just to be there to talk to if she suddenly wants to. Or maybe you have some family-movie videos, movies from thirty-forty years ago when there wasn't as much blown-out brains and blood in them," and he said "We don't have VCRs here. She'll be all right, really. It'll be a good distraction. Look, I have kids too. And I know, for they're around the same age as yours and a third who's a bit older and also because of the patients I see and talk with, that what happened to her today and what she sees on TV and the movies are two distinct things. One's fantasy and entertainment, the other's real and repulsive, but for some reason, even if they haven't seen a lot of it on TV, they're able to separate the two more easily than me or you." "You've kids my age—my kids' age? And two—three? You seem so young to—too young to. Maybe I started too late. Anyway, I'll try to get her away from the TV soon as I can. I won't try to get through with the phone call to my wife soon as I can, but over it after, and maybe sooner to it." You shut the door. Just before you did you said "What happens now to my younger girl? More slicing up? I should ask my wife first if she wants Julie to go through with more of that, but I wouldn't know how to go about it. With both of us so uncollected, there can't be a way," and the doctor said "I'm afraid you haven't a choice, sir. Someone's been killed. We only did an exploratory on her, to see what could be salvaged if you'd agree, though nothing could. But first a few holes for tubes and other medical procedures to try to resuscitate her, even if everything was predetermined the minute we saw her. The county medical examiner will perform a thorough examination of her because foul play's been suspected," and you said "Foul play? She was murdered in front of me, or by two guys in front of me, she was right behind me or to the side in back. Now I forget where she was sitting but she had to be because Margo was right behind. I mean—" and he said "The term's a technicality. He'll also trace and then locate the bullet if it didn't exit. Our preliminary exam indicated it didn't, but it's easy to miss the exit hole. Or even a second bullet, since the entry and exit holes for it may be in some more unyielding areas of her body or they closed. Then his office will contact you to arrange for a funeral home to pick up your daughter. If he can't reach you—before you leave here you'll want to give me all the phone numbers where you think you might be. In fact, let me have them now, I might miss you later," and you gave your home phone number—"I think that's right, I'm so confused now, but up till last year I think I was the only Nathaniel Frey in the phone book"— but couldn't remember at all the numbers of your in-laws and your wife's sister. "This is her folks' names and address: they're listed in the Manhattan book as a couple, his name first, and here's my brother-in-law's name in New Haven. I might just drive north— not drive, take the train or hire a cab or something—to be with my wife, and she might go to her sister's or stay at her folks' or even fly home to be with me and Margo. I'll have to make sure to coordinate it, so we don't get, you know, that'd be terrible, wouldn't it? But I guess it'll all depend where Julie's taken to. And where would we? I don't know of any home where we are, but that shouldn't be tough to find. Several are nearby, not next door but within blocks, and by then friends or my wife's family will help if I want to bring them in. But if he can't reach me?" and he said "The coroner? Then he'll get instructions from one of those close relatives or place her in a home here and tell you when he does contact you. He has a small office and no facilities for storing the subjects he's worked on, excuse me for putting it like that. He should be done tomorrow afternoon, since he's probably picking her up right now." "Maybe I should go to him, help him put her in his truck or van if he didn't come with anyone and you're short-staffed, and go with him to provide information he might want. And to stay with her, but in another room while he's working on her, till she has to go to a home, and maybe even there's where my wife can meet me—the coroner's—but I have to make that call to her first and what would Margo do all that time?" and he said

"It's also not necessary; he has all the data he needs from us and the police." "But there are little specific health details he might want to know about her that only her pediatrician and parents know, and my wife ten times better than I, and he doesn't have her records, does he? Did you call her pediatrician for them? I don't remember giving anyone her name and phone number. That one I could never remember—it didn't have to take something like today—and would always ask my wife for, who'd produce it on the spot. Among other things she has a head of a thousand phone numbers and all our Social Security numbers, but I can give you the doctor's name or the group practice's," and he said "He won't need any of that for what he'll be doing," and you said "So, that means I'm done here. I can go whenever I want with Margo after I make my call. It's hard to believe. There must be something I haven't done, attended to, that sort of thing—answered," and he said "Outside of the call to your wife, if you're still up to it, and what you want the police to do with your car after, I can't think of anything. You will want to contact them before you go if they're through with the car and you're planning to leave it behind, as I don't know how long they'll want to take care of it before they park it in a private lot. Perhaps you'd like me to deal with them, you shouldn't be bothered," and you said "I can call them from where I end up or in a few days, send them the title and registration and tell them to sell it or give it away if they want. Maybe for the hospital; you've all been very kind. But it's almost an old car, lots of miles and stains and banging up and now even worse. It might get a couple of thousand if the buyer isn't repelled by what happened or think there's a curse attached. Though even if it were new and worth umpteen thousands it wouldn't stop me from never wanting to have anything to do with it again or anything we left inside it or even file an insurance claim, other than for going what I probably have to go through, like signing the ownership papers with my wife's and my name, to get rid of it," and he said "It's a generous offer, one you or your wife might have a change of mind about later, but I'd think it'd be too complicated for the hospital to get involved in something like an auction or sale, though thank you." It's a little room, a cubicle as the doctor said. As they were walking to it he said "It's something, isn't it, those floods down South. With only a slightly stronger wind or high pressure—something blown in from the ocean or up from the Gulf—and then a similar weather pattern that stopped the clouds over the South for so long, we would have got a huge dose of it ourselves," and you said "What, because of the rains? I wish we had. I wouldn't have driven back today, or yesterday if I had heard it was on the way, or tomorrow if it happened today, if we started to get what they did or anything near. That is what you mean, right?" and he said "There's never been anything like it in the weather annals there. We've had periodic heavy wettings recently, nothing for several days. But they've had, Virginia on down, twenty-six straight days of rain and five to seven inches of rain in some places for six consecutive days. You can understand why the rivers wouldn't hold—the levees. A few billion acres of land covered over, I read. Entire towns and one capital city under water, or to the first or second story, and one of our oldest universities totally flooded. What a catastrophe. Six states have already been declared federal emergency disaster areas and a seventh is on the way. Municipal water systems knocked out for weeks, the pestilence that can occur if people so much as brush their teeth with tap water in thousands of homes. Billions in property damage, not acreage loss. Maybe a few million acres covered or totally saturated. And to top it off, it's continuing to rain in biblical proportions with no end in sight. What was it, eighty days, forty days, forty-eight? You can almost begin believing that it happened because of something horrific the region's done, for why was every other region spared? Just think what's going to happen to fruit and citrus prices the next year and traveling this summer if some of those major bridges go and highways are ruined," and you said "I've been listening to it on the radio now and then and seeing it in the papers the last few days but for some reason I haven't paid much attention. Could be it's just too big a calamity to imagine or care about as a whole or there hasn't been enough reporting of individual tragedies about it except for things like 'My family farm's gone,' 'The homestead where my ancestors grew up is finished,' 'I can't get to work and I need the money, now even more so to pay off this damage,' 'My car and camper both destroyed along with the carport they were in,' 'Our only family tree's on my mother's computer that floated away,'" and he said "Picture I get is different, sir. Seventy-one deaths so far overall and thousands of livestock, if you care about animals the way I do. An entire Boy Scout troop lost while spelunking, quarter-million people living in shelters now, but all that neighbor-aiding-neighbor attitude down there, with some people driving hundreds of miles to help and even coming from other states when the call went out for sandbaggers to work twenty hours straight. One man who sandbagged for a storeowner he hated like hell, he said, but in times of crisis like this, he added, what else can you do but pitch in?" and you said "Then I must be wrong, didn't read enough or not the right newspapers and wasn't listening to the radio at the right times. I didn't mean to sound heartless about it." Little room, little cubicle, normal-size cubicle, how big do you suppose? Big as three old telephone booths, some height. Big as your second-floor shower-bath at home plus connecting linen closet, same height. Big as two cars of your model and make, one on the other. Your car. What things of hers you leave behind in it? Dollies, clothes, games, toothbrush, you've said all this, her own special toothpaste gel with an unusually large flat cap so the tube can stand on it, books from your local library, let it all go. To the library you'll say, well, you'll say nothing. You'll just pay by check sometime after the bill comes for all your overdue books and never if you can help it go near that library again. No windows, so, windowless, diplomas on the walls, bookcase full of medical books, papers neatly stacked on the narrow desk underneath, pencils, long yellow writing tablets, couple of coat hooks on the door with medical jackets on them, hanger with street clothes on a wall hook, tie on another, running outfit and athletic shorts on a third, running shoes and hightop sneakers so maybe he also plays basketball,

towel on another wall hook, under it a long black rubber tubing
he probably exercises with. You pull out the drawers looking for
what? Phone book because you forget your area code and don't
want to dial Information and speak to anyone for it. It's a new
one, changed the past year when the state divided into two codes,
and all you can think of is the old. Shaving gear, bottle of aspirins,
pint bottle of rye or whatever the smallest size is that isn't the
souvenir kind, half pint. A glass. You shouldn't, it's not yours,
there's barely a quarter-bottle left, which means around two shots.
He may be saving it for a bracer, after this difficult shift with your
dead daughter, for instance, or right after you go. But he wouldn't
mind, he'd understand, not mind that much, you might even tell
him if you see him again and a few months from now send him a
fifth or liter of one of the best Irish whiskeys, if you remember his
name, and pour a finger of it, two fingers, practically emptying it,
and shoot it down and put the bottle back in the drawer. Glass
was clean when you picked it up, no sink in here so unless you
wash it he'll know you drank from it. But again, you're almost
sure he won't mind. He's a nice guy, you can tell by what he said
and the way he smiled and all the time he gave you. What doctor
do you know would do that? Maybe all of them, in this situation,
if they weren't called to another emergency, and anyway by the
time he finds the glass, which could be today if he takes that bracer,
you'll be gone from here though you don't know where yet, and
you look for your hanky, no hanky, you must have used it on her
in the car and left it there or thrown it away, and dry the glass
with your bloody, dirty shirt—even worse than stealing his liquor,
as the hanky would have been, but here he won't know and he'll
probably, since he'll also probably smell the whiskey on it and
notice the bottle almost empty, wash the glass before using it.
Framed photo on the desk of him and his wife and two sons, or
you assume they are, and who else could they be? Framed photo
on a bookshelf of him and this same woman and now three children, so you know they're his. But he said two were around the
same age as yours and one a bit older, which isn't so here. Was

he saying that to show something, do something? What's the difference what it means if he was only trying to help? All facing the
camera, posed in a way you never would with your family, and by
a professional it seems—cloudy blue backdrop that doesn't exist in
real life except as a photographer's prop or maybe it's just worked
into the print, but to you it looks like life after death, to them
maybe it's heaven on earth. Anyway, something else you'd never
do, pay a pro to photograph you, doctor and his wife sitting on a
red Victorian loveseat, three- or four-year-old girl squeezed between
them with a hand on each of their closest knees, same two boys
behind them and looking about three years apart but several years
older than in the desk photo, so that one probably taken before
the girl was born, doctor serious, wife looking giddy to almost
delirious, both seemingly unaged since the earlier photo and doctor
looking even younger in this one, must be the more youthful haircut
and the jogging and exercise or the photographer touched them up.
Do you have family photos where you're all in them? Maybe only
one, or two or three, but one you remember and is inside a plastic
sheath tucked away in your billfold and which used to be pinned
above your desk at home but you haven't looked at since you stuck
it in there: first time Julie was taken outside, when she was a couple
of weeks old. Your mother-in-law had come down to help out and
took it. On the grass in front of your apartment building then,
Margo seated between your wife's spread legs and waving a lolly,
you kneeling beside them holding Julie who's crying hysterically
while everyone else is smiling. Diaper pin or rash, soiled diaper,
stomach bubble or hunger, any one of those could be it, your wife
used to say, but here it might only have been her first airing. So:
outside air on her face and street sounds—cars, trucks, maybe
birds, a dog barking, passerby shouting, motorcycle passing—and
all your excited chatter at having her out. Even a plane overhead.
They often flew by and sometimes it seemed pretty low. Think
what the first one of those must have sounded like. Impossible. The
phone, and you sit at the desk. Got to get it over with. No, that's
not the attitude. The attitude should be what? You don't know.

The attitude, my friend, the attitude! Sorry. How do you call out from here? Same as from your office: dial nine, then one, area code and phone number? The area code, you were looking for a phone book, and you go through the drawers again and look on the bookshelves but don't find one. Some people in tight quarters keep them in corners on the floor and you look at all four of them, none's there. Someone's playing loud music with this thumping beat, probably in a nearby cubicle. Area code you suddenly remember and write it down along with your phone number. But you're not dialing home, you're calling your wife at your in-laws', and you jot down the New York City area code. Their phone number, even after years of calling them now and then, you were never able to remember. You don't know why. You like them and they're easy to speak to so it isn't that you wanted to forget the number and by forgetting it you forgot them or your difficulty in talking to them, et cetera. You even tried to find some memory device to remember it but it was such an odd assortment of numbers, the lower ones all mixed up with the higher ones and none seeming to join another, that you couldn't come up with one. It'll be hard calling your wife—speaking to her with what you have to say—with that music—and then dealing with everything else after it—going on. "Stop, please stop that racket," you say, "if there's a God in heaven, stop it now." But you don't want to try and find the room it's coming from and ask that person to turn it down or off, if anyone's there. You might lock yourself out of this room and you also don't want to confront anyone. You want to get it over with, that's all, done, done, and don't want any more interferences and distractions, and then get on to the next thing and the next thing and so on till ten years from now it's somewhat out of your mind or not in it all the time. Something like that. Just speak, when you do speak, with a finger in your free ear. Which kid did that recently? Not one but with two: Julie, in the car; no, Margo, here. Both—all kids likely—did it with both ears plugged: don't want to hear what you're saying when you're remonstrating, that sort of stuff. You get up and put your ear to the walls till you find the one it's coming from and yell "Stop it, will ya, shut the fucking music up," banging the wall. You listen for about half a minute and no one says anything, music stays; they had to have heard you so probably nobody's there. There's no other way, you'll have to get New York City Information, and it isn't as if you're talking to your wife yet, and you dial nine, one and the Information number there. Man says "Mr. Lewis, what city please?" and you say "Yes, thank you. Listen, this is very tough for me, Mr. Lewis, speaking. I do want a number but there's been—please stick with me through this quick spiel—a death in my family—" and he says "I'm sorry, sir, what can I do for you, what city?" and you say "Manhattan. It was just before, a few hours, and I'm still a little crazy—a car accident—all upset about it and I have to call my wife and need her parents' number there," and he says "The name and address?" and you say "That I have," and give them and he says "Hold on for your number please," and a recorded voice gives it. The music, another piece, almost the same screeching and beat but faster, is that supposed to be relaxation, diversion, rest, something to think with or listen to on your dinner break, maybe just good for sex, but not here, though could be, on the floor, put a jacket underneath, or both on a chair, perfect place with only one key, but if not what is it then, what's it serve? It's so goddamn ignorant, why do people who like serious music keep it low and those who like this kind turn it up so? That true? You don't care what the answers are, but in a hospital, in this part, where people are dying or recently dead, or maybe that's not in this part, you walked a long way, but still, and instead of a bracer, this? What am I missing? Oh that's a lark. Oh shit, forget it, don't let it get to you, it's not going to go away by your praying and raving against it, so are you ready? As I'll ever be. What are you going to say? I'll just see what I'll say. Not good enough, this is the most emotionable of human instances which calls for the rarest most fastidious kind of sensitivity, equableness and self-control. Stop it, stop the words and bullshit, speak to me in plain language, I can't stand any fanciness like that and for sure not now. Okay, so just how will you? How will I? How will you and what, yes, how? I'll say, I'll say, I'll say I'm at a hospital, here, this one, I'll give the name and state, Margo's with me, Margo's all right, nothing's wrong with her, don't worry about that, but there's been an accident, a terrible one, so terrible, couldn't be worse, listen, hold tight, it's a shooting, Julie's been shot, Julie's shot, Julie's dead, I'm at the hospital, Margo's with me, she's okay, unhurt, is anyone there with you, if anyone is, please get that person to the phone or just someone to help you. You'd break the news to her like that? So fast, right off the bat? You wouldn't first ask if anyone's there with her before you tell her, so that person can sort of be there to help her when you tell her or tell her himself? And also, for this is such shocking news, get into it slower and easier with this person before you say what happened? Yes, I'd do that. I'd say to my wife "Hi, dear, how are you, is anyone there with you, your folks, they around? May I speak to one of them, it's something about something, a secret, nothing wrong, don't worry, and one I'm sure they'll give away the moment I get off the phone," as if it were something like a surprise party I was planning for her, and then I'd speak to her mom or dad the way you said. I'd do it quietly, wouldn't break the news quickly, even start off with a bit of small talk. If she said "Which one?" I'd say "Oh, I guess your dad," since I think, though it'd be the worst thing he's ever heard or had to deal with, he'd handle it better. Or I'd just ask for him straight off, "Let me speak to your dad, please, if he's there," and if he wasn't then I'd ask for her mom. But suppose neither parent is there? Or suppose she then says, after I made that pitch, "Sure, I'm at their apartment, why wouldn't they be here? But something's wrong, you're holding it back, don't try to act like you're not, so what is it, tell me, the kids, one of the kids, both?" She might have picked up by my voice, not what I said, that something's wrong, very wrong, couldn't be worse. I might only have to say one word for her to notice. Or one word before I start crying. I might start crying second I finish dialing her folks' or be crying while I dial. Be sobbing, be bawling. I might have to hang up while I'm dialing, try to collect myself and then dial again when I feel composed enough to speak to her and then might start sobbing the moment she lifts the receiver and says hello. Or I might never get that control. I might try very hard, clench my teeth, bite the insides of my cheeks, do some mental preparation—"Now don't cry, don't cry, too much is riding on your staying composed"—think I have it, heart's not beating wild, throat's not tight, and so forth, and dial again and start crying while I'm dialing or the moment my wife picks up the phone. Or when some other person, it doesn't have to be she, lifts the receiver. Though most times I've called her at her folks' place she's been the one to pick up the phone, maybe because she's faster, more energetic or it's just a habit of racing to the phone there from the time she was a kid and they don't even bother trying to answer it while she's there. But if her mother does answer the phone, what then? Do I ask for her husband? If she says "What's it about, Nate, anything I can do?" which she usually does when I ask for him, what do I say? Something like "Something to do with our income tax forms last year, he told me to call him about it if I got the letter from IRS I had anticipated would be waiting for me at home, and we're home, by the way, good trip, everybody's safe, kids say hello, and of course after I speak to him I'll want to speak to Lee." But if I do get her dad, or only her mom if her dad's not home, what then? I don't know. No, you have to know, it's absolutely essential. You're priming them for your wife, right? and the call's to be made momentarily, so you have to think now what you'll say. I'll say something like, I'll say something like, I'll say "Hi, it's Nate, Nat, Nate, but you know that, you know my voice, but there's something you don't know, some very important thing to tell you, some very bad news to tell Lee too but first I have to prepare her through you, prepare you to prepare her for the absolute worst though I wish there was some way to prepare you for it too." I might then say "It isn't Margo, it's Julie." I might put it this way: "Margo's not hurt, Julie is." I might then add "Julie's very hurt, in fact. Extremely. There's been an accident. Not an accident. Listen, I'm going to go nuts with crying if I don't tell you right away and if I do start crying I'll never stop and you'll never find out what it is I have to tell you and you have to, you see, for I have to tell Lee. It's this: Julie's dead," I might say, "Margo isn't. Julie's been wiped out clean, Margo isn't even scratched." No, not like that, not any of it, I have to go back. Why? You're on to it, you are, and almost over it with her folks, so go on, what else? I'll say, or might, "Listen, Julie's been killed, killed, by a freaking mad gun shooter from a car." No, some other way. If I tell them that way I'm sure they'll break down and be unable to prepare my wife for what I have to tell her, what do you say? What do I say? I say you're right but that whatever way you tell whichever parent you tell it to, they'll break down, how can they not? They might be strong, father stronger than the mother as you said, but no one can be that strong if they're not the same type as the guys who killed your child. But even those guys would probably break down the same way if let's say they heard one of their kids was just killed, even if they'd done it to someone else's kid the same way and not long before, but we won't go into that. Or both you and one of your wife's parents might break down the same moment after you say it about Julie and then the other parent might get on the phone after the first one broke down or ask his or her spouse what's wrong. And you might then have to repeat it because the one you told it to would be in no shape to repeat to the other one what you just said. So? So I'm saying you'll now probably have two of them broken down, if you were able to tell the second what you told the first, and you still haven't really begun to get the news to your wife. So? So stop saying "so?" for you don't see that as a problem? I see it, my wife. Where would she be all this time? If she's not home, that's one thing, and it might even be easier that way, for her parents would have calmed down enough to tell her or prepare her by the time she got back. But if she's home and in the room with them, one of her parents breaking down during the call would in a way be a way of telling her something's very wrong. In other words, that might be all the preparation I need, through the crying and probably the hysteria of her parent or both of them, if I was able to tell the second, but not the way I want to begin telling her. What way do you want? That could be the key to how you go about telling her. I'm not sure. I don't know. No, I'm just not sure. I'd love for her to just hear it from me in whatever way I tell it, soberly, hysterically, something in between, either of the three or some other way but no matter what way for her to then say something like "This"—soberly, unhysterically, no in-between—"is the worst news of my life, dear, the worst thing that has ever happened or could ever happen, but we have to begin dealing with it the best way we know how. And I know how it is for you now, Nat, and how hard it was to tell me, just as I know you know how it is for me and how hard it was to hear. But we can't let it overwhelm us where we can't function for each other and Margo, especially for Margo, so that's what we have to do." "What do we have to do?" I can then say if it's not really clear to me and she can say in the same way what she means till I under-stand. Do I want her to say something like that in the way I had her say it? I do, for if she doesn't there'll be nothing but sorrow and we'll just sink in it and Margo will go down with us too. One of us at least should stay in some kind of control like that, either Lee or me, and I should because she might not and also because I've known of it longer than she and probably because of some other reasons, and maybe that's the approach or attitude or tactic I should take now, to take care of them both in their sorrow or despair, but how do I do it, how do I even start? First step is to try to composedly tell one of her parents, second is to try to tell Lee the same way, and so on and so on, and maybe only at the funeral I can crack up for the length of it and then recover till we get to the cemetery, if the entire service isn't at the cemetery, and then crack up for most of the burial ceremony and recover for the ride home with Margo and Lee. And maybe later I can crack up in moments when I'm alone but where I know I can come out of it just about when I want, and then months from now—a month, weeks, even—when Lee will be a little better adjusted to Julie's death perhaps, I can crack up with her when Margo's asleep or out of the house or can't hear, or just on my own when Margo isn't around or can't hear and Lee for those minutes can take care of me. In time in front of Margo but when I can quickly recover again, and maybe even with Margo if it comes to that, and much later on, whenever it happens and in front of whomever happens to be there. Anyway, better to take that approach than total breakdown or any but a momentary breakdown on the phone with Lee now. Certainly if she's in the room when I tell one of her folks about Julie she'll see from their face that something's very wrong—did I say all this before? That something catastrophic and possibly tragic has happened but she wouldn't automatically know it was one of us her parent was screaming and sobbing over. It could be about one of her relatives—an uncle, a cousin—or a good friend of her folks: sudden stroke, someone keeled over and died, news that the husband of the woman on the phone has terminal cancer and only a month to live, that sort of thing. For if my name isn't mentioned—for instance, if my father-in-law doesn't say right away "Nate, how are you, how was the trip?" or Julie's name isn't mentioned—"No, not Julie, oh my God!"—she probably wouldn't know who her parent is crying over or that I was on the phone. She might think it's a call from her sister or brother-in-law about her brother-in-law or sister or one of their kids. Lee's parents would break down if anything tragic happened to one of them too—not to the brother-in-law as much as their other daughter and three grandchildren from them. Lee might say "What is it, what happened?" and if her father or mother continued to sob and scream or acted any way like that, take the receiver away, if she thinks it's about her sister or one of her nieces or her nephew or even her brother-in-law and say "Hello, this is Lee, who's this, what happened, why's my mother (or father) crying so?" and I might be crying. She might recognize my cries. Of course she would. I've cried and sobbed before over the news of people's deaths or the memories of some who were dead. She might say "Nat, what's wrong, tell me, one of the kids? It's one of the kids," and I might be able to say yes or I might not be able to say anything I'd be

crying so hard. She might then say—she'd probably then say—
"Come on, what is it, one of the girls like I think? Which one, and
what, what—a car accident—on the highway—something at home?
Is she alive, is she dead? Both, one? Which, which?" Her parents
would still be crying—one would probably have told the other by
now if both were home—and she might then say to them or just
to the one who's home, since I might not be able to speak—I
probably wouldn't—"What is it, what did he tell you?" and they
might, one might, blurt out "Julie." "Oh no, Julie what? It's the
worst, I know, I can tell by your face and that he can't speak.
What? Oh no," and they might not be able to say anything and
she might get back on the phone and say "What's wrong with
Julie?" or if they told her what, "Dad (or Mom) said Julie's dead—
he (she) has to be wrong, she can't be, she isn't," and I still might
not be able to speak, and then what? She might turn to her folks
again, or one of them—whatever—and say "I'm wrong that you
said that, right? She's not dead, isn't that so? Nat didn't tell you
that, true? It's something bad, I know, but nothing as bad as that,
right, right? So what did he say, what exactly did Nat tell you?"
and one of them might nod that yes, she's dead, or mouth "Yes,
dear, she's dead," or say it, whisper it, or just in a normal voice
"Yes, dearest, Julie's dead," both of them could say it, he could be
saying it on the phone while they're saying it or just calling out
for her, "Lee . . . Lee . . . ," but whatever way she's told she would
then scream, there's no question she'd scream and become hysterical and cry hysterically and yell and tear at her hair and scratch
her face probably and stick her fingers in her mouth maybe and
bite down on her fingers and pull the corners of her mouth apart
till they hurt and even after, maybe till they bleed, but things like
that and I'd be on the other end listening but not knowing what
to do and she wouldn't get back on, by this time she wouldn't be
able to, though I'd stay on, it might take minutes but then one of
her parents might be able to get on and say "Nathan, you still
there? . . . tell me what happened, Lee's hysterical as you can hear,
we all are, but if you can, just some more information, tell me and

I'll do my best in conveying it to her, or withholding it from her, whichever I think best, but please, don't keep us in the dark." That might be a phrase her mother would use, her father would just say something like "What is it, Nate, before we lose our senses again and I can't hear what you have to say? Where you calling from? Home, a hospital, a police station, the morgue?" "Hospital," I might manage and he could say "Did you say it was a car accident?" "Shooting," I might be able to say. I would then probably say I can't speak any longer, for I probably couldn't, but that I want to, to be as cooperative as I can—*helpful*—to do anything I can to help Lee and them now, but I'm unable to, I'm crazy with grief because of the whole thing, out of my gourd, my head, but in control enough to take care of Margo through all this, who as they can imagine is as distraught as anyone but sort of okay, holding it in, I don't know when it's going to come out in a kid's way and if it does if I'll be able to handle it, but so far she and I are okay, and maybe I can get the doctor closest to this to talk to him (or her) if he's still around, but before I get off to get him I'd want to give the doctor's name and name and phone number of the hospital so they don't lose contact with me, for if I do lose contact with them—I could, I'm holding it in too but am underlyingly that overcome—they won't be able to reach me since they won't know where I am. I could be at any hospital from there to where I live, right? "Oh, if we were only home, all three of us, girls and me, dinner done, dishes washed and traveling things put away, place tidied the way I like it, neat piles, rug under the dinner table swept, getting ready for bed, maybe in bed—the kids; if I were that tired from the trip and cleaning up and things, me—for I don't know what time it is, maybe long past their normal bedtime when tomorrow's a school day," I'd probably say if I'd said all the rest of what came before it. So I'd say "Hold on, the doctor's and hospital's name have to be here someplace," and I'd look on the desk for personal stationery or an envelope addressed to the doctor—you do that now, look, nothing there with the doctor's or hospital's name on it, open the top drawer—wait a minute, the diplomas on

the walls would have his name on them—but in it there's a manila
envelope with the doctor's name and hospital address—and I'd give
this information to whichever parent I was speaking to and say the
phone number they can get by calling Information in this state, for
it's not on the phone—and then I'd say "Okay, stay on"—say it if
I was able to—"I'm going to look for the doctor, he might be
outside the door here or down the hall but in hearing distance—
I'm in his cubicle in the hospital, his private room, office, calling
from it, I wanted privacy for this call, and if you're not on when
I get back, don't worry, I'll call back soon as I can, so if you do
get off, keep the line clear, or if you want to get me, ask for this
doctor's private number when you call the hospital, say 'His cubicle,' they'll know . . . so I'm going," though I'd probably say before
I go—I'd definitely say if Lee was home and they told her or I
somehow had before but she wasn't the one I was speaking to
now, "How is Lee now, what's she doing, what are you doing to
help her, how much help does she need? Maybe you should call
your own doctor right after this to see what he can do for her and
for you too, for advice, who can give you a psychiatrist to call and
possibly come now if you don't know of one, she might need
medicine, something for sleep, I don't see how she couldn't, someone professional there like that with those things to help you with
her and also to help the two of you," and then after they told me
I'd say "So I'm going, I'll try to be quick," and put the receiver
down and look outside the door and if the doctor was there or
down the hall I'd ask him to speak to my mother- or father-in-law
and tell them what he thinks they should know about Julie and
answer any questions they may have, or by now even Lee if she
was there, maybe she'd want to talk to him, and if he wasn't there
and he probably wouldn't be and there was no one from the hospital around I could ask to get him, for I now have his name down,
I'd race back to the phone—before I left the room I'd have done
something to make sure the door wouldn't close and lock—and if
one of my in-laws was still on the line—I don't know what I'd say
if I said hello on the phone, "anybody there?" and Lee was the

one now on, though maybe by now I could say something clear
and sound and also maybe she'd by now be somewhat calm—"The
doctor's not around, what more can I say, or maybe I should look
for him more, how's Lee now?" and if it was Lee there, "Lee . . .
Lee . . . what more can I do for you from here, what can either of
us do? We're devastated, but we got to control ourselves somehow,
for our sakes for Margo's sake, meaning that we don't want to
destroy her by destroying ourselves, there's no point in cracking
up—not that, it isn't a question of a point or not, but if one does,
you do, I'll take care of Margo and you, crack up if you have to
and nothing can stop it, I'll be there forever for you, I swear,
though try if it's possible to wait till I get there or you're here or
we're together somewhere soon, please." Anyway, that's some of
what I'd do on the phone. Not the best, no great plan, but the
aim's good. It probably is the best you can muster under the circumstances and considering your limitations and if you're alone on
the phone doing it. What's that mean—the last? It means maybe
you should, after all, have the doctor beside you while you call or
have him be the one calling Lee and her parents about it with you
beside him, and you think about this and you think and think and
think and you think no, best it comes only from you when you're
alone. You can't say why. You could if you really thought about
it perhaps. The doctor might inhibit you somewhat to a lot. It just
wouldn't seem right in a way, saying the deepest most grievous
thing possible to the person closest to you and who'd be most
affected by it, with a medical professional you didn't know till an
hour ago standing next to you and in so small a room, or having
someone like that say it for you to her or one of the two persons
closest to her and who'd almost be as affected by it. And such a
small room, barely a cubicle. Or rightly named one: desk, chair,
but narrower than usual desk and chair, even the bookshelves seem
narrower than usual or is that some sort of illusion because the
room's so small, and so many things hanging from hooks and pegs
on the walls and door, probably because there's so little space in
the room. There was a comedian, when you were a boy, who used

to say either on TV when you still watched or the Paramount Theater stage, so you would have been high school age, "Our apartment's so small the furniture's painted on the—" no, zero in on the phone. You ready? Yes, and you lift the receiver. "To get around we had to walk sideways once past the door." You start to dial. Stomach nervous pains like when dialing girls thirty years ago, forty, or with your hand on the receiver ready to pick it up to dial. Girls you wanted to date but didn't think they'd be interested even a first time. Or girls you'd dated once and wanted to again but didn't think they would. What would you say to them on the phone? You're stalling again and you know it but what would you say? And what digit were you on when you stopped dialing? and you put the receiver down. "Hi, my name's Nathan Frey, you wouldn't remember me," this for the first date but they'll find out you're not that smart or sharp or with it in a way they like or you don't come from a family with dough or go to a private high school or one of the elite public ones, or something else or they already found that out the first time you met or that you're just not their type. You'd thought a lot about what approach to take and what might be the best weekday time to call: around nine, after they might have their homework and house chores done, maybe had a shower or bath, were feeling clean and relieved and relaxed, sort of the start of the quiet time of night and when your mind seemed a bit sharper and line cleverer and voice lower, so you felt more confident, but not much later than nine for they could use the excuse that their parents thought it a little late for someone to call them, even a good friend, especially when the conversations tended to go on for a while, and not earlier because their folks might want to use the phone or were expecting a call. Nine-fifteen to -thirty and if you could swing it, for you didn't want anyone interrupting you and stopping your concentration, when no one was home or wanted to use the phone. For a second date: "Hi, it's Nathan Frey, or Nat, okay, but never Nathaniel, how you doing, what's been happening, have a good week?" Or the first time: "We met at the Dalton dance last week . . . at the Jewish Center party . . . coming out of RKO last Saturday, you were with a friend, I was with a pal who knew her . . . curly brown hair kind of unkempt, about five feet eight without shoes," later "five feet nine . . . ten . . . almost six feet . . . let's say six feet flat though not with flat feet but with shoes that were recently heeled . . . slim," always slim but actually skinny, "in a blue V-neck sweater . . . blue windbreaker . . . blue button-down-collar Oxford-cloth shirt," and if it was a dance, "three-button brown tweed jacket" for about four years, sleeves let out till the lining showed, "dark" or "light gray flannel pants," for a while "scuffed white bucks . . . you mentioned Frankie Laine . . . Johnnie Ray . . . some English singer Vera Lynn and this moving wartime song she sung that's now a big hit . . . Menotti's new opera on Broadway we both said we wanted to go to, about Little Italy, lovers' quarrel that ends with the girl getting stabbed or shot to death but sung in a language you can understand and where there are words in it like, you know, 'bitch' and 'shit,' we both heard about it and agreed better at a regular theater than the Met, well, if you still want to see it . . ." Sweating now as you used to do then before and during the call. Hands, face. Stomach, as if you're going to have the runs. Dizzy too but little did you know. What a jump. One kind of call to an entirely different kind but some of the same physical feelings or symptoms or manifestations you think or whatever the word for it is and push-button now or whatever they call it instead of rotary dial then or whatever it's called. Stop. Dial. Doctor might be knocking on the door soon and you want to get it over with before. Not "get it over with" but— Then to use as an incentive then. Not that either. But ready? Never, of course. There is no right— Just stop all that crap and dial. You dial.

INTERSTATE 7

 uy in the car to the left of ours looking at me. I didn't see the
car till just before this second, nod to him, eyes back on the
road, car he's in stays beside ours maybe four-five feet away;
maybe six. "Yes," I think, "what?" looking at him. "You're aw-
fully close, any reason to be? No answer. Wouldn't think so. Just
the look, the straight stare, oh you're a toughie, bet your kids are
scared shit of ya," and look front and steer the car closer to the
right lane line. Few seconds later I feel—sense—he's doing something with his hand, motioning, or waving something and maybe
even from outside and I look over and car he's in has moved over
to almost cross the lane into mine and his window's down and
he's pointing out of it at me and has this smirk or sneer or I don't
know what, not the noncommittal plain know-nothing to even
dopey look from before trying to be hard but some smart-ass

scorning sarcastic smile if I want to say it in a mouthful, and I think "Why, what's with him, did I do something with my driving he didn't like and for all I know might have, or he thought so, endangered their car for a moment or maybe the driver thought this and told him to let me know for he's closer?" and say through my window "Yes?" and Margo in back says "What's the man pointing at you for, Daddy?" and I say "Beats me. —Yes sir, what, something wrong?" I mouth to him now, raising my eyebrows to show, or by doing that making lots of folds in my forehead, but that I'm asking a serious question and am no wiseguy and maybe something's wrong with my car that he's seen and he wants to tell me but doesn't know how to look at people or really deal with them in any way, or just strangers, but how he's doing, or possibly just normal rather conventional looking guys with kids in tow who he thinks might be some threat to him for some reason, that they do seem so normal and content and polite while he's such a roughneck who can't keep anything, job, woman, family, but I'm no doubt going too far into it, and he starts laughing riotously while pointing at me, to even shutting his eyes and opening his mouth wide and probably making haw-haw noises it's all so funny and then says something to the driver who starts laughing normally—I'm looking back and forth at the road and them—but almost as if he doesn't really want to laugh, his face I mean, but feels he has to for the other guy's sake—honor, whatever—or so the other guy doesn't think he hasn't a sense of humor or something. In other words, his heart's not in it, and out of friendship or fellowship, I mean. They beat up people the same way, I bet: even if you think the guy who's arguing with your friend is absolutely right and your friend's dead wrong you still stomp the guy with your friend because he is your friend. And I look front and I don't know why, out of nowhere perhaps but maybe more so from some nervousness with these guys keeping up this thing with me like they are and their car being closer than I like and still almost in my lane, maybe straddling the in-between line now and staying even with us so long, but I say "So what do you think they find so funny, girls?"—asking them this to distract myself from those guys, is what I'm saying—"and don't look, no staring, don't give them any more cause for continuing whatever it is they're continuing," and Julie says "What is it that they're doing, Daddy, and the driver's doing it too?" and I say "That's just it, I don't know what it is, playing goofy loony games with me is all I can see. There are all sorts of stupid people in this world I'm afraid to tell you, but when they get on the road they're even worse. The car seems to bring something out in people that nothing else does, and it isn't just the speed and enclosure of the thing either—you know, being contained in it, inside, windows shut, cut off from other people. For even the bumper cars at the amusement park do it to people—excite them, make them reckless. But that's a bad example since they're made for craziness and you pay to get in them and drive wildly, but I guess I was saying that those things are wide open and aren't fast at all while most real cars are the opposite. Meaning, fast or slow, open or enclosed, just being in a car, even a kiddy car when you're a kid— I remember how reckless and adult I felt in them—does it. And in a way, though you can't get in them but they can make kids wild and strange a little, those miniature toy cars kids have— Matchboxes, because they come in them or that's the size they are—that they roll against the wall or smash into other tiny cars like it, or off a table and that sort of stuff. So it's cars of all kinds we can say—kiddy and bumper ones, toy cars and real convertibles and Jeeps. Two-seaters, six-seaters, racing and stock cars of course, probably not blood- and bookmobiles and golf carts, but panel trucks, minivans, though not as much, I'd think, possibly because families are usually in them. They're made for parents with their kids, you can say, and families can be kind of inhibiting on the road. Restraining. You know, they keep control of the driver's most reckless and wild emotions when he's outside, while inside, meaning in the house and not the car, it could be another story where all sorts of violent terrible stuff can go on. But anyway, you don't want to drive too fast and carelessly and take chances—that's it—take chances with your wife and kids in the car, so almost any car or minitruck when they're in it and also your cats and dogs and so on. Oh, do I know what I'm talking about? Nobody answer but I'm afraid not. Though what was I talking about way before I started all that about cars and pets?" and Julie says "I don't know, you lost me long ago," and I say "Thank ye, thank ye—oh yeah, about what do you girls think those men found so funny before from their car, anyone have an idea now?" "Not me," Julie says and I say "My face, right? Maybe my face. Got to be that, for we all know it's funny, and can't be your faces for yours are gorgeous and who laughs at that? So, fine, my funny-looking spongy face and maybe my balding scalp—they both had big hairy clumps on theirs—and we'll leave it at that," and Julie says "I don't think your face is so funny, and you have hair," and I say "Not in the right head places, but thanks. And Margo, you've been noticeably quiet, anything wrong?" and she says "I've lost interest in the subject," and I say "Oh, well, that's—uh," for I see without looking right at it that a car's alongside us again when one hasn't been there for a couple of minutes, not that I saw the guys' car go, I was too caught up in my talking, and I say "Listen, and I'm serious, I've a funny feeling those same two palookas are beside us again on my side, anyone want to sneak a peek for me and report back?— maybe it's a different car," and Julie says "The same, they're there for lots more seconds than just now, something the matter, Daddy?" and I say "Are they—do this from memory, neither of you look—were they staring or laughing again?" and Margo says "Staring, at you, the man not the driver was. And now kind of trying to talk to you through your window. And now making these hand movements as if rolling down a car window while also pointing to you as if you should do it with yours," and I say "I told you not to look, goddamnit," and she says "I'm sorry, Daddy, I didn't mean to; I'm now looking straight ahead at only nothing, but are you worried by him?" and I say "The truth is, without trying to scare you kids, the good thing is they're not so danger-

ously close as they were the first time— And continue not to look
at them, just as I'm not and won't, for sooner we completely
ignore them I'm sure quicker they'll go away. But I just didn't
like the looks of those guys. Not the looks so much as what they
did and are still doing, distracting my attention, or trying to,
really, and just being dumb, but real dumb dumb dumb, as if they
want to spook me off the road, for who the fuck they think they
are?—excuse me, but I'm mad at them and with good reason—I
got my kids with me," and I speed up and Margo says "I hope I
didn't make you feel bad before by what I said about losing interest," and I yell "Please, not now," for their car stays beside ours,
"I've got too much to do driving, and sit back tight, make sure
you're buckled in good in case they try to do something crazy
with their car—they could," and Margo yells "Oh no," and I say
"What's wrong?" and Julie says "My gosh, Daddy, what?" and
I shout "It's okay, nothing will happen, but do what I say, and
let me drive," and slow down and their car continues as fast
and the guy sticks his head out and turns it around to me and
gives this sinister big grin and then sticks his hand out the window
and points it at me into sort of a pistol shape and takes aim, one
eye cocked, and I think says "Bang bang," his mouth moves like
that, or maybe "Pop pop," and then puts the pistol hand up to
his mouth and blows gunsmoke off his fingertip and brings his
head back into the car and faces front and they're now about a
hundred feet in front of us, his pistol hand open and dangling
down the door, and now a hundred-fifty, two hundred, and their
car cuts into my lane without signaling and slows down a little
and I think "What're they up to now?" and slows down some
more and then shoots across the next center lane into the slow
one and really speeds up till it must be doing eighty-five, ninety,
no car's in front of it, even a hundred, it seems to be going so
fast. I look around for a patrol car same time I'm keeping my
eyes on the men, or an unmarked car with a trooper in it in
trooper's clothes and maybe the hat. I'd love to see those bastards
caught. If one went after them with the roof light or siren going

I'd follow at a reasonable clip just to stay near and pull up behind
on the shoulder once the trooper stopped them and explain to
him why I was speeding like that myself: what these guys tried
doing to me and my kids, the scare tactics and driving close and
so on. By now their car's way off, half a mile or so, quarter-mile,
third of one, anyway, pretty far in front and still speeding it seems
and now no threat to us, for I can't think of them slowing down
so much where they'd come back and resume what they were doing,
and soon they're out of sight or just mixed in with lots of tiny dots that
are cars and buses and trucks. "It's okay, girls, you can relax,
the idiots are gone," slowing down even more and moving into
the slow lane to be out of the way of any cars that might want to
get around me, for my body has that feeling of having gone
through something very scary, heart pumping where I can feel it,
the stuff in the larynx or neck, and of course the sweat, and
Margo says "It wasn't really ever that bad, was it, Daddy?" and
I say "Nah, though for a moment I thought so, but I'll tell you,
if I ever saw those guys stopped off the road by some cop for
speeding, which they should be, but you know, as they say, 'try
and find a cop when you truly need one,' well I'd pull over and
tell the policeman what they did. But okay, good riddance and
may we never see them or anything like them again," and Julie
says "What's 'good riddance'?" and Margo tells her and though
her definition's all wrong—something like riders no longer riding—I don't correct her. What would I say to the policeman
though? That they drove alongside us awhile, sort of were following us, tried to screw up my driving by trying to frighten me with
those sinister grins and getting too close and also that thing with
the hand shaped like a gun when they tore off? It would be nothing; they could give all sorts of innocent and plausible reasons
why they did it: they like kids, at least the passenger does, but in
a good way and he was trying to make my sourpusses laugh by
making faces. Or he thought my door wasn't closed all the way
and was pointing it out to me, that's why their car got so close,
because I didn't seem to hear him and they thought it too im-

portant to let pass, and that's also what his so-called shooting finger meant: it was pointing to my door, and they never crossed the lane line into mine either, and so forth. The trooper might just laugh at me or tell me to be a good guy and forget it, even if he half believed me, and move on, for he has more important business to take care of, like writing out a speeding ticket—that he has clocked on his radar—and calling in on them to see if their car's stolen or they owe for past traffic violations in this state.

"Those two laughing men before," Margo says a couple of minutes later, "did they actually bother you so much where you got scared? They did us, me and Julie agree," and I say " 'Julie and I, Julie and I,' " and Julie says "I said they scared me only a little but not so much," and Margo says "That's not true, we were just talking about it," and Julie says "Don't lie, I didn't say those men were so bad, only for a little," and Margo says "She doesn't know what she says, even right after she says it," and Julie says "Not so, you're lying again," and swings at her it seems because Margo says "Dada, you told me to tell you when she's hitting me so I'm telling you instead of hitting back, she just punched me in the arm," and I say "Did it hurt?" and Julie says "It couldn't have, I missed her," and Margo says "All right, so she almost did it," and Julie says " 'Almost' isn't doing it," and Margo says "You aimed to hit, that's bad from the start," and I say, "Girls, girls, enough already, arguing over what you said about those men and now this is silly and swinging at anyone about anything, even if you intend to miss, is dead wrong. And now you're distracting me even worse than those guys. Anybody mind some music? I think I know the public radio station in this neck of the woods. 91.1 or 91.9—one or the other, for we're somewhere between Philadelphia and Delaware and I've heard them both on these trips," and Margo says "Not your music, do me a favor; I don't like it. Can't we have some of ours for a change?" and I say "Maybe it'll be interesting talk or folk music or something, even someone reading for kids, but we're not going to listen to your music—that you can do when you're home in

your own room, for it stinks," and she says "That's not nice, I
only said I didn't like your music, I didn't use profanities against
it," and I say " 'Stinks' isn't a profanity and anyway, all of it?—
all my music? You don't like any of it? That Bach Christmas stuff
we listened to last Christmastime, in New York on that twenty-
four-hour radio station that goes—you know, the Columbia University one run by students—all night for eight days or so with
just Bach and maybe some of his family? You said you liked some
of it. That was to me like a breaking-open moment for you with
good music when you said that and without any prompting from
me. I think it was part of the Mass and then those organ preludes
played on the piano. And also, just a few weeks ago when I played
the tape, the Messiaen *Journey Till the End of Time* or *for the
End of Time*—no 'journey,' just a *Quartet for* is what it's called,
with the flute part that you said you especially—clarinet and piano
part, I mean, that you—" and she says "All right, I don't like
most of your music but might have liked them, but you still
shouldn't have cursed mine," and I say "Anyway, not 'stinks,'
your music; just it's so young, so you know, not for me," and
she says "That's not what you want from us for an apology when
we say something you don't like and you're right," and I say
"Okay, okay, I've got a headache, I probably was shaken up by
those men more than I thought. Maybe I've also been driving too
long, I should take a break, it's been an extralong weekend and
I got tired of living in a cramped space in someone else's over-
heated airless home, so cut it, will ya?" and she says "If you
insist," and I say "Don't get cynical with me, don't be sarcastic,"
and she says "If you insist," and I say "Listen you!" and Julie
says "Daddy, stop, for what'd she say?" though she has good
reason to be cynical and sarcastic, or just mad at me. For why
didn't I apologize right off—"That wasn't a smart" or "sensible"
or "tactful" or something "way to express myself, I admit it"—
and end it then? I could still do it but don't feel like it now. I
doubt I could get the right words out, any words about it out,
and she'll also think I'm only saying it to smooth things over

rather than that I believe it. I do believe it, I'm just not a good one for apologizing, but I'll do it later, later will be okay, in the car, at a rest stop, or home; I'll have a drink, look at the mail, newspaper, open a book, just a nice quiet one with the drink, but I'll also have to make supper—what are we going to eat?—and if the kids aren't around or don't want to come in when I need help—they could say they've been in the car most of the day and want to play outside—set the table, do everything, bring all the junk in from the car, put things away, do the wash after three days and what was here before, maybe two loads, and the dryer, mix some fruit juice for them, salad dressing, so on. Maybe we can have—the kids can, I'll just have coffee and then at home a piece of cheese, carrot and celery and bread and wine—dinner on the road. And smoked turkey if any's left and hasn't spoiled, tomato, mustard. Sure, they'll like it and anything they want: sit down at Bob's Big Boy, salad bar which they love going up to a few times—there'd be no rush and then, over that table while they're eating and after I say "Anyone want dessert after this?" say I'm sorry and why. "It *was* probably still those guys," et cetera . . . "My 'music stinks' remark stunk," and so on; but now forget it and I reach for the radio Play button. "Anybody mind some music? Oops, sorry, I already said that, excuse me, and look what it brought, tee-hee." No response, so maybe they didn't hear, and usually when I imitate that kind of laughing they find it funny and laugh. I look at the rearview and flip it around; they're looking at me through it, dour faces, almost scowling, so *there*, wrong again. At least they can see I'm back to being in a good mood but maybe they didn't catch that or don't want to, harboring their, well, hurt, as people do. Harboring? Nothing on the two public radio stations, one of which I thought I could pick up here, and I dial around. What seems like a public station I didn't know of on another frequency: the voices and subject, news analysis or sociological or medical call-in show, something about TB and lack of public awareness of it which is only increasing the current pandemic, and turn it off. "Good, that was boring," Margo says and I say "Boring, and in a car on a long trip I can almost listen to any discussion, debate or talk. Not religious, though, meaning not a religious discussion or lecture unless it's mostly secular, meaning with the emphasis not on holy spirits and God who art in heaven and doctrines and dogmatisms and no-no's and don't-do's and so forth. Common everyday morality and ethics and holy-book interpretations can be okay, and who-am-I's and what-am-I-doing-here's and where'm-I-going's—questions, you see, so long as they're not accompanied by the rigorous—*rigid* self-righteous . . . well, you know." Neither asks what some of these words mean or for me to go over any part of it again because she didn't understand and I don't offer immediate unasked-for definitions and sentence use of them as I often do and maybe say some of what I said in a clearer way. They want to be quiet, or at least not speak to me, let them. Why do people act like those guys before, that's what I'd really like to know. So untouchable, mean-spirited, worse. Maybe killers or brutes as I thought. Hyenas, jackals, if they're not the same thing. Some word or words or term. I don't understand this country, for it really doesn't happen anywhere else, meaning as much. "Oh, it doesn't, and the whole country?" someone could say and I'd say, I'd say, well, "In this kind of wacky pass-by almost violence and also the actual violence other places, yes, or almost. I mean you don't need too many thugs like those guys to make living lousy and unlivable." For why do we produce so many killers and bastards like that, and if not that then people so firmly dumb—not "firmly" but determinedly or something; almost religiously; doggedly dumb. I like that, and into the double D's again for some reason. But also, I read—what did I read? In my head and then it went. Something about how much of the country's functionally illiterate, whatever percent—forty was it, fifty? I mean the comparisons with all other Western countries and the more advanced ones elsewhere were staggering, but what's that got to do with what I was thinking? Well, I thought . . . but maybe it's simply, or this would help somewhat, that directions for everything should be made easier.

But where was I? Something about killer bastards and doggy dumbness. I read and read about it in articles and such and . . . what? I don't know. I forgot. I'm impossible. So goddamn stupid sometimes. Don't be so hard on yourself and fill yourself with guilt, Lee says and she's right, but I am, I do, impossible, stupid, guilty, hard on myself, other things like that, lots of times. I just don't think straight, so often. I just don't . . . but formulate it in your head the point you want to make. Try, as a diversion and maybe a test: what you say inside you can say out. Do it articulately, confidently, not so much eloquently, but comprehensively—comprehensibly?—just *intelligently* and directly, and ask and answer that way in your head too. So: these guys . . . they're in a car . . . they drive up beside us on the highway—no, go into the general thing of it. There, perfect example: "the general thing of it," as if that means anything, and "go into," which is such sluggard speech, almost a slur. What I'm really saying here, and say it well, already, is there's—is that there's a social malaise in this country—good, and good word too, malaise, came out spontaneously, though the "social" should go because it's such a cliché—and it seems to be spreading at its own speed through the—chuck the "at its own speed": familiar, not needed, and what's it mean anyway? It's spreading, period, from here to there and nearly everywhere to the point where just about nowhere's safe. It's global, or almost, or getting there. Brought about by a tremendous—you also don't need the "tremendous"; just simple words and sentences and no superfluous or fancy adjectives. Brought about by societal and familial—society and family changes and increased mobility and home and job transience so no or little strong neighborhood feelings and allegiance anymore perhaps and lots of divorces and drugs don't help, which is—to get deeper into it—to speak about it more deeply—and the movies and songs being played and performed and television and video games, some of them with gang rapes and beheadings in them but yet for kids. And guns, of course, the numbers of them in the dumbest hands, and how's it help to have a strong or tight neighborhood anyway if hoodlums and brigands, you can even say, are zipping through it in cars and robbing and shooting up people and zipping back to the Interstates because of their easy access, invisibility and fast escape? That came out sort of okay. And maybe the scarcity of jobs or just the shortage of them and so many poor-paying ones, but I don't know, and shifting values and morality, though all that's "societal" or "society change," isn't it? People hardly even read anymore, and one has to think that only makes things worse. Anyway, it's all killing things or they are, the malaise is and most of those reasons I gave are, and those guys before—real good books, I'm saying, the ones that say yes this is the way people think, feel and live and life shouldn't be to scare people off the road or shoot them in the head—were an example of—the result— just examples, those guys were, of it, the malaise. See? This couldn't be worse. I just can't think well or straight or at least put words together about what I want to say, inside and probably out. Meaning aloud, and inside should come easier than out, right? Just try to steamroll through, maybe that'll work. For years ago ... Because years ago, thirty, forty, did people drive along and—people didn't drive by your car and do things like those guys did or anything like it. There was such a thing—there was road courtesy and same kind of behavior or thereabouts when you walked past someone on the sidewalk. You didn't stare him down; nobody shot you a look; people weren't provoked so fast; they didn't have this idea that they had to have respect from other people twenty-four hours a day. I'm talking about when I was a kid growing up in a big city and even when I was in my teens, twenties and thirties, almost. Actually, in my teens other teens were a lot like that, they just didn't have the weapons they have today. But as an adult other adults for the most part smiled at one another naturally, genuinely, not hostilely—I'm talking about from another car. But people in almost all situations were less aggressive to and suspicious of one another than they are today. Forget "suspicious of"; it's got nothing to do with my argument, or little. But if they looked into your car from theirs, they—though

my dad did tell me that when I was a boy and sleeping in the front
passenger seat next to him, someone spit through the window at
him from a car when they'd both stopped for the light, but that
was when a race riot was going on in the city and he'd by some
mistake driven too close to it. Or maybe someone ran up to the
driver's window when we'd stopped and spit at him. But people
then were mostly polite, had better manners, I'm almost sure of
that, at least in cars and on the street, and if they didn't they still
didn't bait you over nothing and weren't provoked by the slightest
thing or give you killer smiles. For that's what those smiles were
with those guys. I bet they do have guns. I bet they are up to no
good. I bet by the end of the day someone's going to get roughed
up by them or one of them and maybe a couple of people, even
to three or four, over drugs, being shot in the head. And they're
all around, these guys, that's what I'm saying. It's not just the
newspapers, I hear it from relatives and friends. They're robbed,
their homes are broken into, cars stolen, they're pistol-whipped
without being robbed, they're beaten up in a bar because some
stranger thinks they slipped a laxative into his drink, one friend's
son is intentionally run down when he's changing a tire, another's
caught in a crossfire at high school on his way to class and gets
a bullet in his lung, a woman at work has her apartment cleaned
out one day and is mugged on the bus the next and then stuck
in the buttock by a passerby the third day with what the police
say was a hatpin. I even know two women this year who have
been raped, one by her husband she's separated from, but still,
it's something I think someone like him never would have done
under the same circumstances ten to twenty years ago, so why?
For all of these, I mean: why the increase in their happening, and
all over the place as I said? Just that people are more violent or
prone to it and defensive and short-fused and just argumentative
and angry at things and have less inside them somehow to control
themselves and also the frustration that comes from having no
language or just ability to speak, something like me but much
worse, to say calmly or just some way what's bugging them and

to end it at that, to walk away from it I'm saying, or drive away if that's what it was in today's case. But all those reasons can only be taken so far and don't really go deep enough. For it's also just wanting, this killing and mugging and stuff, quick cash to get whatever they want from it—drugs, flashy cars, hundred-dollar sneakers, you name it—with no feelings for people and the consequences of what they do to them and so on, but what causes that? Parents again, or rather the absence and shortcomings of them, and television, movies, society, et cetera, just examples all around of real people in the legit world doing everything they can legitimately to make a ton of money too without any feelings for who they screw. Oh I don't know. You also hear about lack of religious upbringing or influence of religion today and very little teaching of right-behaving beliefs and such on what people do, but I still don't know and for sure didn't say that clear. This is where I get off or should, when I have to try and figure out the whys of overall things from personal experiences and information I'm not really a good put-togetherer of. But I also have to say that good people are around too, of course, and they make up the majority by a vast lot, but that there are more than enough bad ones to make it rough going for the good, something like that. In other words, to rephrase it, good people vastly outnumber the bad, that's a known, or at least people who don't physically harm or threaten other people, but in the long run—not the "long run" so much as just—

"Daddy," Margo says and I say "What?—whew! you scared me, I was so into—involved with my own thoughts—that I . . . anyway, saved by the girl," and she says "What's that?" and I say "Bell, as in prizefight, boxing, saved by it, the timer's bell, like a boxer who was almost going to be counted out—referee over him; you know, or maybe you don't," and I hold the wheel with my left hand while the right one with the forefinger out wags like a referee's when he's calling off the seconds a boxer's been knocked down, " 'One . . . two . . . three . . .' But the bell ended the round, meaning the girl did, you, ended my confused thinking, before the boxer on the ground was counted out of the fight at ten," and she says "I don't—" and I say "Ten seconds, I mean; that's how long they give the knocked-down boxer to get up if the round's still going on—they're three minutes each," and she says "I don't know boxing, not the smaller things in it, and I don't know what the bell means to the girl," and I say "Good, you don't have to, it's a stupid savage sport—you know, part of our culture so who am I to say and so on. With millions of fiends—*fans*—loving it . . . that wasn't a joke by the way, I actually said 'fiends' for 'fans' by mistake. And some of the boxers make fortunes from it, when they might earn peanuts for their lives otherwise and maybe become street hoods. But like bull-fighting in Spain and southern France or wherever they still kill the bull at the end of the fight, Portugal, or maybe it's the reverse—no, never in France—it's antiquated, out of date, too brutal and too much like gladiators killing off each other in coliseums; that was two thousand years ago. Animals—humans, bulls, fighting cocks, anything—tarantulas—shouldn't be killed for money or sport," and Margo says "Even the meat we eat? For we have to pay for it," and I say "Hamburgers and grilled tuna steaks are another thing. I'm talking of . . . anyway, I forgot I was driving with you kids before, I was so engrossed in my own thoughts. But what were you going to ask me when I said *whew!*" and she says "I forgot too, and this isn't it, what were you thinking that made you so scared then?" and I say "Those guys, their looks while they did it, and especially doing it while there were you kids in the car, the freaking, well, freaking bastards—it's not such a bad word for what they did and I save it for rats like that," and she says "Why did they, do you think?" and I say "Who knows? Bad bringing up, I'll tell you, or maybe they had a great one but the neighborhood toughs or something wherever they lived had a bigger influence on them than their parents did when they were teens or even younger. In other words—why do I always say 'in other words,' or so often? Because I can't say anything straight or unqualified it seems, meaning, well, heck with what it means, I'd just be doing it some more—or clear first time out. Meaning I can't say it, first time out, clearly either. But in other words, their parents lost their influence and these guys, if they were once smart, got dumb because for years being dumb or acting it has been the fashion, you know," and she says "How?" and I say "Talking it, for instance—'Hey man, hey dude, yo, I dunno, I ain't like going, gonna dis this muddy rudder,' and so on. And looking and walking it too—the haircuts that make them look moronic, initials or coded messages scissored into their scalps, or maybe with razors, but some way—what barbershops do they go to? And the sides or just one side completely shaved as if they had brain surgery there while the rest of the mop's floppy and wild, not to mention those bleached and greased spikes that run down the middle of their heads like porcupine quills or warpath Indians. And the slouch, the clothes, caps on backwards like baseball catchers or tough Hell's Kitchen gang members—that's when I was a boy, kids with switchblades, before your time, but just the thought of them ganging up on me used to scare me more than anything," and Margo says "I wear a cap that way sometimes," and I say "Yeah, but you're a little girl, I'm talking about grownups or semiadults. And walking with their pants intentionally belted around their buttocks as if they're about to fall off, or even below the crotch area, I don't know how they stay on, but cuffs dragging up crud and such from the street. And I'm just referring to the guys and not even going into the stick-through studs they got up and down both lobes and through their noses and one woman, I even saw, through her lip and another with a safety pin through her belly-button nub—you know, the piece that—" and she says "Other than for the lip and thing-y, what's so wrong with it? It doesn't hurt you if they have it and if you don't like what you see, turn away but don't say how much you hate it," and I say "One earring or stud per ear should be enough, I'd think; more than that's mutilating the body, and safety pins should be for what they were invented for—fastening things safely and not stylishly and painfully. And please, if you ever think to do this, even with your own money, don't come home with a big gold band clamped through your ear like a freshly killed kosher chicken has through its wing—you wouldn't know of that because I always unclamp the band before I cook the chicken, but young people are ravaging their ears with similar things. And okay, I'm an old fuddy-duddy I suppose and a bit of a crank, and I'll even grant you the cruddy cuffs and stuff—they're funny and actually make me laugh when I see pants worn that way—but buying shirts and pants with holes and rips manufactured into them down to the frayed threads and at probably twice the price these clothes would cost if they were bought whole?" and she says "Dad, nobody wears them anymore except in old TV shows like from two to three years ago. It was a style, like all those things you hate are styles. Kids like styles and looking right. Older people do too but different kinds," and I say "But the boots," and she says "The boots?" and I think "Nah, I've said enough," but I say "The ludicrous boots. Ones that cost seventy, eighty, a hundred bucks for kids, and what kind?—authentic work boots when they're not working, they're schooling or fooling around. I bet they even use them for dances and gyms. Even if they work at McDonald's, these boots are for lumberjacks or people who climb telephone poles to the top to fix downed lines—they're conducted or something to prevent electric shocks; they're permanently oiled to keep out woods-like mud and slush and maybe something else is done to them to ward off snake bites," and she says "I like work boots and I want to get a pair, and most of them are only copies of the real," and Julie says "I like them too, hightops," and Margo says "They aren't boots," and I say "Okay, let's close it, I'm getting nowhere in my argument with you—discussion. But I—this is all I was saying before, that those guys who gawked eerily into our car at us and with theirs got too close reminded me in a way of overage teenagers, even if they were in their twenties—well, that's my point, and the driver maybe thirty-plus. But they had that look of guys who never and will never grow up, which I hope what we're discussing here will help you to never have or not as

long or much. It's such a repugnant puss though I realize as kids
growing up you gotta try all kinds before the more fitting decent
one sticks—all wiseguy and sly smile and insecure oafish to brain-
less grimace and pout. And which probably is the danger that
comes from your parents, if they're good sensible people, losing
their influence on you," and she says "Why, what were they wearing?" and I say "Wearing? You barely took in a word I said and
after all my sputtering muddled effort," and she says "Yes I did,
why?" and I say "Because you could only say 'What were they
wearing?' Oh boy do people try to fool you when they're caught
or might look bad, not that you did or weren't entitled, sweetie—
it was me remissing," and she says "You said clothes has a lot to
do with it, so I'm asking what," and I say "That's right, you're
right. A necklace, the driver; an ear stud, the other," and she says
"You saw that?" and I say "Yeah, the necklace, as if it had long
teeth or white bones from a shark on it, but definitely very primi-
tive. And the window guy not just the stud but I think another
one pierced through his nostril like the ones I spoke of before,"
and she says "You're making it up," and Julie says "I didn't see
it, I had my eyes closed, but I wish I had," and I say "I only
think I saw the nose ring but the ear thing I definitely did and
maybe two," and Margo says "If he had them I would've seen it,
I was looking more than you—I was watching you too and didn't
have to drive. But what else in clothes and things, this is getting
interesting," and I say "Just that, perhaps the ear guy a tie, the
driver a hat, and both with those arrogant contemptuous looks,
but the ear guy the worst," and she says " 'Contemptuous'?" and
I say "Snotty, sniffy, snooty in a cruel way—so, 'Why?' I was
asking myself then, and not just what was making them act like
that but everything years before and all around us today that went
into it, for that was what you wanted to know, right?—what
thoughts I had before you made me jump?" and she says nothing
and I say "You nodding or shaking your head or just thinking?"
and she says "I didn't see any tie or hat, but yes, what?" and I
say "Well, if that's an invite for me to go on, and I'm almost sure

the driver wore a hat, then they, these men, represented something to me—a toughness today, et cetera, that didn't exist so pervasively—all around, so much—and also so maniacally, murderously, prevalently—all around again and as much—as years ago when I was a boy—" and Julie says "Oh-oh, Margo, when Daddy was a boy again," and I say "Yes, sure, a boy and then a teen and so on, same things you'll be except for the boy, but cutting it off, meaning it got worse, when I got to around thirty. Not that I'm saying I didn't get into fights when I was a kid. I did, as my neighborhood, and especially the ones around it, and later my high school, could be rough and boys acted that way then. At a party or right after school, grade or high. Or they suddenly appeared on your street in a big group and got after you—picked fights, we called it—and over nothing. To show they were tough. For dopey or psychological reasons I don't want to go into—having to do with their minds and the way they were raised—and you protected yourself or set a time and place, usually in the park on the grass so you didn't crack your skull on the pavement, and fought them one to one, your friends and theirs standing in a ring around you so nobody cheated in the fight and the winner didn't take it too far. So, all up and up but in a way terrifying because you could still get your wind knocked out and also lose the fight too easily. Though never with a gun, never a knife, not even a rock or club; at the most a hanky tied around your knuckles if you had one. But mostly you just fought in self-defense to stop them from busting your nose or for them to think you're an easy guy to be picked on a second time," and one of them says "How do you mean the nose?" and I say "Who said that?" and Julie says "Julie," and I say "I'm sorry, darling, sometimes you both sound alike. Well, you're sisters. But you were saying I wasn't clear then, right? And I wasn't when I should be, another thing I was mulling over when Margo suddenly scared me, how I should be able to think in my mind more—well of course thinking is in my mind, but—" and Julie says "No, I was saying how can they bust your nose? With a hammer?" and I say "Their fists. Imagine," and I raise my right hand into a fist and jerk it forward several times. "Pow, nose splattered. Half my friends had them, splattered schnozzolas, from that and football and which they were proud of, the fools, showing how stupid we were then too. I wasn't, with that, because I didn't bust mine. If I had I would've thought 'Oh dear, my looks, ruined, I won't be a Greek god to girls anymore,' only kidding, but probably so, while they thought with their broken noses they would because it gave them a rough he-mannish look. But some boys, not any I knew—oh, I knew of them but didn't want to know them because these guns meant bullets in the foot and gang wars—actually only one bullet since it only shot one, and—" and Margo says "What guns? You said before no guns. You're confusing us again, Daddy," and I say "Boys had—some did—not any I palled around with—zip guns then, handmade ones that were made from toy guns or a pipe and a rubberband, if you can believe it, that got the bullet off, and of course the toy gun converted into a zip. They made them then because I suppose you couldn't buy the real ones—they weren't around as much and probably were too expensive and maybe boys were still a little frightened of the real thing and still into—involved in constructing and fashioning things on their own then, bad as what they constructed was—we all had to take two years of shop in seventh and eighth grades while the girls took home economics. But half the time these zip guns backfired in your face when you shot them, or maybe that's only what the police and older people told us to keep them out of our hands. Some other boys though, again not ones I wanted to know, and these to me were scarier than the zip guns, for you at least knew there was a chance the gun would misfire or the shooter of it would get it in his foot or face, while the switchblade never missed. In other words, there was always some part of you it hit. Well, these other kids carried switchblade knives—I didn't mention this before?" and I listen but don't hear anything from them so I go on. "But I wouldn't touch one, because they also reminded me of terror, murder, gang fights with knives and zips and bicycle

chains and guys pinning you to the ground and kicking your teeth
in, stuff I could never do, or do only if I was attacked and my
life depended on it and I saw one of these weapons on the ground,
but I certainly wouldn't do anything to some guy I'd already subdued. I also didn't like—'subdued'; to, you know, win over, beat
by force—didn't like these knives because they could zip open on
your finger, so maybe they should have been called zip knives, for
that's how they opened, zip!—but cutting it. But I guess the
'switch' in the word—never thought of this before, not that it's
important—it isn't—is the thing that springs it open. You flicked
a little switch on the knife's handle near where the blade and
handle joined, if I remember right," and I hold up my right hand
as if there's a closed switchblade knife in it and pretend to flick
it open as if I remember where, thumb and forefinger rubbing—
"and the blade sprung out. Anyway, it did that, cut your finger,
or could, and could also spring open in your pocket by mistake
and cut your thigh or pants, and then you're in a jam, at least
with the pants, with your mom. Because you got to know, the art
of making these knives couldn't have been so perfect, as the people
who wanted them—punks, hoods—wouldn't know the difference
or really didn't care; they just wanted a scary-looking weapon
with a long blade that could fold back into the handle and stay
hidden there, and if it stopped working right they'd just toss it
away and buy another one. I remember as a kid I used to see a
whole bunch of them sticking blade-point-down in wood, or
maybe it was a sort of solid foam, but in store windows in Times
Square and other places in New York, and maybe they're still
there. Also that I used to think when I looked at these knives
'How can the police let the shopkeepers sell these things and put
them in their windows, no less, to interest thousands of potential
customers a day?' I mean, that's the point—that's economics, mar-
keting, business; you think you can sell them so you advertise or
show them in the best possible spots. Or you just want to sell
them, to make money, but what do you think of the creep you're
selling one of these to or about the person or the cop, which is

the other point I had, he's going to possibly use it on? It's too unbelievable. But there they were, and most of the knives in Army-Navy stores they called them. So I'm saying, everything about these knives represented to me—that word again—an ugly dog-beat-dog-to-death life I didn't want to live. I in fact hated it and wanted to become an adult in part just so I wouldn't have to face young toughs with switchblades and guns anymore or just their crazy fists and kicking feet, and hey, look how that turned out. They're all around us now, weapons, and kids are tougher to adults than they ever were, though believe me they were always tough, and believe me also when I say I was no saint then myself but I wasn't a devil either. You know, somehow I don't think I'm making much sense. Repeating myself, often contradicting myself, meaning saying the opposite or near opposite to what I just said but with as much belief. Am I, or should I just drive?" and Margo says "A little, but drive too," and I say "Funny, funny, does this kit have a sense of hummus?" and Julie says "Really, Daddy, you're only making a very little sense; you don't say things to understand and you're not nice to the people you talk about," and I say "Not nice, not nice? After all I said and you're still on their side just because they're kids?" raising my voice, angry, I can't believe it, she's just a little kid, I'm always doing this, where's it come from and how come I can't stop it? From now on I will. Make it that way. From now on you stop! "Okay, I apologize, about the earlier stuff if I offended the ladies, but I'd like to bust some of those boys' faces for what they do to people, at least tackle and slap them, and guys like those schmucks who tried to scare the crap out of us. But okay, okay, but anyway, nobody then—boys—owned the powerful guns they do today. Boys and men, what am I talking about? For they've machine guns and submachine guns and probably semi- and quartermachine guns if there're such things. All the guns. AKA this, ZBT-10 that. Even the initials, numbers and names are a clever come-on by the manufacturers of the guns, like for cars, though the ones I gave aren't them. But a turn-on, a something-on, a buy-

me, use-me, abuse-me, that's what I'm for if I'm affordable and
if I'm unaffordable then all you got to do to get me is rob a few
people with knives or normal rifles or handguns. I mean, boys—
I know you heard Mommy and I discussing it the other night—
boys of fourteen and fifteen getting on buses and maybe even
paying the correct fare to do this ... Okay, it happened recently
with only one city bus and once with a commuter train when it
was at a station for a stop. But Jesse James way-out-Wild-West
style, but instead of holding up stagecoaches, which was bad
enough, they hold up the entire bus and train car with these big
blow-off-your-upper-torso guns with a single spraying round.
Sorry, I'm being too graphic—I'm describing too much—and then
for good measure—'Oh, thank you, kind boys'—slamming two
women in the cheek with the gun butts because they didn't say
thanks when these young robbers emptied their purses into a shopping bag and threw them back in their faces. And on the train
another young hood putting the gun barrel—that's the long part
where the bullet comes out—into a man's mouth far as it would
go and pulling the trigger—nothing was in the first round, ha-
ha—and giving the guy an almost fatal heart attack. So why, I'm
asking, was asking—either of you have an answer? And why do
boys set fire to derelicts—you know, bums on the street, but here
on subway benches where they're sleeping? Hey, subways were
safe when I was a boy. The toilets were even open though so
smelly to be unusable unless you had an emergency. I used to go
downtown myself to Macy's when I was ten or eleven to buy
Christmas gifts for my parents and dog—maybe today during the
Christmas season they're a bit safer too. After all—well, I wanted
to say something about 'bad for business' and especially during
the month the stores make forty percent of their money—but I
won't. But do you think I'd ever let you do that alone at thirteen,
fourteen, even if you were boys and traveling together? Though
your mommy, who's a good deal younger than I, used to do it
too—go to some special genius girls' school in New York when
she was eleven and right through high school, so that must mean

the city was still a lot safer then too, though she can recall incidents she didn't like," and Margo says "Like what?" and I say "Ask her—but on the subway, usually going to school during rush hour when it was crowded and she couldn't get a seat," and Margo says "So she had to stand. So what sort of things?" and I say "You know, you can imagine it, with men," and Julie says "What they do to her?" and I say "They didn't act nice to young girls. Some men didn't with older girls too, but these guys I'm talking about were even worse. Because you know, or you don't, and why should you? though maybe now's as good a time as any to find out—for Margo; you, Julie, you keep your hands over your ears, hear? But older men—I didn't mean to be cute about it; just listen, both of you, seriously to what I say. Older men can be a bit peculiar, *some*; a little dirty—yes, not nice, and they're not nice, I'm not nice to them—in ways boys aren't, with girls, I mean. I'm sure I wasn't clear there, and probably intentionally. Anyway, that's all I'm going to say about it—ask Mommy the rest, though she might kill me for saying as much as I did. But— so what happened, I was trying to think before, but I guess I lost track of it," and Julie says "About what that happened?" and I say "Wait, I didn't hear that, a bus just passed, what?" and she says "That track that happened, you said, and got lost," and I say "Was I referring before, meaning was I talking to you before about what I was thinking way before, about . . . regarding . . . something about civilized life in cities and around them and what happened to it? I don't quite remember, but certainly lots about cities have changed. Maybe it's the overcrowdedness, not only in subways—there've always been rush hours and dirty men—but everywhere, and people just don't know how to deal with it as well as they did. That clear?" and Margo says no and I say "Anyway, it's ironic, though, because—you know, a strange twist, a reverse of what was to—" and Margo says "I know what 'ironic' is; we learned it in English," and I say "Well, then that's a positive part of life today—'positive: good,' Julie," and Julie says "I know 'positive.' 'The man is positive. The nurse is positive,' " and I say

"So, there again: another slice of the good positive part of life today. You both know the word 'positive' and one of you at ten knows what 'irony' is while I didn't probably know it till I was fifteen, or even seventeen, eighteen. I probably was first taught it at fifteen but it didn't sink in and it maybe could have been till I was twenty till it did, and the truth is I'm not so sure I even now know what it means or at least could give a good definition of it. I was not well educated, you can say, and most likely because I hated school. Uh-oh, I wasn't supposed to say that," and Julie says "Why?" and Margo says " 'Irony' has something to do with that opposite-to-what's-expected thing again," and I say "School's—I'm avoiding an answer to Julie because I don't want to give either of you reasons for hating school too—school's just more fun today and the teachers are better paid and the class-rooms are brighter and airier and everything's less regimented in the safer schools, it seems. And the blackboard's green and magne-tized in spots so things can stick to it instead of falling off and something else it has where everybody doesn't get full of awful chalk dust, and instead of solemn Presidents George and Abe on the wall you have gay posters of flashy TV and music stars. And what else? Lots else. Reading corners, Disney movies in class-rooms, cheery librarians and a principal who merrily races through the halls calling you 'sweetie' and greets you with a good morning at the school door. While we had stiff-lipped principals and screwed-down desks and ugly textbooks, and teachers—Mr. Feeny and Miss Brady, call for Mr. Feeny and Miss Brady and his five ruler smacks on your palm and her single face slap if you spoke out of turn or for a second, while they were speaking, turned your back—who often used corporal punishment. That's—" and Margo says "We know, you just said," and Julie says "I don't," and I say "It's when an army corporal punishes you in basic training," and Margo says "You're not funny sometimes, Daddy," and I say "Vat's dat? Anudder bigische bus just vent past and I dint hear," and she says "No it didn't and one didn't before. It's when people," to Julie, "hit your body as punishment but not to kill you. That's capital punishment," and I say "Now that's something. You know it, now Julie does and may continue to—can? may?—while I—" and Margo says "May," and I say "Good, while I probably did think when I was your age, and probably at Julie's never even heard the term—phrase?—that it was a corporal who punished you in early army training. But I'm also almost sure I didn't know the difference between them, capital and corporal. In fact I might have thought—somehow this is all coming back—that capital punishment took place in the nation's capital or even in that capital's Capitol building, and probably not till I was sixteen or so did I think otherwise—and quick, on your toes, tell me the difference between those two capitals or capitols, and for a bonus Q, what two U.S. bodies meet in the Capitol building, which are toughies but winner gets something sweet," and Julie says "Let me think," and Margo says "One's an *a*, other's an *o* and has a capital *C* but I don't know who meets," and Julie says "Not fair," and I say "You're so ehjacated as my dad liked to say, probably anudder reason I wasn't, but how would that account for you girls being so smart? Your brainy mom, who doesn't laugh at my anti-intellectual jokes, while my brainy mom did at my dad's," and Margo says "When do I get my prize?" and I say "At the next rest stop, and Julie too, but smaller," and Margo says "That's not fair." "Anyway," I say, "if you want to continue this till the first sweet stop, another reason for the dismalness of life today is that most people don't read, and I kid you not. What's the figure I read in the paper—fifty percent of the people don't even read a book a year? And if they don't this year, why would they the next, and so on, so maybe the real figure, unless I don't understand statistics—you know . . . well, just statistics—is that they don't read a book in five or ten years—Americans—twenty, maybe the rest of their lives," and Julie says "I read a lot—three books in one day last week and I'm American," and I say "They're small books, and kids don't count in this report; it's for people after they're done with school, and not for the day done but life. But you do, fine, I'm proud of ya, Margo too, what a read-team, and I just hope the habit sticks. But the entertainment or diversion or outside activity or just intellectual pleasure, and I use the word—term—loosely—phrase—is, well, lots of things—music, movies, catalogs, TV, but creepy demonic killer music, movies and TV, where it's cool, dude, to say dumb things and that you hate cops and you take advantage of old ladies and young girls—I'm talking here of the—" and Julie says "What girls, what do they say to them?" and I say "No girls, shouldn't have brought them up. But of talk music I'm talking of—you know, the one with the flat mangled speech and clumsy headachy beat. I mean, when I was a kid your age we couldn't wait—and not seven but ten, eleven, I swear to you—and I don't want to go into my own dad's when-I-was-a-kid routine, though they had some wonderful artful songs then too, something with a honey blonde and the bicycle-built-for-two one and before his time there was 'Beautiful Dreamer' and 'Jeanie with the Light Brown Hair'—but kids my age couldn't wait for the next Broadway musical by Rodgers and—" and Margo says "Well I like rap," and I say "Who said anything about that? I don't even know what it is," and Julie says "Oh sure, Dad, tell us," and I say "Rap, like chitchat, right, or is that the one with the flat popular-ugly-music-one beat?" and Julie says "You know what it is," and I say "Okay, I won't lie, and I dislike it immensely and think it's hateful—I give that music four aspirins, maybe five," and Margo says "You won't lie after you're caught, because everyone knows rap and that must mean it's good," and I say "Oh, 'good'—a great critical word, 'good.' 'It's good, this movie's good, this book's good, this line of poetry's real good,' or 'It's bad, this bassoon quintet's bad, *The Iliad*'s bad, *War and Peace* is both good and bad,' some title of a great work with three names which I can't come up with right now, *The Red and the Black and the Green* or something, is good, bad and I-don't-know," and she says "I still think rap's very good and that life is better for kids today than when you were one. Kids are freer to choose their own things and styles more," and I say "Freer to choose what the advertisers

gorge down their little throats," "and have more selections to do
what they want most times, while you've always said you couldn't
as a boy," and I say "Advertisers, store owners, record company
heads and the piggies who rant these songs, all they want is your
money. And we too could say what we wanted when we were
kids, to adults, but about important things, if we had anything
important to say—racial and religious prejudice, for instance.
Those were big issues for kids then, and the right of people to
live freely—in freedom—you know, so long as they're not killing
other people, I'm speaking of whole countries. But other things,
some not even important, we listened rather than shot off our
mouths every first chance, not that you do that. But anywhere, I
mean anyway, look what your freer freedom's ended up in—I'm
saying rap and music like it that makes kids want to do hateful
things because the rappers encourage them to—'Hey babe, beat,
bleed and bleat, 'cause it feels good'—and the kids think 'Say,
these dudes are cool and cute and just great because they're popular and hip and make a mint, so they must know about life and
what's right, wrong and I-don't-know,' " and she says "You're
not making sense again," and Julie says "She's right, Daddy,
you're not," and I say "Ahh, she's always right to you, but good,
you're inseparable sisses and she's a thinker so a good one to look
up to, and your loyalty's fine too to a certain extent, you two will
be true comrades forever or so I hope," and Margo says "I admit
some rap might be like what you said but there's other nicer kinds
that—" and I say "Look, those guys before riding alongside us
looking as if they wanted to shoot—freedom, oh boy great freedom when they plug us dead, give me five," and I hold up my
right palm for someone to slap though know no one will, and she
says "I don't see the connection," and I say "And you know
something, for a few moments there I almost did think we'd get
shot at—I didn't see any gun but I was sure they had one, for what
other way to travel today? And that face filled with a rapper's put-
down hate, though at least the rapper gets paid for it so his is
mostly fake, while these guys make it for real; they hated me, but

why? They don't know me from Charlie, do they? Someone here snitch on her dad? So we got a man you don't know who's doing nothing to you and with two kids in back who are obviously his—that's who you take out your rage on?" and Margo says "Maybe they didn't see me and Julie," and I say "They saw, you yourself said you were sitting up and staring at them, or at least staring at them so you had to be sitting up and for them to see, and if they didn't, even so, for what I do? What's really to mock and go ha-ha about in me if my driving was okay which I think it was? Before, sure, I laughed at myself in saying maybe they think I look funny. I've seen my mug in the mirror enough to know it's often good for a laugh. But tell me, why am I letting it upset me so? Listen, one good thing from it once the scare was over is that they helped us pass the time for a while talking about them and anything that came out of it, and that's always a relief. This trip's too familiar and the scenery's pretty dull so it can be a longie for me without someone to chat with in the front seat, not that that's an invite for either of you to come up here. You can amuse yourself and each other much better back there and maybe get a snooze in too. And for safety sake, meaning I bet you get a leverage—ooh, I hate that word, it doesn't mean anything and defies definition—an edge, an advantage of maybe ten percentage points in living and skipping injury from being in back rather than up front if let's say, God forbid, there was ever a crash. If anybody's got to get it, let it be me, though nothing's gonna happen, take my word. This is all what they call conjecture—supposing, perhapsing, like that. But I'll never understand why people act so savagely to people, do you? No matter what the reasons—meaning, what disadvantages they might have in life—you both know what I mean by 'disadvantages,'" and Julie says yes and Margo says nothing but I know she knows. "And they were driving an expensive new car, though maybe stolen, but anyway, things seemed to be going okay with them and they didn't look poor by any means. But even if you're poor—hold on, what you've been waiting for, the lecture; even if you're looked down on by a lot of insensitive stupid society who gotta look down on someone to think they're better, all of which you've heard. Even if—" and Margo says *"Daddy,"* and I say "Wait, let me finish— even if lots of things like that. You're knocked about, your parents and their parents were—I don't mean beaten up by people, including your parents, but possibly that too. And there's crime and drugs and all that awful stuff right outside your door day and night if you're lucky enough to have your own door to stay behind, you still have to be nice and polite to people and give them respect if you want to get the same back. Not to the ones doing these bad things to you but to the seventy or so percent of good decent people left in society. There's more than that figure but just for conjecture, for argument's sake, which I think is really what conjecture's for—" and Margo says "Daddy, you're really lecturing now and it's boring, I'm sorry, but it's like Officer Stokes who comes to our school twice a year to warn us against drugs," and I say "So, maybe that's what I should do for a living, lecture, prepare my copious notes, get up in front of hundreds of students, and three months off every summer—college lectures, I'm saying— monthlong Christmas vacations and other breaks—oh what I wouldn't do for it if I had the brains—three teaching days a week if it's a good expensive school, or just expensive, hang the good— but okay. But it's the truth that for a long moment there I did think those guys would not shoot us but try to run us off the road and even ram our car to do it, but just for kicks, you see, for the sheer delight of seeing me squirm with fright for myself but mostly for you kids, and who knows?—maybe also to see— no. But they're reason one we lock our doors at night though others in not-as-safe neighborhoods keep them barricaded all day. That's all I'll say. And we've more locks than the previous owners of our house did—than my folks did when I was a kid, and we lived in the heart of the city. We in fact kept our doors unlocked till dinnertime—New York, New York—can you believe that?" and Julie says "Didn't anybody walk in?" and I say "Nobody, not once, and we had no doorman and were on the ground floor—

we only started locking it all day about the time I was a teen and the crime rate in the city shot up. When people started getting mugged in the park. That seemed to be the first place. When you couldn't walk through it at night anymore," and Julie says "You used to before? That must have been nice with the dark and the outside lights," and I say "Some people on summer nights used to sleep in the park when the city got very hot, or that might have been more in my parents' time when they were kids, but you could still walk through it at night in mine, or maybe only in the safest well-lit parts. Though actually I remember gangs roaming through the park when my friends and I played in it when we were nine and ten and talking tough to us and giving a little shove and when we weren't looking running off with our bats and gloves. Baseball. You know, we used to do it two against two, one pitching and covering the infield and one in the out, but these kids were usually older and came down in droves. So, robbery then but not the kind where if you stood up for your glove you'd get bashed in the head with your bat and possibly even shot. But the talk's getting too dark," and Margo says "What else happened when you were a boy like that? Now it's interesting when you talk of things I know," and I say "Regarding what—crime, play, just growing up?" and she says "Those boys," and I say "Oh, we ran after them and sometimes even got our stuff back if we yelled for some adults up ahead to stop them and they did, though now they wouldn't because they'd be afraid to get shot. And occasional fights in the street, mostly minor squabbles but sometimes this religion or block against that one when we were really young, and later on in high school much tougher fights, but then, again, because they didn't like your face or the way your laces were tied. And some people got their purses snatched if they left them lying around or let them hang too loosely on their arm, but nobody I heard of had a car stolen or apartment broken into and there was never such a thing as a school shooting or a carjacking," and she says "Did you like fighting when you were growing up?" and I say "What a thing to ask of your daddy—of course not. Don't you remember my saying I looked forward to becoming an adult because I thought all that violence around me would stop?" and she says "Just the way you talked about it, you seemed to," and I say "No, there's nothing I said or was in my voice and if you saw me smiling in the mirror it was just at your question, though I will tell you—I'm being honest here—after you win a fight there is a kind of satisfaction with yourself—you feel pretty good just that you were able to defend yourself and if you did it in front of your friends, even better. But I never started fights, I think, and I wasn't also, I want you to know—I'm not proud of this now, or maybe I am a little, but anyway—an easy kid to punch out. I knew how to fight pretty well, maybe because of my terrific temper then," and Julie says "You still have one," and I say "Rarely, very little, and nowhere near as fierce as I was then, because I became almost crazy if I thought I was being attacked for no reason or ganged up on, but that's the only time. But I'd do anything I could then if I couldn't lick them or overpower them in a fair way. Kick them in the groin, pull their hair, maybe not bite anyone's ear or nose but I wasn't against poking in the eyes a little—oh, I don't know about that—but getting some guy in a neck lock and squeezing in his larynx till he choked—you know," and I turn to the side and point to mine. "Women don't have them, the Adam's apple, or just not pronounced, for of course they have a voice box. But things I'd do, this dirty kicking and squeezing, only if I felt myself losing, or as I said before, almost dying—I did say it, didn't I?" and Julie says "I don't know," and Margo says "You did but differently," and I say "So, ferocious, absolutely so, but now I look back at it I bet it was—well, maybe it was, maybe it wasn't," and Margo says "Was or wasn't what?" and I say "Fuzzy bear—only kidding; but that I was . . . you're right: was what? I forget, though maybe that I was only acting against the rough tactics and just the injustice of those tough guys, or what's another word for it?—the . . . the . . . just the injustice of them. That some kid and then later some young punk was starting with me or one of my friends for no reason, for I was, being bigger and usually stronger than most of my friends and a lot more hotheaded, a big protector and defender of them, though I may have only done that to get in their favor and be a good guy to have around. Anyway, I don't think I fought that way, ferociously, for any other reason than that. Though maybe this high concept of injustice, as I call it, gave me the excuse to act ferociously—meaning their injustice and my strong feelings against it. In other words, some punk picks on me or one of my small friends—but I'm confusing things by bringing in defending them. Just me, and I now have the excuse to get back at him and even better—to immobilize and humiliate him, neutralize him by whatever means imaginable, just take him out as I think kids now say, to kick the living shit out of him, really. Excuse me, something we used to say, but he started it, I'll finish it, for when there's a chance you can get hurt bad or even come close to what you think is dying, as I said, you really can do almost anything— meaning you're permitted to—the law of the streets, we'll say, and maybe even the law of the law—if what the other guy's doing to you or threatening to is dangerous, illegal and by everyone's standards totally wrong. You guys following me?" and Margo says "I'm not now but I was," and I say "Hey, if your big brain didn't get it then I know I crossed myself up somewhere," and Julie says "Did you? Beat other people up?" and I say "That's what I've been saying, when I was younger. I probably even broke a couple of guys' noses in high school—that's how bad it sometimes got for me; it was a tough school and all boys. And once at a party when I was in college—by this time I should have just walked away from it. But a very tall guy, in a white turtleneck sweater, and I leaped up and punched him in the face and there was blood from his nose all over the place—I hated myself for it later; I hate myself for it today. He said 'Why'd you have to do that, what I do to you?' and looked at me so sadly because he knew I had sort of ruined part of his looks. His sweater was drenched from the blood also and I was so ashamed after he said it that I left the party and everybody there and my own sweater back there too and never picked it up, and later I should have called him to apologize and pay for the sweater and even the nose or as much as I could afford. So he wanted to fight with my best friend then, or something; maybe I had even misunderstood who started it and my friend had given me a pack of lies about it, saying the tall guy was at fault. If I did anything I should have just stepped in to mediate—work it out, peacemake—and if they wouldn't and my friend didn't walk away from it—out of the party, even; I would have gone with him—then just given up on them. But I had to be such a big damn stupid hero. At worst I should have only grabbed the guy from behind and held his arms back if I could and said 'Stop it, cool it, calm down, someone will get hurt.' For imagine, two to three old guys my age are walking around today, if they haven't died of something else since those fights, with broken noses because of me. Or if they got them fixed—it wasn't the type of high school for the first two to do, though who knows what almost anyone becomes later—and this to me is worse than walking around with it broken—then noses with shiny ugly plastic surgery done on them because of me. Actually, the guy at the party was very handsome—maybe that's what I was hitting, his tall good looks and wavy blond hair. So it could be he was an actor or had gone on into acting, and for good reasons, perhaps—professional ones—got a nose job, or for modeling. But in high school, no hating myself, no feeling bad over it, and not because I had no feelings like that then. I had to hit back when they jumped me. They started it, as I said, so it was— well, you heard this one before—them or me, and by that I mean one guy jumped me one school term, the second guy another term; they didn't gang up on me together. But that's another thing. Gangs today work as gangs—real ones. Where they don't, as they used to do then a lot, just watch one of their gang members beat up some guy or try to or get beaten up himself and once one guy's beaten the other guy up but is still pummeling him, they also don't say 'Okay, fight's over, our guy' or 'your guy won it fair and square, we should stop him now before someone really gets hurt.' No, right from the start today and without warning they all jump someone and beat the hell out of him or kill him and not just with their fists—not with their fists, period. They use—" and Julie says "Think we should stop now, Daddy?" and I say "Why, I'm going on, right—too much?" and she says "At a stopping place I mean," and I say "Oh? I was beginning to think we should drive straight through, since we're only about what?—hour and a half away at most. But if you're hungry—really hungry—not for a crappy snack but a hamburger or even those chicken fingers and some salad, or have to use the john—" and Margo says "What time is it?" and I look at the car radio, 3:47, then :48, and I say "Almost four—quarter to," and she says "If we don't have to stop or not for long and it's only an hour and a half more, maybe I can still go to the end of the ice skating party Lillian's giving," and I say "Maybe. I didn't think we'd get off so early or there'd be so little traffic in the city, so I never thought you'd make it there in time. When's the party again?" and she says "Three-thirty to six, the Ice Arena," and I say "I'm sure we can if we don't stop for anything except to pee and there are no major tie-ups along the way—want to? Okay by me," and she says "Whee, a big yes," and Julie says "Not for me," and I say "My sweetie, you get invited to lots more parties than Margo—you know, she's so old that not all her friends still give them," and she says "But never ice skating," and I say "Uh-oh, Margo, we have the present?" and Margo says "So I can't go, or can we get it at home first?—it's already wrapped and I know exactly where it is," and I say "It'll take us, extra miles to home and then the rink and so on, twenty minutes more—and rush hour; it won't be worth it. —Ah, come on, so you go without one and just say you came straight from New York and the big sacrifice we made rushing to it and you'll give her the present in school next day. No, no lies, we'll just show up and say she'll get it tomorrow," and she says "It won't be right, everyone will have given her one," and I say "It's right, it's right, for what are presents anyway? Yours not so, but usually something the birthday kid doesn't need or like or ever use. When I was a boy—okay, here he goes again—and had a party, lots of my friends didn't bring them—they were too poor or it just wasn't as important, and I never minded. The party was the thing. Soda, ice cream, cake, games, blowing out the candles. Now kids come with a couple of gifts sometimes. One Julie went to last month? I came in at the end to pick her up and saw the birthday girl tearing them open. 'This is from me,' one of the girls said—Rebecca, and I'm not criticizing her; it's the parents who push these things— and handed over three. It's this mentality that's around. Buy, buy, buy and more buy till we're stuffed to the gills with goods, which is probably why people give so many gifts for all sorts of occasions that don't deserve them—to get rid of all the things they bought or were given that they didn't need," and Julie says "It's not that bad," and I say "It's bad, it's bad, though of course not the worst thing in the world," and Margo says "Daddy, you think if we get there I'll have time to skate? Because I'd have to rent them, hand over my shoes, put them on, and with nothing to give I don't only want to be there to see Lillian open her presents," and I say "Sure, it'll be a challenge. Beltway's jammed, I'll go the side routes and I bet we still get there forty-five minutes before the party's supposed to end—six-fifteen at the latest," and she says "It ends at six," and I say "I meant five-fifteen, hour and a half from now—less, hour and twenty. I also bet the party goes on for at least half an hour after six," and she says "Probably not. Probably they'll be done ice skating way before that and the presents and cake and stuff will be around five-thirty to six and then they'll ask us to leave," and I say "Listen, you're having misgivings about getting there for nothing, tell me and I won't bust my chops rush- ing," and Julie says "Go to it, Margo; I would," and she says "Yes?" and I say "I think you should too; you never know, I might be right, once in my life, about something—the extra time," and she says "It won't be too much out of your way? I don't want you getting upset at me later for rushing you and taking too much of your time when you have lots to do," and I say "Don't worry; see my disposition? It's good. And it'll be a roundabout on-my-way. I'll pull in, drop you off, give you some money for skates if Lillian's folks aren't taking care of it," and she says "I'm sure they are, but maybe not now because they'll think all the kids have them already or it doesn't pay for me for just two minutes on the ice—I wouldn't blame them," and I say "Anyway, if you can skate five minutes, then skate, and I'll drive home, unpack and come back with Julie in an hour. Say around six-ten, and then we'll all go home and have dinner, which I'll have started to prepare there, or even eat out; maybe we will," and she says "Okay, I'll go, thanks, Daddy," and I say "Fine," truth is, wishing she'd given up on the idea, and calculate if I can make it in time for it to be worth it to her. I probably can; I know the side routes; there'll be some rush-hour traffic near the Beltway and first few miles on it before I can get off at an exit I know, if I have to, since most of the traffic will be coming from the city. So I pick up speed, stay at sixty-eight, look at the rearview; Margo's smiling; good, I made someone happy and did it with no fuss, bellyaching, "Look how I'm going out of my way for you," and Julie took it pretty well for a change too, so it was good for all of us. I signal, though no one's behind me, get in the fast lane, no cop will stop me at this speed, not even at sixty-nine; seventy, seventy-one's when they start going after you, and I drive like that, kids talking together in back, checking the rearview every minute or two to make sure no car behind mine wants me to move over, pass a few cars, think of those two dopes from before—why, tell me? Well, I'll never know; just fools, big dopes as I said, with a cruel streak in both—drive at sixty-eight, seventy, keeping an eye out for parked patrol cars, but no faster than seventy, for sometimes you don't know where they are. And so few cars on the road around here, chances are even greater they'll grab you. Radio? Why even try? I've never been able to get anything but popular music and religious programs in this area. Kids still talking low. About what? I really don't mind doing it for Margo; so it's a half hour more of my time on the road, big deal. Half hour, forty minutes: same. This way she won't feel she missed out on much because Lee and I wanted to be in New York a few days. Lee did; I would have as easily stayed home, read, rested, done some work of my own and around the house, things with the kids. She always seems to be missing out on a party or sleepover because of our plans; it just happens; bad luck we'll say. For some reason, Julie almost never. Maybe I can get to the rink even sooner than I thought so she can be sure to get some skating in. And really, faster I get there, the better; driving can be so tiring. And this way she'll feel she missed out on even less, and I can go home and get lots of things done—the entire dinner fixed if I decide not to eat out—and it'll be nice just being with Julie alone, when there's a car in front of us, older guy it seems driving at what? sixty, maybe, that's what I'm doing now—and I get close behind him, I don't like to and if he suddenly brakes I could go into him, though I think we're far enough apart for me to avoid that, but what the hell, it's a message, for why's he think he has to set the speed limit for this lane? everyone knows you can go ten miles an hour over and usually fifteen in this lane and just about any other except the slow one, but he still doesn't budge, doesn't seem to have seen me, head hasn't moved in a way where I'd know he's looked in his rearview mirror, so I turn my lights on and blink them, on and off, on and off, that usually does it in a few seconds or until the car can get past the car in the lane to the right with plenty of room to go into it, though no car's there now, nine times out of ten it works, it's what I should have done instead of tailgating him, and I slow down a little to put another twenty feet between us, but he doesn't move, this guy isn't moving, why isn't the sonofabitch moving? he has to have seen some flashing in his rearview even if he wasn't looking right at it, it just flashes, catches his eye, and he'd know something was catching it, even if he thought it might be the sun, and then he'd look right at it and see it was the car behind him flashing and he'd know it was to move over, it can't be for anything else, if a driver knows anything about driving it's that, and if he's only looking at the side mirrors instead—well, nobody does unless he has to, turning right, left, entering traffic and so on, key mirror's the rearview—anyway, I forget what I was saying, something with the side mirrors, if he was looking at them to see what was behind, I think, well, if he did he'd see part of my car too, that's all, but he hasn't looked at either side mirror, far as I can tell since I've been behind him, but the rearview, through that one he'd see the flashing wasn't the sun or some light bouncing off something way behind him even if he wasn't looking right at it, so he's playing games with me or something, not games but probably thinking "Hey, the guy behind's tailgating me, he knows he shouldn't so I'll keep him going slow for a while to teach him a lesson before I switch lanes and let him pass," or could be he still hasn't seen me, not my flashing, nothing, could be he has eye problems, doesn't see well if at all out of the right one and not so good also in the left, but I don't think so, though he is wearing glasses if those bumps on the back of his ears are the sides of the frames, but he'd have trouble getting a license with such bad eyes or, if the condition came after he got one, then passing the eye test most states make you take every time your renewal comes up and his plate says his state's same as mine, if he's not renting the car and comes from somewhere else that doesn't have such a law, it's just probably he's deep in thought somewhere, as I was before when Margo snapped me out of it, and not paying attention, so I turn the brights on and pull up about ten feet closer and flash them on and off a few times and wait for him to signal right, for when someone flashes the brights from behind so close you almost have to see them no matter where you're looking or what you're doing, but he doesn't signal, I wait thirty seconds, nothing, flash some more with the brights, then pull up a few feet closer, now around two car lengths behind him, which is close enough, and then think I haven't looked in the rearview for a few minutes and look and see a car about thirty feet behind me, so there's two of us, maybe three, more, waiting to pass this guy, and I check both side mirrors and in the right one see a car behind the one behind me but that's all, and I flash my brights several times, for this guy and to let the driver behind me know I'm doing my best to get past him, I could use my horn but I don't like to, sometimes it scares drivers in front, he could be in deep thought as I said and hasn't seen me and one horn blast might startle him where he could go off the road or veer into the next lane when a car's coming in it or something dangerous like that but less, the woman in the car behind me—it looks like a woman, the hair—flashes twice with her brights and I say "Oh come on, you can see I'm doing every-thing I can," and point to the car in front and keep flashing my brights and think "That goddamn asshole, that goddamn stupid old asshole, look alive, you putz, look alive," and Margo says "Daddy, you're too close to the next car," and I say "I want to get past it, he's not moving, look at the stupid speed he's traveling at in the passing lane—that's right, this is actually called the pass-ing lane, it's been going on like this for minutes and there are cars behind wanting to get past," and she says "So go in the next road and let them," and I say "But I want to pass him too," and she says "So go in the next road—" and I say "*Lane*, it's a lane, the middle lane," and she says "Lane, then, but go in it to pass him," and I say "You're not supposed to pass from the right, he might not see me even if I'm flashing him, he certainly won't if I flash him as he hasn't seen me flashing since I started doing it, and then, without looking at his right side mirror and signaling me, he might suddenly decide to go into that middle lane himself the moment we're alongside him and hit us. He's supposed to move over when he sees us behind him so we can pass from the left lane. He's like some Maine driver—you know the ones I al-ways complain about up there—on a two-lane back road, but they go fifteen or twenty miles an hour when they should be going the posted speed of thirty-five or forty. He's doing sixty now—not even sixty—fifty-seven or -eight," and she says "So he's right, the speed sign before said fifty-five," and I say "But you don't know, you're not a driver, you're allowed to go at least sixty-five on these Interstates even if the signs say fifty-five, the police allow

it, everybody does it, and especially in the speed lane, this passing
lane," and she says "You're still much too close to him, Daddy;
if he stops you'll crash into him and hurt everything," her voice
shaky saying this and I say "Okay, I give up, you're right, and as
my dad said, 'When you're right, you're right, and no one in the
world should say you're not right,' I just wanted to get you to
that skating thing in plenty of time to skate but I shouldn't take
chances doing it," and she says "The skating's not so important,
I don't even want to go to the party if it means taking chances
with the car," and I say "You're right again," slowing down a
little to put some more room between our cars, check the rearview
and see the car behind me's keeping just as close to mine, "And
you talk like your mommy; you do," and Julie says "I do sometimes too," and I say "Yes, you're both—you're all three very
smart and cautious and the way I should be, I admit it, I admit
it, but that creepo, look at him, I can even see his eyes now in
his rearview mirror, he sees me and he knows I see him and now
he's looking away but that I'm angry and he probably even knows
I don't want to honk at him, no, he couldn't know that, but he
has to know he's going too damn slow for this lane," and I signal
right and look into the rearview and right side mirrors and cut
into the middle lane to go around him and teach him a lesson by
speeding past him and then cutting sharply in front of him and
speeding on, but his car without signaling cuts into the middle
lane second after mine does and when I see I'm going to hit it I
brake and try to cut into the lane we were in but the car that
was behind mine's already there and our sides hit, I brake all the
way, didn't think about it, just did it, and our cars come apart
and mine spins around my side and I try to brake with little pedal
taps and then all the way when that didn't work but have no
control of the car and it spins around again and nothing will help
it it seems till it stops or slows way down on its own and then I
can stop it and I'm screaming and the girls are and I yell "Duck
down, down, duck down," and a car from somewhere, not one
of the other two, smashes into the passenger side in the middle

lane and pushes us about a hundred feet before it stops, all the
time we're all screaming. All sorts of things after. I must have
been knocked out a few seconds. There's a gas smell and a burnt
smell and a metal smell and a rubber one and I can hear cars
screeching and people shouting and I think "No, this can't be, it
can't," my eyes are shut when I think this and then I think "I'm
out of it again, I'm sure I put myself out because I don't want to
know what's happened," and when I open my eyes it's raining,
but really pouring, sky's dark when just a few seconds ago, a
minute, minutes, I don't know, but it seemed it was light, rain's
slashing the windows and banging the roof when before it was
dry, I'm sure it was, there wasn't a drop, I didn't have my wipers
on or even thought I'd soon have to put them on and I tell myself
"Turn them on now, no, that's not where you are," and I think
"I never would have made that lane change if it had been raining
like this, never, ever, I'm afraid of driving in blinding rain and
the rain slicks, cautious of them, extracautious, I hate them, hate
to slide, and I would have slowed down to a hundred feet more
between me and the old guy and gone into the middle lane when
it was safe to and maybe even into the slow lane and then down
to around fifty if the rain continued like this, forty-five, forty,
thirty as I have on this same Interstate when it was raining hard
as this and I couldn't see much even with the high-speed wipers
on," and then I'm quickly out of it again and in my dark shake
myself awake and think "Hey, what's going on, I'm not driving,
who's driving, somebody driving?" the last I either think or say
and I shout "Julie, Margo, Julie, Margo," and Julie's crying and
I think "Where're they crying from, it sounds so weak, were they
thrown out? but it's only one crying, Julie, not Margo," and I
look up, see the roof, hear the rain banging, try to sit up, for
some reason can't, "What is it," I say, "what, where are you
girls?" and try to sit up again, my body's twisted around itself
with the back of my head down on the seat, seatbelt's caught and
I finger around for the clasp, "No no," I say, "no, please tell me
you're both okay, Margo, Julie," and continue fingering, find the

place to press if it's my seatbelt and I press and sit up, my neck, it stabs, head, holy shit, I can't lift it, feel it and feel a big gash with blood or some slick stuff all around it, I reach up and grab the top of the seat and hear whining behind it, Julie's, still not Margo's, and hoist myself up and am now on my shins with my knees facing the seats and get my face between the backrests and look. Julie's still on the seat. Someone's banging the driver's window and yelling "Sir, you all right, sir? How is it in there? Your girl pinned? Can you let us in?" Julie's still in the seat. "Julie, you all right?" and she says "I hurt, Daddy. I'm bleeding. There's blood," and I say "Where's Margo?" and she says "Daddy, your head," and I say "Where's Margo?" and she says "Here," and looks where and I look and say "Margo, my poor Margo." She's on the floor, not moving, eyes closed, not breathing it seems. "Margo, oh my God, oh dear."

INTERSTATE 8

*G*oodbye, darling," and she says " 'Darling'; you never call me that anymore. I can't even remember when you last called me it, or if you ever did. Have you ever?" and he says "Sure, plenty, tons, or a few times at least. I can't recall each one, but certainly when I first met you. That very night at the party we were at, I said to the host 'There's my future darling,' and she said 'Who?' and I said 'There, there, my future darling wife of my future darling kids,' and went over to you—you were with some guy you couldn't take your eyes off of, so I knew I had some doing to do, and I actually had to wrest him away from you by grabbing his wrist and giving it a bit of a twist to get his arm off you— and then I said to you . . . no, don't let me run on, and with such bullshit too, for we gotta go, gotta move, gotta hustle, darling," and she says "I like it though, not said that way, but before with

the more endearing 'darling.' Where the other stuff comes from—
juvenile fantasies of wresting men away from your wench—beats
me. But the 'darling'—I think I like it more than any other sweet
talk from you, even if I can't remember if you ever called me it"—
"I have, my darling, I have"—"and I call you it lots of times," and
he says "That he knows, his darling, and it's perhaps where he
got it from," and she says "Sometimes—no holding me in bed
when we go to sleep, unless it's your first move to making love;
no kiss goodbye and hello when you leave and come home if it's
just to and from work—I even think we're, well, frittering apart
in a way from what we were"—"Saved by the fritters and way"—
"something I've thought a lot about lately and it . . . distresses
me," and he says "You were going to say 'saddens,' yes?" and
she says "Don't play prig," and he says "I only wanted to see
how sharply I was tuned in—you know, reading thy mind, but
okay, what?—I'm an all-ears kind of guy," and she says "One
sure sign of what I see taking place, other than for the two or
three I mentioned—" "Which were they?" and she says *Nate,*"
and he nods, "is that, one, just your being flip about it like this—"
"You mean 'three' or 'four,' if I'm counting right, but I'm sorry,
go on"—"trying to get around it with jokes when years ago you
would have taken it seriously if not gravely . . . well, maybe not
that bad. And, two, and maybe this is trivial, nevertheless I liked
it: you don't say anything affectionate anymore when we make
love or before or after it," and he says "I'm the strong silent type,
and after, a quick quiet sleeper—oops," and she says "I really get
an awful feeling sometimes of what might eventually become of
us, this gradual dribbling away," and he says "And you want
from me that current term I hate, 'reinforcement,' " and she says
"Not right now but sometime soon, like on the phone tonight—
something for you to think about on the long drive home," and
he says "But what a time for you to bring it up, when we're nice
and tight like this, arms locked, pelvises stuck, ready for the big
goodbye-darling pucker-up," and she says "I mean it. You also
don't make love to me as much, with or without the nice words,"

and he says "*We* don't make love, the two-way street, darling,"
and she says "I don't appreciate it when you use it like that, so
please?" and he says "So what do you mean 'we don't as much'?
As much where, here in a public hallway? Or when, since the first
few weeks after we first met? We make it every bit as much or
just a touch less much or however such one should word it—little
less touch, bit less mush, that sorta stuff, but none of those up to
snuff. Look, it just isn't true, despite all the so-called detergents—
deterrents of long-term marriage used-to-itness and the natural
aging process, on my part at least and I've got almost a dozen
years on ya, but we really gotta go—kids, car and me, and your
dad waiting with them downstairs and by now possibly pissed
off," and kisses her lips, digs into them with his, she kisses back
with not as much dig, wishes they had the time, if the gang wasn't
waiting for him and his mother-in-law wasn't in the apartment,
though even there, he'd say . . . he'd say "Darling, and this is no
joke and I'm not playing up to you now with that word, well,
maybe a little *bissel,* but if we could do it in a few minutes from
pants-dropping start to pulling-them-up finish, last time for two
days and nights, you know what I mean, the where and when,
it's here and now, and we didn't do it all day yesterday and today
so that makes three, even if we just go into the guest bathroom
past your mother under the guise of my washing my hands and
you going to the toilet and neither of us wanting to use their
private john off the master bedroom, or other way around with
the washing and toilet, and do it standing up, you leaning over
and me from behind, wouldn't take me more than a coupla minutes and you might even get something out of it, I'm sorry but
that's how it is, and as a parting even a one-sided goodbye-darling
gift to me," and she'd say yes, they'd hold their breath, or he
would, she'd hardly have started, for they'd really have to be
quick—when hasn't she said yes to sex unless she was very mad at
him for something he said or did and she felt he hadn't sufficiently
apologized, but have to go, must, hates keeping people waiting,
one more kiss, does and then says "I mean it, you're my darling,

I love you, okay?" and she says "What a way," and he says "I mean, I just love you, plain and simple, ornate and complex, but I have to—" and jerks his head to the elevator door and she says "Okay, I love you too," and they separate and she takes his hands and looks at them and then him, smiles pining-like, regretting already that he's gone? and says "You should get moving, it's unfair leaving them down there, I guess, and it's funny, I already feel you're gone," and he says "Am I psychic?—I'll tell you tonight why I said that, you just have to remind me, but now's no time to quote unquote boast . . . say goodbye to your momma again for me," and she says "I will," and he's pulling his hands from hers when the elevator door opens and his father-in-law steps out: "Nathan, where are you?—Don't let the door close," to the elevator car, "keep the Open button down—We've been waiting, it's been quarter of an hour," and he says "Just toodle-dee-dooing to your darling daughter, no other harm; we're not used to long separations—Bye, dear," and she nods to him with her eyes closed and he thinks "What's that mean? I mean, surely no tears; that'd be ridiculous. I was only kidding about the long separation. It's only going to be two days, so look at it as a break," and waves and gets in the elevator, "Oh, kids, hi—of course, holding the door open," Julie pressing down hard on the Open button with her whole hand, and Margo says "Daddy, you said you'd be down quickly," and he says "I am—we will be—let's go," and his father-in-law pushes the L button and door closes. "Oh, forgot to say goodbye to your mom, we gotta go back," he says to the girls and Julie says "You're just fooling us now."

"Drive carefully, precious cargo aboard," his father-in-law says through the car window and he says "Horace, don't worry, I'm a good driver and I never take chances with the kids in the car," and Horace says "You shouldn't take them ever. You're a family man with terrific responsibilities now so you should always drive as if they're with you," and he says "That's what I meant—thanks for everything, you've both been wonderful," and Horace says "And thank you for bringing your family—drive carefully, pre-

cious cargo aboard," and he says "You bet, no high speeds, you
can count on it; I don't care how long it takes to get there," and
starts the car, waits thirty seconds less than he usually does for
the engine to warm up—doesn't want to keep looking back and
forth at Horace and smiling and waving for him to go inside—
checks the right side mirror a few seconds longer than he usually
does when no cars are coming, so Horace will see how careful he
is, and pulls out of the parking spot. "Wave to Grandpa," he
says and kids turn to the window and say "Goodbye, Grandpa,
goodbye," and he waves without looking as he drives up the
block.

"You bring any fresh bagels, Daddy?" Margo says and he says
"Did I bring fresh bagels? Did I hear someone say 'Did Daddy
bring fresh bagels?' Does Daddy ever forget to bring fresh bagels
for long trips?" and Margo says "What kind you get?" and he
says "Oh gosh, I forgot the bagels. The poppyseed, sesame, blue-
berry, jalapeño—" and Margo says "I don't like those kinds,"
and he says "Good thing, for I only bought chocolate and plain,
plenty of chocolate and plain, plus a coupla garlic in their own
bag since you can't stand their stink on the chocolate and plain,
and in that same 'own' bag one everything bagel for me. But too
much about bagels already. Your bagel bag's under your seat next
to my briefcase if neither's been moved. Split one with Julie," and
she says "I want one for myself," and he says "Then offer the
bag to her—Julie, sweetie, want a bagel?" and Margo says "Why
you being so nice to us now and when nobody's around?" and
he says "Why do you say that? Julie, you want a bagel?" and
Julie says "I just want to look outside. The city's so gray. I only
like traveling on sunny days. That makes the trip happier. But
when the day's gray it makes everything gray and there's nothing
more grayer than a gray city on a gray day," and he says "Little
quiz: Which came first, the gray city or gray day and, as a bonus
question for extra points, how'd it get across the road?" and Julie
says "I'm glad I don't live here. With all the gray I feel something
awful's going to all of a suddenly happen," and he says "Margo,

don't offer her a gray bagel," waits for a laugh, is none, says "Mommy and I did—lived here—for years. As kids, public-schooled all the way, then when we met and got married, and we turned out healthy, stealthy and okay—we had you two wonderful girls at least," and Margo says "Phooey flattery, Daddy; you won't pick our spirits with that," and he says "Okay, I won't correct you, but listen: people who don't live in this city—" and she says "We know, you told and told us: 'they can't appreciate it,' " and he says "And the day'll get brighter, I promise, though we'll first see it on the road. The weatherman calls for sunny cheerful weather on the whole Northeast coast," and she says "The weatherman said 'cheerful'? That's nice, I like that kind of prediction. What will he mean when he says 'cool'?" and he says "Boy, are you ever getting tuned into life and its meanings. Both, but if I can say this without either of you thinking I'm underrating or deprecating the other, right now Margo more," and Julie says "That's not nice," and Margo says "She's right, you shouldn't choose anybody," and he says "You see? I fail at honesty, fail at fibbing, fail at any imaginative mix of the two and whatever else is left. I'm sorry, and whatever I say now to help my case will I'm sure be taken unfavorably, so, since you have your bagels, books, games, dolls and each other, I'll just dummy up and drive," and Margo says "Daddy?" and he says nothing, something about the things he has to do when he gets home is coming into his head and he wants it to continue, and she says "Daddy . . . Daddy . . . please say something, you don't have to go that far," and he says "Really, sweetheart, I was just using that excuse so I could think for a while, because talking, thinking, the two things at once, it's hard," and she says "Then that's all right."

They pass a sign saying there's a rest area in three miles and Margo says "Can we stop at the next rest place coming up? I have to go," and he says "But you went at home," and she says "No I didn't," and he says "But I told you both to go just before we left. I said 'Julie, Margo, everybody, including Daddy, go to the bathroom before we set out. Mommy, you don't have to because you're staying here,' " and she says "Maybe I did go then but I have to again," and he says "How can you go so soon after you just went?" and she says "I didn't just went; you kept us waiting in the lobby for a half hour when you said you'd be right down," and he says "It wasn't half an hour; it was ten minutes at the most," and she says "Longer. Grandpa said so when he looked at his watch. He said 'Where's your father? He's been kibbutzing' "—"Kibitzing"—" 'kibitzing upstairs for more than a half hour,' " and he says "Grandpa likes to exaggerate, not so much to make me look bad but to make himself—anyway, when he came up he said it was only quarter of an hour. 'Nathan,' he said, 'it's been quarter of an hour we've been waiting'—and it wasn't even that, I don't think," and she says "Grandpa doesn't exaggerate or tell lies," and he says "Wait, can you hold it a second? The music's about to end and they'll give the title and composer of the piece—it sounds like Vivaldi but there's something that tells me it's Marcello. No, it's all right, that was a false end," sitting back again after leaning forward to the radio. "Look, maybe Grandpa's watch runs a little fast and he got the time wrong," and she says "His watch is very expensive and has a battery worth ten dollars in it and he says he checks his watch with the radio every morning so it'll always have the right time. And he said we've been waiting a half hour downstairs, so even if his watch was five minutes fast or ten it'd still be a half hour we were down there. And when we went upstairs to get you it'd be more than a half hour because of the time it took in the elevator and upstairs, so that makes more than an hour altogether since I went to pee," and he says "Wait, you lost me, and you're also cheating yourself with the total time. My point is only that you still shouldn't have to yet—go to the bathroom. We've been on the road"—he presses a radio button and the station numbers turn into the time—"almost an hour, which means it's been at the most an hour and a half since you went. Can't you keep it in another half an hour? That way we'll have gone about seventy miles, if the traffic continues to move the way it is, which will be more than a third of the trip, even if that's fewer miles than when I like to first stop, which is ideally about a hundred—halfway," and she says "I think I can hold it in another ten minutes. But the sign we're passing says the rest area is in a mile and the next one is twenty-six miles and I know I can't hold it in for twenty-seven miles," and he says "All right, and I'm losing the signal to this New York station fast, so I'm sure I'll never find out who wrote the piece—it's beautiful though, isn't it?" moving into the slow lane, "—that oboe and with the harpsichord going in back," and she doesn't say anything and he says "I'm not trying to take your mind off your bladder, Margo, but you don't like this music? It's so soothing, even with the losing-the-station noises," and she says "It's okay," and Julie says "I have to go also, Daddy," and he says "You're just saying that to help your sister, but you needn't, we're here," pulling into the exit road. "You know," he says, walking to the building from the parking lot, "even if you're not hungry, get something to eat, for I don't know if I'll make another stop till we're home," and Margo says "Even if we have to pee bad?" and he says "Then I'll stop, of course; I wouldn't want to damage your insides. But I'm going to ask you both to go twice, once when we come in and then when we leave," and Julie says "We won't have anything to pee," and he says "You can always pee something, always; you'll just sit on the potty till you do," and she says "It's not a potty. These places don't have them and I'm too old for one," and he says "Sorry; but do you want something to eat? Margo?" They're inside now and Margo sees a place that sells tacos and says "Tacos, yes, I want two— can I, and something to drink?" and Julie says "I don't want them but I'll find something," and he says "First you both pee. I'll do it twice too, now and later. Meet you both outside here, and don't go wandering if by chance you're out first," and goes into the men's room.

Passes several urinals till he sees one that's clean. One had a cigarette butt in it and three in a row needed to be flushed. What are the pissers afraid of, germs from putting their fingers on the flush lever? Then use a paper towel to flush it, if they have them here and not just hand dryers, or toilet paper, but that'd be thinking too far ahead, and if you only think it while standing at the urinal, then too much work to get it. And who throws a butt into a urinal? They don't know someone has to take it out? Not with the hand but just any way you take it out, even with pincers or a nail at the end of a pick, is disgusting. Just the idea that someone has to take it out. *Has to* if it's part of his job and he doesn't want to be fired or quit. In that way the people who clean the ladies' room have it better. But they're probably the same cleaning men; they just block off the ladies' room when they clean it, for he's never seen a cleaning woman in one of these places, not to say because he hasn't seen one they haven't been there. At least there aren't cuspidors anymore. Now those things had to be the worst to clean. When he worked in Washington they were all over the Capitol and Senate and House office buildings, even the public hallways. Worse cleaning them than preparing bodies for funerals, he'd think, or as bad. But they're professionals, embalmers, and probably go to school for it or through some long apprenticeship before they start doing it on their own and they're no doubt a lot better paid than cleaning men. They wore white jackets and black slacks, or is he mixing them up with the waiters in the Senate and House dining rooms? But he seems to remember seeing them, in some congressman's office or Senate committee room, in that starched white jacket buttoned all the way up, emptying . . . not humidors. What are they called again besides spittoons? How can he have the word one second and not the next? "Spittoons" will do, but cuspidors, like on a cusp, which is maybe where the word came from—the shape of the thing, the lip—if he knows what cusp is, or exactly, but he bets it's from the Latin somewhere for that's how far back cuspidors probably go. They did it with a big can on wheels, about the size of a water bucket but the top covered except for a wide slit to pour the spit and chewing tobacco crud in. They probably emptied the bucket into a toilet someplace—where else?—and then cleaned and maybe even had to polish the cuspidors and probably cleaned those buckets as well and the toilets and slop sinks they poured it all in and maybe the area on the floor around the cuspidors where the spit missed. They also took care of the offices and committee rooms, vacuumed carpets, rugs, dusted, work like that, emptied trash baskets, made everything shine, while embalmers only work on bodies, he thinks, and have nothing to do with things like selling caskets and seating the funeral guests. So one job's as bad as the other. Or the embalmer's job is worse, especially since there aren't cuspidors around for cleaning men to empty anymore. Though cleaning a bunch of those still couldn't be equal to embalming or just preparing for burial a decomposed or particularly ravaged or mutilated body, and even worse, the body of a child no matter what condition it comes to him in, but he supposes they get used to that too after a few years. He's heard of embalmers, once from a woman he was seeing who answered phones for a funeral home, who used the navels of corpses they were working on as ashtrays, though maybe those were just stories or the very odd case. If a senator still has a cuspidor in his private office, do the cleaning people there have to empty and polish it? He just doesn't see anyone doing that chore anymore, maybe not even for the president, but then who would do it, for you can't let the thing run over? A devoted follower perhaps or a janitor from the old days who sort of got used to putting up with it or some young flunky who wants to become assistant to one of the administrative assistants and for that future job might even do something worse. When he was in the office of a senator or congressman he was waiting to interview—a different era, almost, but that has nothing to do with what he was saying, which was, well . . . he'd be looking around, in a way wasting time till he was called into the senator's or representative's private office, and suddenly find himself staring into a cuspidor on the floor. Didn't do it out of any curiosity or because he was somehow drawn to it, that's for sure, or maybe that *was* it; more like an accident of the eyes, he'd call it, that happened a number of times. But how'd he get into this and here while holding his dick? Something to do instead of just looking at the urinal while he tried to piss. He finally does—had to go when he walked in here so doesn't know why it didn't just come—flushes and goes to the washstand to clean his glasses and wash his hands and throw water on his face to help make him more alert for the rest of the trip, dries his hands—no paper towels, just the dryers, and for his face and glasses, his handkerchief—and leaves, kids aren't there, looks around and doesn't see them, goes to the gift shop and the wall by the exit where there are some video games, two places they'd wander off to without money, starts to get worried, thinks "Wait, who's going to take both of them?" for both would have left the ladies' room at the same time. Maybe they're still in it, and at the door there cups his hands round his mouth and says "Margo, Julie, are you still in there?" and from what sounds like way inside it Margo says "We're coming out," and they come out, he says "What the heck were you doing? Don't you know we're in a hurry to get home?" and Julie says "Why do we have to? We want to see some things here; it's a good place," and he says "There's nothing to see; let's just eat," and she says "There's video games, a good gift shop; we've been to this stop before," and he says "They're all alike, up and down America; they all have everything you want to take all your dough. Come on, a snack—I'll give you plenty of time to eat, and then I want to get home in time to prepare you a proper dinner and give you a couple of hours between dinner and bed to do what you want—read or ride your bikes or just relax," and Margo says "It wasn't our fault we took so long. All the toilets were filled. Ladies don't have those stand-up things to pee in and they take longer than men," and he says "Oh yes, boy oh boy, are you the observant one," and takes Julie's hand and they get on line at the Roy Rogers while Margo goes to a different fast-food place for tacos.

They're off the turnpike, across the big bridge and past the first rest stop on the left and about an hour and a half from home if they don't run into any heavy traffic or tie-ups, or even closer, hour and a quarter, hour and ten, but around that time in the trip when he usually starts thinking of what he has to do when he gets home and in what order and how much time it'll all take before he can sit down with the newspaper for fifteen minutes and have a drink, like unpacking the car—they didn't bring much stuff and this time his in-laws didn't load him down with presents for the kids and a couple of bags of deli and food his mother-in-law made, maybe for some reason because his wife didn't return with them—get the various things in their various places and the emptied valises back to the basement, but what else? Raise the thermostat from the 58 he put it at when they left. Open the curtains and shades, take the automatic light timer out of the socket and reconnect the lamp plug into the wall and replace the bulb in it with the hundred-watt rather than the twenty-five he put in for these few days. Turn the oven on even if he doesn't know what he's going to cook them. Maybe there'll be something in the refrigerator to reheat that hasn't started to spoil, or from the freezer but which can be thawed while baking—he, he'll just have wine and some mustard and cheese on the good bread he brought from New York and part of the salad plate or tossed salad he makes for them, but his own vinaigrette dressing, not their bottled creamy Italian kind they like, when a car in the fast lane a few feet ahead of him starts moving into his lane without signaling and he honks and it keeps coming and he slows down and starts moving into the slow lane and is halfway over the dividing line when he looks at the right side mirror and sees a van coming on fast. The van honks and he cuts back into the middle lane and waves without looking at the van and says "I know, I'm sorry, it's that stupid car," and honks at it, though probably the van will think the honk's for it. The car moves slowly back into the fast lane and honks twice and he says, as the van passes him, "Oh Jesus, honk honk, bunch of geese we all are, heading south for the summer, though, and with no camaraderie or cooperation or concordance or just plain plan or whatever you want to call it—fool, *fool*," in the car's direction and Margo says

"What, Daddy?" and he says "Nothing, I should've expected it or at least expected anything and then corrected it better—it's essentially and evidentially partially my fault," and she says "What is, correct what?" and he says "Oh, again, nothing, just talking faultily to my littlest self with my biggest words," and she says "Huh?" and to Julie "Do you get it?" and he says "You know, you both do, the brain, for that's about how it feels right now, pea-sized, miniaturized, but without the intricate technics—forget it, my honeys, Daddy's just a-kiddin' again and wouldn't want to give you the impression he has a bad image of himself or any command of the language when he this minute does not—just a-kiddin' again, oh, can I never ever stop?—boing boing," rapping his temple, "sorry, getting myself even deeper into what I won't be able to get out of unless I switch subjects or shut up." Car to the left stays beside his and he wants to see who's driving, what kind of person, really, could be such a lousy driver, though he can try and guess if maybe only to see, even when he's thinking seriously, how far off the mark he can be: unaccompanied man, not a woman, alone because the passenger, if it were an adult, and this one wouldn't have a kid, would have tipped him off that he was driving recklessly and he would have corrected it sooner, and a woman wouldn't stay alongside the car she cut off and risk being needled if not taunted and propositioned and cursed, around forty and with a hat on, hunter's or trucker's cap or one they used to call and maybe still do a porkpie, fatty face and about a hundred pounds overweight, torpid from his bloat and also the huge snack with a couple of tall sodas or shakes he had at the last rest stop, so another reason he was so slow to react, package of opened, no, open package of small powdered doughnuts or bonbons on the passenger seat, beanbag ashtray half-filled with butts on top of the dashboard, messy car, lots of dumb bumper stickers and window decals, dirty T-shirt, that should be it and he actually doesn't recall any stickers or decals but he wasn't looking for them then, looks and there are two men, young, passenger must have been bent over when he honked at them or could he have seen him from behind and completely forgot? look like brothers though driver's clean-faced and other's got a shaggy mustache, lean if not weightlifter-muscular, thick necks, beefy shoulders, work clothes or just not dress clothes—fancy catalog-type casual clothes, both staring stolidly at him, driver not glancing front once, as if saying "What's with you, dummy, got a problem?" and he nods and faces forward and thinks maybe he should move to the slow lane—checks the right wing mirror, that's what it is, wing mirror, no car there—nah, that'll just . . . that'll just what?—suggest to them he's intimidated or scared and thinking him weak that could start who knows what with them, where they stay alongside trying to rile him even more: gibes, glares, threats, fingers, fists, as if he almost got them killed in an accident, dumb idiot, but they stay even with him anyway and he'd like to know why, hasn't looked to the side at them since that one time and he didn't do anything then but nod and maybe flash a nothing smile, doesn't try going faster for he's already doing seventy and that's about as fast as he wants to get when the speed limit's fifty-five and if they stick with him at that clip it could make driving even more dangerous than it now is and they also might take his going faster as some kind of whatever they take it as, a contest they're going to win no matter what, and he's seen lots of cars stopped by cops on this road in the past and he doesn't want to get tagged when he's sort of anxious to get home, and really, he might be exaggerating the menacing from them and also with the ticket he doesn't want to pay through the nose, for he thinks the fine's up to around a hundred fifty now. Fact is he's never been ticketed, all his years driving. Been stopped a few times, maybe twice, and once, second the cop reached his window, he said "I'm sorry, I must've been doing ten over the limit," and the cop said "Twelve, but at least you're honest about it; most drivers, you wouldn't believe the excuses. I'll let you off but don't let me catch you going even five over on this street or I'll ticket you for both at the same time," and another time, twenty years ago, made a U on some boulevard and two cops stopped him in their car. Early morning, five-thirty, six and he was driving home from a woman's house because she wanted him out before her kids awoke, didn't want them seeing him in bed with her, just seeing him in the kitchen, even, and they could tell their father and it could hurt her chances in the divorce, and the cops warned him about making a U. "It's not heavy traffic, so no big danger now, but in an hour you could get killed doing it, so don't, as a standard rule, make a U." "What's the law on it, just out of curiosity?" and they said they didn't know. Those, far as he remembers, were the only two. Looks over, casually, blank expression, as if something caught his attention on that side and he's going to have a peek and then look back to the road, hoping those guys aren't looking at him anymore and he can take his mind off them. Passenger's staring at him with a tough look, driver's just driving, pinky reaming his nose. Should he face front quick? but nods, passenger nods and then a little smile and then a broad one, throwing up his shoulders and raising his hands as if "What can I tell you? We made a mistake and we're sorry," and then points to the backseat, still smiling, as if "Hope we didn't scare your girls none," and then salutes him and waves to the girls with wiggling fingers and the car shoots ahead and soon they got to be doing eighty, eighty-five, maybe even ninety or more and he watches them awhile speeding out of sight and then turns on the radio and moves the dial around. Maybe now would be a good time to go seventy-five or so, he thinks, for if anyone's going to get caught by radar somewhere or just a police car on the road, it's them, but no, sixty-five's fine. They could be slowing down, now that he can't see them—all that shooting out and speed for his benefit, for whatever reason—and he could end up being the sole speeder on the road.

Seems nothing much is ever on the radio in this area but various kinds of obtuse music and the same kind of religious bilge—always a male and "I've seen the Lord and He's me and you and you'll see Him too if you listen to me and do what I say which is what He's told me is for you and that's to do

God's work," and so on, and sometimes even worse. How could anyone . . . ?—oh, he knows: people like to believe. Must be the hills—"And don't forget to send me your moolah so I can carry on our cause"—but must be the hills around why he can't get the good stations from his city or Wilmington or is it Newark, Delaware, pronounced "new ark," or even way back and to the right, he thinks, Philadelphia, and shuts it off. What was that look by that guy all about? No, forget it. No, really, think, what started it, continued it, and then the end? Oh, first terrify you or use whatever punk means to try to and then when they've done a pretty good job of it or think they have, smile but really a big phony one and be nice and their gestures even polite and "Oh, hope we didn't disturb your ride and your cute bitty kiddies," for they got what they wanted and now just don't want to get in trouble for it—you could have a car phone and call the police and give them their license plate number and so forth—something, anyway, for them to change their tactics like that, but exactly what he doesn't know. But dopes, that's all, pure dopes. As for their dangerous driving, face it: you've done as bad if not worse. Made mistakes like they did, drove too close behind a car where when it suddenly slowed you almost plowed into it, pulled away from the curb without looking into the street to see what was coming and almost got into you don't know how many collisions, drove dreamily alongside some parked cars and nearly hit a woman holding a kid getting out of the passenger's door, didn't let the truck pass first when you were entering a highway and it nearly went over you and the kids. You even did something like those just before when you started moving into the right lane without looking and that van was coming. But when you have done things like that you usually if you could apologized right off to the driver you did it to, as you did with the van. But you never that you can remember gave the driver of the car you just scared half to death or nearly killed with your lousy driving any kind of terrifying or cynical or "You're to blame, dumbo, you, so just go screw yourself" look. You have, first chance—oh, a few times when you were in a miserable mood or something, you didn't, and you blamed the other driver and a couple of times raised your hand or even once your fist in a threatening gesture and called him an asshole or jerk—but thrown up your shoulders and hand as the passenger only did later, but surely no sinister . . . anyway, usually totally apologetic or close, at times mouthing "I'm sorry," or if your window was open and theirs too, or even if theirs wasn't, saying or shouting it: "Excuse me, my blunder, stupid of me, I'm sorry." Smart, though, not to have messed with those men. They didn't look like nice guys despite the last nice-guy gestures and look of the passenger and you wouldn't have been surprised, if you had looked toughly or cynically back at them or given them any kind of rebuke with your look, if they wouldn't have—passenger, at least, driver as much as he could from his seat—raised a middle finger at you or even shook a fist or done something like point a hand at you in the shape of a pistol and with the index finger made believe they were pulling the trigger a few times. Enough, they're gone, incident's done, think of other things or just don't think. You just hope you don't run into them on the road again or in a rest stop along the way if you have to stop. You'll have to, you always do, if just for a quick take-out coffee to keep you awake for the rest of the trip and for the kids a large box of popcorn to keep them fed and occupied, and if you get that coffee you'll also need to piss, since your bladder always fills up with a couple of cups. But even if you do see them, and odds are slight, by that time you're sure they won't recognize you but you think you'll recognize them. What happened meant more to you than them, that's probably why, and because of the kind of guy you are compared to them: things sink in, you usually try to understand why they happened, and when you do something wrong intentionally or by mistake it hits you harder than what they do hits them. You see them forgetting it, after a quick joking exchange not talking about it, maybe scaring the shit out of someone else if the feeling nudges them and another car like yours with kids or just to them some dumb-looking schmuck at the wheel happens to be driving alongside theirs. Anyway, that's how it is on the big road: so anonymous though tough and scary every so often and sometimes heated and dangerous for a few seconds before the cars go their own way or one or the other disappears.

Few minutes later he's talking to Margo. Starts when he says "So," for he has nothing else to say and nothing much is on his mind and definitely nothing's on the radio and to pass the time he'd like to talk or just hear their voices and what they have to say, "so, anybody missing Mommy yet?" and Julie says "I am, when will we see her next?" Actually, started when he was thinking of his wife and how odd it'll be going to sleep tonight without her, not only because there'll be no one in the bedroom to speak to but they do it what? every day, almost every day, morning, little before he gets up, or afternoon if he's home and kids are in school or away, or night soon after they get into bed and one of them turns off one of the side-table lights, and just holding her, mornings around four or five when it's coldest in the room he almost always snuggles up and holds her from behind, for that's the way she usually faces, his hand on her thigh or breast or in her pubic hair, sometimes clutching a bunch of it but gently so it doesn't hurt or wake her, how he might even masturbate tonight for the first time in he doesn't know how long, could be a couple of years, for he never does it when he knows she'll be there that night or the next to make love with, feels if he jerks off that same day or even the one before it might stop him from getting or keeping his prick even semi-stiff and that when there's less to shoot it reduces the final kick, and at his age when for years he's been feeling there's little by little less thrill at the end he doesn't want to lose any of it, and he won't be seeing her for two nights, no, tonight and two make three, and then what brought all these thoughts and this image of her up: back to him while she's seated on her end of the bed, taking her bra off from behind, so he'd be observing this while lying or sitting up reading in bed, way her hands and arms twist around till the hook's unhitched, light plop of her large breasts against her chest when the bra's pulled away, two-or-so-inch buttocks' crack rising above her old loose-fitting briefs. Came out of nowhere it seemed, just flashed in his pan or maybe something from underneath to temper being alone tonight in bed. Oh, "temper," now where'd that one come from? And he says "In two days from now or, if Mommy's having too good a time without us—only kidding. If she's got something she has to do there that needs a third day, or let's face it, if she just wants to spend another day with your grandfolks or they sort of put the screws on her to because they see so little of her and when they do it's always with us. And she is their favorite child, you know, as much as they love your aunt—then a day more, which means altogether four nights." "Three is how I count it," Julie says and he says "If it makes you feel better, and maybe you're right, for you're tops in your class in math, then three," and she says to Margo "Three, I know it—Daddy's wrong and I'm right." "We'll all drive to the train station to pick her up," he says, "—she's arranging it to come in around five or six so we can do that," and Julie says "Whoopee, I love trains—I want to take one," and he says "One day, to New York—they're faster and all-around safer I bet, with no possible problems on the highway and we won't have to find a place to park or worry about our car being stolen there or pay through the nose for a garage, but Margo," for he hasn't heard from her yet, "my Margo, sweetheart, you love trains too, don't you?" and she says "Can I stay home when you go?" and he says "Of course not, you can't be home alone— not at your age; you're too beautiful and you might be stolen— only kidding. Mommy hates when I make jokes like that, says they scare you," and she says "They do." "Well, don't be, no-body's stealing you; we live in a safe neighborhood and all our doors at night are always locked and windows too. Besides, some-one tries to break in, bam, one sock in the kisser from me and he's gone forever if not knocked unconscious. But why wouldn't you want to go pick Mommy up with us? We can go to the platform when the train comes in and help her with her bags and things—might even be a present or two for you in them," and she says "Mommy's been mean to me lately, I hate her," and he says "No you don't, and if you did, it could only be for a few minutes; your Mommy's a darling," and she says "I do, you don't know," and he says "Okay, why? I'm going to be reasonable, why?" and she says "She yelled at me—she had no reason to," and he says "For not getting out of the bathroom sooner this morning? I heard; you were in there brushing your hair and she had to go to the john badly," and she says "She could have used the other bathroom and she didn't have to scream," and he says "She only raised her voice and that bathroom's in your grandparents' room and they were sleeping, so she didn't want to wake them," and she says "She's their daughter, she could do it like I do when I have to go in your bathroom and you're in bed, and how do you know they were sleeping?—she didn't even knock," and he says "Because their door was closed," and she says "That doesn't mean anything," and he says "It means they're not ready yet to be disturbed even by their favorite daughter unless it's an emergency, but something more serious than just number one," and she says "Number one?" and he says "To pee, to urinate; the other's number two, defecation. And Mommy thought it'd be easier, instead of disturbing them, for they are fairly elderly people, for you to get out of the bathroom if you were only brushing your hair," and she says "How do you know I was only doing that?—there are no peepholes there," and he says "Because you said so. 'I'm brushing my hair, can't you go to the other bathroom? My hair's important; you want me to look nice, you always say.' Sometimes, you know, you can get a little disrespectful and headstrong, kid, so she thought she had to raise her voice to get through to you. But don't worry about it, it's over. Mommy for sure doesn't think any less of you because of it, and when you speak to her on the phone later, you'll see: everything will be fine. In fact, everything's going to be peachy cream cheese for the rest of the day. We'll have some fun when we get home, what do you say?" and she says "What?" and he says "I don't know; reading, maybe playing Scrabble together or Monopoly—something, after supper. I might even break my cardinal hatred of TV and watch it for an hour with you," and she says "Okay, and this is good, talking personal-like; Mommy might be mean sometimes but you're mostly nice," and he says "Isn't that the same thing? So Mommy and I are even in your feelings—great. And when, long as we're talking, haven't I been nice? Only kidding, but really, when?" and she says "Like today when you punched me. I should be madder at you than I am at Mommy for what she did, but we made up," and he says "When did I do that and when did we make up?" and she says "You punched my arm right before you said you were very sorry you did and me and you hugged and made up," and he says "Wait, I don't remember—you kidding me now? And it's something I should remember—I hit you? I mean, I've done it before, not hard, just little hits or smacks, and so few times that I remember every one of them, but today?" and she says "In Grandma's apartment, this morning. You wanted to leave fast and thought I was slow and then when I was out of the door going to the elevator and forgot something and went back in to get it, you followed me and grabbed my arm and punched it. I hurt and it still hurts, my arm," and he says "I never punched you. What do you think, I'm stupid—I'd forget that? I remember the scene now and there was no punch. I did grab your arms, or shoulders. Not 'grabbed' them—held them when you turned around. And besides, I wasn't in such a rush. I still hadn't said goodbye to Mommy and I can't just do it in a second, race over to her, quick kiss and goodbye. It's not the way we do it. I wouldn't be seeing her for a few days so I'd say something, she'd say something to me, we'd hug and stuff—like that, same as I'd do for my kids, but different. But as for you, it's true, I said let's get going, meaning you kids should start for the car, since Grandpa wanted to go downstairs with you. Maybe he did that to give Mommy and me a moment of privacy, but I also had to stay behind a couple more minutes to see if I forgot anything for the car and to say goodbye to Grandma. And you flew out the door and then flew back and I said 'Where are you going, I thought you were leaving?' and you didn't say but continued to run past me and that's when I grabbed you, or held you—sort of snatched you out of the air, you were running so fast—just to get an answer from you, since I didn't like you racing past without giving one," and she says "You grabbed my arms tight—clenched them hard, so it felt like punching and I didn't see all the time your hands, so it could've been one. And you yelled 'Hey, listen, where the hell you going? We've got to go, so stop wasting time,'" and he says "I didn't say that," and she says "You did, everybody heard except maybe Grandpa in the elevator. Mommy must have heard you from wherever she was in the house. And I had a mark where you grabbed or punched me and I bet I still have it—I looked at my arm in the lobby when we were waiting for you and Grandpa said where'd I get that? I didn't tell him; you wouldn't want me to. But you were too rough with me and you have been too rough lots because of little things I do, but you're still nice most times, or half of them," and he says "No, really, I didn't, you're imagining it, no, and unless I convince you otherwise you'll probably think I did this to you today for the rest of your life. I wasn't rough with you this time though I admit I have been a bit too rough with you other times, or just demanding. Or, you know, when the house suddenly looks a chaotic mess to me and I can't find anything or am always stumbling over everything and have to get the whole joint cleaned up in five minutes or I feel it'll overwhelm me. When I get like that, a bit carried away, true, or can't find my wallet or glasses or keys when I'm leaving the house . . . but I always apologized for it or did nine times out of ten. In other words, I think I recognize my mistakes right after they happen but maybe don't do enough to stop them from returning," and she says "I'm not talking of those times with your glasses and things. But Mommy knows what I'm saying how rough you've been, Julie's seen it, almost everyone we know has, but they don't tell you because you're my father and they don't think it's up to them to say. And maybe because they're scared of you when you act like that— pushing people around and screaming and grabbing their arms hard; I know I am," and he says "Mommy thinks I punched you today?" and she says "No, I didn't tell her because I was angry at her too, but Julie saw the mark on my arm downstairs," and he says "Hey, is Julie sleeping?—I have a feeling," and she says "You're just changing the subject," and he says "I'm not, but is she?" and she says "She fell asleep while we were talking," and he says "So let's talk in whispers; she needs the rest and I don't want to wake her anyway. And if I did grab you too hard today—I don't think I did and I certainly didn't punch you, though there could be a chance I forgot on the first score—then I'm sorry. You know I have a temper sometimes and occasionally even go way out of control and my sense of how everything has to be just so-so to perfect, not sloppy, and on time and stuff and how it gets to me when it isn't sometimes, foolishly though and beyond my powers to stop it, or just can't. I don't like it and I'm sorry if I acted that way to you today, let's say, and surely sorry if I left any marks on your arm, but most of all sorry if I ever made you scared of me," and she says "You have, to every—" and he says "Shh, shh, lower," and she says "To everybody in the house but I think especially to me," and he says "Not everybody, or not so much," and she says "Yes, to everybody, and much, too much, where we hate you," and he says "Okay then, I'm sorry, I apologize, to you and through you to everybody, you can even tell them that if I forget to," and she says "All right, and I'm sorry too but glad we spoke about it, are you?" and he says "Sure, it's always smart to talk things out that are bothering you," and she says "I'm glad you think that because that's what I'm starting to think too."

Few minutes later he yawns so big a yawn that his eyes squeeze tight and tears come and he tries opening them but for a couple of seconds can't and he thinks Jesus, what is he, that tired? doesn't want to stop but might have to—concentrate, concentrate, and while he's staring front, head pitched a little over the wheel, trying to keep his eyes from closing like that again, he yawns, tries to stop it and is suddenly out, he thinks after he snaps awake, he's been out, unconscious, but for how long? seconds, even a half minute, a minute, just sitting here sleeping but holding the wheel straight where it didn't leave the lane. Checks and no cars around so nothing much would have happened if he did go into one of the next lanes and then awakened. But never happened, this. Or happened once, on a trip with his wife before she was his wife and they had kids, eleven hours on the road and he'd driven most of them and forty or so miles from the bungalow on a private cove they'd rented for a month ... anyway, stop at the next rest stop. And that was eleven hours, since early morning, so they probably didn't have enough sleep night before and had tired themselves out a little packing and loading for the trip and cleaning the apartment for the couple subletting it for the month, trying to make it in one day to avoid the costs of an overnight stay and to take full advantage of the cottage's thirty-one-day lease. That's right, think like that, of anything to stay awake, or stop on the shoulder to rest his eyes a few minutes, nap for ten, that'd refresh him, and kids won't mind that much. But you never know. He sometimes gets scared like this. Car coming along could go off the road right into them, thinking it was another lane. Not that but a car in the slow lane might come too close or some thugs might stop to rob him, guys like those guys in the car before. They see a man and his kids: easy target, back up on the shoulder, "Say, you don't have a jack we can use, for we think we have a flat," bam, out comes the gun. Sometimes he wishes he kept a weapon in the car to protect himself, like mace. But then the kids could get hold of it accidentally or out of curiosity and then what? That could happen, much as he might warn them. So a baseball bat. Anyway, still thinking, and feeling more alert. Radio, and turns it on. He'll take any show this time, religious, ridiculous call-in, but can't pick up anything but two stations with the same kind of thumping music that makes him irritable it's so ugly, and it'll wake Julie, so turns it off. Talk. Whispers "Margo?" but she doesn't answer. "Margo? Margo?" Quickly turns around and sees they're both asleep. Just a glimpse of them, but little angels; at what age does that look stop? Next rest area shouldn't be that far off, five, ten miles—forgets when he saw the last sign for one and how many miles it said next area was, but he's definitely going to stop, piss, wash his face, have two coffees or just a big large one, though he's not yawning anymore so maybe the crisis is over, though still stop.

Little later Margo says "Julie's up," and he says "Oh, you're awake," and she says "I wasn't sleeping," and he says "You weren't? What is it with you two where you don't like to admit it? Okay," and she says "Can I speak about something serious now without you getting angry like you can?" and he says "Why would I with just your asking me something—what kind of guy you think I am?" and she says "You have before when I asked you to do something you didn't want to," and he says "What is it you want? I promise I'm turning over a new leaf, no more anger or at least not as much—control, control and self-command is the word, or words, and besides, just ask it," and she says "What time is it?" and he says "That's what you were afraid to ask?" and she says "No, don't be silly," and he says "You can read the time—what time is it?" and she says "Do you think, you don't have to if you don't want, we can get home in time to drop me off first at Lillian's ice-skating party?" and he says "That's what you thought I'd get angry about? Anyway, it's already started—I told you this morning I didn't think you'd be able to go when I saw how late we were getting out," and she says "But I've been thinking about it now and I don't want to miss it," and he says "We don't even have a present," and she says "Mommy has a whole bunch home for emergencies, I can tell her I'll give it in school tomorrow," and he says "That'd work but to get there we'd have to really rush and I don't want to, right now what I'm doing's a safe speed and just enough over the maximum, and even if we rushed, really broke the speed laws and everything, you'd

barely make the last half hour of it," and she says "I've been to
two at that rink and they always went on a half hour to an hour
more," and Julie says "That's not fair if she goes," and he says
"I don't want to count on the party going over—it's just too much
out of the way, twenty minutes, then twenty minutes plus twenty
in coming back to get you and returning home, and I'm tired,
sweetie—did you see me yawning before?" and she says no and
he says "You said you were awake so I thought you might have,
but I did, I'm so tired I don't think I should even be driving
now—I want to stop for coffee and rest my eyes and mind a little
from this driving and that'll add another half hour to the trip,
which'll mean you'll get to the party, if we make great time,
exactly when it's scheduled to stop," and she says "I still want to
try," and he says "You should've thought of that this morning
when you dillydallied in the john and I was pushing us to get
ready so we could go, and also when we stopped for your tacos,"
and she says "That's not fair, we stopped for more—your men's
room, and you had a biscuit and coffee and the tomatoes from
Julie's hamburger," and Julie says "I didn't want them but Daddy
told me to put them on so he could have them," and he says
"Listen, if we make exceptional time till the Beltway and if on
the Beltway I see there's no heavy traffic or there's a way where
I can avoid it and I think we can get to the party for at the very
least, half an hour, then okay, but less than that it's not worth
it, don't you agree?" and she says "No but okay," and he says
"*Okay?*" and she says "Yes, what else can I say?" and he says
"Good, for then I'll do my best to get you there, I swear," and
speeds up a little and she says "Like I said, you're very nice and
sometimes easy to talk to. I didn't say the last thing, but easier
than Mommy most times, and you make up with me faster," and
he says "Listen, I'll have no comparative parent ratings please,"
and she says "What's those?" and he says "I said it wrong; I
meant, your mother's a much better parent than I, doesn't get
hotheaded or temper-tantrummy the way I do, she never really
rants or becomes cross, and if I did grab your arms in a pinching

sort of way as you said—left marks there, squeezed the skin too hard, but no punches; that I know I've never done—well, you know she's never acted like that, right?" and she says "That's right, not even a slap, which you once said you did," and he says "So there. She's as easy if not easier to talk to than I, more understanding and a lot quicker to forgive and let bygones be and so on and more patient and sensible about what might be bothering you; while my first reaction, if it's not your health or safety that's at stake, is to joke about it, but overall we're both okay, would you agree?" and "You too, Julie—that we're not total boobs and floperoos as parents or even near to that?" and Margo says "She's shaking yes and I can say I shake along with that too," and he says "Well, good."

Little later he thinks maybe he can get to the rink in time for her to skate even if they stop for a short break, and drives a little faster, for he slowed down last time, soon after he'd speeded up, to what he'd been doing, and reaches seventy-five, more than he likes to and had got up to last time, slows to seventy-one for he doesn't want to get stopped by a cop for that would end it, no party, he's only trying to do something nice for her, hundred- to hundred-fifty-dollar ticket and who knows what else, humiliation, explaining to his wife why he was speeding and with a fine so high and just endangering the kids she'd really be pissed, and what's four fewer miles an hour anyway in what's left of this trip, five minutes, six? when he sees a car ahead in the fast lane, doesn't like passing on the right and why the hell is it in that lane if it's just going to putt-putt along at sixty? so he gets behind it, a man, and judging by the back of him, pretty old, now down to sixty, fifty-eight and the man probably thinks that's speeding, and stays about thirty feet back but it doesn't move over, and he flashes his brights, okay, it's so, he gets a little pleasure or some power thing forcing the cars in front to move over, flashes the brights repeatedly and waits and again and waits and then says "Oh the hell with you, you putz, for what're you doing there, dreaming?" and Julie says "What, Daddy?" and he says "Nothing, I meant some-

thing else," and checks his mirrors, no car behind in the center
lane, none in sight in any of them, and darts into it but same time
car in front does and he brakes and honks and hears a thump
from the backseat into the front and one of the girls screams and
the other car goes back into the fast lane and speeds off and he
yells "Margo, girls, you all right?" and Julie says "Yes, that was
scary, I thought that car would kill us," and he says "That noise—
the bumping sound I heard," and Margo says "It was my hands
against the back of the front seat here, I was pushed forward, my
seatbelt must be on too loose, but I'm okay," and he says "And
who screamed?—but forget it, I'm sorry, it was my fault, I never
should have tried passing him like that," and has slowed down,
other car's already a few hundred feet ahead, and thinks that's
enough, too fast, no sense in speeding up and taking chances, and
that's crap you don't like passing on the right, do it from the slow
lane then if there are three lanes and you feel you have to pass
the car in the fast, and you're not tired anymore and that power
thing before about forcing the guy over is just ego-building horse-
shit you're going to have to can, for think what could have happened if that man had cut into the center lane just one second after
he did, your car would have been clipped, yours doing seventy or
so, his, sixty, it could have been disastrous, you could have
crashed, turned around, spun around, smashed, gone off the road,
over the shoulder, rolled over, kids killed, all of you killed, car in
flames, worst of all, them killed and not you. Oh brother, someone's watching over you—not that, *luck* and maybe that man's
skillful driving in pulling to the left so quick and good brakes on
your part and so on, and stays in the center lane and tells himself
to stay in it rest of the trip, though first get off at the next exit
even if it's not a rest stop but only a regular highway exit with
those little picture signs that say a restaurant's near, but don't
hurry your stay there, coffee, maybe a sandwich, where you can
sit tight and rest your nerves and eyes, and sees a sign for a
highway rest area coming up in three miles, another answer to
his prayers if he believed in them, and says "Hurray, rest stop's

heading our way," and Margo says "We're really going to it?" and he says "I'm sorry, I know what you're thinking, my darling—we'll worry about your party after, but for now I absolutely without question need a break."

Once they're out of the restrooms: "Get anything you want, so long as it's popcorn or something healthy, not sweet, and of course if you want real food too, fine with me," and gives Margo a five-dollar bill for the two of them, "Can we get soda?" Julie says and he says "Only if it's a diet or natural-flavor one; okay, we'll celebrate getting here alive, but I'd prefer just juice—I'll be sitting over there," and they get on line at a take-out stand where there's a popcorn machine and he goes to the Roy Rogers, coffee, sits and thinks Jesus, I still can't shake what happened. So don't shake, think why it's bugging you. One second, that's all, one, or at the most two. How many times has that happened to him? Too many; half a dozen, full, and he didn't start driving till he was twenty-five; never hit but lots of near misses. Did hit a bridge railing once on the outskirts of D.C. but that was the car designers' or engineers' fault, which the company clammed up about before the car was built rather than redesign the chassis or whatever needed redesigning, or that's what the newspapers said: rear-wheel lockup that got about ten people killed, or the accident deaths this independent watchdog group said it knew about, and almost wiped them out too: Lee in the front seat screaming when the car spun around out of control toward the bridge railing "We're dead, we're all dead," Margo in her car seat in back, on their way to the National Gallery to see a show of minor French Impressionists: he remembers it all, discussing whether to drive the junkpile the rest of the way or turn back, drinking cappuccino in the East Wing cafeteria there and thinking, while Lee walked around looking at the paintings with Margo in a baby carrier on her back, Damn, now I gotta go around getting body-repair estimates and deal with my insurance company and rent a car while this one's in the shop. No more taking car chances, as he said. Definitely not with the kids or Lee and not with himself either.

For what would they do without him? Eventually they'd be okay, but they'd be devastated for a while and it could wreck them for years, maybe affect the kids the rest of their lives, if he died or was left severely paralyzed. You want to stay healthy and alive for them long as you can. Sixty-five, that's the max speed anywhere from now on, even in the states where the limit's now sixty-five but where you can go ten over without being touched. You had the kids late and want to be around to put them through college and graduate school if they want to go, and more—if they need help starting out or buying a home or happen to get stuck with some permanent or chronically progressing crippling disease or such, when he sees those two guys from the Interstate an hour or so ago. Driver's dumping their used stuff off a tray into the trash can, other's sticking a cigarette between his lips but making no move to light it, and now they're heading past him—doesn't want to have anything to do with them so looks the other way—and passenger says "Isn't that the fella . . . ?" and driver says "Who?" and passenger says "There, one we almost bashed into on the highway way before?" and driver says "Beats me—you're talking like I got a good look at him," and passenger says "Sure, it's him, you saw," and comes over, he knows it's inevitable so he turns their way and passenger's smiling, cigarette clutched in his fist now, driver's disinterested, just wants to get out of here and on the road again, and says "Excuse me, but weren't you the fella on the road before and we got into your lane a little and where we all like nearly collided?" and he says "That's right, I thought I recognized you—say, I'm really sorry about it," and passenger says "Why? It was our fault and mostly mine—I felt shitty about it, you had these kids in the car, didn't you? Boys or something? Where are they?" and he says "Girls, and up front somewhere getting food," and passenger says "Yeah, girls, but they had short hair," and he says "Actually, both have long, but it was quick and we were all going pretty fast," and driver says "Hey, when have you ever mistaken boys for girls, that's a new one," and passenger says "Kids. And I know I tried apologizing to you back then but I even told my friend here—he'll vouch for me—'You see that worried look on that man? I wish I could tell him more some way how rotten I feel about what we did,' " and driver says "Not in those words so much but something, and he took the blame for he was distracting me. Got me involved in something else where I took my eyes from my driving, which I never do, never," and he says "It's all right, lots of close calls, won't be our last, just a good thing, that's all it was," and driver says "But what I told him too was 'Impossible, no way you'll see that man on the "I" again for your whole life, or if you do, you won't know it's him, it'll be that far along in years, you'll have forgotten his face and he'll have aged like you've never seen, so stop mauling yourself over it, and me too with your groans,' " and passenger says "Oh what're you talking of?" and driver says "I'm being honest for once—you were rattling on like that, making me almost into another close accident shave if there was any other car near," and passenger says to Nathan "Don't listen to him—once he starts, never stops; mouth like a runaway can opener. Anyhow, no harm meant, right?" and driver says "Of course none meant, he knows, you can tell by him there isn't, so let's get with it, we got to go," and he says "No harm meant, certainly, and thanks," and sticks out his hand and passenger says "Hey, good, we get to shake on it, more than I could have asked for—but boy, it's weird, us meeting up again," and shakes his hand and driver waves good-bye and they start to go and passenger turns around and says "One last ask, man—let your girls know what I said too, that I felt rotten for them if I scared them, or if we did, but I'm the one who felt bad," and he says "Will do, thanks again," and they leave.

Raining when they get outside, not much, sprinkles, and he says "Hey, let's make a dash for the car," and Margo says "Why, it's not raining so much," and he says "Hey, man, whataya talking about, it's a good excuse to run and we need it after being cooped up in the car and your stuffing yourself here, for I don't see no popcorn left, is that what I don't see, man, hey, hey?" and she says "We ate it. And why are you talking like that with all the mans and stuff?" and he says "Just pretending, and I didn't want any corn anyway, but let's run," and runs and looks back after about twenty feet and they're walking and talking and he yells "Hey, last one to the car's a rotten you-know-what," and they run and he stays there till they're even and then lags behind them so they can beat him. "You cheated," Margo says and Julie says "Daddy's a cheater," and he says "Yeah, man, that's me," and Margo says "Stop that, you sound mean," and he says "Sorry, man, sorry, man—oops, okay, stop."

They're on the road a few minutes when it starts pouring, then comes down so hard that most of the cars have slowed down and turned on their lights. He can't see well even with the wipers on high speed and says "Look, Margo, we can never make the party now—we're down to half the speed we were going and if it doesn't let up, this is it the rest of the way," and she says "I understand," and he goes into the slow lane, down to thirty-five an hour, at times twenty-five, twenty, sticking his face a few inches from the windshield to see out, rubbing his side window because it's clouded up. "Wish one of you was up here to wipe the front window for me, though that's not an invite and we'll be fine. Oh, by the way, guess who—no, you couldn't, but you won't believe who I bumped into at the Roy Rogers when you were getting popcorn," and they say nothing and he says "Hello, anyone hear me?" and Margo says yes and he says "In fact, one of them told me to particularly tell you girls how sorry he was if he scared you on the road before—now you know who they are?" and Margo says no and he says "I don't really know if I should believe him. He seemed sincere when he was saying it—he's my 'hey, man' man—but then something doesn't quite jive with his attitude on the road when he did sort of scare us, or at least me—know who I'm talking about now?" and Julie says "Stop teasing, who?" and he says "Those two guys from maybe an hour and a half ago or two hours, on the Interstate before the big bridge . . . they almost ran us off—you know, cut into our lane without warning me, not the old dude before but two much younger men from way way before," and Margo says "I don't recall," and Julie says "Did one wave a doll at me?" and he says "I don't think so," and she says "That must've been someone else, a Raggedy-Ann, or Andy," and he says "On this trip?" and Margo says "She's making it up, can't you tell?" and he says "Anyway, right after—" and Margo says "Daddy, she slapped me," and he says "Julie, stop it—anyway, right after they scared us they smiled, the passenger in the front seat did, and wiggled his fingers at you both," and Margo says "No, *ma père*, I don't recall," and Julie says "If it isn't the doll man—he was nice—I don't too," and he says "Okay, recountal closed."

Few minutes later he thinks if there's another rest area soon he'll pull in and stay in the car till the rain abates and if it doesn't in around fifteen minutes, pull up at the entrance and race inside with the kids, holding some protection over them—sweater, jacket, he doesn't care if he gets wet—and then park and run in and dry off and take another piss and tell the kids to use the ladies' room again and he'll have coffee—or tell the kids to use the ladies' room while he's parking—and let them get anything they want this time, sugared artificially flavored and colored soda, Pepsi or Coke, even, lollipop apiece and for each of them one of those Pez, is it? just the refill or with the dispenser, even if they have several empty dispensers at home in the shapes of various cartoon characters, junky cupcakes, any kind of cake, just so they—but no more popcorn, that'll only give them a tummyache—won't be bored and sort of as compensation for the long trip and also as a reward for being so patient and cooperative during it, that's how we'll word it, "gifts for being such nifty kids on this trip."

Rain never abates, sees a rest area half hour after he thought he'd stop at the next but even at thirty-five miles an hour they're at the most forty minutes from home, so passes it. Parks in front of the house; downpour, as they're preparing to get out of the car, turns into a drizzle. "We're saved," he says, "saved," and Julie asks "What's that?" and he says "Means miracle; rain's

down to a trickle when I thought it'd be a twenty-year torrent."
Gets everything inside in several trips, empty trash cans on the
grass and in the street to the side of the house, mail out of the
box, newspapers off porch and walkway. Turns the heat up, oven
on, peels carrots and washes and slices celery sticks and puts a
plate of them with some cherry tomatoes on the dining room table
so the kids can snack, unpacks, puts things away fast as he can,
soiled clothes into the washing machine in the basement and pours
soap powder in without measuring first and turns it on, straightens
up the downstairs, couch pillows plumped up and put in place,
that more than anything for the amount of work put in makes a
room seem neater, all the old newspapers, magazines, catalogs,
drawing and construction paper and children's books lying around
the living room stacked into one pile, something about a room
with lots of things open and mislaid disorients him, makes a salad,
slices bread brought from New York and butters it, asks the girls
when they're taking from the veggie plate to set the rest of the
table, asks them a few times, yells upstairs "Girls, please come
down and set the table," finally says when he sees them reading
in the living room and eating the buttered bread "What am I
supposed to do, everything?—come on, get with it, set the goddamn table, and that bread was supposed to be for dinner," and
they jump up and run into the kitchen for tableware, "That's
better," he says and Julie says "You didn't have to curse," and
he says "You're right, forget the 'goddamn,' but did you get the
cloth napkins out of the linen drawer?" and Margo says "Nor
shout either—ordering, you're always ordering," and he says "I'm
not always, and I guess I'm hurrying too fast and being kind of
a pain in the ass to get everything done so I can rest a second,
excuse me," tells them to get juice for themselves, please? puts a
pot of water on to boil, why didn't he do it sooner and why's he
have the oven on? and shuts it off—spaghetti, salad, bread, veggie
plate (while he's dribbling olive oil and rice vinegar into the salad
bowl), fruit, that should be enough, maybe broccoli if it's still
good, opens a can of apricots and spoons some into two cereal

bowls and places them next to the kids' settings, smells the broccoli in the plastic bag from the refrigerator, mush, stinks, dumps it into the garbage, smells and tastes the tomato sauce from the jar in the refrigerator, still okay and dumps it into a saucepan and puts a very low flame under it, then thinks You know yourself, you'll forget it and pot will burn and it's all the sauce you have, and shuts it off, water's boiling, sticks the spaghetti in, empties the remaining apricots into a container and puts it into the refrigerator, sits for a few minutes with a scotch and water and reads the mail and the part of today's paper that wasn't soaked, calls the girls to dinner, same old mail and front-page news, dumps all the catalogs but one so his wife won't get suspicious that not even one came when she was away, for he doesn't want her getting her hands on the rest and buying what he thinks are a lot of unnecessary things and increasing the number of catalogs they already get, how do the catalogers or whatever the word for them is get her name? every time she orders, or as much as he can, he tells her to insist the cataloger not sell her name to any other company's mailing list or she'll never buy from it again, calls the girls to dinner, catalog he kept is one he's almost sure she won't buy anything from: maternity bras and baby clothes from a time she bought them years ago and catalog's come ever since, calls the girls to dinner, Julie sits and says "I have nothing to drink," and he says "Did you wash your hands?—I should've told you that before you sat," and both girls wash their hands and he washes his in the kitchen sink and heats the tomato sauce and drains and butters the spaghetti and gets everything on the table along with a glass of wine for him, Parmesan cheese! and runs in and gets it, butter and bread knife and more bread, shakes the pepper mill and refills it and sits and Julie says "I still have nothing to drink," and he says "Excuse me, but I think I told you before to get something. Not milk, that's no good with dinner, Mommy says. But one of the flavored seltzers with ice, orange juice in it to make Orangina if it's plain seltzer, or a flavored seltzer with juice, what's the difference really? or just straight orange juice with or without ice and which is on the side shelf of the refrigerator," and Julie gets juice for Margo and her and they eat, he says 'Food okay, there's enough?" and Margo says "I'm not that hungry—it could be the popcorn, to be honest; I'm sorry," and he says "So what did you think about the day today—good day, bad, so-so mediocre day; how does it rate on your average everyday day gauge?" and Margo says "Who?" and he says "Both of you," and Julie says "I don't get the question," and Margo says "An awful boring horrible day, useless and one of the worst. Too much car and stop, car and stop; I wish we could take the train once," and he says "I promise you—once, we will. But the rest of the day today forgotten—the bad, the so-so mediocre, the good?" and Julie says "Still, what do you mean?" and he says "I don't know—those cowboys; that's what my dad liked to call wild and dangerous drivers, and their cars broncos, which is funny, for that's the name of a fashionable expensive car today, isn't it?" and Margo says "You think they got the idea from your father?" and he says "If they did I bet right now he's thinking of suing them from heaven," and she says "That's impossible, but do you believe people go there after they die if they've been good?" and he says "Death, please, not a subject fit for the dinner table, even over spaghetti and cheap wine," and she says "Would you be sad if Julie or me died?" and he says "Where'd you get that thought?" and she says "Would you though?" and he says "Very very very very, a thought so sad that I'm now sad just thinking about it, but it ain't gonna happen so let's not talk about it," and Julie says "But everyone dies, right?" and he says "Yes, or maybe, but it's a hundred years away for you kids at least, so far away and the way science is progressing today that it may never happen to you," and Margo says "But you'll die earlier than us unless Julie or me dies before you," and he says "But I said you won't, you won't, and I asked you to drop the subject," and she says "Why, as long as we're willing to talk about it and are interested, isn't that so, Julie?" and Julie says "I sort of am," and he says "You see, she's not," and Julie says "No, I am," and he says "But I'm not. Neither of my kids will die, not in my lifetime or maybe anybody's, and I'm going to stay so healthy that I'll outlive the oldest man who ever lived—Methuselah, even," and Margo says "I never heard of him," and he says "Ah, he was probably before your time. But during that long long life of mine I'm going to make sure you kids also acquire the means to live that long and even longer, so from now on you don't have anything to worry about when it comes to living—nothing, forget it," and Margo says "And Mommy?" and he says "Mommy too, an exceptionally long life—Methuselah's wife and then some, I'll see to it," and Julie says "And Mommy's parents?" and he says "Now enough, we've discussed it way past the point of interest and amusement and information and spaghetti conversation and really, all I was getting at before with those guys on the road and the endless rainstorm and your not ice-skating and so forth was, well, that it's all been forgotten or put away by you till I just brought it up, and it's not upsetting you and you both can sleep peacefully and get up tomorrow feeling good, can't you?" and Margo says "It was not seeing my friends at the party I minded, not the ice-skating, but it's okay," and he says "Good, great. Now, continuing my duty as reprehensible single parent—only kidding; responsible father and not morbid-mood bringer and chief family scarer, I have to ask if either of you has homework to do," and they say they've done it, but their teachers went over it in class while they were away, and he asks them to and they clear the table for him, he has another glass of wine and salad while they have dessert, he washes the dishes and puts things away and wants to listen to music while doing this but the classical music station has devoted the hour to marches and waltzes and the other public station which often plays serious music has a call-in on AIDS, yells from the kitchen "Someone want to help Daddy some more and sweep the dining room and kitchen? When I was a kid my folks made me do it every night, even when I was Julie's age and no matter how badly I did it," no answer, looks and they're not around so must be in their rooms upstairs or in one of them with the door closed, he sweeps the floors, puts the washed laundry into the dryer, Julie yells down to the basement "Can we watch TV?" and he says "Is that what you and Margo have been doing since dessert—in my room and you're only now feeling you're being deceptive because you know I wouldn't have permitted it?" and she says "What do you mean?" and he says "The answer's no; the mind, let's do something for the mind. Shut the TV off and both of you come downstairs, I'll meet you halfway," and goes upstairs and in the dining room they say "So? . . . yes?" and he suggests Battleship and they say they hate it and he says "It's something I loved as a kid and your grandma's taught you and given you plenty of graph paper for and you've played it with her, but all right . . . how about Scrabble?" and Margo says "If we have to do something like that, since you're forcing us, okay," and he says "I'm not forcing, but let's do it," and has another glass of wine while he plays and in about half an hour says "So, what d'ya know, the old brain's lost again. Almost bedtime, kids, anyone want to call Mommy?—number's on the fridge door. You call and I'll put away the game, for it'll take too long for you two to duel it out to the end," and Julie calls, speaks to Lee and then Margo gets on and both tell her how boring, dull, long and monotonous the day's been and how Daddy's so unfair not letting them watch TV after such a terrible day and Margo must have mentioned Scrabble and Lee must have said she thought it a good idea to play it because now Margo says "It was his, we didn't want to. He said we should learn new words and use our minds more and I already get thirty vocabulary words a week at school and all the ones we used on the board weren't new to Julie or me, though he explained them like they were. And I use my mind all the time in reading and making things and thinking and I'm sure he let us win because he saw how bored we were playing it with him," and then "I know, 'he' is 'Daddy,' but what of it? Our teacher says we're supposed to use the pronoun more in writing and speech," and then "Mommy wants to speak to you," and he gets on and Lee says "So how'd it go?" and he says

"Home, fine; despite what the kids say, I think we've had fun and I got a good dinner without milk in them and I'll probably get them in bed on time. But oh boy, the trip. Listen, I'll be honest, we nearly got hit twice on the road. Once wasn't my fault—two bozos who in fact I later saw at a Roy Rogers at a rest stop, and they seemed awful on the road—angry, dumb, potentially homicidal, even. But at the restaurant they acted like they were my pals, so what do I make of it?" and she says "Perhaps you misconstrued or exaggerated what you saw in them on the road—they weren't just jokers?" and he says "Didn't seem so, on the road. You know, I can read people's faces pretty well and just as often misread them too, but I swear I thought they'd pull out a gun and aim it out the window at me and the kids. I mean, if half the people in this country have a gun and maybe a quarter of those carry it in their cars, we'll say, then these two guys would have to have had one between them—the figures and what I saw in their faces tell me this—if not a semiautomatic something or another and a grenade," and she says "Certainly you're exaggerating here," and he says "Yeah, a little about the weapons, maybe," and she says "But also the aiming the gun and possibly shooting all of you. That's a horrible thought and I'm sure inaccurate and I hope you didn't pass it on to the kids," and he says "Only minimally, inappreciably, fleetingly and undoubtedly mistakenly, but they've indicated since they've forgotten the whole incident. But in the Roy Rogers, I'm telling you, if they sold beer there I bet these guys would have slapped my back and cuffed my chin and said 'Hiya, palsy,' and stood me to a couple of rounds, not that I'd drink when I had to drive, naturally," and she says "I'll remember that for you when we go to our next party," and he says "I meant over long trips." "But what else happened?—you said 'two near accidents,' " and he says "Other one was partly my fault, going into the center lane—middle lane—which do you use?" and she says "What of it?" and he says "Funny, but that's what Margo said before, though about what I forget—she must've got the expression from you; I was wondering where," and she says "Really, what of it? This is long distance, sweetie, and I don't mind the extended call and the expense if it's about something," and he says "So? So? Money, big deal, for you could have what you have when crash, you're gone or forever out of it and what's the dough good for then, except to help take care of you? If anything, that's something you think about when you almost get into a serious collision, but of course mostly what if the kids were hurt or you were—me—and they survived. Hurt and worse. But it was partly my fault, is what I'm saying, darting into the middle lane, I'll settle on, same time this old guy in front of me does from the passing lane—fast lane? . . . sorry. In other words, we're both in the fast lane—one syllable, so in the end that's what decides it for me, but he wasn't budging from it, when he suddenly darts into the middle lane the second after I did—close but not a close call, I don't think, but close enough, at seventy miles an hour, to send scare shivers through me and get me flashing about death and the kids and so on. So he was partly at fault too, since he didn't signal or look. Or just didn't signal, I'm not sure if he didn't look, but if he did he wouldn't have made that sudden reckless move, right? But maybe it was all too fast, my sudden reckless move and his, that he didn't have time, so it's a draw," and she says "Time to what?" and he says "About him? I forget— what was I saying? But that was close call number two, and then, to top it off hour and a half or so from home, the rain," and she says "You had rain? It was gorgeous here all day. Sunny, golden, clear, a light wind that felt like balmy sea breezes—the most heaven-sent weather on the most rhapsodizical of spring days," and he says "Not a drop? No wonder—we got it all. It came down in buckets, barrels, big street Dumpsters, I never experienced rain like it and it didn't stop being this way till we parked in front of the house, where it just sort of decompressed, though it still might have been coming down torrentially everywhere else around us; in other words, with a little bit of stretching, I think we were blessed. I would have stopped at a rest area—rest stop?—service area?—those places with the Roy Rockefellers and Bob's Pig Boys and Taco Bellies, if I could have seen a sign for one through the rain. Okay, I saw the signs but on that neck of the Interstate all the exits to those service areas are from the left side and I was in no way going to drive in the fast lane to enter one and it seemed too chancy to get over," and she says "So what did you do?" and he says "Thought of you. No. Rest of the way drove slowly in the slow lane, of course—twenty-five, twenty, though still with limited visibility. But we're here, trip's over with, so as you and Margo say, what of it, right?" "Good. I'm glad you're all home and safe. Anything else?" and he says "To tell you? Wait, all I've been doing is going on about me—what about you? Besides the beautiful day, anything interesting or exciting or new happen to you?" and she says "It's been nice being with my folks, that's all, and I did a bit of book buying and store browsing and got my hair trimmed and—" and he says "There is something. Before I left, when we were in the hallway outside your parents' apartment—I was holding you, I think—we were holding each other—and I said I was psychic, you remember?" and she says no and he says "Or maybe I only thought it, but I could almost swear I told you it, and just about something specific, not psychic in general. But I was in this rush to get on the road to get caught in that rain and nearly clipped by two cars so I said I'd tell you about it tonight, but you don't remember," and she says "It's beginning to sound familiar but that may be only because you're talking about it now and it's tricking me into thinking I heard it before," and he says "Too bad; I was hoping you'd remember and tell me what I was referring to in my being psychic," and she says "Nope, I'm sorry, the bell's not binging," and he says "Let me think, for I don't know why but I don't want to lose it—I mean how many times in his life is a man psychic, or this one?" and she says "Better you tell me tomorrow after you remember. Write it down if it comes back," and he says "I suppose. Oh— this is it, flash from the front—that you already regretted we were gone, or that I was, or it had to be 'we,' and I had just been thinking, moment before you said it, that you were thinking this," and she says "Come again?" and he says "Step one, I felt by your look but really more by something that jumped into my head that you were regretting that we or I was gone—were? was? . . . I should stop that; I'm so inconsolable—*incorrigible*," and she says "You are and it's getting—" and he says "And step two, that you said exactly what I'd been thinking, that 'we' or 'I' but probably 'we,' or maybe 'I,' " and she says "If you say I did, I believe you, since it's not a thought I'd mind having. And I did, for a few minutes, regret that you and the girls were gone, right after you took the elevator down. But we'll see each other soon," and he says "Of course. So . . . I miss you; you, me?" and she says "Of course," and he says "Of course, of course. And, well, I love you, do you, still, me?" and she says "What a thing. Why would you ask?" and he says "Oh, you know, one acts like a dodo so much, he has to hear it again just to make sure his mate hasn't turned off him, but it really only popped into me like the other things," and she says "You're my one and only, my uno moono, the big man in my life," and he says "Same here, but 'woman.' Never since we started seeing each other . . . no one else," and she says "Good, and same here, and I'll see you in two days, or is it three? We'll talk," and Julie says "Did you hear what Daddy said to Mommy?" and Margo says "Don't be a child," and Lee says "I hear what the girls are saying. You're in for it now. Get a good night's sleep and make sure they do too," and he says "What do you think, I'm going to play pinochle half the night with them?" and she says "Pinochle? Where'd that come from?" and he says "Just another pop-in thought, but it was a game my dad played with his cronies, though I don't think I thought of him once today. No, that's not true either," and she says "What else isn't?" and he says "Nothing, just an expression. We better get. Bye-bye, my lovey," and she says "Goodnight," and he says "And give my best to your parents," and she says "I will."

Later, kids in bed, teeth brushed, flossed, clothes set for the next day and he says "Lights out, everybody," and Margo says "Can I read for five minutes more?" and he says "Fine, for both of you, five minutes' free play, but that's it, deal?" and they say nothing and he says "You have to say something," and they say yes and five minutes later he goes back upstairs to the part of the hallway between their rooms and says "Lights out now, please," and Julie says "Can't we have a story?" and he says no and she says "You said last night you'd give one because Mommy won't be here," and he says "Okay, but a short one. 'There were two sisters ready for sleep—' " and she says "Oh God, Daddy, *two* sisters—real original. Do they have our names?" and he says "No, why would they?—it's a story," and she says "Margo, did you hear that—Daddy's story with two sisters like us?" and Margo says "I'm not listening, I'm reading," and he says "Not like you. Just two sisters, ages a little different and personalities completely unlike yours, who are very tired, yawning, in bed and ready for sleep—remember, this is a short one—when a bear comes into their room—" and Julie says "With you it's always a bear. Why not an elephant?" and he says "Hey, who's telling it? You don't like the way I do it, I won't and it's goodnight, sweet peas," and she says "No, go on," and he says "Not a bear but a flying duck. And this duck—this is the story—'And this duck, Dickie, for all ducks have first names starting with D, says "Hey, gals, let's go outside and cause a major duck ruckus," and they say "No, we're tired and have to go to sleep; sorry, Dickie. Maybe tomorrow or the day after," ' end of story," and Julie says "That wasn't one— it didn't go on and there was no ending," and he says "Best I can do tonight for a shortie. It's late," looks at his watch, "—oh my gosh, past ten and tomorrow's a school day and I promised Mommy and I'm even a little tired myself and still have to make lunch for you for tomorrow and do other things. I'm also not in the right frame of mind and mood for a story—I gotta feel it and I don't, so goodnight, all," and flicks the wall light switch in her room which turns off the night table light and she says "Wait, I'm not done yet, I haven't fixed my animals in bed," and he says "What's it gonna be, all night with you?" and turns the light on and watches her arrange her stuffed animals under her covers with their noses jutting just above and she rests her head on the pillow and says "Okay, I'm set," and he turns the light off and says "Be back in a sec," and sticks his head into Margo's room and says "May I turn the light off now?—I gave you much more than five minutes," and she says "Only half a page left till the end of the paragraph," and he waits while she reads and thinks "Look at that concentration and the way she won't give the book up—I wish I still had it like that," and she puts a bookmark between the pages, closes the book and puts it on the floor and says "All right, I'm ready, thank you," and he turns her night table light off from her wall switch and she says "You have to come say goodnight to me personally," and he says "Orders, these kids are never done giving orders," and sits on her bed and says goodnight and she raises her arms and he leans down between them and kisses her forehead and she hugs him and pulls him down to her and says "Now you're sentenced to prison, you can never get free, what are you going to do, prisoner?" and he says "Willingly stay here for life, I guess—jail is so sweet and a break from everyday things," and rests his face on her cheek and Julie says "What about me?" and he says "Be there soon, my cookie," and lifts his head and looks at Margo in the light from the hallway and thinks "My firstborn, my firstborn, how big and beautiful you've grown, and smart? oh my God," and feels tears and thinks "Now that wasn't cheap sentimentality, was it?" and she says "What?" and he says "Why?" and she says "Way you're staring at me; I do something wrong?" and he says "The opposite; I'm just admiring you," and thinks "Ah, what great kids, incomparable, inconsolable, I'm so incorrigible, I gotta do something about that soon. For starters not to be such a gruffpot, just not be anything I know I shouldn't be and which hurts them and anything like that and in the end me. I know I've said it all before but this is the end of saying I've said it or the end of saying this is the end of saying I've said it, or will try for it to be, right from now," and says "This is really unbeatable, my dear, but please now release me so I can let you get some sleep, you need it," and she takes her arms away and he kisses her lips and brushes her hair back with his hand and she says "You're looking at me in that weird way again," and he says "Honestly, it's nothing; or maybe just the shadows and stuff on my face, making me look gruff—you know, but go to sleep," and gets up and she says "I love you, Daddy," and he says "Say, that's a coincidence, for me too to you too too, now goodnight," and blows her a kiss and goes into Julie's room and says "By all rights I should've gone to my youngest first, who I believe is you"—puts his face right up to hers—"yes, this is definitely recognizable as Julie's, because she needs more sleep. But I shut Margo's light last so went into her room first to say goodnight, does that make any sense or should I reexplain or just forget it?" and she says "What were you talking of with her—did you tell her a full story?" and he says "I was telling her how beautiful, big, smart and grown she's become, just like you with all those and how you two were always like that from day one of birth though not so grown," and gets on his knees and brushes her hair back and says "Now *guten nacht*, my darlink sveetheart, *mut—mit* great sveet dreams to *du*," and she says "And sweet dreams to you and see you in the morning and have a nice night," and he says "And nice night too, I forgot that one, and see you in the morning," and Margo says "You're taking much longer with her than you did me," and he says "Not true but I'll return to give you equal time," and Julie says "And then me," and he says "I'm now giving it," and kisses her lips and says "I love you, *mein wunderbar* kit, now goodnight," and she says "Goodnight and don't forget to come back," and he says "Never, for tonight, that was it," and goes into Margo's room and says "Goodnight again, that's all, I'm on my way out," and kisses her forehead and she tries locking him in her arms and he says "No, really," pulling her arms away, "fun's fun and love's love but it's sleepy-sleep time," and she says "One more kiss?" and he says "Please, no, this can go on forever," and leaves the room and says "I'll stay here for a few minutes," and Margo says "If not a real story, sing?" and he says "Nah, I've a crummy voice," and turns the hallway light off and she says "We need it to see the bathroom—the night light's broke," and he says "You're getting a little light from my bedroom," and she says "But then you'll go to sleep," and he says "I'll leave the bathroom light on with the door quarterway open," and turns the bathroom light on, shuts the door almost all the way and sits against the wall between their rooms and Margo says "Please sing. Mommy always does when there's no story and sometimes even after one and it gets us to sleep faster," and he says "But she has a pretty voice and knows lots of good songs. Okay, only one with my crummy voice and short as can be but sung slowly," and he sings " 'Oh my darling, oh my darling, oh my darling Clementine, I am lost and gone forever, oh my darling Clementine.' I don't think those are the exact words but the tune's right and the feeling's all there. But that's it; now complete utter silence," and Julie says "More," and he says "No! I mean it. I'm not saying another word and neither are you," and they're quiet and he thinks " 'I've been lost and gone forever? She's been lost and gone? You have? She is? I'm?' I don't know which one, they all sound right," and rests his arms on his knees, head on his wrist, blows out a long breath, no thoughts come. Sometime later he thinks "Was I sleeping? Must've been; wonder how long," and whispers "Girls, you asleep?" and Margo says "I'm not," and he says "So sleep, sweetheart, really; I'll sit here a few more minutes," and she says "If you come say goodnight to me one last time, you can leave," and he thinks "Should I give in? What's the harm," and says "Okay, if that'll do it," and goes into her room and kisses her forehead and says "Goodnight now, all right?" and he can't see her well in the dark but she seems to nod and he goes into Julie's room and kisses her head and then goes downstairs to make them lunch.